SWEET DENIAL

"God, you're wonderful," Dan murmured against her mouth, as his hands moved to take the pins from her hair.

Gabrielle's head spun and a glowing warmth surged through her. She clung to him, aware only of a rapidly intensifying hunger for his touch as his hands spanned her waist. "Please . . . " she pleaded after tearing her lips from his, but he recaptured them with a fierce devouring kiss. Then he reluctantly pulled away from her.

"Please . . . don't stop," she whispered breathlessly, unable to calm the furious beating of her heart.

"I have to," he said huskily. "If I don't, I might not be able to stop at all." He gathered her into his arms and held her tightly.

Gabrielle felt a shudder rock his hard-muscled body, and without warning, her passion-charged senses plummeted back to earth as she realized what she had just done. "Oh, no!" she exclaimed, pushing him away from her and struggling to rise. "I'm ruined!"

D1115958

EXHILARATING ROMANCE
From Zebra Books

GOLDEN PARADISE (2007, $3.95)
by Constance O'Banyon

Desperate for money, the beautiful and innocent Valentina Barrett finds work as a veiled dancer, "Jordanna," at San Francisco's notorious Crystal Palace. There she falls in love with handsome, wealthy Marquis Vincente — a man she knew she could never trust as Valentina — but who Jordanna can't resist making her lover and reveling in love's GOLDEN PARADISE.

SAVAGE SPLENDOR (1855, $3.95)
by Constance O'Banyon

By day Mara questioned her decision to remain in her husband's world. But by night, when Tajarez crushed her in his strong, muscular arms, taking her to the peaks of rapture, she knew she could never live without him.

TEXAS TRIUMPH (2009, $3.95)
by Victoria Thompson

Nothing is more important to the determined Rachel McKinsey than the Circle M — and if it meant marrying her foreman to scare off rustlers, she would do it. Yet the gorgeous rancher feels a secret thrill that the towering Cole Elliot is to be her man — and despite her plan that they be business partners, all she truly desires is a glorious consummation of their vows.

KIMBERLY'S KISS (2184, $3.95)
by Kathleen Drymon

As a girl, Kimberly Davonwoods had spent her days racing her horse, perfecting her fencing, and roaming London's byways disguised as a boy. Then at nineteen the raven-haired beauty was forced to marry a complete stranger. Though the hot-tempered adventuress vowed to escape her new husband, she never dreamed that he would use the sweet chains of ecstasy to keep her from ever wanting to leave his side!

FOREVER FANCY (2185, $3.95)
by Jean Haught

After she killed a man in self-defense, alluring Fancy Broussard had no choice but to flee Clarence, Missouri. She sneaked aboard a private railcar, plotting to distract its owner with her womanly charms. Then the dashing Rafe Taggart strode into his compartment . . . and the frightened girl was swept up in a whirlwind of passion that flared into an undeniable, unstoppable prelude to ecstasy!

Available wherever paperbacks are sold, or order direct from the Publisher. Send cover price plus 50¢ per copy for mailing and handling to Zebra Books, Dept. 2667, 475 Park Avenue South, New York, N.Y. 10016. Residents of New York, New Jersey and Pennsylvania must include sales tax. DO NOT SEND CASH.

Temptation's Touch

Linda Andersen

ZEBRA BOOKS
KENSINGTON PUBLISHING CORP.

ZEBRA BOOKS

are published by

Kensington Publishing Corp.
475 Park Avenue South
New York, NY 10016

First printing: May, 1989

Printed in the United States of America

Chapter One

May 1, 1871
Arizona Territory

Clad only in her nightgown and her wrapper, Gabrielle tiptoed down the hall toward her father's study, her bare feet making no sound on the polished floorboards. She could not wait any longer. She absolutely *had* to know what her father and Major Catlin were saying.

She pressed her ear to the door.

"I don't care if she is your daughter, Colonel!" Major Catlin's deep resonant voice boomed through the house like a cannon blast. "I have better things to do with my time than play nursemaid to a goddamned spoiled brat!"

"I will only be away a month, Dan," Colonel DuBois said with a calm finality that signaled the matter closed. "Believe me, if I thought it would be in Gabrielle's best interests to bring her to San Francisco with me, I would, but you know my daughter. She wouldn't be content to sit in a hotel room all day while I am at Division Headquarters, and I certainly do not want her wandering around that rough city by herself. Besides, I am not asking you to be a nursemaid. The strikers know their duties and Gabrielle is sensible enough to look after herself. All I'm asking is that you keep her safe from the misguided intentions of some hot-blooded young lieutenant."

"Pardon me for being blunt, Colonel, but your daughter doesn't have enough sense to fit on the sharp end of a cactus spine, and if anyone needs protecting around here, it's those horny bastards who fancy themselves to be in love with her. Not the other way around."

Gabrielle made a wry face and stuck her tongue out at the closed door.

"That is precisely why I am counting on your help," Colonel DuBois stated flatly. "Not only are you the only one I can trust not to take advantage of my daughter's innocence, you are the only one within five hundred miles of Camp Carleton that she hasn't been able to twist around her little finger. You have known Gabrielle since she was a child, Dan, and you know she needs someone with a firm hand to keep her in tow. If anyone can maintain a tight rein on her while I am at Division, you can. Now, about that dispatch from Lieutenant Whitman . . ."

Suppressing a giggle, Gabrielle tiptoed back to her bedroom, a devilish twinkle in her gray-green eyes. This was working out even better than she had planned! She took an inkpot and some paper from her dresser drawer and hastily scribbled out two notes, finishing just as she heard her father's study door open. Hiding the notes in the back of the drawer, she dove into bed and pulled the covers up over her head, burying her face in her pillow and bursting into sobs when her father appeared in the doorway. "I have had enough of this nonsense, Gabrielle," he said sternly. "The matter is settled. You will be staying here while I am gone, and I don't want to hear any more about it. Now, get out of that bed and get dressed. I won't tolerate your sulking."

She waited until she heard his footsteps retreating down the hallway before throwing back the covers and scrambling from the bed, her long honey-colored hair flying out about her as she hugged herself and danced around in a circle, pure joy illuminating her face. After some moments of celebrating in that fashion, Gabrielle retrieved the notes from her dresser drawer and stuck her head out the bedroom door. "Psst!" she whispered as one of her father's strikers headed down the hallway, broom in hand.

"Yes, Miss Gabrielle?" Corporal Holmes asked, his face reddening when he saw her. If there was one thing he had never gotten used to since coming to work for the colonel, it was the sight of Miss Gabrielle in her nightgown. He shifted nervously from one foot to the other and ran a finger beneath his collar.

Ignoring his discomfiture, she handed him the notes. "I want you to deliver these for me right away, please," she said sweetly, fluttering her thick black lashes at him.

He blushed even more. "Yes, Miss Gabrielle."

"One is for Grace Simmons, and the other is for Lieutenant Epperling. Hurry! And don't let father see them!"

"Yes, Miss Gabrielle."

Whirling around, she bounded across her room to the oversized wardrobe and yanked open the door. She had to find something special to wear . . .

Dan Catlin stormed across the parade ground toward the Headquarters Building, an angry set to his broad shoulders, his tanned face dark as a thundercloud. His wide sensuous mouth had hardened into a brittle line that left no doubt as to the unspent fury roiling within him and his strongly arched black brows, drawn together, seemed to accent his aquiline nose and smoldering hazel eyes. *A month!* An entire month to be spent riding herd on that seventeen-year-old holy terror who needed nothing better than to have her sassy little butt blistered! He knew damned good and well what was behind the girl's timely display of hysterics and it amazed him that the colonel could be so gullible. Gabrielle DuBois had no intention of trying to convince her father to let her go with him when he departed for San Francisco on the morrow, not if it meant spending even one day away from that still-wet-behind-the-ears, cherub-faced first lieutenant who followed her around like a love-struck puppy!

He burst into Headquarters Building and slammed the door shut with a resounding bang, causing Captain Wilcox and First Sergeant O'Donnell to start in surprise.

"Something wrong?" the surgeon asked as Dan removed his black campaign hat and hung it on a peg by the door.

Distracted, Dan ran his long fingers through his thick black

7

hair in a gesture that expressed both anger and frustration. "Get Lieutenant Epperling in here, on the double."

"Sure thing, Dan," Ben Wilcox answered. He grabbed his hat on his way to the door, a look of concern on his face. Dan's working too hard lately, he thought; and he wondered how long it would be before the lid blew off and his superior officer lost all patience.

"First Sergeant, I want B Company ready to move out at dawn. Plan for enough rations to last you at least a month."

"May I ask where we're headed, sir?"

"Camp Grant." One way or another, he was going to get Lieutenant Epperling as far away from Camp Carleton as was physically possible.

The colonel was pushing friendship beyond its limits, Dan decided after the other men had gone, leaving him alone in the suddenly silent office. He had known Stephen DuBois since '52, when DuBois had been a captain of the Dragoons and he had been a tall skinny runaway from the Madison County Boys Home. It had been payday for the Army, and the cocky young officer had been a shade careless about flashing around the three twenty-dollar gold pieces weighing heavily in his pocket, inadvertently setting himself up as bait for two thugs who would have divested him of his hard-earned pay had Dan not intervened, breaking one assailant's nose and giving the other a couple of cracked ribs. In gratitude, Captain DuBois had treated him to a hot meal, a bath, and his first shave. He'd then pressed two dollars into his large, callused hand and had introduced him to the enlistment sergeant at Jefferson Barracks. Before twenty-four hours had passed, Dan, his stomach full for the first time he could recall found himself in the Army.

Six years passed before Dan saw Captain DuBois again. By then the officer had become a major who had a beautiful wife and a four-year-old daughter with sea-green eyes and hair the color of warm honey; while Dan, no longer a gangly youth, had worked his way up through the ranks, from private to platoon sergeant, and finally to second lieutenant, an achievement few enlisted men could boast of. He'd received his commission on the eve of his twenty-second birthday. The two men had been

8

stationed in the same department ever since, usually at the same post, and the major, Lisette, and little Gabrielle had become the closest thing Dan had ever had to a real family. Those first years were a blur to him now, the days melding together in his memory. Then the changes came, and the disappointments, each one leaving scars that never quite healed. War broke out between the states. Lisette succumbed to scarlet fever. And Gabrielle grew from a sweet, adorable little girl into a scheming tyrant who manipulated everyone around her into giving her whatever she wanted—whenever she wanted it and regardless of whom she hurt in the process.

Dan owed the colonel a great deal. Had the other officer not taken him off the streets and set him in a new direction, there was no telling where he might have wound up. Dead, more than likely, or behind bars, for he was a man not given to taking orders. From the half-breed father who had abandoned him as an infant, he had inherited the tendency to use his fists first and ask questions later, a trait that had served to keep him knee-deep in trouble during his years at the boys' home. Still, his loyalty to the colonel ran deep. There was nothing he would not do for him; in spite of his protests, he was even willing to take Gabrielle off the colonel's hands for a month. But God help the little vixen, he swore silently, his frown deepening, if she doesn't obey me to the letter.

He turned as the door opened.

"You wanted to see me, sir?" Lieutenant Epperling asked, removing his hat and dragging his sleeve across his forehead. Sweat dripped from his blond curls and caused his long, almost feminine, lashes to clump together in damp clusters.

"Half an hour ago, I received a dispatch from Lieutenant Whitman, requesting our assistance," Dan said, pulling a folded paper from his pocket and handing it to the other officer for his perusal. "Yesterday morning he got word from Camp Lowell that a large party had left Tucson on the twenty-eighth, supposedly with the intention of killing all the Apaches receiving asylum at Camp Grant. Lieutenant Robinson is on furlough and Captain Stanwood took his entire troop to the field on the twenty-fourth, leaving Whitman with only fifty infantrymen, all of them raw recruits, to defend the post."

Lieutenant Epperling finished reading the dispatch and handed it back to Dan. "What is it you wish me to do, sir?"

"For the time being, provide Whitman with reinforcements and keep me informed as to the developments in Tucson. Whitman has over five hundred Apaches quartered at the post. If necessary, we'll bring some of them back to Camp Carleton and give them asylum here."

One blond eyebrow arched upward. "The colonel knows about this, sir?"

Dan's mouth tightened. "Are you questioning my orders, Lieutenant?"

Lieutenant Epperling bristled. It was always this way with officers like Major Catlin, men who had worked their way up through the ranks and had received their commissions without the proper training. He drew himself up to his full height. They thought they were God, and didn't have to answer to anyone. And the major was the worst of the bunch, though everyone knew the man's father was nothing but a renegade *métis* from Canada. As far as Epperling was concerned, Dan Catlin should never have been allowed in the American Army, much less have been granted a commission.

"No, sir. I'm not questioning you."

Dan knew the officer's response was given begrudgingly. It had never been otherwise, and he harbored no delusions that the situation might change. "Good. I've already given First Sergeant O'Donnell orders to have B Company ready to move out first thing in the morning. If you have any trouble with the quartermaster regarding your supplies, come to me."

Damned breed thinks he owns the place, Lieutenant Epperling thought irritably. Major Catlin had no right to issue orders to his outfit except through him. Epperling knew it and the major knew it, yet there wasn't a goddamned thing the lieutenant could do about it, short of committing murder. *Just wait, Major. One of these days someone's going to blow your red ass away*. "Will that be all, sir?" he asked, careful to keep his thoughts to himself.

Dan had seen that subtle change of expression on men's faces too often not to recognize it for what it was, and he had a pretty good idea just what was going through the lieutenant's mind right then. While he did not begrudge the other officer his opinion, he was annoyed with himself for being affected by it. He would have thought that, by now, he would be immune to the slurs that had followed him since childhood. "Yes, Lieutenant," he said flatly. "That will be all."

"But I don't understand," Grace Simmons said, her forehead puckering in bewilderment. "If you didn't want to go to San Francisco with your father, why didn't you just say so instead of raising such a fuss and pretending you did?"

"Silly goose!" Gabrielle scolded gently from the bed where she lay amidst a sea of petticoats, laughter illuminating her face. "Do you honestly think Father would leave me behind if he knew I *wanted* to stay?"

"I don't know . . ."

"Think, Grace. *Think!* What would *your* father do if he knew you might be spending every day for an entire month with your one and only true love?"

"Gabrielle, if I behaved like you, my father would lock me up and throw away the key."

"You are such a ninny! You are two years older than I, and you don't do anything but say 'Yes, sir' and 'No, sir' and do only what everyone else expects of you. Good heavens!" Without giving her friend a chance to reply, Gabrielle bounced off the bed. "Here, you can help me with my dress. I can't reach all the buttons myself."

Grace's eyes widened as she saw what Gabrielle intended to wear. "That's the dress that makes you look as though you might fall out of the top if you happened to sneeze!" she blurted out, horrified.

"That's the whole idea, Grace darling. Marcus does love looking at my bosoms. He says they're like peaches, and that there's nothing tastier than ripe peaches fresh off the tree.

"Gabrielle, you didn't!"

"Didn't what?" she asked with feigned innocence, for although she knew perfectly well what her friend meant, she could not resist the temptation to make Grace blush.

The other girl's face turned stark white, then red. "I-I

11

mean . . . d-did Lieutenant Epperling . . . he d-didn't . . .''

A naughty smile played at the corners of Gabrielle's mouth. "No, Grace, he didn't. He wouldn't dare! Father would have him busted all the way down to mister if he so much as touched me." She lifted her arms while Grace eased the dress over her head, reveling in the cool softness of the jade-colored silk against her skin. "I just might let him kiss me tonight though," she mused aloud, a giggle bubbling up inside her. "Tell me what to do. Shall I let him kiss me, or should I make him wait awhile longer?"

"I think you should wear something else," Grace said curtly, her lips thinning in disapproval as she caught Gabrielle's reflection in the cheval mirror.

Gabrielle snatched a translucent silk stocking up off the floor and draped it around her neck, boa fashion, flinging the toe end over her shoulder. "Well, I suppose one little kiss wouldn't hurt, Marcus dear," she drawled seductively, batting her lashes and pursing her rose-hued lips as she leaned into the mirror.

"Gabrielle! How do you expect me to button you up if you won't stand still?"

"All right, all right!" Gabrielle retorted, rolling her eyes in disgust as she yanked off the stocking and tossed it on the bed.

"Here, hold this out of the way," Grace ordered, taking her friend's thick mane of red-gold hair and twisting it into a knot.

Gabrielle obeyed, taking the hair up off her neck and then studying her reflection in the mirror while Grace bent over the row of tiny buttons at the back of her gown. *Spoiled brat, indeed!* she thought, recalling the coarse remarks Major Catlin had made to her father. *And not enough sense to fit on the sharp end of a cactus spine!* She grimaced, causing the sprinkling of freckles across the bridge of her nose to disappear as her nose crinkled up. *I'll bet I have enough sense to outsmart you, Major Catlin,* she mused to herself; then she giggled.

"What are you doing?" Grace mumbled, behind her.

Gabrielle took a deep breath and stuck out her chest and tugged on her bodice, exposing even more of her already daringly revealed cleavage. *I have a nice bosom,* she thought,

12

satisfied with what she saw in the mirror. Even someone as stuffy and old-fashioned as Major Catlin would not be able to ignore a bosom like hers. "Just wondering what Major Catlin would think of me in this dress," she answered, more to herself than to her friend.

Grace's head jerked up and she took a step backward. "Major Catlin! Why Major Catlin?"

She chuckled. "Because the poor boy has been given the disgraceful task of being my nanny while Father is in San Francisco."

"Major Catlin?" Grace said yet again, causing Gabrielle to turn around and peer at her sharply.

"Yes, Major Catlin. I don't see why you're looking so surprised. After my father, he is the ranking officer on this post, so it's only natural that he should assume command of Camp Carleton while Father is—Grace, what is it?"

"Sit down and I'll brush out your hair."

Gabrielle eyed her suspiciously. "Only if you promise to tell me what you're thinking."

"It's nothing, really. I was just remembering something I overheard him say to Pa once, that's all." Taking Gabrielle by the arm, she pulled her over to the dressing table and pushed her down on the stool.

"Tell me!"

Grace picked up the silver-backed hairbrush. "I told you, it's nothing."

"If it's about *me*, it's not nothing. It is about me, isn't it?"

"How do you want your hair? Do you want it put up or—"

"Grace!"

"All right, I'll tell you! But only because you are my best friend and I don't want to see you hurt."

"This should be good," Gabrielle murmured sarcastically, not quite loud enough for the other girl to hear. She gave Grace her sweetest smile. "Please tell me. I shall die of curiosity if you don't."

Grace began working on the tangles in the untamed mass of red-gold curls. "I just think you should take care not to antagonize the major while your father is in California, that's all. He thinks the colonel spoils you terribly, and I don't think

13

he will be at all understanding if you try to sneak behind his back to see Lieutenant Epperling."

"Grace, what did he *say?*"

The older girl took a deep breath. "He said that if you were his daughter and you tried to get away with some of the stunts you've pulled on the colonel, he would turn you over his knee and give you a good spanking."

Gabrielle's face paled and her eyes grew wide and round. He wouldn't dare! No one had ever spanked her, not even her father, who simply yelled a lot and thought he was being firm with her when, in reality, she was quite adept at bending him to her will. But, Major Catlin . . . The mere idea was too horrible to even contemplate! Her bottom lip turned out in a pout. "The old goat would have to catch me first," she said sulkily.

Sparks snapped and crackled like heat lightning as Grace drew the brush through Gabrielle's thick unruly hair. "Major Catlin is not an old goat," she said quietly. "He's only thirty-five, and I think he's rather handsome."

Her mouth dropping open, Gabrielle twisted around on the stool. "You think he's handsome?" she queried, a look of sheer disbelief on her face. She had known Dan Catlin almost her entire life and she certainly did not think him handsome. To her, he was too hard-chiseled and severe looking to ever be considered handsome. And he scowled too much. "Why, Grace, are you blushing? You are! You're blushing! Grace Simmons, you sneak! You're in love with Major Catlin, and you never told me!"

"Gabrielle . . ."

"Does he know?"

"No, he doesn't. And you'd better not tell him either, or I'll . . . I'll . . ."

"You'll what?" Gabrielle dared, her eyes narrowing until they looked like a cat's, green and scheming.

"I'll tell the colonel you're planning to wear britches to the Cinco de Mayo festival!"

Her eyes flared. "You do, Grace Simmons, and I'll tell everyone you stuff cotton batting in your chemise!" As if to drive home her threat, she pushed one forefinger right into the middle of one of the other girl's discreetly padded breasts.

14

Grace's face turned beet red and angry tears glimmered in her eyes. "Major Catlin was right. You do deserve to be spanked. You deserve worse than that! You are spoiled and rotten and mean, and I hate you, Gabrielle DuBois!"

"All right! So I won't tell anyone you stuff batting in your bust," Gabrielle said quickly. "I only said that because you threatened to tell on me. And besides, I haven't yet decided if I'm going to wear those britches or not, so you can't very well tattle on something I might not do, now can you?"

In reply, Grace sighed and resumed brushing Gabrielle's hair, but her heart was no longer in the chore and there was a wounded look on her face that pricked Gabrielle's conscience. Even if she was just the sergeant major's daughter, Grace Simmons was her only friend, and it would break Gabrielle's heart if anything, or anyone, ever came between them. She caught her bottom lip between her teeth and studied Grace's reflection in the mirror, trying to figure out exactly what it was that had caused the other girl to fly into such a tizzy. "Are you mad at me?" she ventured at last.

Grace did not answer and the weighted silence made Gabrielle squirm inwardly. Not knowing what else to do or say, she changed tactics. "Do you want to come over for supper one night this week? I'll even force myself to invite Major Catlin."

The hairbrush came to an abrupt standstill and their gazes met in the mirror, Gabrielle's questioning and Grace's skeptical, but interested.

A knowing twinkle danced in Gabrielle's eyes. "I can fix up your hair and make you look so beautiful the major can't help but notice you!"

Grace shrugged and tried to appear nonchalant, but there was no ignoring the change in her expression. *Grace Simmons and Dan Catlin. Grace Simmons and Dan Catlin,* Gabrielle thought, the words tripping through her head, singsong fashion, like a childish chant. And then she felt an unexpected stab of jealousy.

First Lieutenant Marcus Epperling was dead on his feet. He had been up since before dawn, and here it was approaching

15

midnight, yet he still had a number of tasks to finish before moving out in the morning. He thought of the note in his pocket and felt a pang of guilt, but there was nothing he could do about it. Gabrielle would simply have to try to understand that he had been too busy to see her. Closing the door of the stable after him, he started across the darkened parade ground toward the Headquarters Building in which the lights still burned brightly. The colonel was working late, as usual. Sighing wearily, the lieutenant rubbed one hand across his forehead. He was so tired that he did not hear the footfall behind him.

Someone thumped into him from behind, causing his heart to leap into his throat, and two cold little hands slid over his eyes, blinding him. "Guess who?"

"Damn it, Gabrielle!" he swore, seizing her wrists and whirling around to face her. "What the hell are you doing out here?"

She blinked and took a step away from him, hurt reflected in her eyes as she stared up at his boyishly handsome face. Marcus had never used foul language in her presence before; and she felt he must really be mad at her to do so. First Grace had been annoyed with her, and now Marcus. "I-I only w-wanted to surprise you," she stammered, trying hard to keep her teeth from chattering. The temperature had dropped drastically after the sun had gone down and she was beginning to regret her choice of dresses. She had not even thought to bring a shawl. What good was it to tease Marcus with a peek at breasts covered with unsightly gooseflesh?

"Oh, sweetheart . . ." Lieutenant Epperling contritely reached out and pulled her to him. "You did surprise me. You scared the daylights out of me. I'm sorry I snapped at you." He held her close and buried his face in her sweetly scented hair for a moment before taking her by the shoulders and holding her away from him. "But what *are* you doing out here? It's the middle of the night, and you'll catch your death dressed like that." His mouth thinned in reproach as his gaze dropped to her indecently exposed bosom, and Gabrielle wished she could crawl through a hole in the ground and die. You were supposed to be impressed, she thought, wondering just where her plan

16

had gone awry.

"I-I didn't know it would be so c-cold," she stammered, wishing he would hold her again. At least in his arms it was warm, and maybe he would soften up a little and act more like the besotted suitor he was supposed to be.

"Come on. I'll walk you home before you take a chill."

"No!" she blurted out, giving him a petulant look. "I will not go home. I want to be with you. When you didn't answer my note, I thought you didn't love me anymore, and then I found out you had to leave in the morning. I thought I would die if you left without saying good-bye, and I wanted to go to Father and beg him to let you stay. But then he would know that I really didn't want to go to San Francisco with him, and he would probably be angry; and you know how I can't bear to have him angry with me." Her words had come faster and faster until they were all run together, and finally she had to stop to catch her breath. Her chin quivered. "Oh, Marcus, please hold me and tell me you still love me!"

He broke out into a cold sweat. What was the girl trying to do to him? It had always taken all the willpower he could muster to keep his hands off her. If Colonel DuBois saw him out here holding his daughter, he'd have his hide and his rank, too! Still, maybe tonight she would let him kiss her. She had certainly held out on him long enough. After all, though he had not yet asked for her hand, everyone on post knew it was just a matter of time until he did, and all he wanted was a kiss. Just one little kiss. It was worth a try, even if he did risk bringing the colonel's wrath down on his head. Taking her by the arm, he steered her into the shadows between the stables.

"Where are we going?" she asked breathlessly, her pulse racing. Was he going to try to kiss her? "Marcus, it's dark back here!"

Before she could say anything else, he pulled her into his arms, crushing her breasts against his chest, and lowered his face to hers.

Suddenly afraid, Gabrielle turned her head to one side and managed to dodge his mouth, but when she tried to push him away, he held her so tightly she could feel the brass buttons of his blue uniform blouse gouging into her skin. And he seemed

17

to have sprouted six pairs of hands; they were all over her back, her shoulders, her buttocks. "Marcus . . . what are you doing? Please, stop that!"

"Don't be such a baby, Gabrielle," he scolded gently. "All I want is a kiss, just one little kiss to take to the field with me. That's why you wore that dress, isn't it? For me? To show me how grown-up you are? You do want me to kiss you, don't you?"

"No! I mean, yes. But not like—"

Knotting one hand in her hair, he forced her head back and covered her mouth with his, cutting short whatever else she had planned to say. Gabrielle had teased and taunted him long enough; it was time she paid up, he thought, and the tantalizing warmth of her in his arms driving away all reason, he assaulted her virgin mouth with a kiss that was far removed from the gentle, chaste caress he had planned to give her.

Her body went rigid as his mouth devoured hers, filling her with unexpected revulsion. The kiss was hot and wet and demanding and not at all pleasant, and when Marcus forced his tongue between her teeth, Gabrielle almost gagged. He slid one hand between them, squeezing her breast so hard it hurt. "Marcus, no!" she cried out and drew her lips away from his. He immediately twisted her face back to his and smothered her cries with his mouth.

Major Catlin's voice cracked through the night like a gunshot. "Lieutenant Epperling!"

Marcus released Gabrielle so abruptly, she nearly fell backward.

"Yes, sir!" the junior officer answered, snapping to attention, his breath coming in short bursts as his entire life flashed before his eyes. His career was over. He knew it.

Dan Catlin emerged from the shadow. "Colonel DuBois wants to see you in his office, on the double."

"Yes, sir," Lieutenant Epperling replied crisply. He took off for the Headquarters Building at a fast clip, without even glancing back toward Gabrielle, who just stood there with a sullen look on her face as she gingerly touched her bruised and swollen bottom lip.

Coward, she thought angrily, watching his departing back.

Then her attention riveted on Dan as he advanced on her, his face dark and foreboding beneath the broad brim of his black campaign hat. Panic streaking through her, Gabrielle stepped away from him. "What are you going to do to me?"

"Not what I'd like to do, believe me," he retorted, his fingers closing around her upper arm in a grip that caused her to gasp. "Come on. I'm taking you home." He did an abrupt about-face and yanked her along after him.

"Let go of me!" she howled, trying to squirm free, but his hold on her merely tightened as he hauled her across the parade ground, the length of his angry strides forcing her to take two steps to every one of his in order to keep up.

"Shut up before you wake the entire post!"

Outraged by his harsh treatment of her, she dug her heels into the ground, bringing them both to an abrupt halt. "Major Catlin, you let go of me right this minute, or I'll scream bloody murder, and I don't care who hears me!"

He whirled around to face her. "Well, maybe you should care, little one," he growled, taking her by the shoulders and lifting her up until her toes cleared the ground and her eyes were on a level with his. "Did you ever stop to think of what it would do to your father, knowing that his only daughter was gallivanting around post in the middle of the night, dressed like a common whore and behaving like one too?"

"I never—"

He silenced her with a rough shake. "You're lucky I came along when I did, Gabrielle. Another minute and your beloved lieutenant would have had you on the ground with your skirts up and your drawers down, and there's not a goddamned soul on this post who would have blamed him for trying to take what you've been dangling before his nose like fishbait."

When she opened her mouth to protest, he shook her again. "The party's over, little one. When the colonel leaves for Division tomorrow, you're in my hands, and I have his permission to take whatever measures I deem necessary to keep you in line. Do I make myself perfectly clear?"

Color flooded into Gabrielle's cheeks as she remembered what Grace Simmons had overheard him telling the sergeant major he would like to do to her, and her gray-green eyes

19

glistened with tears of humiliation as they locked with Dan's furious ones in silent combat. A painful lump insinuated its way into her throat. Grace was wrong. He wasn't handsome at all. He was mean and horrid, and she didn't know why her father insisted on being a friend of his.

The muscles in Dan's jaw worked convulsively. "Answer me, Gabrielle," he ordered, shaking her yet a third time. "Do you understand what I'm telling you?"

Swallowing hard, she nodded, willing her head to move. He might have her backed into a corner this time, and she knew he wouldn't hesitate to act if she forced his hand, but she would be damned if she was going to say yes, sir to him. She would rather die first.

Dan's gaze dropped slightly, and for the first time he became aware that the way he held her was pushing her shoulders together and causing the front of her dress to gape dangerously, providing him with an unobstructed view of a bosom no self-respecting seventeen-year-old should be allowed to have. Gritting his teeth together, he lowered her to the ground, but did not release her. "I'm taking you home," he said firmly, grasping her chin with one hand and forcing her to look at him. "And if you give me a lick of trouble, I'm going to march you straight up to your father's office and you can explain to *him* what you were doing out behind the stables at this time of night with Lieutenant Epperling."

The urge to spit in his eye was so great that Gabrielle had to clench her teeth together to keep from yielding to the temptation, and Dan mistook the resulting grimace she displayed for a smirk. He released her chin. "Come on," he ordered, turning and giving her arm such a rough jerk that she nearly stumbled against him.

It was all she could do not to burst into tears as he hauled her unceremoniously across the parade ground toward the officers' quarters. All her plans had gone awry. Her first kiss had been a total disaster, she decided, and Marcus would probably never speak to her again. She really wasn't sure she wanted him to after the way he had forced himself on her and then run off like a coward, leaving her to face Major Catlin alone. And now, she had nothing to look forward to except an entire month of having to answer to the major who was dragging her home as if she were some measly little NCO's brat rather than the daughter of an officer, and a high-ranking one at that. He had even called her a whore. She was the post commander's daughter, and he had no right to treat her this way!

Dan roughly pulled Gabrielle up the front steps of the large sprawling adobe house that she shared with her father, and yanked open the door. "Move!" he ordered, placing a hand at the middle of her back and shoving her into the dimly-lighted entry hall with such force that he nearly sent her sprawling. He leveled a warning finger at her. "If you ever again go chasing after a man, dressed in a getup like that, you had better be prepared to pay the consequences. The next time, little one, you might not be so lucky."

Before Gabrielle could say anything, the door slammed behind him. Her hands knotted into fists which she pounded against her thighs. "You just wait, Major Catlin!" she shouted at the closed door. "I'll make you sorry you were mean to me!"

Her threats met with silence. A terrible, echoing, aching silence. It reminded her that she was very much alone in the big empty house. The strikers had already returned to the barracks for the night, and it might be hours yet before her father came home. Angry tears stung her eyes. She hated being alone. She just hated it! Pressing her hands over her ears to shut out the awful stillness, Gabrielle turned and fled to her room.

She flung herself across the bed. It wasn't fair! Her father had no right to go off to San Francisco and leave her to the mercy of that barbarian! And that was all Dan Catlin was, a barbarian with a lowborn half-breed for a father and God only knew what for a mother! A nobody! Why, he'd never even been to West Point! How the Army could have seen fit to grant him a commission was beyond her. The man was mean and coarse and odious, and she hated him with all her heart.

But the worst part was knowing that he was right.

Gabrielle knew she should not have slipped out to meet Marcus, but when she had heard that he was being sent away, she had become desperate. She'd wanted to see him one last

21

time before he left to show him how much she loved him. And she'd wanted him to take her in his arms and kiss her, tenderly and gently, like lovers were supposed to kiss. Yet he had betrayed her! He had taken advantage of her and had tried to force himself upon her. If Major Catlin had not happened upon them, there was no telling what Marcus would have done to her!

Dan's harsh words returned to taunt her. *Another minute and your beloved lieutenant would have had you on the ground with your skirts up and your drawers down, and there's not a goddamned soul on this post who would have blamed him for trying to take what you've been dangling before his nose like fishbait . . . The next time, little one, you might not be so lucky.*

Gabrielle seized her pillow and pulled it over her head, but even that failed to shut out the sound of Dan's voice.

Next time, little one . . .

Corporal Bates opened the front door and eyed Dan with a combination of curiosity and speculation. It was all over the post that Miss Gabrielle had pitched a fit yesterday about having to remain behind when her father went to Division Headquarters, and that Major Catlin had been assigned the task of being her guardian while the colonel was away. Bates liked Miss Gabrielle—he liked her a lot, in fact—but he could not help feeling sorry for the major. Keeping Miss Gabrielle in line for an entire month was going to be a little like trying to break a wild mustang to the saddle. The ride was liable to kill you.

Wiping his hands on the towel tied about his waist, the soldier moved aside to let Dan into the house, a trace of a limp in his step.

Dan removed his hat. "How's the knee, Corporal?"

"Doin' all right, sir. Still gives me fits once in a while, but most of the swelling is gone." He took the major's hat. "The colonel and Miss Gabrielle are in the dining room, sir."

Colonel DuBois glanced up from his breakfast when Dan approached and beckoned toward an empty chair. "Have a seat, son. Corporal Bates, bring the major some coffee." He turned back to Dan. "Care for breakfast? We still have some of those fresh eggs I ordered from Prescott. A little puny, but good all the same."

"Thank you, sir, but, no. I've already eaten." Dan's gaze fell on Gabrielle who was sitting directly across from him. Her head was bowed, and she was toying absently with the fried egg on the plate before her, pricking the yolk with her fork so that it ran. Except for the few wayward tendrils that curled about her face, her hair was pulled back in a single long braid that hung down her back, giving her a look of youthful innocence, and this morning she seemed unusually subdued, quite unlike the rebellious little wanton he had rescued from the advances of Lieutenant Epperling the night before. How like Lisette she looks, he thought, his gaze skimming over her and taking in the faint pink blush of her cheeks and the smattering of freckles across the top of her small straight nose. So delicate. So innocent. So—

Suddenly the thick black lashes lifted and Gabrielle impaled him with a glare that all but dared him to speak of what had transpired the night before. His mouth tightened in annoyance, and he silently cursed his musings. How could he have been so misled? She was not like her mother at all. Indeed, how that gentle woman could have given birth to such a conniving little witch as Gabrielle was just one of the incomprehensible perversities of life.

Corporal Bates returned to the dining room with coffee, and Dan brought the cup of steaming black brew to his lips, thankful for the diversion. He did not know why Gabrielle could get under his skin like a thorn and rub raw what little patience he possessed. "Lieutenant Epperling will be ready to move out within the hour, sir," he told the colonel and then felt, rather than saw, a stiffening in Gabrielle. He glanced up at her, but she had lowered her eyes and was occupied with dragging the tines of her fork through the yolk on her plate. "B Company should be able to provide Lieutenant Whitman with enough reinforcements to defend Camp Grant. In the meantime, I am going to send a dispatch to General Stoneman suggesting that he order Captain Stanwood back from the field. The garrisons cannot be expected to enforce the general's reservation policy if they lack sufficient manpower."

23

One shaggy white brow lifted and Colonel DuBois eyed Dan with a mixture of concern and disapproval. "I would tread lightly where the general is concerned, Dan. He doesn't take too kindly to hotheaded young officers telling him what to do, no matter how diplomatically they couch their words. He is likely to interpret your suggestions as insubordination."

"Then the general should get his tail out of California and move his headquarters to the Territory where he can see firsthand just what is happening here," Dan said, his voice rising and his amber-flecked eyes snapping like live coals. "What good does it do to have Stoneman headquartered in Los Angeles? Things are no different now than when we were a part of the Department of California. It's still going to take six weeks to get responses to our dispatches, if, of course, they aren't returned for something as insignificant as improper format. We're out here risking our hides, and Stoneman is sitting in an office five hundred miles away, wringing his hands over petty details!"

The colonel leveled his fork at the younger man. "You know as well as I do that the Department of Arizona has been a separate entity for less than three weeks. Give it time. Sooner or later, the general will see the validity of moving his headquarters closer to where his troops are quartered. Until then, we will just have to exercise some patience. So what if it takes time to get a response to our requests? We issue orders as we see fit and rescind them later if Department disapproves."

"And risk getting court-martialed in the process," Dan retorted, his ill-humor heightened.

Colonel DuBois wiped his mouth with his napkin and pushed back his chair. "It is not my place, son, nor is it yours, to question the general's methods," he said, standing up. "We are soldiers. We follow orders." He threw an indifferent glance at his daughter. "When you are through mutilating that egg, Gabrielle, you may join us on the parade ground." He motioned toward the dining-room door. "After you, Major."

Gabrielle waited until after they left before slumping down in her chair and expelling her breath in a silently mouthed *whoosh*. Her fork clattered to her plate as she dropped it and relief settled across her features. She had been so certain Major

Catlin was going to tell Father about what had happened last night! She did not believe he had kept silent out of regard for her. More than likely he intended to hold the incident over her head, to coerce her into doing his bidding. She groaned inwardly. A month. An entire month of trying to stay out of the major's way! She hoped all the ruckus going on down at Camp Grant would be sufficient to keep his attention diverted from her during the next few weeks. She didn't think she could bear it otherwise.

When she finally joined her father and Major Catlin in front of the Headquarters Building, the sixty men of B Company had already formed a single mounted line, shoulder to shoulder, facing the flagstaff; and to the right of the formation, the gold and white Cavalry guidon fluttered gaily in the early morning breeze. Marcus, who was embroiled in a discussion on the Camp Grant problem with her father and the major, did not see her approach, and she was careful to keep out of his line of sight, not being quite ready to face him yet. Wives and children of Cavalry troopers had gathered to bid husbands and fathers and friends farewell. Gabrielle spotted Grace Simmons in the crowd, and lifted a hand to wave to her, but her friend's gaze was fixed on Dan Catlin, undisguised adoration in it. Gabrielle found it odd that she had never before noticed Grace was smitten with the major, for the girl made no attempt to hide her infatuation.

She stole a peek at Dan from beneath her lashes and studied him covertly, trying to determine just what it was Grace saw in him. At well over six feet, he was taller than any other man on post, something she supposed some women might think attractive, although she tended to find his height a bit troublesome since the top of her own head barely reached his shoulders and she was always forced to crane her neck in order to look at him whenever he scolded her. He was broad of shoulder and lean of hip, and, she admitted begrudgingly, he cut an impressive figure in full dress blues and black Wellington boots so highly polished one could see one's reflection in them. Still, he frowned too much for her taste. It made his darkly tanned face seem hard and unyielding, as she knew his heart to be, and she secretly suspected that if he were

25

to smile, both face and heart would crack into a million irreparable pieces. And yet, there was something fascinating about him. She couldn't quite ignore that, no matter how hard she tried. And, though she was loath to admit it, she was just a little bit afraid of him.

Marcus snapped to attention and crisply saluted her father before doing an abrupt about-face and approaching the waiting formation. Gabrielle watched him as he took his horse's reins and swung up into the saddle with practiced elegance, and she sucked in her breath as he turned and caught her eye. How silly he must think her to have recoiled from his kiss the way she had. How childish and inexperienced. Her cheeks became uncomfortably warm.

But, if he was thinking those things, his expression did not reveal it. He gave her a ready smile, as though nothing had happened, then reached up to touch the brim of his hat; and Gabrielle completely forgot that last night she had thought him a coward. "Take care, Marcus," she said softly, her voice little more than a whisper. Oh, what she wouldn't give to be able to go back and relive the past night. This time, she would be grownup and sophisticated, and she would give him a real kiss and not act as though he'd offended her.

Lieutenant Epperling turned his horse around to face the waiting soldiers. "By column of twos . . . to the right . . . move out!"

Gabrielle's throat constricted. These good-byes always seemed so final, and in a sense they were, since one never knew when a company or a patrol would ride out never to return. Deeply regretting the way she had treated Marcus on the previous night, she watched his back until she could no longer see him through the cloud of dust raised by the horses' hooves.

The crowd broke up and everyone began to drift away.

Slowly Gabrielle's gaze moved upward and took in the mountains that surrounded the high desert valley, their jagged peaks silhouetted against the pale sky. A person could simply disappear into those ranges and be swallowed up by them, never to be seen again, she mused morbidly, suppressing a shudder as a sudden chill traced an icy path up her spine, raising prickles on her skin. The desert could be a cruel and

26

unrelenting master. If the heat and the sun didn't kill you, then the *banditos* might. They roamed the Territory, taking what they chose and murdering any who stood in their way. And there were the Indians—the Apaches were said to be the worst. Apaches thought nothing of stripping their victims, smearing their bodies with honey, and then staking them out on anthills so they might be eaten alive. They also strung captives up by their heels and built fires beneath their heads to slowly roast them until—

Gabrielle closed her eyes to shut out the gruesome picture. *Oh, Marcus, please return to me safely! Please!*

"Gabrielle, are you listening to me?"

She started and her eyes flew open. "Did you say something, Father?"

Annoyance was reflected in the colonel's expression. "I want you to give Major Catlin your full cooperation while I am away. If I return to hear that you have been a problem, I will not hesitate to send you to Baltimore to stay with your Aunt Charlotte."

Gabrielle cast Dan a sideways glance and said woodenly, "Yes, sir."

The crease between Dan's brows deepened as he watched the color slowly return to her face, and he wondered just what it was she had been thinking a moment ago that had caused her to blanch so. In the bright sunlight he could make out the faint pink blotches that marred the delicate skin around her eyes, and he knew she had probably cried herself to sleep last night. For a split second, his heart softened. She looked so young and vulnerable. Instantly, he gritted his teeth and abruptly closed the door on whatever sympathy he might have felt for her. To let down one's guard for even a moment where Gabrielle was concerned was like kissing a rattlesnake. It didn't require much intelligence to know better.

Colonel DuBois issued his final instructions and mounted his horse, and, without so much as a glance behind him, he set off in the opposite direction from that which B Company had taken. He did not even wave. Gabrielle's heart sank. Although she knew her father was not one to show affection—in public or in private—she could not help wishing that just once he would forget himself and hug her as she'd often seen the other fathers do. Her spirits drooping, she turned and started back toward the house.

A big hand descended upon her shoulder with an iron grip. "Not so fast, young lady."

Gabrielle bristled. The dust hadn't even settled behind her father's horse and already the major was harassing her. She turned to face him. "Why don't you just go away and leave me alone? I haven't done anything," she protested, giving Dan a wounded look. It was no secret that he hated her. He had always hated her, for as far back as she could remember.

A muscle in Dan's jaw jerked. "I never said you did. I simply want to know your plans for today. Where I can expect to find you."

Angry sparks snapped in her gray-green eyes as she returned his glare with unbridled vehemence. "Well, let's see . . ." she drawled sarcastically, rolling her eyes skyward and placing one forefinger against her chin as if giving his question serious consideration. "First I thought I'd go to the trading post, and then possibly to see Grace Simmons, and—oh, yes—about midmorning I just might need to pay a visit to the privy. That is, if I have your permission."

His face darkened ominously. "Don't get smart with me Gabrielle. I'm in no mood to spar with you this morning."

"I noticed," she shot back, her chin jutting out in defiance. "What happened? Did you get up on the wrong side of the bed? Or perhaps the thought of being my watch dog for the next month is a little more than you can stomach so early in the day."

"Gabrielle . . ." he cautioned, his eyes narrowing.

Undaunted, she opened her mouth to continue, then stopped as the memory of her father going away without so much as a good-bye wave struck her, knocking the stuffing out of her and leaving her with a burning ache in her chest. She clamped her mouth shut and lowered her gaze. "I'm sorry," she mumbled. "May I be excused?"

Dan eyed Gabrielle warily, wondering just what was going on in that deceitful head of hers. Never in his life had he known anyone whose moods could change with such lightning

28

swiftness. "Your father doesn't want you to be alone in the house while he is away," he said, bracing himself for the coming explosion. "After the stunt you pulled last night, I tend to agree with him. I'll be moving some of my belongings into the spare bedroom later today."

Her head snapped up. "You most certainly will not! I won't sleep in the same house with you!"

"You have no say in the matter, Gabrielle. The decision was made by the colonel."

She looked incredulous. "Do you have any idea what everyone will say when they find out you're—"

"I don't give a damn what anyone has to say about it," Dan declared, his patience eroding. "With all the trouble brewing among the Apaches, it's better to take extra precautions, even if it means swallowing your pride and contending with a little gossip. You're not staying in that house alone, and that's final."

Her bottom lip curled out peevishly. "And I suppose you plan to torture me with your presence at supper, too?"

The question did not warrant an answer. "I'll see you tonight, Gabrielle," Dan said wearily, and, tired of her needling, he turned and headed toward the Headquarters Building.

She watched his retreat, a puzzled frown on her face, and it took her a moment to realize that she had just been dismissed. *Damn him!* she swore silently, her fingers positively itching to pick up a rock and heave it at him. The man was impossible. It would serve him right if she just didn't show up for supper at all. Even going hungry would be preferable to enduring a meal in his company. Too angry to think clearly, she whirled about and started home, her heels pounding mercilessly against the ground and her hands knotted at her sides. A shadow that was not hers fell into step alongside her. "Go away," she snapped without looking up, thinking that it was the Major coming back to aggravate her further.

"And a good day to you, too, Miss Gabrielle." The pleasant masculine voice brought her up short.

"Lieutenant Dalton!" she blurted out, hot color fusing into her cheeks as she stared up at him in confusion. "I-I didn't know it was you."

The corners of his mouth turned up in amusement, and the feral gleam that appeared in his dark eyes would have made Gabrielle uncomfortable had she not been too distraught to notice it. "Am I correct in assuming that you just had a run-in with your favorite major?"

She had the distinct feeling that Lieutenant Dalton was laughing at her, not openly, but laughing all the same. "He's just being a horse's ass this morning," she said offhandedly, feeling somewhat pleased with herself when the officer's brows angled upward in surprise. There were a lot of things she could get away with, that people had come to expect of her; using foul language wasn't one of them.

"I'm sure Major Catlin has a great deal on his mind," he prompted, his tone guarded. "After all, with all the problems that have cropped up recently with the Apaches—"

"If he's mad at the Apaches, then why doesn't he take his bile out on *them?*" She was sick of hearing about the Apaches this and the Apaches that, and she was doubly sick of everyone jumping to Major Catlin's defense rather than hers, when he was the one who was being a royal pain in the neck. Grace had done it to her yesterday, and now Lieutenant Dalton, who didn't like the major much more than she, was doing it to her. What in the hell was wrong with everyone anyway? She put her hands on her hips and faced the officer squarely. "Do you know that he is moving into my house while Father is away? My house! And I wasn't even consulted. It's for my own protection, or so His Majesty says."

Lieutenant Dalton looked thoughtful. It was becoming more and more obvious that he had no intention of sticking his neck out and opposing Dan Catlin. "I was wondering what kind of an arrangement the colonel was going to come up with. A little awkward, I agree, but you must admit, it's better than having to spend the night with Bates and Holmes." He chuckled, more to himself than to her, and Gabrielle blushed a bright crimson.

"I don't see what's so funny," she shot back, her irritation flaring. "And besides, no matter what everyone seems to think, I don't need a nursemaid!"

"Don't fret so," Lieutenant Dalton chided gently, his eyes

still twinkling as though he were enjoying some private joke. "It's not such a monumental thing. The major puts in long hours at Headquarters anyway. I don't think you'll see much of him. At least not enough to warrant that sour face you're making."

She shot him a pained look, but said nothing.

"What I wanted to speak with you about before you got your nose so out of joint," he said, lightly changing the subject. "is this. I wish to invite you to be my dinner partner tonight. Captain and Mrs. Wilcox are giving an informal dinner for some of the officers, and afterward we shall indulge in a few hands of cards. Would you like to go?" He leaned toward her and whispered conspiratorially, "Major Catlin won't be there."

It was on the tip of Gabrielle's tongue to tell him that perhaps he should ask the major for permission, but she bit back the remark, knowing full well she was merely being spiteful. Instead, she caught her bottom lip between her teeth and peered up at him from beneath her lashes, a frown worrying her brow. "Do you suppose Marcus will mind?" she asked, suffering another twinge of guilt over what had happened between them on the past night.

"Of course, he'll mind!" Lieutenant Dalton said, laughing. "Why do you think I waited until he was safely out of the way before inviting you?"

"Oh!" In spite of herself, Gabrielle blushed again. She had secretly hoped Marcus would be jealous of her being courted by other men. Especially by Chase Dalton. With his dark good looks, he was one of the handsomest men she had ever seen, and though he had a reputation for being somewhat of a rake, it was this that intrigued her. Besides, she reasoned, accepting a dinner invitation wasn't really the same as being untrue to Marcus. Or was it? Her pulse quickening, she coyly fluttered her lashes. "I would be delighted to be your dinner partner tonight, Lieutenant Dalton. At what time shall I expect you?"

"I'll come for you at seven."

She gave him a dazzling smile. "I'll be ready."

The officer bade her good day, and Gabrielle, her bad mood dispelled, whirled about and made a beeline for the non-

31

commissioned officers' quarters. She could not wait to tell Grace!

It was Mrs. Simmons who answered the door. "Why, good morning, Miss Gabrielle," she said, her broad face frozen in a smile that Gabrielle suspected was forced. Even though Mrs. Simmons generally treated her with kindness, she could never quite shake the feeling that it was because the woman felt it was her Christian duty and not because she wanted to.

"I've come to see Grace, Mrs. Simmons. Is she busy?"

"I'm sure Grace will welcome taking some time out from her chores to visit with you," Mrs. Simmons said, letting her into the house. "But only for a little while, you understand. There are a million things that need doing around here today and we aren't lucky enough to have household help like you and your father."

"Yes, ma'am," Gabrielle said as politely as she could manage, though the response left a peculiar taste in her mouth. She did not understand why Mrs. Simmons should begrudge them the services of Bates and Holmes. After all, having the strikers was one of the privileges of being an officer, and it wasn't her fault the sergeant major was not an officer.

"You just wait right here," Mrs. Simmons said as she led Gabrielle into the front parlor. "I'll go fetch Grace."

"Thank you, ma'am." Gabrielle breathed a sigh of relief when Mrs. Simmons left the room. She didn't think she could stand living in this house under that woman's watchful eye. Grace had not been exaggerating when she'd said her father would lock her up and throw away the key if she misbehaved, only Gabrielle was inclined to believe it would be Mrs. Simmons who would do the locking up, and not the sergeant major.

After what seemed an eternity, Grace came into the parlor. "I can't visit long," she said, a wary look in her eyes as she dried her hands on her apron. She perched on the edge of one of the straightbacked horsehair-covered chairs and motioned for Gabrielle to do the same.

Gabrielle thought her friend seemed a little jumpy this morning. "I waved to you at the formation," she said offhandedly, wondering what was wrong.

"I-I didn't see you."

Gabrielle could not resist a giggle. "I know. You were staring at Major Catlin. Really, Grace! You should show a little restraint. Even I don't gawk at the men like that!"

Grace flushed a brilliant crimson and looked down at her hands.

"But that's not what I came to tell you," Gabrielle said impatiently, eager to change the subject. "Lieutenant Dalton has invited me to dinner tonight!"

Grace threw her a horrified glance. "You're not going to accept, are you?"

"I already have."

"Gabrielle, how could you? I thought you were in love with Lieutenant Epperling."

"I am. And it's only a dinner invitation, not a betrothal!"

"But Lieutenant Dalton is . . . is . . ." Grace frowned, searching for the appropriate word.

"Exquisitely handsome?" Gabrielle volunteered.

"Immoral would be a more apt description," Grace countered.

Gabrielle's sea green eyes twinkled mischievously. "I know. Isn't it exciting?"

"No, it's not! That man is dangerous. He seduced Sergeant Patterson's wife!"

"Oh, Grace, don't be a ninny! He didn't drag Alice Patterson into his bed. She went willingly, I daresay, and I'll bet all he had to do to get her there was smile at her. He has such a gorgeous smile, don't you think?"

"I think you should stay away from him, or everyone on post will be gossiping about you instead of Alice."

"Well, I don't intend to give them anything to gossip about. And I'm certainly not going to his quarters. We're having dinner at Captain Wilcox's house."

"Did Major Catlin give you permission to go?"

A smug smile spread across Gabrielle's features. "He doesn't know." She leaned forward and lowered her voice. "And I don't intend to tell him either."

"But, what if—"

"What if what? What if he's worried? I hope he does worry.

33

It would serve him right. Do you know I have to give him a full accounting of where I intend to be, every minute of the day? He's even moving into our house while Father is away so he can keep an eye on me!"

The color visibly siphoned from Grace Simmon's face.

"I almost wish I could be there to see the look on his face when I don't make an appearance at supper," Gabrielle continued, heedless of the change in her friend's expression. "But then, that would defeat the purpose, wouldn't it? I'll show him he can't boss me around!"

Grace picked at an imaginary spot on her apron. "Did you see Lieutenant Epperling last night?"

"Yes. For all the good it did," Gabrielle retorted, rolling her eyes in disgust. "He was just starting to kiss me when Major Catlin barged in on us."

Grace became very still. "What did the major do?"

"What do you think? He said Father wanted to see Marcus in his office right away, and then he dragged me home like I was some naughty two-year-old incapable of finding my own way. He even bawled me out for gallivanting around the post like a common whore. Do you belive that, Grace? He actually called me a whore!'

"Did he say anything else?"

"Nothing I'd care to repeat. I swear, sometimes that man is insufferable! Just because he's the Acting Commander while Father is away, that doesn't give him the right to—"

"Grace—!" Mrs. Simmons called out from the kitchen, signaling that it was time to bring the visit to an end.

Grace gave Gabrielle a tight lipped smile and stood up. "Just don't do anything foolish tonight," she said in a voice too low for her mother to overhear. "I don't trust Lieutenant Dalton and I don't think you should either."

Gabrielle chuckled. "Major Catlin's the one who is supposed to worry. Not you! I'll be fine. And with Captain Wilcox and his wife for chaperones, I'll certainly be behaving myself!"

"Will you tell me what happens?"

"Nothing is going to happen, Grace. Really! But, yes, I'll tell you everything tomorrow. Now don't you breathe a word of this to anyone, do you hear?"

If at all possible, Grace seemed to pale even more. "I won't," she said hoarsely, not quite meeting Gabrielle's gaze.

"Grace—!" Mrs. Simmons' piercing voice intruded again.

Gabrielle sighed. "I'd better go. But remember what I said. Don't tell anyone! This is our secret."

Grace showed Gabrielle to the door. "Just be careful around Lieutenant Dalton," she warned.

Gabrielle laughed gaily. "Don't worry!"

The rest of the day passed with incredible slowness. Gabrielle went to the trading post, but nothing in the store caught her eye, and she finally went home. With her father away, there was very little for the strikers to do so they had been assigned to dig the pit to be used for roasting a whole steer at the Cinco de Mayo festival. The house was empty and there was no one for her to even talk to. She tried working on the sampler she had started months before, but became frustrated when the thread persisted in knotting up on her. When she tried reading, her mind wandered, and after realizing she had just read the same paragraph for the third time, she slammed the book shut and took an angry swipe at the trickle of perspiration that slid down behind her ear. It was only noon, yet the mercury had already reached one hundred degrees and she felt listless and out of sorts.

Wandering aimlessly throughout the house, she thought about inviting Grace to spend the afternoon with her, then changed her mind. Grace had behaved oddly this morning, she mused. Nervous. Guilty. She chuckled at the thought of Grace feeling guilty. It simply wasn't possible for Grace to feel guilty about anything because she never did anything wrong. Gabrielle frowned, recalling the times she had been compared unfavorably with Grace Simmons. "Why can't you be more like Grace?" everyone repeatedly asked her. "Grace Simmons is a good girl." "Grace Simmons doesn't give her father even a fraction of the trouble you give yours." "You should try following Grace's example." "God forbid that the colonel should have been cursed with a daughter like you, Gabrielle!"

She winced. That last remark had come from Dan Catlin, and even though she had grown to expect such hostility from him, the words had hurt all the same. Furthermore, she did not understand why everyone wanted her to be like Grace Simmons. She did not want to be like Grace. Grace was boring and plain and obedient and . . . and . . . Grace was just Grace.

"You don't want me to be like Grace Simmons, do you, Mama?" she whispered, coming to a stop in the middle of the hall and looking woefully up at the painting of her mother. It had been commissioned shortly before Lisette's marriage, and she had only been eighteen at the time—a year older than Gabrielle was now. The resemblance between mother and daughter was astonishing, so much so that, upon seeing the painting for the first time, people often mistakenly thought the portrait was of Gabrielle. How Gabrielle loved that painting, and the pretty young girl who stared back at her from the canvas; for she knew in her heart that her mother would understand. Her mother would love her just the way she was.

Then why could she not shake the feeling that even her mother would not approve of what she was about to do?

Lieutenant Dalton called for her promptly at seven. It was obvious that he had just bathed because his hair was wet and he was freshly shaven and reeked of bay rum. It was all Gabrielle could do not to crinkle up her nose in disgust. She hated the smell of bay rum.

"I'm ready," she said breathlessly as she pulled the front door shut and grabbed his arm. "Let's hurry and get out of here before Major Catlin shows up."

Lieutenant Dalton grimaced. "You certainly know how to shatter a man's vanity, Gabrielle," he said wryly as she all but dragged him away from the house "And here I thought you were glad to see me."

She gave him a startled look, wondering where he had gotten that idea, then blushed to the roots of her hair as she realized her mistake. "Don't be silly. Of course I'm glad to see you. I just don't think the major will be, that's all."

"So you didn't tell him I was calling on you?"

"Of course not! You know he would never concede to letting me go with you. Like it or not, Lieutenant Dalton, your reputation around this post is a bit tarnished."

Though it was precisely what he wanted to hear, Dalton was careful to keep his expression neutral, and his footsteps slowed as they neared the end of Officers' Row. "Gabrielle, there's been a change in plans . . . Mary Wilcox wasn't feeling well, so the captain canceled dinner."

She stopped in her tracks, her eyes riveted on his face. "But, you promised—! I mean . . . I thought . . ." Gabrielle clamped her mouth shut, annoyed with herself for stammering, but she was unable to conceal her disappointment. Her plan to make Major Catlin worry about her was falling apart before she had even had a chance to carry it out.

"I would still like to have dinner with you, Gabrielle," the officer said quietly, his dark eyes fixed on her. "What do you say? At my quarters? Just the two of us?"

The sea green eyes widened ever so slightly.

As if reading her thoughts, Lieutenant Dalton added hastily, "All I had in mind was dinner, love. I don't intend to force myself upon you, if that's what you're worried about."

She started to shake her head. "I-I'd better not."

"Please? I may not get another chance to ask you before Epperling returns from the field."

Her heart pounding in her ears, Gabrielle caught her bottom lip between her teeth and looked away. Her mind was a battlefield of warring emotions. She knew she should not go with Lieutenant Dalton to his quarters, but she so wanted to get back at Major Catlin for the way he had treated her. Still, there was that scandal with Alice Patterson to consider. Suddenly she wasn't so certain that all the lieutenant had done to get the woman into his bed was smile at her. Suppose he really had seduced Alice? Suppose he tried to seduce her too? She cast the officer a wary glance from beneath her long dark lashes, and asked hesitantly, "Just dinner? Nothing else?"

The injured look he gave her appeared so genuine she wasn't sure if it was real or feigned. "Of course, just dinner! What did you think I intended to do with you?"

Again she blushed. "I'm sorry," she said hastily. "I didn't

mean to imply . . ." Her voice trailed off and she shifted uneasily. Now he was confusing her.

He gave her a sympathetic smile. "Listen, if it will make you feel any better, you can get up and go home anytime you want. I won't make you stay if you're uncomfortable with being alone with me."

Don't! a warning voice shouted in the back of her mind.

"Well?" he prompted.

She shook her head. "I-I don't know. . . ."

You little idiot! Everyone will talk about you the way they talked about Alice Patterson!

He suddenly took hold of her arm and turned her around. "On second thought, maybe I'd better just take you home now."

She jerked her arm free. "No . . . please. I don't want to go home," she blurted out childishly. "I-I'll have dinner with you!" There! It was done. She took a deep breath, not certain whether her knees were shaking from relief at having made a decision or from fear of having made the wrong one.

Thinking of the bottle of champagne he had packed in sawdust and ice, Dalton grinned broadly. The stupid girl didn't have any more sense than he'd thought. "Like I said, you can go home at any time. I won't force you to do anything you don't want to do." I won't have to, he added silently, placing a possessive arm about her shoulders and turning her in the direction of his quarters. Uncertainty clouding her eyes, Gabrielle looked up at him and gave him a wan smile as he swept her along.

Chapter Two

Dan locked the door to the Headquarters Building and started across the parade ground, a dull ache that reached from his neck to halfway down his back putting him out of sorts. It was late, he still hadn't had a chance to move his belongings into the colonel's quarters, and he was in no mood to put up with Gabrielle's sulking. He hoped she'd already had her supper and gone to bed.

He reached up to rub the back of his neck, a frown deepening the crease between his brows as he recalled last night's incident behind the stables. He doubted that the scolding he had given Gabrielle had done much good, for she was about as hardheaded and contrary as an Army mule. She was also dangerously naive, and he knew that she was probably totally unaware of how close she had come to being raped. The girl simply had no idea of the lusty feelings she was capable of arousing in a man. He thanked God that Sergeant-Major Simmons' daughter had been worried enough about Gabrielle to come forward and warn him of her intent to meet Lieutenant Epperling in secret, though he was somewhat puzzled as to why Grace Simmons had come to him instead of going to the colonel.

The instant Dan stepped into the house he sensed that something was amiss. Not bothering to light a lamp, he made his way down the darkened hallway to Gabrielle's room. Her door stood ajar and her bed, as he had anticipated, was empty. "Blast her!" he said aloud, his voice harsh and cutting in the stillness. He had a pretty good idea why she had taken off without telling him where she was headed, and he would be damned if he was about to allow the little minx to get away with it. Gabrielle was going to learn to obey orders if it was the last thing she ever did!

By the time he reached the Senior MCO's quarters, his anger had escalated into a slow-burning rage, and Sergeant-Major Simmons had no trouble recognizing the deadly calm in Dan's voice or the unyielding glint in his eyes. He had seen grown men reduced to tears when the major was in one of his quiet rages; a mere child stood no chance at all. "Grace Meredith, you get your tail out here!" the sergeant major bellowed from the front door before turning back to Dan. "One way or another, sir, we'll find out where she went."

Grace Simmons had long since gone to bed, and she was bleary-eyed and a little disoriented as she stumbled down the hallway, clutching her robe closed over her nightgown. "Yes, Pa?" she mumbled sleepily.

"You saw the colonel's girl today, didn't you?" the sergeant major asked, his brows puckering when he noticed the expression on his daughter's face change as her gaze rested on the major.

"She came by here this morning," Grace said, suddenly coming awake, her eyes still fixed on Dan's face. She clutched her wrapper even more tightly around her and gave him an incongruous smile "Is something wrong, Major Catlin?"

Uncomfortable with the way she was staring at him, Dan felt his stomach muscles tense. "Gabrielle's not at the house. I was hoping you would know where she might have gone."

"Didn't she tell you?" Grace asked, feigning astonishment with such aplomb that, had a gut feeling not told him otherwise, Dan might have believed she was truly surprised.

Suddenly, he knew.

"No, she did not." He returned the cow-eyed look the girl was giving him with an icy glare. The little chit was in love with him! That was why she had come to him last night instead of going to the colonel. She had not been worried about Gabrielle at all, but had merely used her as an excuse to further her own concerns.

"I don't want to get Gabrielle into trouble."

Dan knew that, too, was a lie. "Gabrielle got herself into trouble," he said with a little more brusqueness than he had intended. "You had nothing to do with it."

Grace had the distinct feeling that the major was more annoyed with her than he was with Gabrielle, and she did not know what she had done to incur his anger. "Lieutenant Dalton invited her to dinner at Captain Wilcox's house, sir," she said nervously, her attempts at being coy failing miserably. Why was he looking at her like that?

Anxious to be away from there, Dan curtly thanked her and then apologized to the sergeant major for the intrusion. If he was angry with Gabrielle for defying him, he felt only revulsion for Grace Simmons and her professed loyalty. He had once told Gabrielle she should try being a little more like Grace, but now the advice stuck, like a gall, in his throat.

Both the surgeon and his wife denied having seen either Gabrielle or Lieutenant Dalton that day. "We didn't invite anyone to dinner," Ben Wilcox replied to Dan's query, and each man knew what the other was thinking. "Dan, do you want me to go with you?"

Catlin shook his head. "No, I'll handle this myself."

"Poor little girl," Mary said quietly just as Dan started to leave, "growing up without a mother, and with a father who can't be bothered to give her the time of day."

Dan turned and stared at her in surprise, thinking at first that the captain's wife was joking. Mary Wilcox was a pretty woman, with warm eyes and a gentle smile, though now she was not smiling.

Ben Wilcox shifted uncomfortably and threw Dan an apologetic glance. "It's her condition," he said with a low chuckle, referring to his wife's obvious state of pregnancy. "Tends to bring out the maternal instinct in her."

"Don't make excuses for me, Ben. I meant what I said. I feel sorry for the child. It must be a terrible thing not to be wanted or needed. Gabrielle only behaves the way she does in order to get attention."

"I'll give her some attention," Dan retorted dryly. "I'll blister her rear end. She'll think twice before she pulls

41

another stunt like this one."

Mary placed a hand on his arm "Go easy on her, Dan," she said softly, her eyes dark with concern. "Sometimes those who are the most difficult to understand are the very ones who need our love and understanding the most. Gabrielle's not a bad girl. I just think she's very, very unsure of herself."

Unsure of herself, my ass, Dan thought as he headed toward Lieutenant Dalton's quarters. He decided Ben was right. It had to be Mary's maternal instinct. He'd known Gabrielle since she was a child, and the girl had never wanted for anything. She was about as spoiled and indulged as anyone could get. And for growing up without a mother, he was thankful Lisette was not around to see what a little bitch her only daughter had become. Still, Mary's words had unsettled him more than he was willing to admit.

Whether it was the sound of Gabrielle's laughter that set Dan off as Lieutenant Dalton opened the front door, or the overwhelming smells of wine and bay rum that clung to the younger man, Dan did not know, but something inside him snapped. Without stopping to think about what he was doing, he drew back his fist and planted it on the lieutenant's jaw, sending him flying.

"Who's at the door, Chase?" Gabrielle called out from Dalton's apartment before wandering out into the hall, none too steadily. There was an unnatural flush to her cheeks and she hiccuped and her eyes widened as she looked at Dalton, who was sprawled in the middle of the hall floor, then at Dan standing in the doorway and rubbing the knuckles of his right hand, his face dark with fury as he glared at her. Never in her life had she been so relieved to see someone. For the past hour, she had been trying to find a tactful way to leave Chase Dalton's quarters, yet Dalton had succeeded in detaining her and had gotten her to drink four full glasses of champagne, three and a half more than she had really wanted.

Suddenly, the scene Gabrielle viewed made her want to laugh, for Major Catlin's behavior did not remind her of a disgruntled guardian's, but of a cuckolded husband's, and if she didn't know better, she would have thought him jealous!

Bringing one hand up to her mouth to suppress a giggle that managed to slip out anyway, she hiccuped again and there was a silly, almost dazed look on her face.

His eyes glittering with unspent anger, Dan leveled a warning finger at Lieutenant Dalton who was struggling to sit up. "I'll deal with you in the morning, Lieutenant. Be in my office at oh-eight-hundred hours." Stepping over him, Dan seized Gabrielle's wrist. "You, young lady, are coming with me," he said sharply, and jerked her out the door.

A little too stunned and much too inebriated to make any sense out of what was happening, Gabrielle twisted around to glance back at the officer still sitting on the floor. "Why did you hit Lieutenant—" she began, then gasped as her foot missed the step and she plunged headlong off the veranda.

Dan caught her, breaking her fall, but he had no sooner set her on her feet than her knees buckled beneath her and she sat down hard.

She tilted her head back and grinned up at him.

"Stand up!" he ordered, placing his hands under her arms and pulling her upright.

Gabrielle swayed as the ground seemed to move of its own accord and everything reeled around her. "Oh . . . oh, my!" she muttered inanely, pressing one hand against her spinning head.

"Come on. I'm taking you home."

He turned her toward the house, but her feet refused to follow, causing her to stumble.

"Damn it, Gabrielle," Dan muttered, catching her. "You're so stinking drunk you can't even stand on your own two feet." He rammed one arm behind her knees and swept her up onto his arms.

A panicked cry rose up in her throat as her feet left the ground. "Don't drop me!" she begged, throwing her arms around his neck and holding on tightly, her eyes squeezed shut against the dizzy spinning in her head.

"For chrissake, girl, you're strangling me!"

She immediately relaxed her hold and, when the spinning finally subsided, opened one eye to peer at him as he carried her across the parade ground. *He's jealous!*" she thought again, choking back a giggle; and a warm and wonderful feeling that was one part champagne and three parts pure joy surged through her. He's jealous! He's jealous! Closing both eyes, she snuggled closer to him and nuzzled her face against his neck.

Dan's heart slammed against his ribs as he felt the warm softness of lips moving up his neck. Good God! She was kissing him! "Gabrielle!"

Keeping her hands clasped about his neck, she bolted upright and stared at him in wide-eyed innocence. "No one ever fought for me before," she said breathlessly. "No one."

Annoyed at being reminded of the disgraceful way he had lost his temper with Lieutenant Dalton, Dan frowned and said nothing, but there was no mistaking the anger that reverberated through his strides.

Ignoring the silent warning, Gabrielle placed one small hand up against his cheek and stroked it gently, her young face illuminated by wonder, a pensive look in her eyes. "Grace was right. You are handsome. You're very, very, *very* handsome." She caught her bottom lip between her teeth and giggled.

"Gabrielle, behave yourself!"

Mirth bubbling up inside her, Gabrielle clasped his face between her hands and gave him a big noisy kiss on the mouth.

"Jesus Christ!" Dan jerked his head back as though he'd been burnt. He hastily set her on the ground and put her away from him, but she flung herself at him and wrapped her arms securely around his waist, and an unexpected heat rushed through his loins at the feel of her soft young body pressed seductively against his. Gritting his teeth and cursing inwardly, Dan took her by the shoulders and pried her away from him. "Stop that!" he commanded, shaking her so hard her head snapped back. "Either stop this silliness right now, or I'm going to stick you under the pump and drown your ass! Do you understand me?"

For a moment, Gabrielle just stared blankly at him, unable to move; then her eyes widened and, in spite of herself, she let out a most unladylike belch before clamping one hand over her mouth and dissolving into another fit of giggles.

44

It was all he could do not to throttle her on the spot. Seizing her arm, he whirled her around and half pushed, half dragged her the rest of the way home, hauling her through the front door just as she burst into a rousing chorus of "Oh, Don't You Remember Sweet Betsy From Pike."

"Stay here," Dan commanded, and left her in the darkened hallway as he went into the front parlor to light a lamp.

She tottered after him.

His voice sliced through the darkness. "Where do you keep the matches?"

She giggled. "Under the lamp."

"Damn!" he exclaimed as he banged his knee against a gateleg table. He felt for the lamp, found it, and finally managed to get it lighted. Distorted shadows flickered throughout the room as he adjusted the wick and replaced the glass globe. Then he straightened up, nearly knocking Gabrielle down. He had not known she was standing right behind him. "I told you to stay in the hall!" he scolded, grabbing her to keep her from falling.

She slumped against him and slid her arms around his middle. "You were wonderful," she mumbled drunkenly into his shirtfront. "No one ever fought—"

"Gabrielle, stand up!"

"I liked the way you punched his lights—"

"Gabrielle!"

"Like that!" She took a swing at him, plowing her fist into his chin, then stepped back and blinked up at him in surprise, her mouth dropping open in horror as she realized what she had just done. Dan did not move, but stood there glowering at her, amber lights snapping in his hazel eyes and undisguised anger hardening the planes of his face. There was an odd buzzing in Gabrielle's ears now, and her stomach was knotting painfully. She clamped her mouth shut and swallowed hard, suddenly feeling as though she would be sick.

He took a step toward Gabrielle and she instinctively threw her arms up over her face to protect herself, thinking he meant to hit her in return. Instead, he gripped her wrist so tightly it hurt, spun her toward the door, and pulled her, none too

45

gently, down the hall toward her bedroom. "I've had about all I can stand of you for one day, miss! You're to stay in this room until I give you permission to come out!"

Lieutenant Dalton stood stiffly before Dan's desk, his dark eyes brittle with undisguised insolence, his mouth set in an angry line. A blue-black bruise spread from his chin up along the left side of his jaw and there was no mistaking the raw hatred that radiated from him.

"This is not the first time I have had to counsel you regarding your behavior toward the women on this post," Dan said sternly as he leaned back in his chair, his eyes never leaving the younger man's face. "The incident with Alice Patterson was bad enough. But this time, Dalton, you have gone too far. I'm finding it difficult to believe you would be so reckless as to try to force yourself on the colonel's daughter."

Chase Dalton snickered inelegantly. "I didn't have to force her, sir. The girl is like a bitch in heat. She practically threw herself at me."

Dan stiffened. "Before or after you got her drunk, Lieutenant?"

"All I did was invite her to dinner—"

"Dinner at Captain Wilcox's house?"

"Yes, sir. But then Mrs. Wilcox took sick and—"

"Drop the crap, Dalton! I know damn well Wilcox and his wife never invited you to dinner. You simply used that as a ploy to get Gabrielle to agree to go with you. Then you gave her a trumped-up excuse about Mary being ill and convinced her to have dinner with you instead. Alone. In your quarters."

The younger officer shifted uneasily. He had never expected the major to check up on him.

"And then," Dan continued, pushing back his chair and getting to his feet, "with no regard for the damage that you would cause to her reputation, you proceeded to get her so damned drunk she didn't know if she was coming or going. Of course, being the gentleman that you are, I'm sure you fully intended to put a stop to the situation before it went any further." There was no mistaking the sarcasm in his voice.

Lieutenant Dalton met Dan's icy glare with one of his own. "Not exactly," he retorted, his tone derisive. Everyone on post knew Gabrielle DuBois was just itching to get laid. The way she'd been chasing Marcus Epperling these past few months proved that. Why should he stand aside and let someone else have what could just as easily be his? He didn't give a shit if she was the colonel's daughter. A piece of ass was a piece of ass, and he was just as entitled to an easy screw as the next man.

Dan pushed a paper across the desk toward the other man. "This is a list of the charges against you," he said, grinding out each word with measured deliberation, his face dark with unbridled anger. Right now he wasn't sure who he wanted to strangle more, Lieutenant Dalton or Gabrielle. "Read it and sign where I've indicated. For the next thirty days, you are restricted to post and you will report to Captain Wilcox for additional duty. This is your last warning, Dalton. Another incident like this one and I will personally see to it that you are court-martialed and removed from the Army."

Chase Dalton picked up the paper and scanned it; then, in a move Dan had not anticipated, he ripped it in two. "I'll save you the trouble, Major," he said, a devil-may-care look settling over his darkly handsome features. "You'll have my resignation on your desk this afternoon. I was willing to take my share of the blame in all this, but I'll be damned if I'm going to accept responsibility for a two-bit tramp. I'll be out of here by the end of the week." Ramming his hat down onto his head, Dalton raked his eyes over Dan then turned away. On his way out the door, he said scornfully, "Looks like you're as big a sucker for her Little Miss Innocence act as the rest of us."

"O-oooh!" Gabrielle groaned, clutching her head as sunlight streamed in through the open window, stabbing her eyes. Her nightgown was on backward and was bunched up around her hips, revealing her long slender legs, as she huddled in the middle of the bed, certain that she had died during the night and gone straight to hell. He head pounded so miserably and she thought she would be sick to her stomach and her tongue felt as though an entire Infantry battalion had marched across

47

it in stockinged feet. She silently swore that if she survived the next twenty-four hours she would never, never touch another drop of champagne for as long as she lived.

There was no sympathy in Dan's expression as he handed her a tin cup filled with freshly squeezed lemon and lime juices, to which he had added a measure of fermented maguey and ground cascabel chile. "Drink it all, and fast."

Gabrielle threw him a disparaging glance, hating him for the way he stood there with that holier-than-thou look on his face as though he derived some perverse satisfaction from her agony, but at the moment she felt too miserable to argue with him. Brushing a tangled curl back from her face, she obediently took the cup, brought it to her lips, then backed away. "What is it?" she asked, screwing up her face in disgust.

He folded his arms across his chest. "Drink it."

Suspicion flashed in her eyes. "Not until you tell me what it is."

"Drink it!"

"No!"

Dan's earlier encounter with Chase Dalton had worn his patience perilously thin, and he was in no mood to put up with Gabrielle's antics. Bending down, he placed a palm flat on the mattress on either side of her, his face only inches from hers, and looked her straight in the eye. "Either you drink it, young lady," he said slowly, his eyes boring into her with unrelenting hardness, "or I'll pour it down your goddamned throat."

Her heart coming to a complete standstill, Gabrielle lowered her gaze and brought the cup to her lips, convinced that he would indeed pour the foul-looking concoction down her throat if she did not obey. When she hesitated and threw him a pleading glance from beneath her lashes, he said tersely, "All of it."

Taking a deep breath, she downed the obnoxious brew in a single gulp.

For several seconds, she sat without moving, a bewildered look clouding her face. Then, suddenly, her eyes flared wide and her hands flew to her throat. The tin cup clattered to the floor, and with a shriek that could be heard clear across the parade ground, Gabrielle bolted from the bed. But her foot caught in the tangle of sheets and she hit the floor hard, landing on her hands and knees.

Dan shoved the chamber pot in front of her.

Fiery spasms ripped through her, and her stomach, mouth, and throat were ablaze with a white heat that threatened to cauterize everything it touched. "I'll kill you!" she swore between gasps, oblivious of the steadying hand he had placed on her shoulder as she retched into the pot. "I'll kill y— Arghhh!"

An empathetic smile softened Dan's features, and he gently stroked a lock of the honey-colored hair that spilled over her shoulders to fall down her back in impudent tangles that refused to be tamed. That'll teach you, little one, he thought. And he had every reason to believe it would, for this was one cure that was far worse than it's respective ailment.

Gabrielle sputtered and struggled to catch her breath. "What w-was . . . it?" she managed to get out in a choked voice. Even the tears that pooled in her eyes burned like fire.

He chuckled softly. "Old Mexican remedy for hangover, sweetheart. Rattlesnake piss."

Gabrielle groaned and, with an immense effort, staggered to her feet and crawled back into bed, burying her face in the pillow.

"I'll deal with you when I get back," Dan said, untangling the sheet from around her legs and drawing it up over her. Picking up the chamber pot on his way out the door, he stopped to look back at her and, shaking his head, chuckled again.

It was midday when a persistent rapping at the front door finally jolted Gabrielle from a deep seemingly drugged sleep. "I'm coming, I'm coming." she mumbled irritably, clutching a handful of sheet to help her work her way out of the bed. Every time she tried to move, the room seemed to fly into a crazy spin that left her feeling dizzy and a little nauseated. Only with a great deal of effort did she finally make it to the door.

"Gabrielle, you'll never believe what happened!" Grace Simmons burst out excitedly as she pushed the door shut. "Lieutenant Dalton resigned his commission, and everyone's saying he got into a fight last night with Major Catlin and that you—" She broke off suddenly, her eyes growing wide as they took in every inch of Gabrielle's disheveled appearance. "Goodness! What happened to you?"

Holding onto the wall to brace herself, Gabrielle screwed up her face and forced one eye open to peer at her friend. It hurt even to breathe, and the act of swallowing sent a stabbing pain up the back of her nose and brought tears to her eyes. "Please don't . . . shout," she whispered hoarsely.

For a moment, Grace simply stood there, her mouth agape; then a peculiar look swept over her face and she said, "Gabrielle, why is your nightgown on backward?"

"W-what?" Gabrielle muttered. Her eyes followed her friend's bewildered gaze, and she moaned inwardly and closed her eyes as the memories of the past night came rushing back with frightening clarity. She saw Chase Dalton lying on the floor and Major Catlin standing over him, rubbing his knuckles.

"Gabrielle, do you feel all right?"

No, I don't feel all right, she wanted to snap. But she choked back the retort, knowing Grace meant well, and since she couldn't say what she wanted, she didn't say anything at all. She felt miserable. It was probably all over the post by now that she had disgraced herself last night, but even that mattered little compared to the mortification she felt at knowing she had kissed Major Catlin. *Major Catlin!* She had to have been out of her mind; she hated Dan Catlin! She hated him! Her hands knotted into fists as a wave of confusion swept over her. Just who was she trying to convince, anyway?

Seeing Gabrielle's discomfort, Grace made a sympathetic clucking noise with her tongue and immediately took control of the situation. "Tell you what," she said with a cheerfulness that made Gabrielle want to gag. "You go back to your room and get out of that nightgown and splash some cold water on your face, and I'll go out to the kitchen and make you some tea. That should have you feeling better in no time. And then you can tell me all about last night, and I'll tell you what happened this morning. You won't believe it, Gabrielle. It's simply too incredible!"

By the time Grace had returned from the kitchen with the tea tray, Gabrielle had washed up and brushed her teeth, and she felt almost human again. But dark smudges ringed eyes that were, this morning, too large and too luminous in her pallid face, and an angry fire raged in the pit of her stomach. When she got her hands on Dan Catlin, she was going to kill him. It would be a long time before she forgave him for trying to poison her with that so-called Mexican curative.

Gabrielle pulled her wrapper on over her chemise, but there was a sulky expression on her face as she sat down on the bed, tucking her legs up beneath her. Leaning back against the pillows Grace had plumped up for her, she accepted a cup of steaming tea with what Grace considered a pronounced lack of graciousness. Long lashes threw violet shadows against Gabrielle's ivory cheeks, and unruly curls spilled like red-gold flames around her slender shoulders as she bowed her head over the teacup. For a long agonizing moment, Grace allowed herself to be consumed by envy. It wasn't fair, she bemoaned silently, that Gabrielle should have been born beautiful while she was so plain; but then, she thought smugly, getting a grip on her jealousy, true beauty came from within, and she knew she was beautiful in a way that Gabrielle would never be. Gabrielle was selfish and spoiled and willful, all the things Grace knew men hated in a woman. All the things she knew Dan Catlin hated about Gabrielle.

Careful not to let her thoughts show on her face, she began picking up the clothes scattered carelessly on the floor, chatting cheerfully as she moved about the room. "Did I tell you Lieutenant Dalton resigned?" she asked, going to the wardrobe and retrieving a hanger.

Gabrielle looked up from the teacup, her eyes nervously following Grace's movements. "Why?"

Grace shook her head. "I don't know. He and Major Catlin were locked in the major's office for the longest time this morning, and everyone says that when the lieutenant came out, he was quite angry about something. And . . ."—she turned an inquisitive gaze on Gabrielle, no longer able to contain her curiosity—"his face is all bruised and everyone is saying that Major Catlin beat him up last night when he found . . ." She hesitated. "Is it true? Did Lieutenant Dalton really seduce you?"

51

Gabrielle's mouth went white. "No. It's not true!" she protested hotly. "Lieutenant Dalton did not seduce me. And Major Catlin did not beat him up. He . . . he only hit him once." She did not know why she suddenly felt the need to defend Dan Catlin. He had never thought of her as anything but a stupid, silly, spoiled little girl, lacking *enough sense to fit on the sharp end of a cactus spine.*

Grace shook her head in bewilderment. "Major Catlin was so angry when he came by our house last night looking for you, I would not have put it past him to beat up Lieutenant Dalton. Not in the least. But I was more worried for you than for the lieutenant, because Pa said the major told him that when he caught up with you, he was going to—" She broke off. "Why are you looking at me like that?"

"It was you, wasn't it?" Gabrielle demanded, coming off the bed like a shot, eyes blazing. "You were the one who told Major Catlin where I was last night!"

"It was late," Grace explained, moving with deliberate calm throughout the bedroom, picking up stockings and under-garments and draping them across her arm. "I was afraid something might have happened to you. And I didn't tell him you went to the lieutenant's quarters, because I didn't know about that. I simply told him that Captain and Mrs. Wilcox had invited the two of you to dinner."

Gabrielle's hands shook so badly that she sloshed tea down the front of her wrapper. Setting the cup in its saucer, she slammed both down on top of the dresser with a force that drove the tea up out of the cup in a small wave that spilled on to the starched white doily.

Grace's forehead puckered in disgust. "Now look what you've—"

"You sneak! You told him I was with Marcus too, didn't you?" she demanded. And when Grace did not answer, Gabrielle drew back her hand and slapped her as hard as she could.

For a moment, the two girls simply stood staring at each other in mute horror, Grace rubbing her bruised cheek and Gabrielle fighting down an overwhelming wave of nausea at the thought of what she had just done. Tears pooled in Grace's eyes. "Gabrielle, please . . . I didn't mean to get you into trouble."

"Like hell you didn't! You did it on purpose, just so you could cozy up to Major Catlin and show him what a perfect little angel you are!"

"I didn't!" Grace blurted out defensively, but the angry flush that engulfed her only served to confirm Gabrielle's suspicions.

"That's why you were so jumpy yesterday morning when I visited you, wasn't it? That's why you could hardly look me in the face. You knew you had betrayed me. And you had the gall to call *me* selfish!"

These accusations forced a sob from the older girl's throat, and flinging the armful of clothing aside, she headed for the door.

"Oh, no, you don't!" Gabrielle stepped into her path. Preventing her escape, she faced her squarely, arms akimbo and raw fury roiling like a summer storm in her eyes. "What did the major do when you tattled, Grace?" she taunted spitefully, not caring if her words hurt. "Did he pat you on the head and tell you what a good little girl you were for coming to him? Did he tell you how well mannered and sensible you are and how he wished I were more like you? Did he tell you—"

"That will be enough!" The enraged masculine voice came from the doorway, causing Gabrielle to whirl around in surprise and Grace to lower her eyes in humiliation as hot tears spilled over the hand she held to her smarting cheek. Dan stood just inside the doorway, feet apart and arms folded across his chest, his black brows knitted together above hard, unforgiving eyes that missed nothing in the scene before him. His mouth was set in a grim line, and his tanned skin was stretched taut over his high cheekbones, emphasizing their prominence and lending an exotic, almost savage, air to his already formidable countenance.

Gabrielle's nerves were drawn as tightly as a bowstring, and cold prickles rose on her skin; but she would not let Dan Catlin see her fear. With a haughty toss of her head, she turned her back to him.

For a moment, no one spoke, and the only reprieve from the

awful silence was Grace's muffled sobs. Finally Dan stepped to one side of the door, and held it open. "Miss Simmons, I think you had better leave now."

Grace did as she was told without arguing, and Dan had to catch himself to keep from falling into the old trap of wishing Gabrielle were so pliable. He saw Gabrielle flinch at the sound of the front door closing. Her back was still toward him, but he did not need to see her face to know she was still hurting. And he had witnessed enough of the incident between her and Grace Simmons to know the reason why. Something knotted inside him, for he knew only too well the pain of betrayal, and suddenly felt an unfamiliar surge of compassion for her.

Gabrielle was the first to break the thick silence between them. "I suppose you're going to yell at me for hitting Grace." she said tartly, her shoulders held rigid in anticipation of retribution.

Another long, uneasy moment passed before Dan spoke, and when he did, his answer caught Gabrielle by surprise. "I can hardly fault you for losing your temper when I have yet to learn to control mine," he said quietly, feeling her anguish as acutely as though it were his own.

She spun around to glower at him, suspicion darkening her eyes, and for an instant only a thin layer of cotton batiste stood between her nakedness and his gaze. Then, face flushing maddeningly, she grasped the front of her wrapper and yanked it shut over her chemise.

"However," Dan continued sharply, jerking his eyes back up to her face, "that does not excuse what you did last night. Not only did you fail to keep me informed as to your where-abouts, you behaved in a manner you knew I would find objectionable. I don't tolerate willful disobedience from my men and I certainly won't tolerate it from you. For the next week, you will remain in this house. You will go nowhere. You will receive no visitors. If, at the end of a week, you have learned to conduct yourself appropriately, the restriction will be lifted. If you have not, it will be extended for another week, and then another, and another after that, if necessary. The choice is yours, Gabrielle. You can either grow up, or you can continue to behave like a spoiled child, in which case, you will be treated like one."

She had become very still, her expression almost trancelike, as he chastised her. Suddenly it bloomed into outright fury. "You will do this! You will do that!" she mocked, angry with herself for being so weak as to want to defend him to Grace Simmons earlier. Her hands knotted into fists, and it took every ounce of willpower she had not to fly at him and scratch his arrogant eyes out. "I am not one of your troopers, and I refuse to be treated as one! You have no right to keep me prisoner in my own home. I will come and go as I please, and if you don't like it, you can just . . . you can just . . . stick it in your ear!" It was a mighty weak threat, but she was so furious, she could not think of a better one.

He eyed her evenly, his own anger carefully held in check, and leveled a warning finger at her. "You just remember one thing, young lady. I know you've never had a spanking, but if you try to leave this house without my permission, that is precisely what you are going to get!"

Gabrielle's chin jerked up defiantly, and Dan missed not a single one of the conflicting emotions that rippled across her face in rapid succession. Outrage. Fear. Confusion. Scorn. Doubt. The man was insane! First he'd tried to poison her, and now he was threatening her with physical harm. "Father would have you court-martialed if you hit me," she said, the haughtiness of her tone marred by a tremor of uncertainty.

A cruel cold smile twisted his mouth. "I wouldn't be so sure of myself if I were you, Gabrielle," Dan said, raking his eyes over her in undisguised contempt. "One of these days, you are going to get a rude awakening, and I can assure you, little one, it won't be pleasant." He shot a scornful glance about him on his way out the door, then ordered tersely, "Clean up this room!"

For the remainder of that day and all of the next, Gabrielle was careful not to cross him. But, by the morning of the third day, the mere thought of spending even another hour confined to the house made her snappish and contradictory, and it took a large measure of self-restraint for her not to bring her ill mood to the breakfast table with her. "The Cinco de Mayo festival is today," she ventured with a contrived sweetness, casting him a sideways glance from beneath lowered lashes.

Dan raised his eyes and peered at her over the rim of his coffee cup, but said nothing.

Gabrielle poked aimlessly at a slice of toast that had long since grown cold and unpalatable. "Corporal Holmes says the mess sergeant is stuffing a steer with chiles and onions and roasting it whole in that pit they dug."

"That's right," Dan said flatly, refusing to be drawn into her game. Whenever Gabrielle was up to something, it showed in her face. She was not subtle.

Her patience flagging, Gabrielle took a deep breath and tried again. "Everyone is going to be there. I heard that Bryce Edwards is letting his men have the day off from the ranch so they can attend. They're even bringing their own entry for the—"

"You're not going."

"But—"

Dan set his coffee cup down with a thud and turned a stern gaze on her. "In case you have forgotten young lady, you are being punished. Your restriction doesn't end for another four days. You will stay in this house today, and that's final."

Despair flickered in Gabrielle's eyes. "But the festival only comes once a year, and you know I've been waiting months for—"

"You should have thought of that before you disobeyed me."

"But, all I want to do is—"

"No!"

"But—"

"Damn it, Gabrielle! I refuse to argue with you. You will do as you are told!"

Before she could say anything else, they were interrupted by Sergeant-Major Simmons. "Need to speak with you, sir," he told Dan, while casting a glance in Gabrielle's direction.

Her stomach did a nervous flip-flop. He had not been too pleased when he'd found out she had slapped his daughter.

56

Dan pushed back his chair and got to his feet. "What's wrong?"

"Sergeant Plunkett just rode in from Camp Grant. A mob from Tucson attacked the Apaches quartered near the post. Murdered a hundred and twenty-five or so, most all of 'em women and children."

A cold, congested expression settled on Dan's face. "I take it Epperling didn't get there on time?"

The sergeant major shook his head. "It happened Sunday morning, sir, before you even got Lieutenant Whitman's dispatch."

Dan swore inwardly. "What about the survivors?" he asked, reaching across the table for his hat.

"Skimmy and his men took to the hills, and they're leaving a trail of blood behind them. There have already been more than a dozen reported outrages against white miners and settlers since the attack." Sergeant-Major Simmons paused, then added, "Seven of the dead were members of Skimmy's immediate family. He was only able to save one daughter from being killed."

Eskiminzin, or "Skimmy," was a Pinal Apache who had married into the generally peaceful Arivaipa band, but there would be no peace in these hills now, Dan knew. A crippling feeling of helplessness knotted inside him. He accompanied the sergeant major to the door. "Is B Company on it's way back?"

"Plunkett didn't say. Oh . . . and another thing, sir. There's a courier from Department waiting in your office."

Gabrielle bolted from her chair. "Major Catlin—"

Dan turned on her. "Not another word out of you, young lady!" he bellowed, fire snapping in his eyes. "You are not going to the festival, and that's final!"

The front door slammed after him, and for a moment, Gabrielle just stood there, too numb to move; then, blind fury welling up inside her, she grabbed Dan's coffee cup up off the table, ran out into the hall, and hurled it at the closed door, wantonly smashing the delicate bone china. "I wasn't even going to ask you about the festival, you old goat!" she shouted, but her anger was far from vented and she stamped her foot in frustration. She had wanted to ask if Marcus was all right, but Catlin had not even given her the chance.

Mumbling under her breath, Gabrielle stormed into her bedroom and sent the door crashing shut. Marcus was right. Dan Catlin was a crude, boorish *breed*, just like his father. Yanking open the bottom drawer of her dresser, she took out the faded brown corduroy pants she had hidden beneath her petticoats. She refused to stay in this house a moment longer, just because *he* said so.

The britches encased her hips and her well-proportioned legs like a second skin, which was just as well, Gabrielle thought as she put them on, since she didn't have a belt to cinch the waist. She had gotten them, along with a boy's blue chambray workshirt, from a batch of used clothing she and Grace had collected and mended and washed and then donated to charity. Grace had been appalled by her action and had, upon more than one occasion, threatened to tell on her. But Gabrielle didn't give a hoot what the uppity Miss Simmons thought. She was sick to death of kowtowing to Grace and to Dan Catlin and to anyone else who professed to know what she should or should not do.

She hastily brushed out her hair and bound it into two tight plaits, which she wound about her head and pinned into place; then she wedged one of her father's hats down over her head to hide the braids. There! She pursed her lips and studied her reflection in the cheval mirror, a gleam of satisfaction illuminating her eyes. As long as she didn't get too close to the major, he'd never recognize her as being anything other than a twelve-year-old boy. Maybe. She frowned and hunched her shoulders slightly, but even that failed to hide the distinctly feminine bosom that lurked beneath the blue chambray shirt.

Just in case Dan Catlin was watching the house, she slipped out the kitchen door and circled around behind the officers' quarters, emerging on the far side of the quadrangle. White canvas field tents had been stretched over tall poles to provide shade to the otherwise barren parade ground, and the air was filled with the smells of mesquite smoke and chile and fresh corn tortillas and the pit-barbecued beef and apple pie. Gabrielle's mouth watered and her stomach rumbled. She had

58

never seen so many people in one place in her entire life, she thought as she worked her way through the noisy crowd, her hat pulled down low and her eyes peeled for any sign of Dan Catlin.

Corporal Bates was the first to recognize her. "That you, Miss Gabrielle?" he asked, his mouth dropping open as he gazed at her, astonished.

She threw him a sharp look. "Shhh! I don't want anyone to know I'm here. Not yet anyway." She moved in close to him where she would be half-hidden by his height. "Have you seen Major Catlin?" she whispered, casting an anxious glance over his shoulder.

He shook his head. "Ain't here. Been tied up at Head-quarters all morning. Miss Gabrielle, does the major know you're out here running around in them britches?"

Her eyes narrowed menacingly. "No, he doesn't. And you'd better not tell him either!" She glanced around. "I don't even 'know half these people."

He raised a hand and pointed. "There's Mr. Edwards from the Rocking P. You seen their entry for the regatta? Sergeant Wilson calls it *The Ark*. C'mon. I'll show you."

She started to follow, then clutched his arm and dodged behind him. "No! Not that way!"

"W-what?" He twisted around to see where she had gone.

"It's Grace Simmons. I can't let her see me," Gabrielle said. She jerked her hat even lower over her eyes. "She'll run and tell the major I'm here."

"You mean, you're not supposed to—"

"No, I'm not supposed to be here, you fool! Darn you, stand still or she'll see me!" Gabrielle ventured a peek over the soldier's shoulder. Wearing a new white dress with a blue sash, Grace Simmons was standing with her mother not fifty feet from them, her eyes scanning the crowd. Probably looking for old lover-boy Catlin, Gabrielle thought peevishly as she ducked out of sight when Grace's gaze swung in their direction. She grabbed Corporal Bates' hand. "Let's go around the other way."

The soldier good-naturedly allowed himself to be pulled along as fast as his limp would allow. "I thought you and the sergeant major's daughter were friends. How come—"

"Because she's mad at me, that's why." Figuring the only way she was going to put a stop to his questions was to tell him the whole story, Gabrielle did just that. Starting with her plan to meet with Marcus, she went on to describe the ill-fated dinner invitation from Lieutenant Dalton, the fight she had gotten into with Grace, and ended by saying the major had restricted her to the house. She was careful, however, to leave out the part about kissing the major. She didn't want *anyone* to know about that.

Corporal Bates stopped dead in his tracks and shook his head in dismay. "Miss Gabrielle, if the major finds out—"

"He won't find out! Besides, if the old goat shows his face out here, I'll go home. I promise!"

He eyed her warily.

She threw him a coy glance from beneath her lashes, and a dimple appeared in one of her cheeks. "You can always say I threatened to bust your other kneecap."

The corners of his mouth twitched uncontrollably. Miss Gabrielle was about the most engaging thing he'd ever seen in his life, and she looked especially fetching today with that mischievous twinkle in her eyes and her pert little nose peeking out from beneath the brim of the oversized hat. "I really shouldn't do this . . . ."

She could tell his resistance was crumbling. "Please?" she said sweetly, tilting her head to one side and giving him a look that would have melted iron ore.

"Oh, what the hell! C'mon. We'll find Holmes, and between the two of us, we should be able to keep you outta the major's gunsights."

Gabrielle's spirits soared. She was going to enjoy this day more than any other in her entire life. And when it was over, she would simply slip back inside the house and His Royal Majesty would be none the wiser. She would just have to remember to sulk all through supper so he didn't get suspicious.

Corporal Holmes was well on his way to getting shit-faced drunk by the time they located him. "Tulibai," he said, grinning and turning bright red all at the same time. The sight of Miss Gabrielle in britches was even better than the sight of her in her nightgown. "Wanna sip?" he asked, holding the cup of homemade Apache corn mash out to her.

She wrinkled her nose in disgust. "You'll need a dose of rattlesnake piss come morning," she stated with a nod of authority.

Corporal Holmes choked and sprayed tulibai everywhere. Bates guffawed loudly. "She's right about that one, Charlie!"

Charles Holmes dragged his sleeve across his mouth when he finally stopped sputtering. "And just what do you know about rattlesnake . . . er . . . uh—"

"Rattlesnake piss," Gabrielle prompted, silent laughter illuminating her beautiful green eyes.

The soldier's face reddened considerably. If the major heard her, he was liable to wash her mouth out with soap! Bending down to her level, he looked her straight in the eye. "And who told you about this rattlesnake whatever, Miss Smarty-pants?"

"The major made her drink it," Al Bates volunteered, winking at her and slapping her affectionately on the back. "You should've been there. She screamed so loud the fellas heard her all the way over in the barracks!"

Gabrielle's mouth dropped open. "*You* were there?"

"Uh-huh. I helped the major fix it. Someone had to stand there and pulverize all them chiles!"

"Why, you!" She put her hands on her hips and gave him a wounded look.

Bates chuckled. "Aw, c'mon! It was for your own good, and you know it. Besides, you were lucky. We only put one chile in yours."

Gabrielle's distress did not run deep, and before another ten seconds had elapsed, a dimple flitted in and out of her cheek and a satanic gleam appeared in her eyes. "Will you tell me how to make it?"

Bates jerked his head back, and his eyes narrowed suspiciously. "Just what are you up to?"

She blinked at him with studied innocence, and affected her best Southern drawl. "Why, kind sir, whatever gave you the idea that I am up to something?"

This time it was Holmes' turn to laugh. "I think she means

to pay back the major for making her drink that shit!"

Gabrielle giggled.

Shaking his head, Corporal Bates rolled his eyes heavenward and pleaded, "Why me?"

The conspirators agreed that Bates and Holmes would take turns keeping an eye out for the major, and then, the soldiers armed with mugs of tulibai and Gabrielle fortified with a round of Fry Bread smeared with honey, they headed toward the wash where the regatta was about to begin.

Cinco de Mayo, the fifth of May, was celebrated every year in honor of the Mexican victory over French forces at Puebla nine years before, and, at Camp Carleton, the highlight of the festivities was the annual Mule Creek Regatta. A dry arroyo during all but the rainy months, Mule Creek became, once a year, host to the most unlikely assortment of "yachts" known to man. Anything that could be towed, pushed, or dragged along the sandy creek bottom was eligible to enter, the only stipulation being that participating vessels had to be rigged with at least a semblance of sailpower. Over the past couple of years, entries had become quite imaginative, and this year was no exception.

"There's *The Ark*," Corporal Bates said, pointing toward the wash.

Gabrielle licked off the honey that had run between her fingers and raised up on tiptoe, but too many people stood between her and the wash. "I can't see."

Bates and Holmes exchanged glances, then, before Gabrielle had time to realize what they were about, they bent down and hoisted her up between them.

Giggling impishly, she clung to her lofty perch upon their shoulders, her eyes growing wide with wonder at the panorama spread out before her. *The Ark* was easy enough to spot. A rickety old wagon had been harnessed to two half-grown calves, and in the bed of it, beneath a billowing white bedsheet that served as a sail, were wood and wire livestock crates holding live chickens, geese, a pig, and two wild coatis! Cy Harmon, Mr. Edwards's foreman, held the reins. Surrounding *The Ark* were buckboards and handcarts, and even a travois; all fitted with some kind of improvised rigging. Mrs. Mendoza and her brood of laundresses commanded a fleet of washtubs while Captain Wilcox was driving the blue-painted Army wagon that served as an ambulance. It had been decked out like a California clipper, with three masts and dozens of union suits flapping in the breeze in place of canvas.

But the best entry by far was the one from the cantina. Being pushed into place alongside the others was Ruby Collins' big iron bedstead, which had been painted white and mounted on wagon wheels. Ruby herself was standing up in the middle of it. Her voluminous skirts spread over the makeshift yardarms that had been lashed to the headboard, she threw kisses to the crowd and received bawdy encouragement from the men who frequented her establishment. This was the only entry in the bunch that could boast "sails" of red satin.

From the sidelines, a man whistled between his teeth and called out, "Hey, Ruby! The wager's ten to one that you don't got no drawers on!"

A gasp went up among the crowd, and all heads turned to see who had made the crude remark.

"Who's that?" Gabrielle asked as her shocked gaze rested on a short, rangy, mean-eyed man who looked as though he had not bathed in months.

Al Bates snorted in contempt. "That's Jack Doolen. A walking slop bucket if there ever was one. Used to work at the Rocking P until Edwards fired him."

Just then, Gabrielle spotted Sergeant Major Simmons coming toward them. "Oh, hell," she muttered. "Put me down! The sergeant major's coming."

The two men hastily lowered her to the ground and Gabrielle pulled her hat even lower over her eyes. "Do you think he saw me?" she whispered frantically into the back of Corporal Bates's shirt. Her heart was pounding so hard it hurt, and she hardly dared to breathe.

"He's saying something to Cap'n Wilcox," Corporal Holmes said; then he added after a moment's hesitation, "The cap'n just got down from the ambulance and Sergeant Clancy is taking over." He shook his head. "Naw, I don't think he saw you. Him and the cap'n are headin' on back to Headquarters."

Gabrielle let out her breath in a single long *whoosh* of relief.

"Think we can get a little closer? I can't see from here."

"Maybe. C'mon over here."

The rules were explained to the contestants. They would "sail" their vessels a quarter of a mile down the dry wash, circle the orange-painted water barrel, and head on back. They were not to move any obstacles that had been placed along the course, but were to maneuver around them; and anyone who deliberately tried to "capsize" another vessel would automatically be disqualified. The first one to cross the finish line would win first place in the chow line—and one of Mary Wilcox's homemade pies. Sergeant Covington, the post armorer, raised a revolver into the air. The crowd fell silent. Sergeant Covington fired.

They were off!

The travois immediately moved into the lead, to the astonished wails of poor Private Sykes who had been coerced into making the bumpy ride strapped into the contraption. One of the calves harnessed to *The Ark* panicked and sidestepped into a washtub, causing the laundress occupying it to scream and exit her vessel in great haste. Chickens squawked noisily and the pig tried to escape its pen. "Get that animal out of my washtub!" the offended laundress yelled at Cy Harmon.

Then a roar went up from the crowd. Gabrielle laughed gleefully and pointed. "Look"

Ruby Collins' iron bedstead had sunk up to its wheelhubs in the sand and was going nowhere, despite the efforts of her "oarsmen" to get the bed unstuck. Ruby, her makeup melting in the heat, turned large kohl-enhanced eyes on the onlookers and asked demurely, "Would one of you gentleman care to give a lady some assistance?"

For a split second, no one moved. Then someone laughed, and, to the amusement of everyone in the crowd, men began falling all over themselves trying to get to her. Gabrielle clapped and cheered as Corporal Holmes hurled himself into the middle of the fracas; then she winced and moaned as a man twice his size picked him up and literally threw him out of the way. The bedstead came up out of the sand, the sudden jolt causing Ruby to momentarily lose her balance. Then, not even bothering to use the wheels, about thirty men hoisted the bed up into the air and began running down the wash after the other contestants. Holmes staggered to his feet and, with a sheepish grin, began bowing to the howling onlookers as though he had accomplished freeing the bedstead all by himself. "You fool!" Gabrielle shouted good-naturedly, laughing until she had tears in her eyes.

Out of nowhere, a strong hand descended on her shoulder and spun her around.

"What the—" Gabrielle started to say. Then she broke off, her protest lodged in her throat as she found herself staring up into Dan Catlin's darkly furious eyes.

Chapter Three

"Let me go!" Gabrielle demanded as Dan hauled her roughly through the crowd, her vehement protests turning heads and drawing stunned stares. "You have no right—!" She dug her heels into the ground, but even that failed to slow him down, and she was nearly jerked off her feet. She clasped her hands together and yanked hard, throwing all her weight into the act, but his fingers merely tightened around her wrist, cutting painfully into her skin. She tried to pry his fingers loose. Finally, she bit him.

"Why, you little—" Without thinking, Dan dropped her wrist and took a swing at her, but she ducked and his hand clipped the brim of her hat, knocking it from her head.

"You have no right to treat me like this!" Gabrielle railed at him, stepping out of his reach. Anger smoldered in her sea green eyes. "I wasn't causing any trouble and I sure as hell wasn't bothering *you!*"

"I told you to stay in the house!"

"I don't care what you told me! You've been picking on me ever since Father left, and for no good reason. If you were so bent out of shape by the idea of looking out for me, then you should have told him *no,* instead of taking your frustration out on me. I don't like this arrangement any better than you do, but I'm the one getting the rotten end of the deal. Do this. Do that. Stay in the house. Be quiet. Clean your room. You can't even open your mouth without bossing me around! I'm sick of you always telling me what to do!"

His eyes narrowed dangerously. "Well, maybe if you'd grow up and act your age, I wouldn't have to tell you what to do! First you sneak out in the middle of the night to meet Lieutenant Epperling. Then you go into Lieutenant Dalton's quarters without my permission and without telling me where you are going to be. And now this. Did you honestly think that by disguising yourself as a boy, you were going to get away with leaving the house after I ordered you not to?"

"You don't have any right to order me around. You're not my father. You're not my guardian. You shouldn't even be an officer. You're nothing but a no-account *breed* who should never have been allowed into the Army in the first place!" The words were out before she could stop them, and she knew from the cold, unsparing look that flashed across his face that she had gone too far.

He closed the space between them in a single stride and snared her arm in a bruising grip. "You're coming with me."

Fear coursed through her. She had not meant to make that awful remark about him being a breed, but it had been on the tip of her tongue for so long, ever since Marcus had first told her about it, that it had just slipped out, and now it was too late to take it back. She almost had to run to keep up with him as he dragged her across the parade ground. He was gripping her arm so tightly it hurt, and from the anger on his face she knew it would not go well for her once he got her home. Panic dissolved all reason. She had to get away from him.

Her lips pressed together in last-ditch determination, Gabrielle swung at him, catching him in the middle of his chest with her fist, and when his stride faltered, she kicked him as hard as she could in the shins, then threw her feet out from under her, breaking his grip.

Dan swore as a sharp pain shot up his right leg. Gabrielle scrambled to her feet, but before she could get away, he lunged, knotting a massive hand in the waistband of her britches and hauling her in.

"Bastard!" she spat and drew back her fist, but he threw up his arm, deflecting the blow, then caught her wrist and twisted her arm behind her back, bringing a yelp of pain from her. He did not move quickly enough to restrain Gabrielle's other

67

hand, however, and she lashed out, raking her fingernails down the length of his face.

Before she realized what was happening, he swung her around, turned her face downward beneath his left arm, and brought his right hand down across her backside with a resounding *crack*.

Her body went ramrod stiff and air left her lungs in an undignified grunt. A shriek of outrage tore from her throat as she writhed to get away from him, but he kept her pinned securely against his thigh, her feet flailing and the blood rushing to her head. As his right hand lifted and descended again and again, Gabrielle bit down on her bottom lip to keep from crying out. Tears of pain and humiliation stung her eyes. To her, there was no mercy in the blows he dealt her.

He righted her and set her on her feet, and before she could flee, he gripped her arm and propelled her toward the Headquarters Building. Red-faced, she stumbled along blindly, painfully aware of the stares that bore into her back and followed them across the parade ground. She was certain she would never again be able to hold her head up after what he had done to her.

Dan yanked her up the steps and into the Headquarters Building, slammed the door after them, and pushed her down onto a chair next to the wall. "You sit right there and don't move an inch. I'm not letting you out of my sight!"

Choking back a sob, she slid back on the chair, her stinging posterior feeling as though it were on fire. With a pang of agony, she realized that they were not alone. Captain Wilcox and Sergeant-Major Simmons were standing not ten feet away and she did not have to look up at them to know they were staring at her. No one asked what had happened. No one needed to. It was obvious.

"Get Dalton in here," Dan snapped, his voice sharp with anger that was far from vented.

Gabrielle threw him a horrified glance from beneath lashes that glistened with unshed tears. Why Lieutenant Dalton? Just what was he trying to do, anyway? Humiliate her further? A lump to big to swallow stuck in her throat. She would rather die than face Chase Dalton now. She started up off the chair and said in a choked voice, "I'm going home."

"*Sit down!*"

She flinched and sank back onto the chair, shaken by the look of sheer hatred Major Catlin had flashed at her. Her face burned bright red with shame, and fresh tears welled in her eyes.

Dan turned to Captain Wilcox. "Let me know as soon as you are ready. I want to go with you."

"You may have to translate for me. Also, I'll need a couple of wagons, and we'll have to find a way to get water out to those people until a well can be dug."

Gabrielle twisted away and rested her cheek against the high back of the chair, chewing on her lip and blinking hard to forestall tears as she stared morosely out the window. Her heart felt swelled to twice its normal size, and it hurt to breathe. Never in her life had she felt so degraded, so humiliated. Everyone would laugh at her now, and point at her and say it was about time someone gave her what she had coming; but they were wrong. She didn't deserve to be spanked like that, and certainly not before the entire post.

Yet something inside her told her she *had* deserved it.

A tear coursed down Gabrielle's cheek, and she hastily wiped it away with the back of her hand. No matter what he'd done to her, she would not give Catlin the satisfaction of seeing her cry.

She could see the mountains from where she sat, those big, scary, dangerous mountains. She wanted to run away, and if she weren't so afraid of being captured by wild Indians or of being bitten by a rattlesnake or even of getting lost, that was precisely what she would do. She would run away and hide where no one would be able to find her. Ever.

Chase Dalton entered the building just as Captain Wilcox was on his way out of it. Gabrielle glanced up in time to see the look of amusement the lieutenant threw her way, and her face turned scarlet. She glowered at him. How dare he laugh at her! If he didn't wipe that silly smirk off his face, she was going to get up and do it for him!

Dan was the first to speak. "Before you leave, Lieutenant, there is a matter I wish to discuss with you."

Lieutenant Dalton snickered. "Pardon me for saying so, Major, but I don't believe there's anything left to be said. So if you'll just hand over my out-processing papers, I'll be on my way."

"Not so fast, Dalton. I haven't signed your release yet, and I don't intend to until I've had my say."

The younger officer shifted impatiently.

"I received a dispatch this morning from a Captain Moreland at Department," Dan said, leaning against his desk and folding his arms across his chest. "He's on orders for Ehrenberg, but he doesn't want it and is looking for another officer to trade assignments with him. It's a one-man operation. You'd be customs officer at the supply port. That is . . . if you want it."

Lieutenant Dalton looked skeptical. "You'd do that for me?"

"My argument was never with your duty performance, Lieutenant," Dan said dryly. "You're a good officer, and if you resigned, it would be the Army's loss."

The Lieutenant seemed to give the matter some thought. "When would I have to report?"

"You may take a few week's furlough first if you wish. However, I must give the courier from Department an answer today."

Lieutenant Dalton did not hesitate. "I'll take it," he said, then added. "Thanks."

Dan opened his desk drawer, took out the letter of resignation Lieutenant Dalton had given him several days before, and ripped it into quarters. "Don't thank me yet, Lieutenant. Ehrenberg is the hottest place on earth. Before long, you're going to wish I'd sent you to hell instead."

Gabrielle had listened to the exchange with mounting fury, and now she flew up out of her chair. "It's not fair!" she burst out, her nostrils flaring and her hands knotting into fists. "I get punished and he gets away with—"

"Gabrielle!" There was no mistaking Dan's tone or the look he shot her. Blood had beaded along the three long scratches on his face where she had clawed him, and the injury only added to the severity of his expression. Fire snapping in his

70

eyes, he pointed to the chair!

He might as well have been speaking to a dog! Gabrielle jerked her chin up, and, for a moment, she did not move but met his glare with one of her own. Tension crackled between them. If it was a battle of wills he wanted, she fumed, she could be just as stubborn as he could. Except that he was bigger and when he started toward her, she quickly backed down and returned to her chair, but not without first flashing him a venomous look.

Dan finished with Lieutenant Dalton and penned a dispatch to Department. As the minutes ticked slowly by, Gabrielle sulked.

Dan wrote out two more dispatches.

Gabrielle squirmed restlessly. The least he could do was let her go home.

Sergeant-Major Simmons stuck his head in the door and said the captain was ready.

Finally! *Now* she could go home!

But Dan had other ideas. He seized her by the arm and hauled her out the door with him.

"Where are we going?" she asked, fear knotting inside her. She had the terrible feeling that he was going to punish her again.

He did not answer, but steered her across the parade ground to where Captain Wilcox waited with the loaded wagons. The celebration was still going on strong, however, Gabrielle was careful to keep her gaze from wandering in that direction. Her face burned with embarrassment, and she knew that if she were to look up and catch someone staring at her or pointing or laughing, she was liable to burst into tears on the spot. Dan Catlin was going to pay for what he had done to her today. She intended to make certain he did!

He boosted her up onto the seat of a wagon loaded with water barrels and climbed up next to her. She started to ask him again where he was taking her, then decided against it. He was being so rotten, he probably wouldn't tell her.

As if reading her thoughts, Dan said without looking at her, "Some of the Apaches who were driven out of Camp Grant have come here for asylum. We're taking them food and supplies."

She threw a surprised glance at him, his words giving her a twinge of smug satisfaction. His turn was coming. Father was going to have a fit when he returned to find out Dan Catlin was harboring hostile Indians at this post. The colonel was very much against turning Camp Carleton into a haven for the Indians, because that was merely the first step into establishing a reservation, and Gabrielle knew the last thing he wanted was to be responsible for feeding and clothing a bunch of no-good renegade Indians who didn't have the sense to look after themselves. "Then why are you taking me?" she asked testily. "I don't want to go out there just to see a bunch of dirty old Indians."

"You're going because I can't trust you to stay out of trouble otherwise," Dan retorted, making no effort to disguise his displeasure. He turned the wagon down a faintly marked trail to the north, and Captain Wilcox followed in the second wagon along with the half-dozen men from A Company who had been drafted to help unload the supplies.

The Indians were camped in the foothills about two miles from the post, but the ride seemed ten times that long to Gabrielle. She sat stiffly on the wagon seat, gritting her teeth and trying hard not to wince whenever they hit a rock or a pothole, and she could have sworn the major was going out of his way to run over every one he could find. The air was hot and hot and heavy, and the sun beat down on her head, making her wish she still had her hat. Dan guided the team down through the wash then back up the opposite bank toward the ridge. Gabrielle swiped at a swarm of gnats that hovered annoyingly about her face. It was not until they crested the rise that they were able to see the Apache encampment sprawled out across the narrow valley below them.

They rode silently into it.

The camp was a sorry affair. A large brush ramada had been constructed to provide shade, but, apart from that, there was no shelter for the families who were being quartered here, not even a tent to protect them from the elements. Several Apache women, their expressions hostile, turned to stare at them; and small children hid behind their mothers, black eyes set in the dirt-smeared faces that peeked out from behind the women's full skirts. Gabrielle had never seen such a ragged, dirty bunch of people in her life. Her heart pounded erratically. Major Catlin was crazy! They had no business riding into an Apache camp like this. They'd be lucky if they weren't scalped!

Dan brought the wagon to a halt.

Her heart beating so hard it felt as though it would break through her chest, Gabrielle ran her tongue across her parched lips and looked around. If only they would not stare so. She forced a wan smile and nodded at a young woman dressed in a full calico skirt and loose-fitting deerskin top. The woman bent down, scooped up a scantily clothed toddler and hurried away. Gabrielle watched her disappear and felt more uneasy than ever. It occurred to her that these people were as afraid of her as she was of them, but she could not ignore the simple fact that the Apaches outnumbered them by about twenty to one.

After barking a curt order at her to stay out of the way and out of trouble, Dan began to help unload the supply wagons. More resentful than ever over being dragged to the camp against her will, Gabrielle found a spot of shade under a mesquite tree and sat down on the ground. Drawing her knees up to her chest, she rested her chin on them. There was a surly look on her face as she watched Dan help the men unload the wagons, and her mind raced to devise some trick mean enough to pay him back for the grief and humiliation he had caused her.

Finally, the sensation of being watched drew her attention away from the major, and Gabrielle turned her head to find a little girl who looked to be about three or four years old, naked except for a torn cotton top that did not even cover her lower half, standing several feet away, her dark eyes alive with undisguised curiosity. *Little urchin*, Gabrielle thought, glowering at her. Doesn't the child have anything better to do than stare at me as if I were some kind of freak?

Annoyed, she screwed up her face and stuck out her tongue.

The little girl did not move.

Determined to get rid of the pesky child, Gabrielle leaned toward her, a wicked gleam in her eyes, and suddenly said, "Boo!"

The little girl laughed.

Gabrielle shook her head. "You just don't scare, do you?" She noticed that the child's arms and legs were pitifully thin and covered with scratches, and her belly was distended. In addition, the little girl was filthy, and her black hair was matted and hung in tangles about her unwashed face. Gabrielle's stomach knotted. Never in her life had she seen anyone so dirty that just looking at that person made her ache inside. She ventured a contrite smile and looked away. Several minutes passed and still the little girl did not leave. Gabrielle wracked her brain for something to say. "See that big man over there?" she said, inclining her head in Dan's direction. "Did you know he's really a wolf in disguise and he eats little girls for breakfast?"

The child did not move, but continued staring at her.

Leaning back against the mesquite tree, Gabrielle picked up a small stone and tossed it back and forth between her two hands. "He tried chewing on me this morning, but I think I'm too old and stringy for his liking. So you'd better watch out. He's in a bad mood today, and he's probably just itching to find some tender little thing to gobble up." She glanced at the little girl and cocked an eyebrow. "You don't understand a word I'm saying, do you?"

The girl bent down, picked up a stone of her own and tossed it up in the air.

This time it was Gabrielle's turn to laugh. She patted the ground beside her. "You want to come sit by me?"

When the child did not budge, Gabrielle shrugged. "Can't say that I blame you. You're not the one being punished, so why should you sit over here beneath this old tree?" Drawing back her arm, she threw the stone as hard as she could in Dan's direction. Her heart leaped into her throat as it hit the ground and skidded expertly between his feet. "Oops!" she blurted out, and hastily laid her head down on her knees, her gray-green eyes alight with mischief. "Is he looking?" Gabrielle whispered to the little girl, her face turning red as she tried hard not to giggle. She'd never be able to repeat that stunt again if she tried. Her aim had been a matter of pure luck.

The little girl stared, first at Dan and then at her, and then, in a swift move that made Gabrielle want to burst out laughing, she picked up another stone and brought it to her.

Gabrielle grinned. "So you want me to ping him again, huh?" she asked as she took the stone. The child was so skinny Gabrielle's heart ached for her, but she had a face that belonged on an angel. A lump welled in Gabrielle's throat. "Well, to tell you the truth, I'd like to get him good, but he's so testy today, he'd probably come over here and smack me. Tell you what we can do, though," she said, then paused to draw a circle in the dirt. "This rock is about the size of a good shooter. You take it and hook it in your forefinger like so . . . " She showed the girl how to hold the stone, then placed another that was about the same size inside the circle. "You hold your shooter right about here . . . aim. . . ."

Kerplunk!

The child hastened to try out the game for herself and, in no time at all, had mastered the basics.

Her own troubles temporarily forgotten, Gabrielle laughed. "You're pretty good at that, squirt!" She reached out and touched the little girl's hand. "Can't make any promises, because I'm not sure I still have them, but tonight I'm going to look for my old marbles, and if I can find them, they're yours. There's a real pretty agate, and a cat's-eye even!" It mattered not that neither of them could understand a word the other said. They communicated in a language of their own that required no interpreter.

The sun was low in the western sky by the time the men finished unloading supplies and erecting tents and getting the Apaches settled into the makeshift shelters. Dan had kept an eye on Gabrielle all afternoon, and was both amazed and pleased to see her befriend the little Apache girl. He had half expected her to spend the afternoon sulking. Instead, she seemed truly happy for the first time in a long while, and something twisted inside him when her smile faded and the light in her eyes died when she saw him approach. A taut silence hung between them as they rode back to Camp Carleton.

Corporal Bates was waiting for them when they returned to the house. "Saved you some of that pit barbecue and some peach pie," he said, glancing tentatively from one to the other.

Gabrielle said nothing. She did not even look at him, but went to her room and closed the door.

The crease in Dan's forehead deepened, and he rubbed one hand across his eyes. "You can go home now, Bates," he said wearily.

The soldier left.

For a long time, Dan stood in the hallway, trying to decide whether to go speak to Gabrielle or just let the matter ride. He regretted losing his temper with her earlier. Much of the frustration he had taken out on her had arisen because of problems he faced, and he felt like an ass for having shamed her in public the way he had. Camp Carleton was a small post, and it would be a long time before the incident was forgotten. Finally, deciding that he had no choice but to apologize, he went down the hall and knocked on her door.

When she did not answer, he knocked again and he knew even before he opened the door that something was wrong.

The window stood open and the white dimity curtain billowed in the breeze that swept down off the mountains. On the dresser, weighted down by a small leather pouch containing a set of children's playing marbles, was a hastily scribbled note that read, "These marbles are for the little girl who was with me today. If you show her how to shoot one, she will know what they are for. I'm sorry I can't be more like Grace."

A cold dread gripped Dan.

She was gone.

Gabrielle ran until a stitch in her side forced her to stop. Her breath coming in huge gulps, she pressed the heel of her hand into her side and fought against the tears that stung her eyes. She hated Dan Catlin! He had ruined her. He had made it impossible for her to face anyone at Camp Carleton again. They would all be laughing at her now, laughing about how he had turned her over and paddled the daylights out of her, right there before God and everyone.

A sob broke in her throat and she choked it back. There was

76

no time now for tears. She had to get as far away as possible before a search party came looking for her. She had no idea where she was going or what she would do. She didn't even care. If the major caught up with her and made her go back to the post where she couldn't even hold up her head, she would just as soon be dead.

She had not intended to run away. At least, not until Corporal Bates had made that remark about the pit barbecue and the peach pie. Then a vision of Grace, as she'd looked at the festival had flashed before Gabrielle's eyes. Grace Simmons, all prim and proper in her white dress with the blue sash. Grace Simmons, who was good and kind and never gave anyone a moment's remorse. Grace Simmons. Everyone liked her even though she wasn't very pretty or very smart. Even Gabrielle's own father wished she were more like Grace Simmons. Her heart felt near to breaking. No matter how hard she tried, she could never, never be like Grace.

Now she wished she had not left that stupid note. She did not *want* to be like Grace Simmons, and she didn't understand what had prompted her to apologize for being different, except that for a fleeting moment she had wished that, just once, Dan Catlin would look at her with something other than disappointment or disgust in his eyes.

Steeling herself against the conflicting emotions that raged inside, her, Gabrielle brushed a curl, damp with perspiration, back from her face and then continued on into the night-shrouded foothills, methodically placing one foot before the other until she lost all track of time and distance, and could no longer see the lights of Camp Carleton when she turned and looked back. The only thing that mattered now was getting away. She never wanted to see any of them again, not Grace, not her father, and especially not Dan Catlin.

Captain Wilcox had to lengthen his stride in order to keep up with Dan as they neared the Headquarters Building. "Don't worry," he said, squinting into the early morning sun. "I can handle everything here. Just find the girl and bring her home. And, for crying out loud, quit blaming yourself!"

A muscle in Dan's jaw jerked. "If I hadn't humiliated her in front of everyone, this would never have happened."

"She deserved it. Even Mary was appalled by her behavior yesterday and you know how she is always making excuses for the girl."

Dan's angry footfalls reverberated from the front steps and he jerked open the door. "Still, I shouldn't have lost my—" He broke off at the sight of a wiry little man dressed in buckskins sitting behind his desk, his chair tilted back, his hands clasped behind his head and a merry twinkle in his sharp blue eyes.

The front legs of the chair hit the floor with a *thunk*. "When'd you start keepin' bankers' hours?" the man said with a broad Missouri drawl as he stood up. "Hell, it's nigh on six-thirty. I was beginnin' to think I was gonna have to come drag your mangy ass out of bed."

A rare grin broke across Dan's face. "Bandy Moreland, you ugly rascal! When did you get here?"

Captain Moreland came out from behind the desk and clasped Dan's hand in a firm grip. "About an hour ago. Didn't want to take any chances on you turnin' down my request, so I came to plead my cause in person."

"I only received your dispatch yesterday. As for turning you down, there's an officer en route to Ehrenberg now to report in your place." Dan shook his head, disbelief etched across his face, and his voice dropped. "It's been a long time, Moreland. I never thought I'd see the likes of you again. I could have sworn you'd have gotten yourself busted and booted out of the Army by now."

The other officer chuckled. "You kiddin'? And miss out on all them big bucks from Uncle Sam?" His blue eyes dropped to the three parallel scratches on Dan's cheek. "What she-cat you been tanglin' with?"

Dan shook his head. "I don't have time to go into it now. The colonel's daughter is out in those mountains somewhere and I have to find her. Ben here can fill you in on what happened."

Moreland grabbed his dust-covered hat up off Dan's desk. "I'm goin' with you."

One black eyebrow arched upward. "You've been riding all

night. You're tired."

"My horse is tired. I sure as hell ain't. You know me; I can sleep sittin' up and with one eye propped open. Loan me a fresh mount and I'll help you round up this missing filly."

Dan knew he should refuse, but he didn't. Right now, he needed a friend.

The trail he had not been able to find last night was clearly discernible in the light of day. The depth of her footprints showed that Gabrielle had run hard and fast the first half-mile, but had slowed the higher she climbed. She had the hardiness of youth on her side, Dan knew, but the pampered life she had led would soon prove a disadvantage. Without food and water, she would not get far. As long as her trail stayed clear, they would soon find her. He only hoped they got to her first, before someone—or something—else.

The search party was limited to Sergeant Reikowsky and Corporal Gilly who both knew those mountains inside and out, Bandy Moreland, and himself. None of the men wore the blue uniform that risked drawing attention; they were all clad in old faded civilian clothing that would allow them to blend in with the surrounding hills.

Moreland listened without speaking while Dan told him all that had happened. Then he shook his head and let out a long low whistle. "Set her ass on fire, huh? You know what they say about a woman scorned."

"She's not a woman," Dan shot back, annoyed, but by what he did not know.

"Then what is she? An armadillo?"

"She's a seventeen-year-old *girl*."

"Shee-it! Another year and she'll be an old maid!"

Another year and I'll be exactly twice her age, Dan thought irritably, then wondered what had brought that on. "She's immature," he said instead.

"What seventeen-year-old ain't? She'll grow up. Is she purty?"

Dan gritted his teeth, remembering the day he had happened upon her and Grace Simmons quarreling, anger flashing in

Gabrielle's long-lashed eyes and thick untamed tresses cascading down around her shoulders. Her robe had hung carelessly open, and the sight of her full round breasts straining against the revealing fabric of her shift had stirred him more than he was willing to admit. Even now, just thinking about Gabrielle's scantily clad form sent a rush of heat through his loins. He forced the disturbing vision from his mind. "She's passable," he said curtly.

Moreland threw him a sharp glance. "You in love with her?"

"Of course not!" Dan shot back, then wished he had not spoken so quickly.

The other officer chuckled.

"For chrissake, Moreland, she's the old man's daughter!"

"What's that got to do with anything?"

Before Dan could answer, Sergeant Reikowsky reined in his horse and called out, "Take a look at this, sir."

Dan dismounted and hunkered down, his brows drawing together as he studied the ground. A second trail had joined Gabrielle's and paralleled it, at several points obliterating hers completely. A terrible pressure welled in Dan's chest.

"Unshod horses," Captain Moreland said matter-of-factly, and though no one said anything more, the men were all thinking the same thing.

Apaches.

Chapter Four

Gabrielle sat up, her mind still fogged with sleep, and rubbed the back of her neck. She did not know how long she had dozed, but the sun was well above the horizon and every bone in her body ached from lying on the hard ground. Her stomach rumbled noisily. Having nothing to eat, she pulled out the hairpins that gouged her scalp, letting two thick braids fall to her waist, and slowly dragged herself to her feet. She had to keep going. It didn't matter that last night's anger was but a hazy memory that no longer seemed to warrant running away. She had committed herself to a course of action, and she was determined to see it through.

There were mining communities in these mountains, she reminded herself as she forced her feet to move on. If she could only reach one of them, she would be all right. She could find work, though doing what she did not know. She couldn't cook. She couldn't sew worth beans. She didn't know anything about doing laundry. She didn't even know how to run a household. The only things she did know were reading and writing and ciphering. *And getting into trouble,* a small inner voice interjected. She frowned at the intrusion and quickened her pace. Finding work couldn't be all that hard. Surely there was something out there she could do.

The deeper into the mountains she ventured, the more everything changed. The ground became rockier. Prickly pear and mesquite gave way to juniper and scrub oak, and several thousand feet above her, the hillsides were dark green with thick stands of pine forest. She wished she could find a stream. Her throat was parched and her lips were beginning to crack. The delicate skin on her face felt taut, and Gabrielle knew she was getting sunburned. Worse, whenever she blinked, she could feel the cutting grains of sand that had worked their way beneath her eyelids. She had to find water.

Finally, she stopped to rest. Her head throbbed from having strong sunlight beating down on it, and it hurt to swallow. Sinking to the ground, she drew her knees up to her chest and laid her forehead on them, struggling hard against the feelings of despair that now threatened to overwhelm her. If she had ever felt alone before, it was nothing compared to the way she felt now. Before, there'd always been someone to come to her aid whenever she was in trouble. Here there was no one. She wanted to go home. It would mean swallowing her pride and admitting that she had made a mistake, and she didn't even want to think about what Major Catlin was going to do to her. His words to her father echoed through her mind: *Your daughter doesn't have enough sense to fit on the sharp end of a cactus spine. . . .*

And what had she ever done but prove him right?

The sound of a pebble rolling over rock jolted her back to the present. Gabrielle jerked her head up to find herself staring into the frightening visages of four mounted Apaches. A fear unlike any she had ever known welled up inside her, and her heart seemed to come to an abrupt standstill. She glanced hesitantly at each Indian, then her gaze returned to the tallest one, drawn by something in his obsidian eyes that she did not understand, but which filled her with dread. A scarlet band circled his head, and his face was blackened with warpaint. His features were more angular than those of his companions, and there was a cruel twist to his thin lips. As his eyes lingered on her the look in them was both frightening and sinister. Gabrielle's pulse quickened. The Apache began to dismount, and she caught a glimpse of naked powerfully muscled thigh. Seized by blind, unreasoning panic, she scrambled to her feet and took off, running.

In an instant, he was upon her, a low, animal-like growl sounding in his throat as he slammed into her from behind.

She screamed.

They hit the ground with a force that drove the air from Gabrielle's lungs, and she lay, pinned beneath the Apache, her face pressed against the rocks, unable to move. Then her captor's weight shifted, a strong hand seized the back of her shirt, and she was hauled roughly to her feet. Driven by terror, Gabrielle half turned and flung herself at him with all the force she could muster, planting an elbow into his belly and lashing out at his face. She raked her nails down one bronze cheek before he seized her wrists and forced her hands down. Twisted with fury, his face loomed over her, his teeth bared. He circled an arm about her, trapping her arms at her sides, and brought her up hard against his chest in a viselike grip. Raising one foot, she brought her heel down hard against one moccasin-clad instep.

The Apache gave a startled yelp. Swinging her around, he dragged her, screaming and kicking, back to where his companions had dismounted and now waited, amusement etched on their faces. One of them said something Gabrielle could not understand, and the others laughed. Suddenly releasing her, her captor planted a hand in the middle of her back and gave her a shove that sent her sprawling.

For a moment, she just lay there on the sharp rocks, fighting back the wave of nausea that swept over her. Nothing mattered now except getting away from these men who held her life in their hands. She harbored no illusions that she might be spared, for she had heard too many stories not to know what lay in store for her. If one of them wanted her for his own, she would be taken prisoner. If not, they would simply have their way with her, then kill her. She took a deep breath, trying hard to calm herself. This was no time for panic. She had to be able to think clearly. She had to make each move count. She needed a weapon.

Gabrielle struggled to sit up, and was surprised and a little puzzled to see that the Apaches seemed to be quarreling among themselves and had momentarily forgotten her. Glancing hastily about, she spotted a black sharp-edged rock just the size to fit securely in the palm of her hand. Careful not to let anyone see what she was doing, she groped behind her. Her fingers closed about the stone.

The Apache who had captured her motioned angrily to the others and then toward her, the gesture raising icy prickles on Gabrielle's skin. Her heart pounded with the slow steady beat of a death knell, but whatever fate they chose for her, she was determined to resist. Her fingers worried the rock in her hand as though she could somehow draw strength from the hard granite. She would not let them take her captive. She would not let them rape her. And if they killed her, she would take at least one of them with her. No matter what they did, she would fight until she had drawn her last breath.

Her captor went to his horse, then came toward her, carrying several strips of rawhide. Gabrielle's eyes widened and her breath caught in her throat as she realized what he intended to do. He knelt before her, his face, hard and cruel and dark with undiffused anger only inches from hers. Blood had clotted and dried on his cheek where she had clawed him, and a crippling pain wrenched her heart as she was suddenly reminded of the terrible way she had clawed Dan Catlin only the day before. Was it only yesterday? It seemed so long ago now. So unreal. A sob rose and stuck in her throat. She had never even said she was sorry. . . .

The Apache grasped a foot in each hand, causing her to wince as he pulled her legs straight out in front of her and bound her ankles together with a rawhide strip. He tightened the knot with a jerk and reached for her hands.

It was her only chance.

She swung hard. But his reaction was swifter than she had anticipated. He blocked her arm, deflecting the intended blow to his head, and knocked the rock from her hand. Hampered by her bound feet, Gabrielle rolled away from him, but he seized one of her braids and jerked, causing her to cry out in pain as she fell back against him, sending him toppling backward. He brought her down with him, wrapping one arm around her neck while he strove to restrain her flailing fists with his other hand. She bucked and kicked, but to no avail.

Then he shifted his hold on her.

Without thinking, she twisted her head around and sank her teeth into the flesh of his upper arm.

He howled and flung her away from him, the back of his hand catching her across the mouth. Gabrielle uttered a strangled cry and her hand flew instinctively to her mouth as she tasted blood. Her eyes smarted with sudden tears; she had bitten her tongue when he'd hit her.

Grasping her wrists, the Apache pulled her hand away from her face and pushed her roughly onto her stomach. After wrenching her arms behind her back, he tied her wrists together with the other strip of rawhide, passing one end through one of the belt loops on her pants and securing her hands firmly in place.

He left her lying face down on the ground. Her swollen tongue throbbed painfully and her mouth had filled with blood. She spat it out and tried to wipe her lips against her shoulder, but merely succeeded in smearing blood across her cheek. She managed to roll over onto her side and sit up just as he led his horse up alongside her. Effortlessly scooping her up in his arms, the Indian deposited her face down across the animal's back, causing her to release her breath in an undignified grunt. Then he mounted behind her and turned his horse down the same trail his companions had taken.

It was Gabrielle's screams that brought Dan out of his saddle. A fear unlike any he had ever known knifed through him and he hit the ground running. If anything happened to Gabrielle, he knew he would never forgive himself. He moved recklessly, forgetting his military training, forgetting everything save the need to get to her before it was too late.

Realizing what was happening, Captain Moreland immediately took charge. Signaling instructions to the other men, he turned his horse around and spurred it to a gallop. He owed Dan one, and he wasn't about to let him down now.

Dan slowed as he reached the rocky outcropping, knowing that a slip on his part would give away his position and endanger Gabrielle's life. Hidden from view by a jojoba thicket, he crouched on the ledge and watched as the small procession moved along the trail below. He saw Gabrielle, face down across her captor's horse, struggle; and relief surged through him.

She was alive! Then the Apache knotted his hand in her hair, yanked her head back and slapped her full in the face. Rage and loathing filled Dan and he instinctively reached for his gun. For the first time in his life, he wanted to kill someone.

But the angle was bad. He stood too great a chance of shooting Gabrielle instead of the Indian. Moving with the swift but quiet stealth of a mountain cat, he worked his way along the ledge until he was just ahead of the Apaches, and waited. They passed directly below him, so close he could see the cracks on the warpaint on their faces, and when one of them glanced up in his direction, he looked right into the warrior's eyes for one long interminable second before the other man withdrew his gaze. The Apache with Gabrielle brought up the rear. Dan waited, his breath checked, until they moved into alignment . . . then he lunged.

He caught the Apache broadside, knocking him from his horse, and rolled to the ground with him. A shot rang out. The Apache's horse reared. From the corner of his eye, Dan saw Bandy Moreland ride into the clearing at breakneck speed.

Dan rolled to his feet.

Sunlight glinted off metal, and he kicked the knife from the Indian's hand, then crashed his fist into the Apache's jaw.

The warrior staggered back, rage contorting his features; but he regained his balance.

The Indian's horse reared again, its hooves pawing dangerously in the air, and a scream tore from Gabrielle's throat as she was hurled to the ground.

Another warrior leaped from his mount, rifle in hand, then was brought up short as a bullet caught him between the shoulder blades.

In the confusion, the riderless horses whinnied and bolted.

"Gabrielle, run!" Dan yelled. He saw too late that her feet were bound.

The Indian scooped up a handful of dirt and gravel and flung it in Dan's face.

Dan ducked and threw one arm up over his eyes, but not soon enough.

The Apache dove for his knife.

Dan sidestepped his attacker and threw out his foot, tripping him, but the Indian grabbed his shirt and pulled him to the ground. The two men rolled over and over in the dirt, locked in a death grip. Then searing pain ripped through Dan's arm, and the Apache sprang away from him, the bloodied knife raised above his head, poised to kill. Dan drew his gun.

As quickly as it had begun, it was over.

"You all right?" Captain Moreland called out, running to Dan who had shoved the dead Apache off him and was staggering to his feet.

Dan pushed him aside and went to Gabrielle.

She was lying facedown in the dirt, motionless.

Yanking out the knife he kept sheathed in his boot, he sliced through the leather straps that bound her wrists and ankles. Fear and rage and desperation coursing through him, he rolled her onto her back and felt the hollow of her neck for a pulse.

Her long black lashes fluttered against dirt-smeared cheeks and she whimpered.

"It's all right, little one. You're safe now," Dan said, breathing hard. He gathered her into his arms and held her close. His heart banged so hard against the wall of his chest each beat hurt. "It's all right," he murmured again, more to himself than to her.

She blinked up at him, her eyes glazed with pain. "I-I'm sorry," she whispered hoarsely. "I won't d-do it again."

"Shhh! It's all right."

"I-I'm . . . s-sorry. . . ."

Dan glanced up as Corporal Gilly came toward him.

"Those sons-of-bitches got better weapons than we do," the corporal said disgustedly as he held out the four brand-new Winchester repeating rifles that had been taken from the prisoners.

Bandy Moreland touched Dan on the shoulder. "You're pumping blood faster'n Texas changes flags. We'd better see to that shoulder."

Dan shook his head. "I'm okay, but she was trampled by that bastard's horse."

Bandy looked down at the girl in Dan's arms. Her eyes were closed and her face ashen; yet, even covered with dirt the way she was, she was the most beautiful thing he had ever seen. If his old buddy wasn't in love with her, he should be, Bandy thought. He glanced up and met Dan's penetrating gaze. "I'll get your canteen."

When he was alone with Gabrielle, Dan brushed a strand of hair back from her face and a muscle in his jaw knotted at the sight of the angry red handprint emblazoned on the cheek the Indian had slapped. "Gabrielle?"

Her eyes flew open. She tried to swallow. "It h-hurts when I breathe."

He lightly grazed his knuckles against her cheek and stared solemnly into her eyes. God, how young and vulnerable she looked! He was certain she had a couple of broken ribs, and did not even want to think about the internal injuries she might have sustained. Just the thought of that horse's hooves coming down on her helpless form made him ill. "Shhh . . . don't try to talk now." She was trembling. Or was he?

Her eyes filled with tears. "I c-called you a *breed* and an old . . . an old goat."

An involuntary smile tugged at the corners of his mouth. An old goat?

"I-I ran away. . . ."

"Shhh . . . It doesn't matter."

"I caused you . . . to get h-hurt." Her voice cracked and a tear streaked through the dirt on her face.

Dan pulled her close and rocked her gently. "Shhh," he murmured into her hair, torn by the powerful emotions she aroused in him. Moreland was wrong. He wasn't in love with her. He didn't especially like her. And yet, he had never been so scared in his life as when he had heard her scream, nor had he ever felt such an uncontrollable rage as when he'd seen the Apache slap her. He brushed his lips against her eyelids and tasted the salt of her tears. "It's all right, little one. Don't talk."

Bandy returned with Dan's canteen. "There's a spot a couple hundred yards off the trail where we can make camp."

Dan held the canteen to Gabrielle's lips, but when she tried to drink, an excruciating pain stabbed her chest. Fresh tears stung her eyes, and she shook her head and pushed the canteen away.

Bandy raised an eyebrow. "Ribs?"

Dan nodded. Keeping one arm around her shoulders and sliding the other beneath her knees, he got to his feet, trying not to hurt her any more than necessary. Gabrielle's mouth went white and she squeezed her eyes shut. She did not cry out, but he could tell from the white-knuckled grip she had on his shirt that she was in pain, and before he had taken more than a few steps, she sagged in his arms and her head lolled against his chest.

Bandy led the way, glancing once over his shoulder to see Dan press one cheek against the top of Gabrielle's head. He chuckled to himself. Whether Dan was aware of it or not, he was crazy in love with that little girl. And some girl! They sure didn't make 'em like that when he was seventeen!"

The spot Captain Moreland had found was smooth and sandy and cloaked in shade. "I spread your bedroll out over there," he told Dan, though his eyes, cool and assessing, were on Gabrielle. "Good thing she passed out. Might as well get them ribs bound while she's out cold; then I'll take a look at your shoulder before you bleed to death."

Dan lowered her to the blanket, and began removing her clothing while Bandy went back to get his saddlebags. The corduroy britches and white cotton drawers were ripped, and dirt stuck to the torn flesh beneath. Dan pulled the ruined garments down over her hips, exposing the bloody scrapes along Gabrielle's hip and thigh; then he unbuttoned her shirt and pulled it open. He sucked in his breath. Her entire left side was scraped and bruised, but beneath her left breast the discoloration was a deep purplish-black. Vicious dark streaks radiated from it across her rib cage and down her abdomen. Probing gently, he slid his fingers slowly over ribs, feeling for a break.

Bandy dropped his saddlebags onto the ground and squatted beside him, a frown creasing his brow as he watched the movements of Dan's hand. "Is it broken?"

Suddenly Dan didn't want anyone else looking at her. "Just bruised," he said brusquely, drawing her shirt closed. "I'll take care of her. You get the clean shirt from my saddlebags and start ripping it into bandages."

Amused by the possessive look on his friend's face, Bandy chuckled. "Anything else?"

Dan threw him a sharp glance. "You still carry unauthorized rations in your canteen?"

In reply, Bandy reached behind him, grasped the strap, and tossed the canteen onto the blanket.

For several seconds, their gazes locked, Dan's flinty, Bandy's faintly mocking. Moreland was the first to break the silence. "If you're worried about me havin' designs on your woman, don't. I want one of my own, not one I've gotta wrangle my best friend for."

Dan turned his head to look at Gabrielle, and this time he saw not her injuries but long lashes resting against her sunburned cheeks, freckles dotting the bridge of her nose, and the clean line of her jaw. Her torn shirt failed to hide the fullness of her breasts or the slenderness of her waist, and as his gaze slid down her long, well-shaped legs, Dan felt an unbidden surge of desire. He took a deep breath and said flatly, "She's not my woman."

Bandy shrugged. "Suit yourself."

Gabrielle only came to once while Dan bathed her scrapes and bound her ribs, and she immediately slipped back into unconsciousness after he gave her a drink of the whiskey in Moreland's canteen. He covered her with the blanket, as much to protect her from his own conflicting desires as from the curious stares of the other men; then he let Moreland tend to the knife wound in his shoulder, which, in spite of the amount of blood he had lost, was minor.

That done, he spoke to the two Apaches they had taken prisoner, and ascertained that they were of the Cibecue band and had ventured this far south of the Mogollon Rim to steal horses and cattle from ranches in the Tonto Basin. He questioned them about their use of warpaint and they replied that it was only to scare off some Yavapai who did not want them raiding in their territory. They did not want trouble with the white-eyes, the Americanos.

"I'm going to let them go," Dan told Moreland later.

Bandy looked skeptical. "You think that's smart?"

"We can't take them back to Camp Carleton. They haven't

done anything for which I can legally arrest them, and they could stir up trouble among the other Apaches quartered near the post."

"They can stir up trouble anyhow."

They didn't talk much after that, and when Bandy went to take the first watch, Dan moved closer to Gabrielle. She slept fitfully, pain clearly etched on her face. He brushed the stray curls back from her forehead, then sat stroking her hair. Gradually, the pucker between her brows lessened, and she turned her head and pressed her cheek against his hand. The gesture was so childlike and trusting that Dan was suddenly filled with self-loathing. He had done this to her. If he had waited, if he hadn't been so anxious to take down the Apache who held her captive, she would not have been thrown from the horse and trampled. And if he had not lost his temper and humiliated her before the entire post, she would not have run away.

He turned away from her and ran one hand over his eyes, suddenly feeling decades older than his thirty-five years.

He did not know why he disliked her so much. She was not all that different from her mother, and he had loved Lisette. He had loved the way Lisette's red-gold hair defied the constraints of her hairpins and curled about her face, the way the light danced in her gray-green eyes. And he had loved her guileless laughter and the gentle joy she'd brought into the lives of everyone who knew her. He had loved her, but from a distance; for she had belonged to someone else and could never be his.

Gabrielle was so much like her, yet so different. Whereas Lisette had been gentle, Gabrielle was reckless and sometimes overbearing. Lisette had been giving; Gabrielle was demanding. And Lisette had been content to be wife and mother, but Gabrielle would never be content. Not with anything. Like a prairie fire, she was wild and unmanageable and consuming. And, like fire, she could suck the very life out of a man and leave only a hollow, blackened shell. Only a very strong man would be able to hold his own against Gabrielle, for he would have to be all things to her—husband, lover, father, mother, friend—and Dan knew of no one, least of all himself, who could tackle the job and emerge unscathed.

91

Yet, how many times had he closed his eyes only to have her image flicker through his mind? How many times had he toyed with the idea of taking her in his arms and kissing that sweet mouth? He had often wanted to caress her soft white skin and cup her breast in his hand, to touch her where no man ever had. And he had wished she were not Stephen DuBois' daughter. He was not proud of these thoughts. He didn't love Gabrielle, but he wanted to make love to her, to possess her, to bend her to his will. And if the colonel had known that, he would never have entrusted Gabrielle to his care.

Gabrielle's eyes fluttered open and she lay without moving, staring up into the clear night sky at stars that seemed almost close enough to touch, and trying to remember where she was and what had happened. Then, when she tried to move, a grueling pain stabbed at her chest and it all came back to her— the Apaches, falling from the horse, Major Catlin holding her and telling her everything would be all right. She turned her head and saw the major staring into the fire, lines of worry creasing his brow, and she felt ashamed. He had just risked his life for her, yet all she had done in return was call him names and cause trouble for him. He had been right about her all along. She was selfish and childish and inconsiderate—a spoiled brat. A lump wedged in her throat.

As if sensing her gaze on him. Dan turned his head and looked at her. Relief passed over his face. "Welcome back, little one."

At any other time, a sharp retort would have sprung to her lips; now she could think of nothing to say. Nervously, she looked away.

Dan took a deep breath. He was as uncomfortable with the awkward silence as she was. "We'll leave for Camp Carleton in the morning. Wilcox needs to take a look at those bruised ribs."

Bruised ribs? So that was why she hurt so much. Beneath the blanket, Gabrielle placed a hand on the bruised area, feeling the binding he had wrapped tightly around her to protect the injury, and she realized with a start that she was naked. Her gaze riveted on him. "Where are my clothes?"

"I had to remove them."

Her eyes grew wide, her face hot. "But, b-but . . ."

"Gabrielle, I couldn't very well tend to your injuries with them on." He paused. "They're folded up at the foot of your blanket. I'll help you get dressed in the morning."

In the morning! He had to be jesting. Surely he didn't expect her to sleep *naked*? Clutching the blanket over her breasts, she started to sit up and reach for her clothes, then fell back with an agonized cry.

Dan sprang to his feet. "Christ, girl! What in the hell are you trying to do?"

"I want m-my clothes," Gabrielle said through clenched teeth, as she squeezed her eyes shut against the white-hot throbbing in her chest.

"I told you, I'll help you put them back on in the morning. For tonight, however, you'll rest more comfortably without them."

Disregarding him, she rolled onto her right side and struggled to sit up, but the pain the movements caused took her breath away. Her head reeled and perspiration broke out across her upper lip, and, for a moment, everything went black before her eyes.

Dan dropped to his knees beside her, and his arm went around her shoulders just as she started to collapse. "Damn it, Gabrielle," he muttered into her hair as he held her close. "Just once, can't you do as you're told?"

She rested her forehead against his chest until the spinning subsided and she became aware of the large work-roughened hand that caressed her back. Delicious tremors rippled down her spine at his gentle, but firm, touch, and, for a fleeting second, she longed to settle deeper in his arms. Suddenly remembering herself, she pulled away, horrified by the madness that had temporarily possessed her. The blanket had slipped down between them, exposing her to his view, and with a gasp, she grabbed it and yanked it back up over her breasts, her face burning with embarrassment as she glanced up at him and caught him studying her with amusement.

"It's a little late to hide," Dan said dryly, barely able to control the smile that played at one corner of his mouth. "I've already seen everything you have to offer."

Tears of mortification smarted in her eyes. "You *looked?*"

"I'm a man, Gabrielle. Of course, I looked." He reached up to brush a stray curl back from her face, but she slapped his hand away.

"Here I was, feeling badly about the way I had behaved, and all the time you were enjoying yourself at my expense!" she blurted out, her voice wavering in spite of her efforts to keep it steady. Holding the blanket in place over her breasts with one hand, she reached past him for the shirt he had folded and placed at her feet. Jutting out her chin, she glowered at him. "I assume you did enjoy yourself?"

At least her pigheadedness hasn't suffered any permanent damage, Dan thought. Piqued, he allowed a lusty gleam to creep into his eyes as he raked his gaze over her and then said, "Immensely."

Gabrielle had never felt so disconcerted in her entire life. On the one hand it gave her a wicked stab of pleasure to think that he had looked at her and had liked what he saw; on the other hand, she wished the ground would open up and swallow her. Haughtily tossing her head, she turned away from him and began putting on the shirt, but the pain in her ribs hampered her movements and it was all she could do not to give in to tears of defeat.

"Would you like some help?" Dan asked from behind her.

"I can do it myself," she shot back. She wouldn't ask him for help if he was the last person on earth.

Despite her attempts to keep herself covered, it was only the front of her that she had remembered, and Dan knew that she was totally unaware of the tempting display her bare back presented, not only to him, but to the men sitting around the campfire as well. Their attention was fixed on her slender form as she struggled with the shirt. Dan allowed his gaze to travel along an expanse of smooth skin and down over her buttocks before saying sternly, "Madam, I think you had better let me help you."

Wondering at his change in tone, she turned her head to look back at him, but saw instead the other soldiers who hastily looked away when she caught them watching her. Her eyes flared wide and a cry of indignation rose in her throat, but before she could further disgrace herself, Dan took control of the situation and snatched the blanket away from her, holding it high to protect her from prying eyes.

"Don't always be so hasty to refuse help, little one." he said, more gently this time, yet his tone was still slightly scolding. Even in the darkness he could see the tears that glimmered brightly in her eyes as she flashed him a proud but wounded look, then turned away.

With her face set in a look that was somewhere in between a pout and a grimace, for pain threatened to consume her, Gabrielle finally managed to get her arms through the sleeves and to button the shirt. It annoyed her no end to know that the major was sitting behind her, calmly watching her dress, for though he was shielding her from view of the others, he had made no attempt to divert his own gaze. Damn him! Why can't he just leave me alone? she screamed inwardly as she worked the corduroy trousers up over her scraped and bruised legs, her eyes brimming with the tears that she refused to shed. She was not a crybaby, and despite his insistence to the contrary, she did not need his help.

Refusing his proffered hand, she stood up.

Dan raised one brow and eyed her skeptically as she swayed on her feet.

Gabrielle glanced about seeking some place where she could go relieve herself in privacy and her gaze inadvertently met Dan's. Suddenly embarrassed, she blushed. He inclined his head. "Over there."

"Thank you," she said stiffly and turned in the direction he had indicated, eager to be away from his mocking gaze.

Tossing the blanket aside, Dan got to his feet. "Don't go too far."

"I can take care of myself," she retorted over her shoulder, then heard him make a noise that sounded like a snicker.

"If you faint, I'm going to leave you to the coyotes."

"Bastard," she muttered under her breath as she stalked off into the shadow. She wished now she could take back the apologies she had uttered earlier when she'd been so relieved to see him she'd spoken without thinking. He had almost led her to believe he really cared about her, but she now knew that she had imagined it. Dan Catlin was a man without a heart, and she had been a fool to ever think otherwise.

By the time she finished taking care of her personal business and started back, the pain in her ribs was so unbearable that even the most shallow breaths hurt, and she was beginning to feel sick to her stomach. Her footsteps faltered and the ground seemed to move beneath her as everything shifted in and out of focus.

A steadying hand fastened on her elbow. "It's all right," Dan said gently. "I'm here."

Swallowing her pride, she leaned against him and allowed him to lead her back to the camp. Nor did she fight him when he helped her to the ground and covered her with the blanket. "I-I guess . . . I guess rattlesnake piss won't m-make this go away," she stammered miserably and squeezed her eyes shut. She hated the feeling of being so utterly helpless.

Dan chuckled softly. "No, little one. I'm afraid good old rattlesnake piss won't be of much help to you now. But, maybe this will." Unscrewing the cap from Bandy's canteen, he lifted her head and held the canteen to her lips.

The whiskey burned her throat as it went down and she tried to pull away, but Dan held her head firmly and would not release her until she had taken several small sips as he directed. "It tastes awful," she gasped, trying to catch her breath.

Dan smiled, surprising her by the way that transformed his countenance. "Don't let Moreland hear you say that. He's liable to take offense."

Gabrielle turned her head to one side and saw the man in question go to the fire and refill his coffee cup. "Is he the one who's taking Lieutenant Dalton's place?"

"He is," Dan said, then tilted his head back and drank deeply of the whiskey.

Gabrielle's forehead puckered as she studied the short, grizzly little man. "He's kind of runty looking for an officer, don't you think?"

Annoyance glittered in Dan's eyes as he screwed the cap back on the canteen. "He helped save your life, little one."

She turned a questioning gaze on him, but the hard set to his jaw told her he was not going to go into that, and she had an uncomfortable twinge of conscience. She was beginning to realize that liquor loosened her tongue considerably.

Dan sat back and carelessly draped one arm across a bent knee. "I've known Bandy Moreland ever since we were both kids at the Madison County Boy's home. His folks were killed in a riverboat accident when he was four. He always was a little scrapper, just itching for a fight. But he's also the type of person who would give you the shirt off his back and ask for nothing in return. He's a good man, and I suggest that in the future you keep any unkind remarks about him to yourself."

He had spoken quietly, but there was something so hard and unrelenting in his tone that he might as well have yelled at her. He had made her feel small and unworthy, and it was all she could do not to burst into tears. Trying hard not to let him see how much the rebuke had upset her, Gabrielle swallowed and then asked in as proud a voice as she could muster. "And if I don't?"

The look he gave her made her squirm inwardly. "I would have thought you'd learned your lesson the last time you tried my patience, Gabrielle. Are you so anxious to be punished again?"

"You know I'm not." Her voice cracked.

"Then, why? Why are you always testing me? Always trying to see just how far you can push me before I lose my temper? My God, girl! Do you get some fiendish delight out of tormenting me?"

"Tormenting you!" She bolted upright, then clutched her side and fell back with a gasp of pain. Sobs of agony rose in her throat, but she choked them back. "Go ahead and snicker." she said through clenched teeth. "You're obviously enjoying the fact that I'm practically your prisoner. I can't even move without your help, much less haul off and bust your nose like

I have half a mind to do!"

For a moment, he simply stared at her, his expression unreadable. Then, moving closer to her, he planted his hands on the ground on either side of her head and bent down until his face was only inches from hers. "I'm at your mercy, Gabrielle. Go ahead. Hit me."

Chapter Five

Struck speechless, Gabrielle searched his unfathomable eyes for some sign that he was jesting, then realized with a pang that he was not. "I-I can't hit you," she stammered, punctuating the declaration with a small shake of her head.

One dark eyebrow lifted, but the penetrating expression in his eyes remained unchanged. "Why not?"

Her mind raced, frantically seeking an answer that was not forthcoming. Why not, indeed? More than anything in the world, she wanted to draw back her fist and plant it squarely in the middle of that arrogant nose.

"Are you afraid of me?"

"No," she lied.

"Then go ahead and do it. Hit me. Bust me in the nose as you so graciously stated you wanted to do. I promise you I won't retaliate."

Her heart thumped mercilessly. "I-I can't."

"Why?"

"Because . . ." She swallowed hard. "Because I don't enjoy hitting people the way you do."

This time his brows drew together in an expression that was more surprised than menacing. "Do you honestly think I enjoy hitting people?"

She nodded. "Y-yes."

He was so close to her that he could feel the velvet warmth of her breath on his face, and he might have been tempted to kiss her had her revelation not disconcerted him so. Instead, his brows dipped and he asked, "Whatever gave you that asinine idea?"

"You enjoyed hitting me."

"When?"

Good Lord! Did she have to spell it out for him? She nervously moistened her lips and wished her heart would be still. "Y-yesterday . . . morning . . ." She winced. Never, for as long as she lived, would she forget the humiliating sting of his broad hand on her backside.

"Contrary to what you think, Gabrielle," Dan said, with a deliberation that made her uneasy, "I did not enjoy punishing you yesterday. But that doesn't mean I won't do it again if you continue to defy me."

A sob of defeat and despair broke in her throat. She glared up at him through the tears that pooled in her eyes, and said in a choked whisper, "I hate you."

With a sigh, Dan drew away from her and said wearily, "Somehow, little one, that does not surprise me."

In the morning, minus their horses and weapons, and having received a warning to keep away from the Tonto Basin, the two surviving Apaches were left to bury their dead. Captain Moreland did not like the idea of setting them free, but Dan once again insisted he had no reason to hold them, and so the issue was settled, though far from forgotten. A tense silence hung over the group as they started home.

During the night, Gabrielle's condition had worsened. Her pulse was rapid and uneven, and a low-grade fever brought an unnatural flush to her face, but what frightened Dan most was that the fight seemed to have left her. She did not protest when he unbuttoned her shirt to check the binding around her ribs, or when he made her drink a healthy portion of the water in his canteen, though he knew from the glazed look in her eyes that the effort pained her. She did not even protest when he informed her that she would be riding with him.

He kept his horse at a steady gait, not wanting to bring her any more discomfort than was necessary. She rode in front of him, cradled in his arms, her cheek resting against his chest.

He could tell when she slipped in and out of consciousness, by the changes in her breathing and the movements beneath her eyelids, but she never complained; and his pride in her swelled, along with his worry.

Bandy glanced at him occasionally from the corner of his eye, then looked down at Gabrielle, and he knew the lines of torment on Dan's face stemmed from more than mere feelings of responsibility for the girl's welfare. He knew Dan blamed himself for what had happened to her, and he also knew, despite his friend's denials, that Dan was in love with her. He smiled inwardly. From the little he had learned of Gabrielle, he'd gathered that what the little minx needed most in her young life was some consistency, someone strong and dependable; Dan certainly was. And Dan needed someone who would peck away at the protective wall he had erected around his heart, someone who would make him learn to laugh again. It would be a good match, Bandy thought, almost as good as if I'd arranged it myself. Satisfied, he chuckled.

Reluctantly drawing his attention from Gabrielle, Dan threw Moreland a questioning glance. "Did you say something?"

Bandy wisely kept his musings to himself. Instead, he waved a hand in a dramatic flourish and asked, "Well, what d'ya think of it?"

"Think of what?"

"The land. This valley."

"What of it?"

Moreland gave him a sly grin. "It's mine. Six thousand acres of it. At least it will be when I get the deed back from Prescott."

For a moment, Dan just stared at him; then he allowed his gaze to scan the valley and the surrounding mountains. "You bought all this?" he said at last, his tone edged with disbelief.

"No, you ass, I stole it! Of course, I bought it! Why else do you think I busted my butt tryin' to get assigned to your outfit? It sure as hell ain't 'cause I'm in love with you!" He surveyed his surroundings, a look of wonder on his weathered face. "Saw it first last spring when I was on a patrol out of Camp Bowie, and bought it with the money I've been savin' up ever since I joined the Army. Figured I'd give Uncle Sam a few more months, just 'til I'd saved up enough to stock up a year's worth of supplies, then come up here and try my hand at ranchin'. So, what d'ya think?"

Dan shook his head. "I'm amazed. Why didn't you tell me this yesterday?"

'Cause you had enough on your mind worryin' about her, Bandy thought, casting a surreptitious glance at Gabrielle. He grinned broadly. "I was tryin' to think up some easy way to ask you to go into partnership with me without you gettin' your dander up."

Dan speared him with a look and said dryly, "You're just looking for someone to foot half the bill."

"Yup."

"You rotten son-of-a-bitch!"

Bandy laughed good-naturedly. "Yup!"

Gabrielle moved in Dan's arms, and he looked down to find her staring up at him without blinking, a dull glaze clouding her gray-green eyes. "Do you want to stop and rest?" he asked.

She opened her mouth to speak, but when nothing would come out, she shook her head.

One of her braids had come undone, and when he reached up to smooth the wayward tendrils back from her face, he was startled by the fire that radiated from her hot dry skin. "It won't be much longer now, little one," he said, trying to keep his tone light. "We'll get you home and have Wilcox take a look at that rib."

Her eyelids drifted shut and several moments passed before Dan realized she was staring at him again, her face ashen with undisguised pain. This time he did not hesitate to issue the order to stop.

"A fire, sir?" Sergeant Reikowsky asked, not certain he had heard right. They never took time to make a campfire when they stopped at midday.

Dan carried Gabrielle to a sheltered spot that backed up on to rocks and gently lowered her to the ground. "Yes, a fire. And I want fresh meat and a pot of coffee."

Sergeant Reikowsky glanced down at Gabrielle, then back up at the major, and saw that taut lines of worry in his face. He nodded reassuringly. "Not a problem, sir. Gilly and me, we saw some nice fat quail back down the road a ways. We'll have the colonel's little girl here fixed up right in no time."

Gabrielle struggled to open her eyes, vaguely aware that they were talking about her. "I—I'm not . . . hungry."

Dan reinforced his orders to the enlisted man with a silent nod, then turned his attention to Gabrielle. "No arguments, little one," he said firmly, unbuttoning her shirt. "You need meat to build up your strength."

He did not like what he saw when he pulled her shirt open. Though the binding was still snugly in place, the flesh around it was puffy and discolored, and he didn't know what else to do for her except rewrap the bandages. "This is cutting off your circulation. I'm going to undo it and rewrap it. It will probably hurt like hell."

When she did not respond, he shifted his gaze to her face and caught her watching him, stoic determination in her expression. His own demeanor softened and he smiled tenderly, wishing at that moment that he could trade places with her, if only to ease her pain.

The corners of Gabrielle's mouth turned up uncertainly. "I always thought the first time a man undressed me would be on my wedding night. Does this mean I've been . . . compromised . . . and you'll have to marry me?"

Absolutely not! he nearly blurted out. His eyes riveted on hers, but he was so caught off guard by her comment that it took him a moment to see the faint glimmer of mirth behind the pain in her eyes. Relaxing slightly, he chuckled inwardly as he untied the knots and eased the bindings from around her middle. Then he said, in as serious a tone as he could muster, "I'm afraid marriage would be the only acceptable solution. What do you think, little one? Could you tolerate having me for a husband?"

Tears of agony stung her eyes as his fingers moved along her bruised flesh. "I think we should make a fine pair, Major, always sniping at each other like a couple of—" She sucked in her breath and threw her head back as searing pain exploded inside her, wrenching a tortured scream from her throat.

The next thing Gabrielle knew, she was in Dan's arms, sobbing disconsolately into his shirtfront.

"Shhh . . . It's all right, little one. I'm sorry. I didn't mean to hurt you." He held her close, his face pressed against her hair, rocking her as one would a child.

Her body jerked convulsively, with spasms she could no more control than the bitter tears that came in relentless, scalding waves, soaking the front of Dan's shirt. "It hu-urts. . . ."

"I know, I know," he murmured as he rocked her, his face ashen, feeling as though someone had rammed a knife between his ribs and given it a cruel twist. His hands glided over her back, pressing her to him, and his lips moved in a silent prayer that knew no words because it came from somewhere deep inside him.

Gabrielle's head reeled from the intense, burning pain. "I-I tried to be . . . brave," she stammered between sobs, and clung desperately to him as she fought the delirium that threatened to overtake her. "I tried. . . ."

"I know, sweetheart. Don't cry. You'll only make it hurt more if you cry."

"I wanted to show y-you . . . to m-make you p-proud. . . ."

His heart slammed against the wall of his chest. "Shhh . . . Don't talk anymore."

"I'm s-sorry. . . ."

A hand descended on Dan's shoulder, and he looked up, meeting Bandy's troubled gaze over the top of Gabrielle's head. Bandy held out his canteen of whiskey, but Dan shook his head. "Not now. She'll only choke on it."

"Not her, Dan. You."

Gabrielle felt a cool hand brush against her forehead, and she opened her eyes to find her mother smiling down at her. "Mama, you came back," she whispered, incredulous.

"Of course I came back, child. I only went to Mrs. Fergusson's."

"But you were gone so long. Father said you weren't coming back."

"I was only away an hour, Gabrielle. Must you always exaggerate so?"

104

"Father told me you were dead. He said you weren't ever coming back."

Her mother smiled indulgently. "You have a fever, dear. Rest now. You'll feel better in the morning."

"Mama, it's hot in here. . . ."

"Drink this." A deep voice interrupted and strong but gentle hands lifted her head and held a cup to her lips.

Gabrielle smiled. "Marcus, you silly boy! Whatever are you trying to do? Of course you can't kiss me. Father will have you court-martialed! Marcus, don't! You're hurting me!"

"You're just a child, Gabrielle. A child pretending to be grown-up. That's why you wore that dress, so I would think you are grown-up."

"Marcus, don't go! Don't leave me to face Major Catlin alone!" A sob broke in her throat. *"Marcus!"*

"Shhh . . . it's all right. It's just a dream." It was her mother again, but not her mother's voice.

"I hate him, Mama," she sobbed, throwing her hands up over her face. "I hate him! He called me a brat and he spanked me. Oh, Mama, he's always so mean to me. He said I was a whore and that I should be more like Grace Simmons, but I don't want to be like Grace. Mama, you don't want me to be like Grace, do you? She's in love with him, and she stuffs batting in her bust so he'll notice her. She's the one who told on me. Mama, you still love me, don't you? Mama, don't go away!"

"Gabrielle, stop this nonsense right now!" the colonel said sternly. "Your mother is dead. Do you hear me? She'd dead! She died of the fever. The scarlet fever *you* gave her!"

"No! I don't believe you! She's not dead! She's coming back. She said she was coming back!"

"Gabrielle, go to your room!"

"Fine! Go to San Francisco and see if I care! You don't want me to go with you because you think I'm too much trouble and you don't want to be bothered with me. You wish I had died instead of Mama! You don't love me. You only love *her*."

It was hot, unbearably so. She kicked her feet, but something tangled about her legs, trapping her. Someone was lifting her head and making her drink, then swabbing her burning skin with damp cloths. She twisted away, but the hand would not leave her alone. They turned her onto her side and she felt something cool and wet slide over her back and down her legs.

"Shhh, darling, don't cry. Your father didn't mean it. He's just being cross because of the war. He has a lot on his mind. Now take your medicine like a good girl."

"Yes, Mama."

Gabrielle felt herself being lifted into the air, and a sharp pain knifed through her ribs. She thrashed frantically, but her hands were tied and she was falling, falling. . . . The horse reared up and she saw the hooves coming at her. She screamed.

"It's all right, little one. I'm here for you."

Strong arms tightened around her, and she was safe again. Then she felt herself being lowered onto her own bed, the sheets cold and crisp against her skin.

Again someone raised her head and made her drink, but when she looked to see who it was, no one was there. "Mama?" she cried out. It was dark and she was afraid of being alone.

"I'm right here, Gabrielle."

She breathed a sigh of relief. "Father told me you weren't coming back."

A soothing hand brushed the hair back from her face. "Go to sleep, little one."

"I love you, Mama."

Gabrielle awoke from a deep sleep to sound of rain steadily drumming on the roof. It was night and she was in her own bed, though, try as she might, she could not recall how she had gotten there. Through the partially closed door, she could see the table that had been placed in the hall outside her room, and on it a lamp burned brightly. She frowned, wondering why it was there. She had not been afraid of the dark since she was a small child.

Her frown deepened as she noticed the Army cot set up next to her bed. A blanket had been carelessly tossed across the foot and at the head was a pillow, rumpled and packed down as though someone's head had been lying on it. Who had been sharing her room? Unable to contain her curiosity, Gabrielle threw back the covers, dropped her feet over the side of the

106

bed, and started to rise. A sharp pain just below her left breast caused her to gasp and fall to her knees. She clamped her hands to her side and gritted her teeth to keep from crying out, the searing torment in her chest bringing sudden tears to her eyes and sucking the air from her lungs. For what seemed an eternity, she huddled there on the floor, resting her head against the cot, trembling violently, and trying to catch her breath.

When a shadow fell across the shaft of light that came from the hall, Gabrielle lifted tear-filled eyes to see Dan standing in the doorway.

"Good God!" he exclaimed, and rushed to her side, bending down to scoop her up in his arms and hold her close against his pounding heart. "What in the hell are you trying to do? Injure yourself all over again?"

She clung to him, digging her nails into his shoulder and burying her face against his chest, and as the pain that had overtaken her ebbed, she became aware that she was totally naked except for the white cotton bandages tightly wrapped about her rib cage. Her first reaction was to recoil in righteous horror, but that response died when she remembered that he had already seen her thus, more than once, and that to try to retrieve her modesty at this late stage would be pointless, and a little silly as well.

Dan lowered her on to the bed, and a small cry of dismay burst from her lips when his arms slid away from her. Bewildered by her own reaction, Gabrielle turned away from the amber-flecked gaze that bore into her. What was wrong with her? This was Major Catlin. He had treated her like a child, and had threatened her with bodily punishment if she did not obey him implicitly. She wished he would go away and leave her alone. Or did she?

She kept her head turned away from him as he pulled the bedclothes up over her, unable to look at him for fear he would see the confusion in her eyes. Several long agonizing moments passed before he spoke. "Captain Wilcox says you are going to be fine," he said dispassionately, his tone clipped and formal. "You don't appear to have any serious internal injuries, and now that your fever has passed, it won't be long before you are up and about."

This time she did look at him, puzzled by his sudden coolness toward her. Fever? She glanced at the cot beside her bed and vague memories danced before her, coming closer, then retreating, yet always eluding her grasp. Had he been the one tending to her? How long had she been ill? More than a day, surely, or he would not have set up a cot in her room. Her eyes dropped to the shoulder that had sustained the knife wound, and she realized with a start it did not seem to bother him to move it and no bandage bulged from beneath his shirt. It could not have healed so soon, she thought, and was gripped by the odd feeling that she'd lost a large chunk of time which she would never be able to recover. How much? Four . . . five days? A week? Even the scratches she had gouged into his face the day of the festival were no longer visible. She swallowed hard. "How long . . . was I sick?"

"Six days," he said flatly. He had tossed his pillow and blanket onto the foot of her bed and was dismantling the cot.

Six days? Again she was haunted by vague memories. Someone holding her head and making her drink. Strong hands turning her and bathing her fever-scorched body with cool cloths. Someone holding her and murmuring words that had brought her comfort. An odd feeling came over Gabrielle as she watched him fold up the cot. "Did you take care of me . . . all that time?"

Their gazes locked, and for a fleeting second she saw in his eyes an uncertainty that matched her own. Then it was gone. He carried the collapsed cot across the room and propped it up against one wall, then said in his most unapproachable manner, "I did what had to be done."

At other times, his icy tone would have sparked Gabrielle's ire, and she would have casually attributed it to his irascible nature. Now, his coolness hurt. Taking as deep a breath as her sore rib cage would allow, she steeled herself against the tumult of conflicting emotions that battered her already exhausted and confused mind, then said, "I'm sorry I caused you so much trouble."

He reached for his pillow and blanket and said flatly, "Apology accepted."

An ache unlike any she had ever known swelled inside Gabrielle. The gentle, caring man who had saved her life, tended her wounds, and sat by her sickbed—that man was gone, replaced by the Dan Catlin she knew, the cold and unfeeling major who always treated her like a child. Another thought entered her mind—a dark thought that sent a tremor of fear up her spine. Clutching the covers high up under her chin as though to protect herself, she asked uncertainly, "Are you going to punish me?"

He stopped, halfway out the door, and turned to stare at her in amazement. Then his brows knitted and sudden anger snapped into his eyes. Good God! What breed of monster did she think he was? Had she no idea what this past week had done to him, first the worry of not knowing where she was and whether she was safe, and then, once he had found her, wondering if she would live? For six goddamned days and nights he had sat with her, nursing her through feverish delirium and praying his guts out for her recovery. Now she was cowering beneath the covers and looking at him as though she expected him to haul her out of bed and apply his belt to her bare backside. In spite of his vow not to let her get under his skin, Dan couldn't keep irritation out of his voice. "I'm going to get you something to eat," he said. Then he tersely ordered her to stay in bed and stalked out of the room.

Gabrielle sighed with relief the instant he was gone, though relief was not exactly what she was experiencing. Her heart was thumping so wildly it had begun to feel bruised, and she was shaking. What was happening to her? Something had changed between them, of that she was certain. But what? She knew he didn't care about her; he was only concerned with the scene her father was going to make when he returned, although at this point she wasn't sure whether the colonel was going to be more angry with her or with the major for letting everything get so out of hand. Yet, if Major Catlin's feelings for her hadn't changed, was it possible that she was beginning to care—just a little—for him?

Before Gabrielle's tormented mind could provide her with an answer, Dan appeared in the doorway. Picking up the table that stood in the hall outside her room, he carried it within, lamp and all, and placed it beside her bed where the cot had stood only moments before. Then, without a word, he went to her dresser, opened a drawer, pulled out a nightgown, and returned to the bed with it. Gabrielle started to sit up, and immediately his arm slid beneath her shoulder to assist her. The sheets fell away from her breasts, exposing them to his view, but before she could cover herself, he had drawn the nightgown over her head and was working her arms into its sleeves. She bowed her head as he reached behind her and extricated her long hair from the gown, then lifted a wary gaze to his face as his strong tanned fingers worked the fastenings at her throat.

For the first time, studying his strongly chiseled face in the flickering lamplight, she realized just how gaunt and tired he looked. His skin seemed more tightly drawn than usual over those prominent cheekbones, and there were shadows of fatigue beneath his eyes. His black hair, usually neatly combed, now fell across his forehead in weary disarray, and the frown lines between his brows appeared to have deepened into permanence, like a scar. He's worn himself out, she thought, caring for me. Guilt pricked her, and that and her own exhaustion brought a lump into her throat and tears to her eyes. Not wanting him to see them, she hastily lowered her gaze.

Not a word had passed between them since he had come back into the room, and the resulting silence, coupled with his indulgent patience in helping her dress, wore heavier on Gabrielle's already taut nerves than if he had yelled at her. Her mind whirled in a frenzy of remorse and self-reproach, and by the time he had gone from the room and then returned with a tray bearing a bowl of steaming broth and a large glass of milk, she had resolved never again to disobey him, to talk back to him, and to give him cause for disappointment. Unlike the singular promises she had made in the past not to repeat specific misdeeds, it was a sweeping pledge, frightening in its scope. Never before in her life had Gabrielle committed herself to anything so all-encompassing, or with such earnestness.

Her first test came almost immediately, when he set her supper tray on the table in front of her. Gabrielle's throat constricted as she eyed the milk, though she knew he expected her to drink it—All of it. She hated canned milk, for it had a peculiar taste as opposed to fresh, but it was all they were able to procure at the post, and it did have the advantage of keeping for long periods without spoiling. Determined to see her newborn resolution through without fail, however, she scooted to the edge of the bed, pushing the hem of her nightgown down over her knees as she dropped her feet over the side, and picked up the napkin he had placed next to the bowl.

His mood much improved, Dan pulled up a chair opposite her and lowered his tall form into it, stretching his long legs out beneath the table until his feet nearly touched hers, careful to keep the bemusement from his expression as he watched her delaying tactics with the napkin, unfolding it, smoothing out the creases, the daintily spreading it across her lap. He knew full well how much Gabrielle disliked canned milk, and he was prepared to dodge the glass that was certain to come flying in his direction at any moment.

His good humor faded and his brows rose as she picked up the glass and, without so much as a word or a look of protest, raised it to her lips. He watched in fascination the working of her long slender throat as she tilted back her head and drank deeply, until the milk was gone. For a full minute after returning the glass to the tray, Gabrielle just sat before him, a peculiar expression on her face as though she might gag, and then, slowly, the color began returning to her cheeks. Obviously more relaxed now she dabbed at her milk "mustache" with her napkin, them flashed him a triumphant look and calmly picked up the spoon and began to sip the beef broth.

Not quite believing what he had just witnessed, Dan watched her closely. There was something wicked going on in that devious little head of hers, he was certain of it, though he was at a loss to determine what. It was not that he could find fault in her behavior, because he could not. For a change, she was actually doing what was expected of her without putting up a fight. Yet he knew damned well that she did not like canned milk, and he had given it to her thinking he would have to deliver a lecture on why she needed to drink it. It had never once crossed his mind that she would pick up the glass and empty it without argument.

Gabrielle finished the broth, wiped her mouth, neatly folded her napkin, and placed it on the tray. Then, clasping her hands demurely in her lap, she gave Dan her full attention. "Thank you for the supper. I feel much improved already," she said sweetly, adding as if it were an afterthought, "sir."

Dan felt the hairs along the back of his neck bristle, along with his temper, and it was only with great restraint that he managed to keep himself firmly planted in the chair. Since when had she ever called him *sir?* He did not trust himself to speak without giving vent to his mounting fury, so he remained mute and the taut silence between them grew to awkward proportions.

Gabrielle shifted nervously and her palms grew damp. She could sense Dan's growing displeasure in her, yet she could not figure out what she had done to provoke it. She was trying, really trying, to behave in the manner she thought he would find acceptable, yet her actions seemed to be having the opposite effect on him. His pointed scrutiny was making it increasingly difficult for her to drum up the courage to voice what she knew could no longer go unsaid, and the odd pressure in her chest made her feel as though she were suffocating. Finally, before she lost her nerve entirely, Gabrielle lowered her gaze and began to speak in a monotone. "I know running away was stupid and childish, and that I endangered not only my life but yours as well, and for that I am truly sorry." Her voice wavered, and she paused to moisten her lips and take a breath. "I would appeal to you for mercy except that I know I don't deserve it. So, what I ask instead is that you punish me now and get it over with because I don't think I can bear the waiting much longer."

When he did not respond, she ventured a hesitant glance at him, and was taken aback by the dark rage that gripped his features. His brows were drawn so closely together, they seemed to touch, and his eyes blazed as he regarded her with a look so damning that she instinctively shrank away from him. The sensation of suffocating became all too real, and Gabrielle wondered if this was how a condemned prisoner felt at the moment of execution.

When Dan finally did speak, there was a cold edge to his voice. "I believe, young lady, that my exact words were, 'apology accepted.' The matter is closed. I see no reason to discuss it further."

Her eyes widened in disbelief. "Then, you're not going to punish me?"

No sooner were the words out of her mouth than she wanted to retract them. Dan flew up out of the chair, bumping the table with his knee and causing the lamp to tip precariously. Gabrielle froze, unable to dodge the slap she felt was coming, then wilted in exhausted relief when, miraculously, it did not materialize.

Catching the lamp just as it was about to fall, Dan moved it to her dresser, and returned to pick up the table. "I think, Miss DuBois," he ground out between clenched teeth, his face dark with barely controlled anger, "that you are sufficiently recovered to spend the rest of the night unattended." With that, he turned and left the room, stopping only to set the table in the hall and to cast a scathing glance at Gabrielle before yanking her bedroom door shut with an explosive bang.

Gripping the edge of the mattress so tightly her knuckles had turned white, Gabrielle could not stop quaking as she stared at the closed door in stunned horror. What, pray tell, had she done? Never, in all the years she had known him, had she seen him so angry, yet her intention had been to please him. She felt betrayed. She had never imagined that being good was going to be so hard.

To her immense relief, Dan was gone when she awoke the following morning. "He went out to the Indian camp already," Corporal Bates told her when he brought a breakfast tray to her room. "Captain Moreland's been handling things out there while the major was here looking after you. You sure gave all of us a scare. The major wouldn't let no one but himself and Doc Wilcox get within ten feet of you. Took care of you himself, he did, all day and night for the past week, and wouldn't let up for nothing except to wash up and change clothes now and then. We all thought he was going to drop, he was so tuckered out,

113

but he just kept on going like there was demons driving him." Bates stopped when he saw her eying the glass of milk on the tray. He wondered if he should explain why the major had wanted her to drink it, then decided against it. He knew how much Miss Gabrielle hated tinned milk, and, if need be, he'd decided he would quietly dispose of it and tell the major a little white lie about her having polished it off.

What Bates had said about Catlin tending her all that time had captured Gabrielle's attention. Would Dan have gone to such lengths to help her recover if he did not care for her? And yet, he had been so angry with her last night. Or had he merely been exhausted? She recalled the dark shadows beneath his eyes and how worn he had looked, and was pricked with the awareness that, even though she had known him most of her life, she reallly did not know him at all.

Ill at ease with the turn her thoughts had taken and suddenly aware that Corporal Bates was staring at her, Gabrielle suddenly blushed. In a fit of modesty she pulled the covers higher up over her nightgown and then reached across the tray for a piece of toast. "Is Corporal Holmes in the kitchen?" she asked, anxious to change the subject.

This time it was the soldier's turn to look nervous. "Charlie ain't a striker here anymore, Miss Gabrielle."

Her brows lifted in surprise, and several seconds passed before she could make herself swallow a bite of toast that had suddenly turned to sawdust in her mouth. "Why not?"

"The major relieved him and put him on K.P. duty," Corporal Bates said, busying himself with gathering up the cot and the bedding Dan had left in her room the night before. "It happened when the major was giving you cold sponge baths to bring down your fever. He caught Charlie standin' in the doorway staring at you, and you didn't have nothin' on." His face turned bright red. "The major was fit to be tied. I thought he was goin to skin Charlie alive!"

It did not especially disturb Gabrielle that Charlie Holmes had stolen a peek at her. He was always looking at her, any chance he got, and everyone on the post knew it. But learning of Major Catlin's forceful reaction to the incident sparked a tingling warmth in her and brought a flush to her cheeks.

Gabrielle DuBois, whatever on earth is wrong with you? she moaned silently. She was spared having to give Corporal Bates a response since Captain Wilcox appeared in the doorway and the striker excused himself and left the room, taking the cot and bedding with him.

"Well, well, how's my prettiest patient this morning?" the surgeon asked, closing the door after Corporal Bates had gone. He placed his medical bag on the floor next to her bed. "Dan told me your fever broke during the night. How do you feel?" He placed a hand against her brow.

Well, well, how's my prettiest patient this morning? Gabrielle mimicked mentally, struggling to keep annoyance out of her expression. She hated it when people treated her like a child. Still, remembering her resolution, she took a deep breath and gave the doctor her most serene smile. "I'm a little tired. And sore."

He chuckled. "I don't doubt that. Mind if I move this tray? I need to take a look at those ribs of .yours."

Gabrielle did mind, but she refrained from saying so, and though it embarrassed her to have him see her and touch her so intimately, she dutifully spent the next ten minutes in tight-lipped silence, her nightgown hiked up under her armpits, while Captain Wilcox examined her and rewound the bindings.

"Healing quite nicely," the doctor pronounced when he was through. "In a few days, you can get up and start moving around. In the meantime, however, I want you to stay in bed."

Instantly rebelliousness showed on her face. "But I wanted—"

"You're still very weak," Captain Wilcox declared, not giving her a chance to finish. "I don't want to take a chance on you falling and bruising those ribs again. You're lucky they weren't broken."

"But—"

"No arguments, Gabrielle. And I intend to repeat my instructions to the major so he can insure that they are carried out. You are not to leave this bed. Is that clear?"

For goodness sake, all she wanted to do was take a bath! "Gabrielle?"

She nodded glumly and said, "Yes sir."

115

Satisfied, Captain Wilcox placed her breakfast tray back on the bed. "And another thing. If you want those bones to heal, you must have at least three glasses of milk a day."

It was all she could do not to hurl the tray in his face. Go and be damned! she fumed to herself as he left the room. She was not going to drink three glasses a day of that vile brew if he forced open her mouth and poured it down her throat! And she *would* have a bath, whether he authorized it or not. Why did people have to be so blasted contrary? She was trying so hard to be good, and not a single person was making it any easier for her. "And you!" she said aloud, giving the offending glass of milk her most contemptuous look. "You're nasty-tasting, you look like gutter scum, and I'm not going to drink you! I don't care what anyone says!"

Yet, not a half hour later, when Corporal Bates came to take the breakfast tray away, the glass was empty, and Gabrielle, her face pinched and pale with exhaustion, was sound asleep. The soldier looked first in the water pitcher and washbasin. Nothing. He ventured a peek in the chamber pot, but that, too, was empty. Then he went to the window and peered out, but no telltale puddle marked the ground below.

"By God!" he whispered aloud, his brow puckering in disbelief. "She actually drank it!"

Not even strong drink could drive Gabrielle from Dan's mind. She was always there, taunting him with her woman's body and her childlike innocence. Pricking him with sharp words at one moment and clinging to him for comfort the next, she flashed those stormy green eyes at him and seduced him with lips he was not permitted to kiss. She was an urchin. She was a temptress. She scared the hell out of him! He had bathed her and bandaged her and spoon-fed her until he'd thought he would lose his mind if he were forced to touch her exquisite body one more time. Only his respect for her father had kept him from giving vent to the lust that churned within him. "Witch!" he cursed drunkenly as he made his way up the front steps of the house that had become his temporary home—and prison. "What is it, little girl, that makes me want you even though I can't stand the sight of you?"

It was the irritating voice of the sergeant major's daughter that brought him up short and deepened his scowl. "And what the hell is *that one* doing here?" he muttered under his breath as he made his way down the hall toward Gabrielle's bedroom.

"Grace, you must tie it tighter!" he heard Gabrielle say, and through the open door, he saw her standing in the middle of the room in all her naked glory, her back to him and a towel wrapped around her head, that half-wit Grace Simmons fumbling ineptly with the bindings around her ribs. Neither girl saw him.

"I'm afraid I'm going to hurt you," Grace whined.

"You're hurting me now! Please, just leave it. I can't bear to have you touch me anymore."

Grace wrung her hands together. "Maybe I should go get Captain Wilcox."

"No! I don't want to see Captain Wilcox," Gabrielle ground out angrily, pulling the towel from around her head and letting her wet hair fall in a tangled mass down her back.

Folding his arms across his chest, Dan leaned against the doorjamb and a wry smile twisted his mouth as he watched Gabrielle don a fresh nightgown. *You can't hide your nakedness from me, litle one. I've already seen and touched that perfect body of yours so many times the memory of it is burned into my brain.*

"Gabrielle, I don't like this. What if you had injured yourself getting in and out of the tub?"

"Well, I didn't. I simply overdid it for my first day out of bed. That's all. Really, Grace. I'm fine."

Liar! Dan thought, noticing that she was standing a bit crookedly, and was holding her left arm in close to her side. *You're hurting, little one, yet you're too damned stubborn to ask for help.*

Grace shook her head. "You don't look fine at all. I'm going to get Captain Wilcox."

"Grace Simmons, you do and I'll never speak to you again!"

"Why won't you let me get help? Your face is all white like you're going to swoon, and if we could just get the doctor to take a look at—"

"No!"

117

"But why?"

"Because he'll tell the major I—" Gabrielle broke off in midsentence as her gaze fell on Dan, and the little color that remained to her drained from her face.

Grace followed her friend's stare, and she, too, paled.

A guiltier pair I've never seen, Dan thought, his annoyance rising along with his brows as he glanced from one to the other. Finally his gaze rested on Gabrielle. Her chin automatically came up, and he saw fury flash through her eyes. But it quickly disappeared and her expression became blankly passive. Damn her! he swore silently. Whatever she was up to, he would not stand for it. Pulling himself up to his full height, he impaled Grace Simmons with a glare that made her recoil, and then jerked his head over his right shoulder. "Get out!"

Chapter Six

Gabrielle felt as though every nerve in her body was stretched to the point of snapping. How long had he been standing there? Unable to make herself respond in defense of her friend as Grace fled the room in tears, she stood without moving, her heart hammering wildly, her eyes fixed on Dan's face. There was an unnatural flush beneath his dark tan, and anger crackled like heat lightning in the hazel eyes that raked over her. What was wrong with him? Why was he looking at her like that? Then he took a step toward her, nearly stumbling, and she knew. Taking a deep quivering breath, she willed herself to speak. "You've been drinking."

He laughed, but it was a harsh sound, devoid of humor. "No, little one, I haven't *been drinking,* as you so diplomatically put it," he said, sarcasm failing to disguise his slurred speech. "I'm drunk. I'm roaring, stinking drunk." He lurched as he stepped farther into the room, then caught himself and regained his balance. He seemed to fill up the small space; making it even smaller, and his drunken state made his presence all the more frightening.

Gabrielle moved cautiously away from him and nervously moistened her lips. "This isn't like you," she ventured, her voice strained and uneven as she pressed her elbow into her throbbing side. "In all these years, I have never known you to get drunk."

"There's a great deal you don't know about me, Gabrielle," Dan said tersely. Going to her dresser and yanking open the drawer in which he had found her nightgown the night before, he rummaged through it, pulled out a pair of lace-trimmed cotton drawers, and flung them at her.

She reacted instinctively, throwing her arms up to protect herself as the undergarment sailed straight for her face. But she caught it and clutched it against her breast, bewilderment clouding her eyes.

"Put it on!" Dan barked.

Raw heat consumed Gabrielle, turning her face a deep crimson, as she realized that he must have stood there in the doorway quite a long time, at least long enough to watch her put on her nightgown. How else could he have known that she was not wearing anything beneath it?"

When she did not move, Dan's anger soared. "Damn it, girl! If I have to look at your bare butt one more time, I'm liable to forget my promise to the colonel to keep you out of harm's way! *Put that on!*"

Misinterpreting his meaning, Gabrielle unwittingly let her gaze drop to his right hand. She saw it flex, then flushed even more as she remembered the last time he had raised it against her in anger. A small cry born of fear and indignation sounded in her throat as she spun away from him and did as he ordered, unaware that in the process she provided him with an unobstructed glimpse of that very part of her anatomy he had expressly said he did not want to see. Her hands shook as she tied the drawstring at her waist with fingers that suddenly felt clumsy and uncooperative. Though she cursed herself for letting him intimidate her, she was too afraid to defy him. For as long as she had known him she had not seen him drunk. It was an ugly sight, and it frightened her.

Smoothing her nightgown back down over her hips, she turned back to face him only to find him glowering at her with a look that bordered upon hatred. Dear God, what have I done this time? she wanted to scream, but did not. She had long since lost count of the number of times he had been angry with her, but never had she been as scared as she was now; for this time his ire was fueled by whiskey and was unpredictable.

He said nothing at first, but crossed the room to sit on the edge of her bed. Resting his hands on his thighs, he lifted an

120

expectant gaze to her now-ashen face, and said in a quietly ominous tone, "Come here."

Terror rose in Gabrielle, and though it briefly occurred to her that she stood between him and the door, the part of her that bade her to obey him outshouted the part of her that longed to turn and run. Dragging her feet like a recalcitrant child, she stepped before him. "I'm sorry!" she blurted out before he even had a chance to speak. "I know Captain Wilcox said I was to stay in bed, but all I wanted to do was take a bath and wash my hair. I felt so grimy and—"

"Shut up and turn around!" Taking her by the hips, Dan turned her sideways and hooked one foot around her ankles, imprisoning her between his long legs.

Then he began pulling her nightgown up from the bottom, and Gabrielle, visibly shaking, squeezed her eyes shut and held her breath. *Please don't!* she screamed silently over and over in her mind, certain that he intended to strike her.

"Hold this," he barked and shoved the bunched-up nightgown into her hands, causing her to gasp in surprise and turn a questioning look on him.

She was so close to him she could smell the whiskey on his breath and see the red in his eyes.

"Hold it up!"

She snapped her head around to the front so he would not see the tears that glimmered in her eyes, and held the nightgown up higher, though even that did not seem to please him.

"Not that high, damn you! I have no wish to sit here with your goddamned breasts staring me in the face. Cover yourself!"

Biting down on her bottom lip, Gabrielle lowered the gown several inches and then waited for the next sharp command to fall. What had ever given her the idea that he cared for her? He hated her, that was plain from the look on his face. And there was no gentleness in his touch as he removed the bandages from her ribs and began rewrapping them properly. Gabrielle's breath caught in her throat, and it was all she could do not to cry out in pain. "I—I didn't mean to m-make you angry," she stammered in a choked voice.

121

"Angry? You're not making me angry. You're driving me out of my mind! Always taunting me. Always pushing to see just how far I'm going to let you go. Damn it, Gabrielle! You would try the resolve of a castrated saint!"

The lump in her throat seemed to be strangling her. "All I did was take a bath," she protested, in a voice that was little more than a hoarse whisper.

"To hell with your bath! I'm talking about you and your goddamned feminine scheming! This is my last warning! Go ahead and twitch your butt and flaunt your breasts for the rutting stags you have wrapped around your fingers, if that's what pleases you, but, for chrissake, don't try to play your games with me, little one! I'm not a man to be toyed with, but I am a *man*—which you consistently seem to forget!"

What he was talking about suddenly dawned on Gabrielle and she turned on him, a shriek of outrage tearing from her throat. "How dare you speak to me like that, you drunken—"

He silenced her with a stinging smack to her bottom. "Stand still!"

Choking back a sob, she obeyed, her head held high and her eyes swimming as he fashioned a knot in the bandage and jerked it tight. She hated him. Oh, how she hated him!

Snatching the hem of the nightgown from her hands, he yanked it down, then took her by the shoulders and set her away from him with such force that she almost fell. "You're not to leave this room," he ordered, standing up, his face dark with something that went beyond fury. "I don't want to see you. I don't want to hear your voice. I don't even want to be reminded that you are here!"

She stared at his retreating back in stunned silence, her ribs heaving with hurt and anger. Then, just as he reached the door, she grabbed the hairbrush up off the dresser and hurled it after him, but it glanced off the doorjamb and clattered to the floor. *Damn him!* she said to herself. Then, her breath coming in painful gasps, she clutched her throbbing side. If he hated her so blasted much, why didn't he just get out of the house and leave her alone?

Not two minutes later, she heard the front door close after him. He had done just that.

Gritting her teeth in steely resolve, Gabrielle marched down the hall to the front door and rammed the bolt into place. Then she bolted the kitchen door. Finally, she went from room to room and methodically closed and locked every window in the house. Dan Catlin was going to have to do more than just waltz through the front door if he wanted to get it back in!

It was already dark when a loud knock at the front door jolted Gabrielle from a restless, troubled nap. Dazed and feeling a little nauseated, she sat up and rubbed the heel of her hand across her eyes, her befuddled mind groping for reality. Her bruised rib cage burned, and her nightgown clung, in clammy folds, to her perspiration-drenched body. In the suffocating closeness of the room her head began to ache.

The knock sounded again, louder and more persistent this time.

"All right, I'm coming," Gabrielle muttered thickly, getting to her feet and slipping on her wrapper. She peeked into Dan's room as she made her way down the dim hallway, finding it empty and her anger returned the instant she remembered that she had locked him out of the house.

For several moments she just stood in the middle of the hall, undecided. Should she let him in? Or should she just go back to bed and leave him standing on the doorstep? She had already made her point. But then, considering the state he was in, he was liable to want to make a point too, and *that* worried her.

Leave him on the doorstep, she decided. He's liable to be cursing up a blue streak come morning, but at least he'll be sober.

Careful not to make a sound, Gabrielle turned and started back to the sanctuary of her room. She had not taken more than a half-dozen steps on tiptoe when the silence was shattered by a great pounding on the front door. She froze, suddenly terrified that Major Catlin was going to shame them all by breaking down the door. Locking him out of the house no longer seemed like such a commendable idea.

"Dear Aunt Charlotte," Gabrielle mumbled aloud, mentally penning a request for asylum with her Baltimore relative as she made her way back down the hall. She paused at the front door and nervously wiped her damp palms on her wrapper, all the while contemplating the quickest possible escape route. Then, taking a deep breath, she slid back the bolt and eased open the door.

It was not Dan Catlin, but Bandy Moreland who stood on the threshold, his hat in his hand and a look of concern deepening the lines on his leathery face. "Is the major here?" he asked, taking in her disheveled appearance with his quick blue eyes.

Gabrielle's terror left her, along with her breath, in a *whoosh* of relief, only to be replaced by supreme pique. "No, he's not," she snapped ungraciously, annoyed with Captain Moreland for pounding on her door like a madman, and with herself for having been such a goose. "And I don't know where he is, so don't bother to ask!"

If Moreland was bothered by her rudeness, he gave no sign. "I take it he weren't in the best of moods when you seen him last."

She gave him a contemptuous look. "He was drunk. He came tottering in here half-pickled, yelled at Grace, and made her run out of here crying. Then he bawled me out for no good reason and accused me of playing games with him . . . and . . ." Gabrielle's voice faltered as she realized that she was clad only in her gown and wrapper. Folding her arms across her chest, she lifted her chin in outright defiance of the discomfort clearly etched on her face. "No, Captain Moreland," she said, struggling to regain her composure, "Major Catlin was not in the best of moods."

Bandy studied her for a moment, and was once again struck by her beauty. Even half-dressed and without her face dolled up and with her damp hair spilling about her shoulders in a mess of tangles, she was lovely. *Damn!* If he had to spend his nights in the same house as this one, he'd be so blasted horny he'd never be able to sleep! Giving his head a sharp shake as though to clear it, Moreland stepped into the house, uninvited, and closed the door after him.

"Captain!" Gabrielle wailed in protest as she followed him into the parlor. "I told you, Major Catlin isn't here!"

"I ain't deaf, little lady. I know what you told me. And I figure this is as good a time as any for you and me to have us a little talk."

Gabrielle ground her teeth together, and eyed the short,

buckskin-garbed officer suspiciously as he sank down onto a chair and propped up his booted feet on an ottoman that Lisette had decorated with needlepoint shortly before her death. "Captain Moreland, this is most unseemly! I am not dressed and I did not invite you in here, so please be a gentleman and leave."

He chuckled. "I managed to live this long without turnin' into some fussbudget gentleman, and I don't plan on becomin' one now. No, ma'am, I think I'll stay right here until I've had my say."

"You, sir, are impertinent!" Gabrielle finally blurted out, no longer able to contain her anger.

"In that case, Miss DuBois, you and I should get along just fine, 'cause you're about the most impertinent little split-tail I ever seen in my entire life." He grinned at her outraged expression. "Now, quit standin' there shootin' arrows at me with them big green eyes of yours and sit your fanny down. We got us some serious jaw jackin' to do."

Too dumbstruck to do anything else, Gabrielle perched primly on the edge of a chair that was far too close to him for her liking, then placed clasped hands in her lap. But, with her chin thrust out and her eyes snapping with undisguised anger, her demeanor fell conspicuously short of being even remotely ladylike.

Bandy fixed an infuriating grin on her. "Seein' as how we've never been formally introduced, maybe I should start off by tellin' you—"

"I know who you are, Captain Moreland. I also know you helped save my life and that I should be grateful. But right now I'm too mad at you to be able to thank you properly, so you'll have to forgive me if I don't fall at your feet and shower you with appreciation." He was still grinning at her and she was beginning to get nervous.

"Please, Miss DuBois, don't trouble yourself with bein' nice to me just 'cause our friend Dan threatened you with dire consequences if you didn't. I'd rather sit face-to-face with a woman I can speak my mind to than have to coddle up to some prissy lady whose delicate sensibilities might be upset by somethin' I gotta say. Now, if you think I'm kinda runty lookin, well then, that's all right with me. Just you do me the courtesy of tellin' me so to my face, and don't go whisperin' it behind my back."

Gabrielle's mouth dropped open and the color completely drained from her face as she recalled the comment she'd made. She could not believe the major had been so unprincipled as to repeat it.

As if reading her thoughts, Bandy said offhandedly, "And don't be thinkin' Dan went and told me what you said, 'cause he didn't. I got pretty sharp ears. I heard you myself."

"Oh." It was all Gabrielle could manage to say. Suddenly feeling ashamed of herself, she lowered her eyes and said tonelessly, "I'm sorry I said that about—"

"No, Miss DuBois, I don't want apologies, 'cause we both know you don't really mean 'em. Under the circumstances, I think it's best we just start over from the beginning." He paused as though waiting for his words to register before continuing. "My name is Wilbur Moreland, but when I was a sprout someone stuck me with the name Bandy 'cause my knees don't quite meet up like they're supposed to, and that's what folks have been callin' me ever since. I'm a captain with the Fifth United States Cavalry, and I got me six thousand acres of prime ranchland in the Tonto Basin where I'm hopin' to settle down one of these days. I'm five foot, eight and one-half inches when I choose to stand up straight, and I refuse to put on one of them peacock uniforms unless it's to get my picture took. I ain't never been married, though I'm thinkin' I might like to be, and you can stop lookin' at me like you're scared I'm gonna offer for you or something, 'cause you're too ill-mannered for my tastes. All I want is for us to be friends."

Ill-mannered! It was all Gabrielle could do not to fly up out of her chair and scratch his grinning face to smithereens! Instead, she lifted her chin haughtily and, fighting the wavering of her voice, said, "I don't think, Captain Moreland, that you and I could ever be friends. The truth is, I don't like you very much."

He slapped his thigh and guffawed. "Well, now, we're finally gettin' somewheres. You don't like me and I don't especially cotton to you, but our friend Dan does, only he's about as bullheaded as you are and he won't admit it."

Gabrielle stared at him, not quite comprehending what he was saying.

"Dan Catlin cares about you, little lady," Bandy continued, his tone serious now. "At first I thought you'd be good for him and all, 'cause you're not some silly bit of fluff who would expect him to cater to you like you was a helpless babe, but now I'm not so sure. I'm beginnin' to think you're too damned selfish to have a care for anyone but yourself. I know I ain't got no business buttin' in, but Dan's a good man, the finest, and if you think I'm gonna just sit back and watch you cut him to the quick, then you got another think coming."

Gabrielle shook her head in disbelief. "Major Catlin doesn't care about me. He doesn't even like me!"

"That's where you're wrong, Miss DuBois. The major cares about you so much every little thing you do keeps him so churned up inside he don't know if he's comin' or goin'."

"Believe me, Captain Moreland, you are mistaken. Besides you're new here. You haven't seen the way he treats me."

"I saw him risk his life to save yours, then sweat over you day and night to pull you through that fever."

"He's mean to me. He confines me to this house and won't let me—"

"He worries about you."

"Right!" she shot back sarcastically. "He worries about me so much he doesn't think twice about humiliating me in front of everyone."

"So, he blistered your rear end. From what I heard, you had it coming."

Good God! Did everyone know about that? "Well, I didn't deserve what he did to me today."

"And what was that?"

"I already told you. He came home drunk and ripped into me for no good reason, said I was playing games with him and flaunting myself. And he accused me of being a . . . a . . ." Her brow puckered as she searched for the word.

Bandy eyed her quizzically. "A cock-teaser?"

"No!" Gabrielle blurted out, a stricken look coming over her features. Then she lowered her gaze and nervously toyed with a fold of her nightgown. "I'm not really sure what that is, but I know it must be something awful—and I was trying so hard to be good and not anger him." Her voice wavered. "I don't even know what it was I did this time to make him mad at me."

"Maybe you're not the one he was mad at," Bandy said quietly.

She nearly contradicted him out of sheer habit, but the thought that the major might not have been angry with her was too great a temptation to ignore. She ventured a questioning glance at Captain Moreland.

The officer was a long time getting around to explaining, and when he did, he opened with a question. "Miss DuBois, do you have any idea what Dan was doin' all day today?"

She shrugged. "I know he went out to the Indian camp."

"Do you know there's well over two hundred families out there now?"

Remembering the day Major Catlin had forced her to go there with him, she shook her head. There had not been more than a score of families at the camp then. Still, she didn't see what that had to do with anything.

"Well, there are, and most of 'em from Camp Grant. This past week, while Dan was here takin' care of you, I was out there gettin' 'em settled in and all, but there weren't much else I could do for 'em, since I don't talk their lingo. Dan does, and when he went out there today, he had to take their reports of what happened down at Camp Grant, for the government records. He didn't say nothing, 'cause he's the kind of man who keeps things inside himself, but I know it was hurtin' him to hear about all the burnin' and murderin' that went on down there."

Gabrielle thought of the little girl she had befriended that day, and a sick dread knotted in the pit of her stomach and pushed upward against her lungs, cutting off her air.

Bandy continued, "Them folks seen their loved ones hacked to pieces with axes that day, and their little girls raped, babies' heads smashed in with rocks and —"

"Stop it!" Gabrielle cried out, her face ashen, she pressed her hands over her ears.

Bandy reached across the distance that separated them and

firmly pulled her hands down.

She tried to pull away from him, but he would not let her go. "No, please!" she begged, shaking her head from side to side. She felt as though she would be violently ill. "I don't want to hear any more!"

"Dan didn't want to hear it either, Miss DuBois. But he did. For eleven and a half hours he sat there listenin' to them folks tell about what happened that godawful day. And my guess is, when he finally did up and go home, he got drunk so's he could forget. But that didn't work, so he came here and took his frustrations out on you."

"But, why m-me?" she stammered, feeling more confused than ever. "I didn't do anything to him."

"You didn't have to."

"I don't understand."

Bandy shook his head and frowned at her as though he could not believe he had not been able to get through to her. He released her hands. "No, I guess you wouldn't. But you mark my words, little girl," he warned, getting to his feet, "Dan Catlin is about the finest man on the face of the earth, and I won't stand back and let you make a fool of him. You so much as try it and by the time I get through with you, you'll wish you'd never been born." He rammed his hat down on his head. "Don't bother gettin' up. I can find my own way out. And one more thing . . . you might try openin' a window or two before you suffocate in this oven."

For a long time after the front door slammed shut, Gabrielle sat in the parlor, rubbing her aching temples and struggling with the myriad of emotions that pummeled her. She did not believe for one moment that Dan Catlin actually cared for her, but even if he did, that still did not explain his outrageous behavior earlier. Then another incident came to her mind, one so far removed from the issue at hand that she did not know what had made her think of it.

She had been a child of six when it happened, yet she was able to recall the scene with such frightening clarity, it might have happened yesterday. Her father had come home from work spitting fire because he had been turned down for promotion to lieutenant colonel, and she had cowered in terror behind the

129

sofa while he'd slammed doors and cursed and shouted loudly enough to be heard clear across the post. Yet, through it all, her mother had listened with a sympathetic and most serene expression on her face, and when it was over—this was the closest Gabrielle had ever come to witnessing a display of affection between her parents—her father had sat down on the sofa, gripped her mother's hands, and said in a pained voice, "I don't know what I would do without you, Lisette. You're the only one who understands how I feel."

The scene had haunted Gabrielle for a long time afterward simply because she had not understood it, and even now she was not quite certain she comprehended what had transpired between her parents that day or why she should suddenly think of it after all these years. Feeling unaccountably wretched, she dropped her face into her hands, too tired even for tears.

The following morning, Corporal Bates found her curled up in the chair, sound asleep. He touched her on the shoulder. "Miss Gabrielle?"

Jerking awake, she bolted upright with a startled cry and blinked at him while the terrifying images slowly faded from her consciousness. Her heart was pounding furiously and terrible pressure in her chest made it nearly impossible to breathe.

"Sorry, Miss Gabrielle. I didn't mean to scare you."

"I-I was having a . . . dream."

"Must've been a bad one. You look like you seen a ghost."

"It w-was," she stammered, trying to still the pounding of her heart. For as long as she lived she would not be able to forget the sight of Dan Catlin lying dead, a warpaint-smeared Apache warrior leaning over him, bloody knife in hand.

Grimacing at the dull ache in her muscles, she rose unsteadily to her feet and glanced up to find Corporal Bates watching her with a questioning expression in his eyes. Too ashamed to have him know that she had spent the entire night in the chair, and why, she produced the first excuse she could think of. "I woke up and couldn't get back to sleep, so I came out here." She uttered a wan laugh and rubbed the small of her back. "I think maybe that was a mistake." To her relief, he accepted her explanation without question. Nor did he ask her why all the windows were locked, and for that she was glad. She was not sure she could think up a suitable lie to explain away that one.

"Oh, before I forget," the soldier said just as she was about to leave the room, "do you want me to set an extra place for supper?"

Holding onto the doorjamb to steady herself, Gabrielle turned and gave him a bewildered look. "W-What?"

"What I meant was, you and the colonel usually have Lieutenant Epperling over for supper whenever he comes in from patrol, and well, I didn't mean to assume nothing, but—"

"Marcus!" Gabrielle blurted out, suddenly coming fully awake. "Is Lieutenant Epperling back?"

"B Company returned yesterday evening. I thought you knew."

She shook her head, a stunned look clouding her features; then, suddenly, a burst of sunshine spread across her face. *Marcus was home!* "Oh, Corporal Bates, you're so wonderful I could kiss you! Of course, do set an extra place!"

Her thoughts leaping ahead to the moment when she would see Marcus again, Gabrielle could hardly contain her excitement as she started down the hall. She paused at the door to Major Catlin's room. His bed had not been slept in, and a flush of embarassment stained her cheeks as she wondered where he had spent the night. Locking him out of the house had been an incredibly childish act, even for her. Then another thought occurred to her. How was she going to explain her own appearance at the dinner table, much less the presence of a guest, when she had been ordered to stay in her room? No, not a guest, *guests,* she mused, a slow smile spreading across her face. She could give a dinner party to welcome Marcus home. Surely Major Catlin would not create a scene before all the other officers and their wives. Gabrielle decided she would even swallow her pride and invite Captain Moreland in spite of the awful things he had said to her the past night, including his preposterous allegations that the major cared for her. She had known Dan Catlin for nearly fourteen years, and while she could think of a few choice descriptions of how he felt about her, most of them were unrepeatable and *caring* was not one of them.

She grimaced and rubbed her bandaged ribs, wishing they did not hurt so much. Maybe giving a dinner party wasn't such a good idea after all. There was so much to do. Food to be ordered. Invitations to write. And the house needed to be scrubbed from top to bottom. On top of all that, Captain Wilcox had ordered her to stay in bed, and she wasn't at all certain he would buy any excuse she tried to foist on him. Still, it was for Marcus, the man she loved, the man she hoped to marry. And, she thought ruefully, the man she had allowed to ride away from Camp Carleton with only the memory of her childish reaction to his kiss. Above all else, she had to make him forget that awful night.

Determined to see her plan through in spite of the odds against her, Gabrielle turned and headed straight for the kitchen to ask—beg, if necessary—Corporal Bates to stay late and handle all the preparations.

"Sorry, Miss Gabrielle," the striker said when she presented him with her plans. "I got a barracks inspection this afternoon."

"Can't you get out of it? This is so much more important."

"I wish I could, but I can't. Tell you what, though. I can put the house in order for you and get supper started, but after that, you're on your own. And if you want something special for dessert, you'll have to make it yourself."

She barely had time to digest his words when another idea occurred to her. Grace! Grace would help her. "Corporal Bates, you must do me a favor. Go to the sergeant major's and tell Grace to come right away. Tell her it's important!"

But Grace was not so enthusiastic. "Gabrielle, how can you even ask such a thing of me? Major Catlin doesn't want me here. He made that clear last night."

"He was upset over something that happened out at the Indian camp. It had nothing to do with you."

"But he told me to get out!"

"He didn't mean it. Honest! Oh, Grace, if you only knew how many times I've heard him say, 'Why can't you be more like Grace Simmons?' or 'Grace Simmons doesn't cause even a fraction of the trouble you do.'"

"He really said those things about me?" Grace asked, her eyes widening in surprise.

"Yes. And more," Gabrielle begrudgingly admitted. "Please say you'll help me. I want so much for this to be a nice party for Marcus, and I can't do everything by myself. Besides, it's not like I only want you to help with the work; I want you to come to dinner too. It wouldn't be nearly as much fun without you here. And we can fix up your hair and make you so beautiful Major Catlin can't help but notice you."

Grace looked doubtful. "Do you really think he will notice me?"

"I know he will!"

"Oh, Gabrielle, I don't know . . ."

"Please?"

"All right, all right, I'll stay. But only if I get to sit next to Major Catlin during dinner."

Gabrielle released her breath in one long *whoosh* and beamed. "Grace, darling, you can sit anywhere your little heart desires."

By the time everything was ready and they were expecting the guests to begin arriving, Gabrielle had worked herself into a nervous knot. "Do I look all right?" she asked for at least the tenth time, reaching up to smooth an imaginary stray tendril into place and biting her lips to redden them.

"You look fine," Grace assured her, taking a turn before the cheval mirror in Gabrielle's bedroom. "But your lips are going to get chapped if you don't stop doing that. Goodness, Gabrielle! What is the matter with you?"

Gabrielle clenched and unclenched her hands. In spite of a concentrated effort to relax, she could not. "I don't know. I just have this awful feeling that something is going to go wrong tonight." She knew exactly what was going to go wrong. Major Catlin was going to come home and raise holy hell because she had disobeyed him. Perversely, she almost wished he would. Being out of bed all day had exhausted her far more than she would have imagined possible, and she was beginning to feel sick to her stomach. She pressed her elbow into her aching side, but the added pressure did little to relieve her discomfort.

Realizing that Grace was waiting for her opinion, Gabrielle gave her a wan smile and said, almost ruefully, "You look absolutely lovely. That dress is very becoming on you." It was the dress Gabrielle had worn the night Marcus had tried to kiss her, and though she hated to admit it, the dress really did look well on Grace. And it was certainly less revealing.

"I still can't believe you actually gave it to me," Grace said, a look of wonder on her face as she smoothed out the folds in the jade green silk. "It's one of your favorites."

It *was* one of my favorites, Gabrielle thought, painfully remembering the night she had worn it for Marcus and the disparaging remarks he'd made. Earlier, not thinking Grace would know the answer and unable to contain her curiosity, she had drawn Corporal Bates aside and had asked him what a cock-teaser was. He had given her an explanation that made her blush, and now she could not help wondering if that was, indeed, what Marcus thought of her. Grace felt she was being generous in giving her the dress, but in truth, she never wanted to wear it again.

All too soon, the first knock came at the front door, causing Gabrielle to jump in near-panic. "You get it," she told Grace, and she reached up to adjust the high collar of her white muslin day dress. Even though this was a special occasion, she had taken care to dress both simply and modestly, in part so that she would not outshine Grace, and in part to deprive Major Catlin of the opportunity to find fault with her attire.

She took a step forward as Marcus entered the hall and found herself looking up into incredibly blue eyes. His tall form was silhouetted against the evening sun that streamed in through the open door, making his hair seem even more golden than usual and his shoulders broader. Gabrielle could not remember when he had looked more handsome. Desperately needing his approval, she said in a low voice that was little more than a whisper, "Welcome home, Marcus."

He bent down and touched his lips to her cheek, but it was a dutiful kiss, lacking in feeling, and Gabrielle realized with alarm that he was not smiling. "Hello, Gabrielle," he said flatly, his gaze raking over her with what could only be interpreted as contempt, and her own smile faded.

Before she could say anything, he had turned to Grace. "I don't recall ever seeing you look lovelier, Miss Simmons," he said, giving Grace his most charming smile. "That dress is quite becoming on you."

Gabrielle felt as though Marcus had punched her between the eyes. When she had worn that dress, he had treated her like a whore, and here he was, fawning all over Grace as though she were royalty. "I think," she cut in, unable to keep the hurt from her voice, "that we would all be more comfortable in the parlor."

Just then, Captain Wilcox appeared in the open doorway. He looked tired and sweaty. He was not dressed for dinner, and Mary wasn't with him. "Gabrielle, I want a word with you," he said curtly after giving Marcus an acknowledging nod, so she had no choice but to stand and watch while Marcus escorted Grace into the parlor and led her to a chair.

Captain Wilcox rounded on Gabrielle the moment they were alone. "All right, young lady, just what are you trying to pull?"

She cast a nervous glance toward the parlor door. The last thing she wanted was for Marcus to overhear her being scolded like a naughty child. "I can explain—"

"I told you to stay in bed."

"I know, but—"

"It's only been ten days since you were injured. Your ribs are badly bruised, possibly even cracked, and until two days ago, you were delirious with fever. How do you expect to get well if you don't follow instructions?"

"I only wanted to surprise Marcus, and besides—"

"Answer my question."

"I feel fine!" she lied.

"Well enough to spend all day preparing for a party?"

"I hardly lifted a finger. Grace did most of the —"

"Well enough to disregard my order that you stay in bed and rest?"

"But, I did rest."

"Well enough to—"

"Please stop interrupting and let me explain!" She gave the

surgeon an imploring look. "I have not been disregarding your orders. I've been very careful not to do anything too strenuous, and I even drank the milk as you requested. All I want to do is give a special dinner to welcome Marcus home. Just one dinner. This is really important to me, and it's only for tonight. Tomorrow I'll stay in bed all day. I promise."

"At this point, Gabrielle, I couldn't care less what you promise. You are going to do what you want anyway, regardless of what anyone tells you. You always have. It's no wonder the colonel didn't want to take you to Division with him. You would have ruined any chance he had for promotion. Dan can deal with you. I absolve myself of all responsibility for your welfare."

The remark about her father stung, and it hurt to speak over the thick lump that swelled in her throat. "Does this mean you and Mrs. Wilcox won't be coming to dinner?"

He threw her a disparaging glance before stalking off without so much as a reply.

Wondering how she was going to explain the surgeon's absence, she cast a frantic glance toward the parlor just in time to see Marcus laugh over something Grace had said.

Damn you, Marcus Epperling! Gabrielle screamed silently, she speared the young officer with her most venomous look and balled her hands into fists, which she hid in the folds of her skirt, but he was looking at Grace and did not see her. She did not know why he was angry with her, but she intended, by God, to find out!

"Ahem!" The loud, sound came from behind her, and Gabrielle turned to see Captain Moreland standing in the doorway, grinning at her. "Can I come in?"

"That all depends," she retorted with undue sharpness, unintentionally taking her wounded pride out on him. "Have you come for dinner, or merely to insult me?"

He grimaced and said, "Ouch!"

Then Gabrielle relaxed a little, and was sorry she'd snapped at him. "To be honest with you, Captain Moreland," she said, giving him an apologetic smile as she approached him and extended a welcoming hand, "I am a little surprised that you accepted my invitation. After last night, I wasn't certain you

136

would even speak to me again."

He laughed good-naturedly and clasped her small slender hand tightly in his sun-browned, callused one. "You oughta know by now, little lady, that I ain't one to hold a grudge. If I was, I'd still be takin' you to task for callin' me a runt."

"I'm afraid I don't have such a generous nature," Gabrielle admitted sheepishly. "I still haven't forgiven you for calling me a . . . a . . ." She felt her face grow warm and could not even bring herself to say the word, but it was obvious from the look on his face that he knew exactly what she was talking about.

"What d'ya say we just start this dance over from the beginning?" he suggested, giving her hand a conspiratorial squeeze. "Who knows? Maybe one of these days we'll get the steps right." Before she could respond, his gaze traveled over her shoulder and he inclined his head and said, "Are you gonna introduce me to that vision in green, or do I gotta do it myself?"

As Gabrielle followed his gaze, she could not help but feel a stab of jealousy at seeing Grace perched primly on the edge of a chair, enjoying Marcus's undivided attention, while she herself was struggling to hold tears in check and to maintain a cheerful front for her guests. Steeling herself against another encounter with Marcus, Gabrielle turned to Bandy and said in as gracious a tone as she could manage under the circumstances, "Captain Moreland, if you will be so kind as to follow me, I would be delighted to introduce you to Miss Simmons."

Gabrielle approached Grace and Marcus on legs that felt as though they were made of lead. While she was careful not to look at Marcus, she could feel his icy gaze on her, and it was all she could do not turn and run. Somehow, she managed to stumble through the introductions.

"Miss Simmons," Bandy drawled elegantly as he bent over and raised Grace's hand to his lips. "I do believe you are the most beautiful woman I have ever seen in my entire life. Are you spoken for?

Grace, never having been the object of so much male attention, blushed.

Only then did Gabrielle venture a glance at Marcus, she caught him glowering at her, his blue eyes hard, like flint; and something inside within her withered and died. "Lieutenant Epperling, may I have a word with you?" she asked, barely able to keep the quiver out of her voice. To her immense relief, he did not refuse, but politely excused himself and followed her into the hall.

"What do you want?" he asked stonily the instant they were alone.

Her heart pounding furiously, Gabrielle whirled to face him. "I want to know why you are acting like this!" she demanded in a tear-choked voice. "I've tried so hard to make this a nice homecoming for you, yet you are behaving as though I have done something unforgivable."

"Are you in love with him?"

Her eyes widened in surprise. "Wh-What?"

"Don't play the innocent with me," Marcus hissed, his face dark with barely contained anger. "Are you in love with Major Catlin?"

To stunned to speak, Gabrielle simply stared at him, but his face blurred before her eyes, and the terrible pressure in her chest made it nearly impossible to breath. Finally she got out an embarrassed little laugh. "Marcus Epperling, you must be out of your mind!"

The blue eyes turned hard, like flint. "Answer me, Gabrielle! Are you or are you not in love with Dan Catlin?"

"No!"

She had spoken so loudly that all conversation in the parlor ceased, and a full minute passed before it resumed. Hurt that he could doubt her feeling for him, Gabrielle glared at Marcus through a haze of angry tears. "I love *you*," she said, her voice wavering. "I have loved you for months. I thought you knew that."

"No, Gabrielle, I don't know that. What I do know is that, for months, you have taunted and teased me with your hot little body, yet when I merely try to kiss you, you recoil as though I were a snake."

Cock-teaser. The vile word danced around and around in Gabrielle's mind and she flushed with shame as she recalled that terrible evening. "Marcus, you didn't merely try to kiss me. You had your hands all over me."

"What about the major? He had his hands all over you, yet you didn't mind that, did you? You like having that stinking breed touch you."

Just then, Lieutenant Johnson, the quartermaster officer, and his wife arrived, and Gabrielle, choking back a retort, went through the motions of welcoming them and taking them to the parlor. Despite the angry flush on her cheeks, her face was drawn, and it took an extraordinary amount of effort for her to smile for the dull ache in her side had become a persistent throbbing.

"It's a mighty cozy arrangement the two of you have here while the colonel is away," Marcus ground out when she returned.

"It was Father's idea that Major Catlin stay here and act as my guardian. You know how he hates for me to be in this house alone while he is away."

"Was it the colonel's idea that the two of you share the same bedroom? Was it his idea that Major Catlin undress you and bathe you and—"

"Marcus! I was trampled by a horse. I could have been killed. And then I came down with a fever. Major Catlin took care of me because I couldn't take care of myself. Yesterday was the first day I've been able to do anything on my own since the accident."

"Captain Wilcox is the post surgeon, Gabrielle. Had you really been ill, he is the one who would have cared for you. Not Major Catlin."

"I *was* ill!" Gabrielle protested, stunned that Marcus did not believe her.

Marcus waved his hand toward the parlor. "Then what would you call this? A miraculous recovery? Do you honestly expect me to believe that you are well enough to throw a party when only days ago you were supposedly near death? Don't insult my intelligence, Gabrielle. Wilcox would have never given you permission to leave your bed if you had been as ill as you claim."

Bitter tears stung her eyes as she realized what she had done. She had wanted to give Marcus a nice homecoming, but had only succeeded in trapping herself in her own scheme. The only way out was to swallow her pride and admit that she had disobeyed the surgeon's orders, something she stubbornly refused to do. If Marcus loved her, he would believe her. Her throat constricted. "I might have died if the major hadn't been there for me," she said in a low voice edged with pain, her brimming eyes silently pleading with him to try to understand. "Doesn't that mean anything to you at all?"

"And what about your reputation, Gabrielle? Doesn't that mean anything to *you?*"

"My reputation is spotless, and you damn well know it!" she shot back, stung by his insinuation.

"Your reputation, my dear, like your language, has slipped considerably. You're lucky I am a forgiving man. Otherwise, I would never be able to bring myself to follow through on my intention to speak with your father when he returns. As it is, you are making it exceedingly difficult for me to call you my betrothed."

"Your betrothed!" Gabrielle blurted out, the words she had longed to hear now hitting her like a slap in the face.

"Don't look at me like that, Gabrielle. You were well aware that I intended to marry you and I still do, in spite of your shameful behavior."

"And what makes you think I want to marry you?" she retorted, too hurt and angry to think clearly.

"What you want is irrelevant, Gabrielle. The matter of our betrothal will be discussed between the colonel and myself. All I ask of you is that, in the meantime, you have a little concern for my feelings and refrain from causing me any more embarrassment than you already have."

Gabrielle stared at him as though seeing him for the first time, and she suddenly hated what she saw. His feelings! What about hers? Or didn't they matter? Marcus turned and headed for the door, and she knew without asking that he would not be staying for the party she had gone to so much trouble to plan for him. Visibly shaking, she followed him, determined to try once more to reason with him. "Marcus, please, don't leave like this. I know you are angry with me, but I also know that I haven't done anything to deserve your anger."

"I have no wish to discuss this with you any further,

Gabrielle," Marcus said over his shoulder. Then he stopped and with one hand on the door, turned to glare at her. "There is one thing I would like to know, however. Are you still a virgin?"

Without even thinking, Gabrielle drew back her hand and slapped him as hard as she could.

Marcus stiffened and the muscles in his jaw worked convulsively while his cheek slowly reddened. "I will forgive you for that," he said coldly, regarding her with contempt, "because you are young and you obviously don't comprehend the import of my knowing whether or not I will be bartering for used merchandise when I speak with your father. And I do intend to speak with your father."

With that, he jerked open the door, leaving it standing wide as he stalked across the parade ground, his shoulders rigid with anger; and Gabrielle, her arm throbbing from the force of the blow she had dealt him, watched him go, scalding tears streaming down her face and a rent in her heart that felt as though it would never mend. Nothing would ever be the same between them. All she had ever wanted, all the love she had ever felt for Marcus, had been totally and ruthlessly destroyed. A wretched cry burst from her throat as she whirled about and fled down the hall to the sanctuary of her room, slamming the door behind her.

In the parlor, a shocked silence gripped the guests; they had overheard enough of the conversation between Gabrielle and Lieutenant Epperling to be able to ascertain what had happened. No one moved. No one knew what to do or say. Finally, Grace, her face drained of all color, rose unsteadily to her feet and said in a small voice, "I think it would be best if everyone went home."

Grace and Captain Moreland were the only ones remaining when Dan entered the house and stopped in the middle of the hall, his brows knitting as he became aware of muffled sobs coming from Gabrielle's room. "What happened?" he asked, turning a weary gaze on Bandy, who remained stubbornly silent about the matter, and then on Grace who was on the verge of tears herself.

In broken sentences, Grace haltingly explained as much as

141

she could of the plan for Lieutenant Epperling's welcome-home party and the argument that had ensued between him and Gabrielle, including the officer's coarse remark about Gabrielle's virtue—or lack of it—and as she talked, Dan's anger slowly built.

He had learned of Gabrielle's dinner plans earlier in the day, and at first, his head throbbing from his excesses of the night before, he had been angered by her outright defiance of his order confining her to her room. But as the day had worn on and his reason had returned, he'd found himself begrudgingly admiring her spirit. Grown men seldom dared defy him, either openly or behind his back, and the thought of a mere slip of a girl blatantly thumbing her nose at his command had brought a reluctant smile to his lips.

He turned his head toward the sound of Gabrielle's sobbing and clenched his hands, wishing they were around Marcus Epperling's neck; then, his voice quiet with carefully controlled rage, he said, "I'll go see if she's all right."

Grace started to follow him down the hall, but Bandy put a restraining hand on her arm. "But, Gabrielle needs me," she insisted.

Bandy shook his head. "Dan can handle it. What d'ya say you and me go for a nice walk?"

The sound of Gabrielle's weeping grew louder as Dan opened the door to her bedroom and stood on the threshold a moment, watching her. She was lying on her side in the middle of her bed, curled into a tight ball, her back toward him. Bitter sobs convulsed her entire body, and he knew that whatever he said to her over the course of the next few moments, he would risk driving a permanent wedge between them. There was a note of finality in the click of the door as he pushed it shut and, without further hesitation, went to her.

"Go away!" Gabrielle pleaded wretchedly as Dan sat on the edge of the bed and took her by the shoulder, pulling her up off the mattress and onto his lap. She tried to fight him, but his arms closed around her, holding her tightly; and when she would have jerked her head away, he reached up to hold that too, pressing her face against his chest. "Go ahead and cry, little one," he murmured, rocking her and stroking her hair, until she finally gave up resisting him and wept freely, soaking the front of his uniform with her tears.

After what seemed an eternity, her sobbing began to ebb until, before long, it was reduced to an occasional choked hiccup. Threading his fingers in her hair, Dan tilted her face up to his and brushed his lips against her eyelids, tasting the salt of the tears that clung to her lashes. "Feel any better now?" he asked gently.

Her head resting against his shoulder, Gabrielle opened her eyes and nodded weakly as she looked up at him through her tears. Exhaustion showed in the lines of his face, and there were dark shadows beneath his eyes. But his expression was warm and gentle; he was smiling at her. Not mockingly. She felt a twinge of conscience at the realization that she was sitting on his *lap*, in her *bedroom*, with the door *closed*, but his arms felt so strong and secure around her that she was not ready to give up the wonderful, yet unfamiliar, feeling of being held and comforted. Shyly, she reached up to touch a finger to one corner of his mouth as she said in a low voice, full of wonder, "I used to think that if you ever smiled . . . your face would . . . crack. . . ."

A cloud passed over his eyes and he said quietly. "I'm not made of stone, Gabrielle. I don't crack. I only bruise."

His words jarred something inside her and, without warning, her misery erupted anew. Turning her face against his chest, she wrapped one arm about his neck and clung to him as harsh sobs wracked her slender body and scalding tears spilled from her eyes. So great was her desolation that several moments passed before she became aware that he had lowered her to the mattress and was lying beside her, still holding her securely in his strong arms. Though cognizant of it, Gabrielle did not pull away as she knew she should. Instead, she clung to him, like a child terrified that he might let go of her. "I-I tried so ha-ard," she said brokenly between sobs. "I w-wanted the party to be nice for h-him."

"I know you did," Dan said quietly, stroking her hair.

"And n-now it's all ruined and Grace will be m-mad."

Dan said nothing, knowing there was nothing he could do to ease her hurt except be there for her as long as she needed him.

Closing his eyes, he pressed his lips against the top of her head and tightened his arms about her in silent reassurance.

"It hu-urts so much."

"I know, little one."

"I-I loved hi-im."

Dan said nothing.

"He wa-ants to marry m-me, but he doesn't . . . lo-ove . . . me. He said I-I teased him and then wouldn't le-et him touch me." Fresh sobs wracked Gabrielle, and several minutes passed before she could continue. "I didn't m-mean to be a . . . a cock-teaser . . . I-I didn't. I just wa-anted him to hold . . . me-e."

Stunned by her words, Dan raised up on one elbow and gripped her chin, making her look at him. "Is that what he called you?" he demanded harshly, and Gabrielle, seeing the fury in his eyes, thought he was angry with her.

"You said I played games and I didn't m-mean to. I'm sorry . . . I never m-meant to." Her watery green eyes filled with remorse, begging his forgiveness. "I-I tried to be like you w-wanted. I tried to be like G-Grace. I even d-drank all the milk and c-called you 'sir'. I-I didn't want you to be s-sorry you saved my life. . . . Please don't h-hate me."

"Good God." Dan groaned, and drew her back into his arms, to hold her so closely he could feel her heart beating against his chest. He had never meant to hurt her. The last thing he had wanted to do was harm her, yet he had; and in that he was no better than Epperling. "I don't hate you, little one," he murmured thickly into her hair, his voice sounding choked. "I never hated you. You must believe that. And, for God's sake, the last person I ever wanted you to be like was Grace Simmons!"

She pulled her head back to stare at him in agonized bewilderment. "But you s-said—"

"I know what I said, and believe me, I wish like hell I could retract the words." He leaned over her and, cupping her tear-streaked face between his hands, brushed his thumbs across the curve of her cheekbones, his hazel eyes serious as he studied her. Then one corner of his mouth turned up in a bemused smile, and he asked, "Do you remember the first time

I ever saw you?" She sniffled and shook her head. "You were wearing a white dress that had a sailor collar with dark blue piping, and you had the longest damned lashes I had ever seen in my life and the biggest green eyes. Not a clear, vivid green, mind you, but a soft gray-green, as I always imagined the sea would look. And your hair wouldn't stay braided. It refused to be tamed even then," he mused aloud, brushing a tendril back from her forehead and watching in wonder as it curled around his finger like a baby's hand. "I remember thinking it was the color of warm honey." He paused as other memories came back to him. "You hid behind your mother's skirts, and at first I thought you were afraid of me. But then, when you didn't know I was looking, you stuck you tongue out at me."

"I d-didn't," she protested, uttering a small choked laugh. It was the longest speech she had ever heard him make when he wasn't scolding her.

"You did."

Gabrielle shook her head and smiled at him through her tears. "I did not!"

Dan's thumbs moved down her cheeks to play with the corners of her mouth. "You did. I remember it quite clearly, little one. Your father was saying something serious which I was supposed to be paying attention to, yet wasn't, because *you* kept peeking at me from behind Lisette's skirts and making faces, and I was trying like hell not to disgrace myself by laughing."

"You must have thought I was . . . terrible," she said, her voice dropping to little more than a whisper.

"No. I thought you were the most beautiful, most priceless thing I'd ever set eyes on." He paused, then added solemnly, "I still do."

His gaze dropped to her mouth and held, and Gabrielle knew that he was going to kiss her. Her heart did a crazy flip-flop and she had a sudden fear that it was going to be awful, as it had been when Marcus kissed her; yet, in her fright, rather than withdraw, she unthinkingly lifted her face to his, meeting him halfway as he lowered his head. Firm, yet gentle, his lips moved tenderly against hers, and Gabrielle began to relax, thinking how she was not at all repelled by his closeness. Indeed, it

145

seemed the most natural thing in the world to be lying here in Dan's arms, kissing him. Sighing contentedly against his mouth, she lifted her arms up to encircle his neck, and threaded her fingers through his dark hair, drawing him closer.

In response, his kiss deepened and became more compelling. But it was a request rather than a demand, and under his gentle urging, her lips parted and she hesitantly, shyly, received him.

Feeling her trembling beneath him, Dan moved slowly, taking care not to frighten her or demand more of her than she was ready to give. To his delight, Gabrielle responded to the signals he gave her and began to kiss him back, timidly at first, then with a boldness that caused his heart to leap in his chest and his blood to surge. "God, you're wonderful," he murmured, his tongue flicking over her swollen, throbbing lips, caressing them, teasing them, before plunging inside to explore every corner of that sweet recess, her mouth. His hands moved up to take the pins from her hair, and it spilled over his fingers and onto the pillow in silken honeyed waves.

Gabrielle's head spun and a glowing warmth surged through her as she clung to him, aware only of a rapidly intensifying hunger for his touch as his hands moved downward to span her waist and pull her hard against him. "Please . . ." she gasped and tore her lips away from his. But he recaptured her mouth in a fierce devouring kiss that took her breath away and left her violently trembling, and when his hand slid upward over her breast, she unknowingly arched her back, pressing the soft swell against his palm.

Her breast fit perfectly into the cup of his hand as though it belonged there, and Dan felt the sensitive nipple harden beneath the fabric of her dress. Only when Gabrielle moaned and writhed against him, bringing his own sharply curbed passion to the brink, did he realize he had to stop or risk destroying the special bond that had formed between them, bridging years of discord. Reluctantly, he pulled away from her.

Feeling as though she were floating on a cloud high above the earth, Gabrielle blinked up at him through a warm passion-induced haze as she gently stroked his firm, sun-bronzed cheek. "Please . . . don't stop." she whispered breathlessly, unable to calm the furious beating of her heart.

He caught her hand and pressed a kiss into the palm. "I have to," he said huskily, his strong fingers closing securely around hers, a sympathetic smile warming his eyes. "If I don't stop now, I might not be able to stop at all."

Gabrielle caught her bottom lip between her teeth and looked away, feeling a surge of guilt over what she had just asked of him, yet wanting nothing more than for him to continue what he had started. Her heart would not be still, and her entire body ached, longing for a release that was not forthcoming.

As though reading her thoughts, Dan touched her chin and turned her face back toward his. "Don't be ashamed of what you're feeling, little one," he said gently, his voice heavy with emotion. "I want it too. God, how I want it!" He gathered her into his arms and held her tightly a moment, his face buried in her thick, luxuriant hair.

Gabrielle felt a shudder rock his hard-muscled body, and it filled her with awe to think he, too, was wrestling with conflicting desires. Then, without warning, her passion-charged senses plummeted back to earth and she was jolted by the realization of what she had just done. "Oh, no!" she exclaimed, pushing him away from her and struggling to rise. "I'm ruined!"

Chapter Seven

"Gabrielle, wait!" Dan dropped his feet over the edge of the bed and sat up, trapping her skirt beneath his legs.

"Get off!" she cried out, trying to tug her skirt free, but he would not budge.

He grasped her chin and forced her to look at him. "I would never do anything to hurt you, least of all compromise your virtue," he said, both tenderness and compassion in his expression as he looked down into her stormy green eyes. "You are far from ruined, little one. Believe me."

She jerked her head free of his grasp and stared up at him as though he had lost his mind. "I just left my dinner guests stranded in the parlor and you are worried about compromising my virtue? Good heavens! No one will ever accept one of my invitations again!"

Gripping a fistful of skirt, she tried to yank it free, but Dan's hand closed around her wrist, stilling her. "Grace sent everyone home," he said quietly.

Gabrielle stared at him, disbelief frozen on her face. First Captain Wilcox, then Marcus, and finally Grace and the others had abandoned her. In spite of her efforts not to cry, fresh tears pooled in her eyes. "They're gone?"

Dan released her wrist and extricated her skirt from beneath his leg. He motioned toward the door. "Go see for yourself."

Her stricken gaze dropped from his face to the closed door, and in her mind Gabrielle saw the dining-room table with its white damask cloth and centerpiece of bluebonnets and golden poppies, every bone-china place setting, every crystal goblet, and every newly polished piece of silver right where she had left them. Unused. Dan saw her throat work convulsively several times. Pain and exhaustion showed in the dark hollows beneath her eyes. She looked worse now than she had the night her fever had broken. A tear slipped down her cheek, and she hastily wiped it away with her fingertips. "I guess it's no more than I deserve," she said thickly. She sniffled and dragged her sleeve across her eyes. "I should have stayed in bed like you told me."

"Yes, you should."

She looked at him, expecting to see condemnation in his eyes, but there was none. She swallowed hard. "It meant so much to me."

"I know," he said, taking her hand and brushing his thumb across the backs of her knuckles. He knew all too well just what this party had meant to her. For Gabrielle, it was no trifling social occasion that would soon be forgotten. It had been her one opportunity to redeem herself in the eyes of those who chose to dwell upon her shortcomings rather than her virtues. For one evening she was to have been Gabrielle DuBois, a perfectly brought-up young lady and a charming hostess, rather than Gabrielle DuBois, the despair of her father and the bane of Camp Carleton. His fingers closed around her hand and he held it securely. "Miss DuBois, will you do me the the honor of dining with me tonight?"

Guilt streaked across her face. He was the only officer she had not invited. "But . . . the dinner is . . . ruined."

"Not unless your guests confiscated the food on their way out the door."

The corners of her mouth twitched involuntarily. "The only one I can imagine even doing such a thing is Captain Moreland; but he was being so nice to me tonight, it wouldn't be fair to accuse him, would it?"

Dan was glad she was still able to see some humor in the situation, no matter how devastating it had been for her. "I wouldn't be so quick to discount Moreland until you've had a look in the kitchen," he said, silent laughter making amber flecks dance in his eyes. "As a kid, he was the wiliest little

149

pantry rat I knew."

By the time Gabrielle had washed her face and treated her swollen eyes with cold compresses and brushed out her hair, Dan had partially cleared the table so that it appeared her dinner had never been anything other than a carefully planned tryst for two. There was something so intimate about those two place settings laid at right angles to each other at the head of the table that Gabrielle's heart missed a beat at the sight of them. And the thought that he cared enough about her to try to salvage this evening for her caused an unfamiliar warmth to unfold inside her. It was humbling to realize that, of all the people she knew, the one person who had been her bitterest enemy over the years should turn out to be her most caring friend.

She turned at the sound of a movement behind her and saw him lounging against the doorframe, watching her. He was not wearing his uniform, but had changed into civilian clothes. Gray trousers hugged his narrow hips and long legs, and the white silk shirt, which he wore open at the neck, served to emphasize his broad shoulders and his dark tan. As Gabrielle stared at him in stunned silence, she could not help wondering why she had never before noticed—really noticed—how incredibly handsome he was.

She gave him an uncertain smile, then, realizing that she was staring, blushed and tried to hide her embarrassment by thrusting out her chin and raking her eyes down the length of him and saying in her most imperious tone, "What? No peacock uniform?"

"That sounds suspiciously like something Moreland would say," he retorted, his broad shoulders shaking in silent mirth.

Barely managing to keep a straight face herself, Gabrielle nodded firmly. "He did."

"What else has Moreland been filling your ears with, little one?" Dan teased, his smile fading as he saw a pained look flash across her face before she turned away.

"He said you cared about me," she stated offhandedly as she pulled out her chair and sat down without waiting for him to assist her. "And he said I was much too selfish to ever care about anyone but myself. Amazing isn't it, what an astute judge of character Captain Moreland is?" Her voice cracked and her shoulders hunched forward. "I did so many mean things to you," she whispered brokenly, her head bowed. "I never cared how much I hurt you."

He pulled out the chair beside her and sat down. Leaning toward her, he rested his forearms on his thighs, and let his folded hands dangle between his knees. "We all make mistakes, Gabrielle."

"Mine weren't mistakes. I did those things deliberately."

While he couldn't refute her words, he knew how much it had cost her to say them.

"But I tried so hard to be good and show you how sorry I was."

He watched her pick nervously at the tablecloth. "Is that why you've been emulating Grace Simmons these past few days?"

"I was trying to make up for all the times I had been mean and spiteful. But it didn't work. You kept getting angry at me."

And he had thought she was doing it to antagonize him. "Gabrielle look at me," he said, and when she complied, he continued. "Moreland was right about one thing; I do care for you. It's hard not to care for someone you've spent the last fourteen years watching grow from an adorable little girl into a beautiful young woman. And, no, I do not want you to be like Grace Simmons. I don't even like Grace Simmons. I just want you to be yourself. And, if you say 'sir' to me one more time, little one, I'm going to wash your mouth out with soap! Do you understand me?"

She cracked an involuntary smile. "Do I still have to drink all my milk?"

"Yes!"

For the next several hours, they shared what was probably the most enjoyable evening Gabrielle could remember having had. They talked of the happy times before her mother's death and of the not-so-happy times afterward, and Major Catlin was so attentive over dinner that Gabrielle felt as though she were being courted. Nor did it end with dinner. "Do you remember the Christmas pageant at Bent's Fort, when the mule bit Sergeant Blevins?" she asked as she sat opposite him in the

151

parlor, studying the cards in her hand.

Dan chuckled and placed his cards face down on the table. "How could anyone forget? Blevins was certain he was going to die of blood poisoning."

"It got him out of going to the field."

"It got him three weeks of yard detail, little one. I think he would have preferred going to the field."

She eyed his cards critically and raised an eyebrow. "Are you folding?"

"No," he said in a lazy drawl, a meaningful undertone in his voice, and leaned back in his chair. "I'm waiting for you."

Gabrielle glanced up and caught him studying her with thinly disguised amusement. "And what, may I ask, is so funny?" She pulled two cards from her hand and tossed them on the table with a jaded air.

Gold flecks danced in his eyes as he watched her. She presented such a picture of youthful innocence sitting there with her stockinged feet tucked up beneath her skirts and her luxuriant red-gold tresses cascading down over her left shoulder as she bent over her cards that he was hard put not to burst out laughing, for he was well aware that she had been cheating from the moment they'd begun playing. "I was wondering when you were going to stop coveting my queen of spades."

Her head jerked up and she feigned complete ignorance. "Now, what would I want with the queen of spades?"

Dan said nothing, but there was a wicked gleam in his eyes as he dealt her another two cards.

Her expression deadly serious, Gabrielle studied her hand, then selected two pieces of salt-water taffy from her store of "chips" and added them to the ante in the middle of the table.

Trying to decide whether to expose her scheme now or let it ride awhile longer, Dan settled on the latter option. Knowing full well he was going to lose, he called her bet.

She smiled prettily and laid her cards face up on the table. "Two pair, jacks high."

He shrugged indifferently and showed his hand. "You win again. Your deal." He rose to his feet and went to the sideboard. "And no trying to work all the aces into the middle," he cautioned over his shoulder as he poured himself a brandy.

Though Gabrielle's expression did not change, a flicker of alarm shot through her. How did he know she had tried to do that the last time she'd dealt? She attemped to divert his attention by arching a brow at his brandy when he returned to his seat.

With an enigmatic half-smile, he raised his glass in a silent toast and brought it to his lips, his half-closed eyes never leaving her face.

"Don't I get any?" she asked sweetly.

"No."

She expelled her breath in an exaggerated sigh and said wistfully, "I know . . . when I've grown up."

"Actually I was thinking of all the milk you drank at dinner. If I were to let you have a brandy now, the results could be disastrous."

She stifled a giggle and started to reach across the table. "I do seem to have a problem holding my liquor, don't —Ow!" she yelped as Dan rapped her knuckles sharply, and jerked her hand back to safety.

"Keep your hands off my chips," he ordered, giving her a stern look and leveling a warning finger at her.

Gabrielle picked up a piece of taffy and held it out to him. "I'll trade you my green one for one of your pink ones."

He shook his head. "No."

"Please?"

"No!" He took the cards away from her and began to shuffle.

"You're just sore because I won the last three hands," she gloated, her expression a happy one as she leaned back in her chair and unwrapped the candy.

One corner of Dan's mouth twitched, but he said nothing as he dealt the cards, all the while watching her take tiny bites out of the taffy and chew pensively.

Gabrielle set the taffy aside and picked up her cards. "Actually, I'm not so certain I'm very fond of spirits," she said, arranging the cards in her hand. "I've only had two experiences with hard drink in my life, and both of them ended in disgrace."

"Including the time you allowed yourself to be coerced into

having dinner with Lieutenant Dalton?"

She felt her face grow warm. "That was the second time." She weeded a deuce of hearts from her hand and discarded it.

"And the first?"

She allowed her hands to rest on her lap and lifted her head to stare off into the distance. "It was when I was twelve," she said, her brow puckering as the memory came back to her. "Remember when we were at Jefferson Barracks?" Her frown deepened. "No . . . you weren't there. I think you were on furlough at the time. Anyway," she continued, placing her bet, "I discovered that Corporal McGinnis, our striker, had been nipping at the sherry, so I decided to play a joke on him." There was a devilish twinkle in her green eyes as she grinned at Dan over her cards. "I poured out some of the sherry and replaced it with vinegar."

Dan felt his stomach twist at the mere thought. "Go on."

She shook her head. "He didn't even notice. So I poured out a little more and added more vinegar. And he still didn't notice!"

"So what did you do then?" Dan asked, struggling to keep a straight face. He knew there was more to come; Gabrielle had never had the foresight to quit while she was ahead.

"I poured every last bit of Father's best sherry into the flower bed and refilled the bottle to the top with raspberry vinegar."

'I'll bet that was an eye opener for McGinnis the next time he dusted the liquor cabinet," Dan said, chuckling.

"Not for him," Gabrielle quipped, her eyes twinkling. "But it was for Colonel . . . Colonel . . ." She cast him an inquiring glance. "You know, the tall skinny one with the big bushy sideburns who was always quoting scripture." ·

"Colonel Shiplett?

She nodded. "That's the one. Anyway, Father had invited him to dinner and we'd spent a perfectly boring evening listening to Colonel . . . Shiplett expound on the moral degeneration of modern youth. Well, after dinner, Father offered him a whiskey and he declined, saying that he preferred sherry."

Dan grimaced. "How many swallows before he caught on?"

"Only one. He was obnoxious. Not slow."

Dan lifted his glass toward her. "I'll drink to that."

"Colonel Shiplett turned purple like he was having a fit of apoplexy and pitched a screaming fit, and Father, thinking our striker was to blame, hauled Corporal McGinnis into the parlor and threatened him with court-martial."

"And you?"

Gabrielle studied her nails in feigned indifference. "I did the honorable thing, of course. I confessed."

This time Dan did laugh. "What did Stephen have to do to drag the truth out of you?" he asked, his hazel eyes twinkling.

Gabrielle lifted her head and peered down her nose at him. "I never said I told the truth," she declared saucily. "I said I *confessed.* I told Father I had accidentally spilled the decanter and had put vinegar in it thinking he wouldn't notice since none of his *friends* ever drank sherry."

Dan winced as he imagined Shiplett's reaction to that one. "And did he believe you?"

"He might have if Colonel Shiplett had not chosen to launch into another tirade. He swore to Father that I was in communication with the devil, that he had seen me sneak spirits on many a previous occassion—which was a lie—and that I should be soundly whipped for my sins."

Dan could picture Colonel Shiplett as clearly as though he were sitting across from him now. The man had been an unmitigated bastard, and he could not recall a single soldier who didn't dread being assigned to Shiplett's command. He looked at Gabrielle and saw her sitting with head bowed, picking nervously at an imaginary spot on her skirt. "I find it hard to believe Stephen would raise a hand against you," he prompted gently, and when she did not respond, he asked, "Did he?"

She shook her head, and her eyes sparkled as she peeked up at him from beneath her lashes. "He told Colonel Shiplett that he did not believe in corporal punishment and that he had a better way of dealing with me."

"Which was?"

"He filled a wine glass from the decanter and told me to drink it," Gabrielle said laughingly. "You know me. I wasn't about to give in without a fight. I kicked up a fuss and pleaded with Father to find some other way to punish me, but he wouldn't listen. He made me stand there and drink the entire glassful of raspberry vinegar, and then I had to apologize to Colonel Shiplett."

Dan was no longer smiling. It filled him with silent rage to think that Stephen DuBois would do something so cruel as force a child—his daughter—to drink a glass of vinegar simply to appease someone like Shiplett. For the first time in almost twenty years, the time he had known Stephen DuBois, he began to wonder if he might have misjudged the man.

"Of course, I had the last laugh," Gabrielle continued gaily, oblivious to the look of tender concern in Dan's eyes as he watched her. "You see, I had had milk with my supper that night too."

Dan's expression softened, and one corner of his mouth curved upward. "You didn't."

Gabrielle beamed. "I did. All over the front of Colonel Shiplett's brand-new dress blues!"

Their gazes met warmly across the parlor table and held, and for several breathless seconds, Gabrielle had the odd sensation that she was suspended in time. Past and future ceased to exist and nothing else mattered but that moment, which she wanted to last forever. Suddenly feeling self-conscious, she lowered her gaze and nodded toward his cards. "Are you going to draw?"

"Not until I've figured out whether you are going to play your two pair or your full house," he said in mock seriousness, his eyes never leaving her face.

She threw him a pointed glance. "Don't be absurd. Even I know a full house beats out two—" Suddenly broke off and her eyes grew wide and round as she stared at him. "How do you know I have a full house? Did you see my cards?"

Reaching across the table, he touched a long tapered finger to each of her cards in turn. "Four of diamonds. Four of hearts. Four of clubs. Ten of clubs. Ten of spades."

"You saw my cards!" she accused.

Dan reached for the undealt portion of the deck. "Six of spades," he said knowingly, arching one dark brow at her and

156

pausing for a second before turning the top card faceup on the table, a six of spades. "King of diamonds." The king now lay beside the six. "Ace of hearts. Three of hearts. King of spades. Need I go on?"

Hot color flooded Gabrielle's face. "How . . . how did you know?" she asked, choking back a laugh as she wondered how long it had taken him to realize she had been cheating.

He lifted a card and held it up before her eyes. The pencil markings across the blue diamond-patterned backing, while not obvious at first glance, were clearly visible once one knew where to look. "Next time, little one," he said slowly, carefully enunciating each word, "I choose the deck."

In spite of the severity of his tone, Gabrielle could not help noticing the warm sparkle in his eyes, and she knew he was not really angry with her. With all the magnanimity of a gracious loser, she put down her cards and, with both hands, pushed her entire accumulated treasure of saltwater taffy across the table toward him. "I surrender," she said solemnly.

Not *I concede,* but *I surrender.* As he studied her beautiful face across the expanse of table that separated them, Dan wondered if she knew just how much of herself she had given to him that day. Not merely a few hands of poker or even the sweet kiss which he would remember for as long as he lived. She had surrendered a piece of her heart. Though his voice was gruff, there was a smile in his eyes as he jerked his head toward the door and said, "It's past your bedtime, little one."

With a sigh that was more of a concession to fatigue than a protest, Gabrielle dropped her feet to the floor and then bent down to retrieve her shoes from beneath the chair. She did not get up right away, however, but sat where she was for several seconds, trying to drum up the courage to ask him something that had been on her mind all evening.

Dan did not miss the troubled look that came to her face. "Is something wrong?" he asked, bending forward to place his empty glass on the table before leaning back in his chair and raising a questioning brow.

Her heart was thumping so loudly she was certain he could hear it. "Major Catlin," she began uncertainly, forcing herself to meet his gaze, "why . . . why did you kiss me earlier?"

157

Why did he kiss her? Good God, if he knew the answer to that! . . .

Instead of trying to give her a reply when he himself did not know the answer, Dan simply said quietly, "Go to bed, Gabrielle"

His response told her more than he had intended.

Upon rising, Gabrielle did not go straight to the door, but walked around behind him and, bending over the back of his chair, wrapped her arms around his neck and pressed her cheek against his, assaulting his senses with the clean unadorned scent of her. "Thank you for giving me the most wonderful evening of my life," she whispered. "And thank you for being my friend."

Then, before he could say anything, she reached around him, snatched one of the pieces of pink taffy from the table and sprang away from him with a musical little laugh. She waved the taffy in the air as she blew him a kiss from the door. "Good night!"

For a long time after she left the parlor, Dan sat there by himself, trying to drive the soft warm feel of her from his memory with another brandy. He swore silently, his brows drawing together, as he stared angrily into the amber liquid in his glass. Just why in hell had he kissed her? What was he trying to do? Torture himself? He wanted her; that much he would admit. But did he love her? No. Was he fond of her? Not especially. Did he care for her? Deeply. Only one thing was certain. He must never, never let it happen again.

His attention drifted, and after a time it was not the feel of her in his arms that was uppermost in his thoughts, but the haunting image of a motherless child who had been made to stand and drink a glass of vinegar.

"I'm going with you," Gabrielle flatly announced at the breakfast table the following morning.

Dan put down his coffee cup, eyed her sharply, and said with equal bluntness, "No."

"But, I—"

"Don't argue with me, Gabrielle. I'm not taking you out to

158

the camp today and that's final."

Her chin shot up mutinously. "Why not?"

He pushed back his chair and stood up. "For one thing, you need the rest Wilcox ordered you to get."

She jumped to her feet and started to follow him to the door. "But I feel fine! My ribs don't hurt all that much anymore—"

He turned on her, nearly knocking her over, she was so close on his heels. "Gabrielle, I have too much to do today without having to worry about you!"

His words had the effect of a slap. The feeling of contentment with which Gabrielle had retired and with which she had awakened, drained from her and was replaced by a terrible raw ache. "I thought we were . . . friends," she said in a strained voice, her eyes wide and dark with disbelief as they searched his face.

"Don't start," Dan cautioned, leveling a warning finger at her. "Please, *don't start.*" There were purple smudges of weariness beneath his eyes, and he was in no frame of mind to deal with her quicksilver moods.

Gabrielle continued anyway "Last night we were friends. Last night you were warm and kind and gentle, but this morning you're right back to being cross and unreasonable. It's almost as though when you put on that uniform you become a totally different person. What's the matter with you? Don't you know how to be an officer *and* a friend?" Her voice had risen until she was almost shouting, and she clenched and unclenched her fists, fighting desperately against the scorching misery that seemed to be burning a hole right through her heart.

The muscles in Dan's jaw knotted, and it was all he could do to keep a grip on his dangerously escalating temper. 'What happened between us last night, young lady, has nothing whatsoever to do with why I don't want to take you out to the camp with me this morning," he said slowly, carefully enunciating each word so that he would not have to repeat himself. "The reason I want you to stay here—"

"The reason," she interrupted recklessly, too hurt to think of what she was saying, "is that you think I'm just a silly child who will cause mischief and get in your way. Well, I have news for you, Major High-and-Mighty, there are laws against seducing *children!*"

"Gabrielle!" Dan called after her. But she was already halfway down the hall, and before he could go after her, someone knocked loudly on the front door.

"Christ!" He muttered under his breath as he turned and yanked the door open.

Marcus jerked to attention at the sight of him, then gritted his teeth together, annoyed by that reaction. "I've come to see Gabrielle," he said stiffly, cringing inwardly under his commanding officer's condemning gaze.

"After what you did to her yesterday, Lieutenant, you have a lot of gall to be showing your face around here. Gabrielle's not accepting visitors. Return to your post."

Marcus caught the door just as Dan started to push it shut. "I don't know what she's been telling you, Major Catlin, but the truth is—"

"The truth is, Lieutenant Epperling," Dan ground out harshly, sickened by the mere sight of the boyishly handsome younger man, "Gabrielle didn't tell me a thing. She didn't have to. There were plenty of witnesses to your little display of jealousy here yesterday evening."

The junior officer's cobalt eyes were brittle with anger as he regarded Dan with the arrogance of a pampered youth assured of getting his way. "Pardon me for being blunt, sir, but this is between Gabrielle and myself. It does not concern you."

"On the contrary, Lieutenant. As long as I am responsible for Gabrielle's welfare, it does concern me. Until the colonel returns and gives you permission to do otherwise, you will stay away from this house. You will not speak with Gabrielle. You will not even try to see her. Is that understood?"

Marcus bristled. The veins along his temples became distended and he knotted his hands, fighting the urge to smash them against the major's face. *Goddamned breed.* He hated Catlin, but knew he would have to tread carefully where the major was concerned lest he be charged with insubordination. There was a subtle change in the glint in Epperling's eyes; then he drew himself up to his full height and said with clipped formality that was the epitome of respect, if not sincerity, "Yes, sir, I understand you perfectly well. And I will honor your request to stay away from Gabrielle until her father returns."

"It wasn't a request, Lieutenant. It was an order," Dan said in a voice that was honey smooth, though the taut planes of his sun bronzed face hinted at the controlled rage he felt.

Marcus brought his right hand up to the brim of his hat and an enigmatic smile touched his full lips. "Give Gabrielle my regards."

Dan swore inwardly. The man was an inveterate liar. He knew Epperling would be back to see Gabrielle the moment he left the house, and he had no intention of leaving her to face him alone. Slamming the door shut, he turned on his heel, the sharp clicking of his boots on the floor sounding like gunshots as he marched down the hall. He stopped abruptly at the door to his bedroom. "What are you doing in here?" he demanded, his eyes blazing with the anger he had not been able to vent on Epperling.

Her eyes bright with unshed tears, Gabrielle slowly turned to face him and he saw that she was clutching the small leather bag of marbles that he had left lying on the dresser. "You never . . . gave them to her . . . ." she said in a broken whisper, and her chin quivered in spite of her efforts to control it.

"You can give them to her yourself," Dan retorted, and when she flinched at his harsh tone, he realized she had misunderstood his meaning. "You wanted to come along," he explained, though his tone was no less severe. "Put your shoes on. I expect you to be out front in five minutes." With that, he did an abrupt about-face and stormed out of the house, leaving her standing there to gape after him in stunned bewilderment.

What, had gotten into him? Gabrielle wondered. Last night he had been the warmest, kindest man she had ever known. He had treated her as though she were someone special. He had talked to her and comforted her. He'd even sat and *listened* while she'd prattled on about childish things that she knew couldn't possibly interest him. And for an entire evening they had actually enjoyed each other's company. But today! Today he was right back to being antagonistic.

Fine! Gabrielle gritted her teeth as her anger grew. If that was the way he was going to act, then so be it! The last thing she was going to do was let him know how hurt and confused she was by his unexplainable behavior. If he was going to be obnoxious, she was going to be obnoxious right back. If he chose to be stubborn, she could be equally stubborn. His Royal Highness would learn once and for all that Gabrielle DuBois was not about to jump simply because he ordered it. Having decided that, she took her sweet time in putting her shoes on and a good twenty minutes had passed before she left the house.

She knew from the scathing look Dan threw her as she approached the wagon that he was aware she had deliberately kept him waiting, and it gave her a perverse satisfaction to know that she could so easily antagonize him. So the old boy wasn't immune to her after all, she thought smugly, ignoring the hand he extended and climbing up onto the wagon seat unaided.

Dan's face was dark with thinly disguised anger as he circled the wagon, though Gabrielle pretended not to notice. His thigh brushed against hers as he settled beside her onto the seat, and when he jerked his leg away as though he had been burned, an involuntary smile quirked Gabrielle's lips. She hastened to erase it before he saw it, and folding her hands around the bag of marbles in her lap, she straightened her back and fixed her gaze straight ahead, refusing to acknowledge that he even existed. Without so much as a word to her, Dan picked up the reins and gave them a vicious snap, sending the team lurching forward.

But his anger began to ebb as the post fell farther and farther behind. After a few minutes; he stretched his legs, and shifted on the seat to ease some of the tautness out of his back. Glancing down at Gabrielle, he instantly regretted having vented his ire on her. It wasn't her fault that he was tied up in knots because he'd forgotten himself and kissed her last night. She was so young, so innocent. He doubted she was even aware of the dark passions she stirred in him. He knew what he had done was wrong; he was supposed to be guarding her virtue, not trying to take it from her. Yet, he wanted her. He wanted her so badly he was even toying with the idea of stopping the wagon and making love to her right there, on the ground, surrounded by the mountains and the desert and the pale blue sky. Good God, she was beautiful! Even with her back stiff and her bottom lip turned out in a childish pout, she was the most beautiful girl-woman he had ever known, more beautiful than her mother had even been, for though they were similar in appearance, Lisette had lacked her daughter's indomitable spirit.

The morning sun reflected brightly off Gabrielle's shiny red-gold tresses, making them seem to be on fire, and fire of another sort spread through Dan's loins as he remembered the feel of those silky locks when they'd been entwined in his fingers. As though sensing his gaze on her, Gabrielle lifted her head slightly, her eyes still looking straight ahead; yet he could see that there was an unnatural flush to her cheeks and a white ring about her mouth. "You forgot your bonnet, little one," he said gently, suddenly longing to return to the closeness they had shared the past night.

He saw her mouth tighten in annoyance. "You didn't tell me to put on a bonnet," she snapped belligerently, not looking at him. "You told me to put on my shoes."

Dan felt tensed at her insolence. He knew why she was behaving this way, and while he couldn't entirely blame her, he had to double his efforts to keep his temper at bay. "Here," he said, taking off his hat. "Put this on."

She slapped his hand away. "I don't want it."

He sucked in his breath and choked back the rebuke she was quickly earning. He knew she was deliberately goading him and he wasn't going to be sucked in by her childish antics. "I'm only trying to keep you from getting heatstroke," he said, careful to keep his voice even.

Even though Gabrielle was trying not to let him get to her, his solicitous tone was accomplishing just that. She felt the sting of tears, and quickly turned her head away before he could see them.

Thinking he had just been dismissed, Dan swore under his breath and rammed the hat back down on his own head. He'd had about enough of her rebelliousness and her sulking for one morning, by God! The little tart was going to get the back of his hand if she didn't shape up.

Gabrielle took a deep breath and squared her shoulders, wishing she had not been so hasty in refusing his offer of the hat. The sun was beating mercilessly down on her head, and she was beginning to feel sick to her stomach. Worse, to her chagrin, she found herself wanting to turn to him for comfort. She hated this spiteful bickering that inevitably cropped up between them. Why couldn't they be friends as they had been last night? Why were they always lashing out at each other as though the only thing that mattered was who could get in the last cruel barb? She ventured to glance at him from beneath her lashes, and flinched at the dark fury that marred his handsome features, knowing full well that she was the cause of his anger. He was the angriest man she had ever known, especially where she was concerned. It was almost as though he used his anger as a shield to protect himself from her. Why? she asked herself, her throat aching with a swell of emotion that she could not put words to. Did he hate her so very much that the only way he could stand to be around her was to build up an impenetrable wall of anger around himself?

For several long agonizing moments, neither of them spoke, but the tension between them became so painful that Gabrielle felt like a tightly coiled spring, ready to break at the slightest provocation. What is wrong with me? she wailed inwardly. Why did it matter so much to her *what* he thought of her? She hated him. She had always hated him, for as far back as she could remember. And yet, she had let him kiss her. Worse, she had kissed him back. And even worse than that, she wanted to do it again! She wanted him to take her in his arms and hold her and kiss her and tell her—

Tell her what? That he loved her? No! She didn't want him to tell her that! But, if not that, then what? Gabrielle's head reeled with the unanswerable question. What? What? What? She squeezed her eyes shut and clung to the edge of the seat with a white-knuckled grip, totally unaware that the bag of marbles was sliding off her lap to hit the floorboard with a dull thud.

Without warning, Dan jerked on the reins so hard that Gabrielle was nearly thrown from the seat as the wagon came to an abrupt halt. Jumping down, he stormed around to her side and captured her wrist in a painful grip. "Get down!"

Seized by panic, she shrank away from him, then scrambled to obey, if only to keep from being dragged off the seat. "Sit down," he ordered, pushing her to the ground in the shade of the wagon. "I'll be damned if I'm going to have you fainting on me simply because you're too stubborn to wear a hat in this heat." He unscrewed the cap from his canteen and shoved it into her hands. "And, for God's sake, have enough common sense to drink *slowly*."

Gabrielle's hands shook as she brought the canteen to her lips. Her ribs ached and her head was beginning to throb, and right now she wanted nothing more than to just go home and crawl into bed and stay there forever. As Dan hunkered down before her the concern in his eyes confounded her.

"Are you all right now?" he asked, reaching out to lift a damp curl away from her forehead.

Was she losing her mind? "I was all right before," she retorted, jerking her head away from the hand that had dropped to caress her cheek. Why was it that every time she decided she hated him, he did an about-face and was nice to her?

Dan took a swig from the canteen before replacing the cap. "You were so pale, I was afraid you might pass out. I should have known better than to let you leave the house without a hat or a bonnet of some sort. Next time I'll make damned certain you have one with you."

Gabrielle's green eyes glittered with hatred as they fixed on his ruggedly chiseled face. "There won't be a *next time*, Major Catlin," she spat out. "I wouldn't go anywhere with you again if you got down on your knees and begged me." She started to rise, but he put a detaining hand on her arm.

"Stay here in the shade until your coloring returns to normal. I don't want to take a chance on losing you to heat stroke."

Don't worry," she shot back irritably. "I wouldn't dream of doing anything so crass as to die of heat stroke and leave you without someone to carp at."

His mouth tightened and white-hot anger exploded in his eyes. Then he drew his hand from her arm and stood up, his shoulders rigid as he turned his back to her and walked several paces away. His large hands clenched and unclenched convulsively, as though he wished they were tightening around something tangible—like her neck.

In the silence that followed, Gabrielle's irritation crumbled beneath a crushing wave of guilt. As she watched him try to get his anger back under control, she wished the ground would split open and swallow her whole. She was the one who had wanted to be friends, yet she didn't even know *how* to be a friend. Why was she always goading him? Why did she never seem to know when to keep her mouth shut? Her cheeks burning with shame at her childish behavior, she swallowed her pride, then took a deep breath and said, a little unsteadily, "I—I'm sorry I said . . . those things about—"

"Shut up!" Dan whirled around, his face dark with barely contained rage. "I'm sick to death of your apologies. You do what you want. You say what you want. You couldn't care less who you hurt. And then you seem to think all you have to do is say you're sorry and everything will be forgiven. Well, it won't work anymore, Gabrielle. Do you understand me? It won't work!"

Desperate to make him understand, she tried one more time. "Please . . . just listen to—"

"I don't want to hear it! All I want you to do for the next five minutes is sit there and keep your mouth shut!"

"And if I don't?" she blurted out without thinking, blindly sidestepping all caution. "What will you do then? Wash my mouth out with soap? Or perhaps spanking is more to your taste. After all, you do it *so well.*"

The words were out before she could stop them, and she knew the instant they passed her lips that she had gone too far. Immobilized by fear, she stared at him as he bore down on her. Oh God, he was going to kill her! At the last second, she threw her hands up over her face to protect herself, and a strangled cry was wrenched from her throat as he seized her arms and hauled her to her feet with a vicious jerk that caused her head to snap back. "I didn't mean it!" she cried out. "I-I didn't—" Then a searing pain knifed through her chest and her lips went white. "Please . . ." she managed to gasp as his terrifying visage blurred before her eyes. "You're . . . hurting . . ."

The painful grip on her arms slackened and her knees buckled beneath her and she was falling, falling down through a black abyss of pain and darkness. Then, slowly, gently, Gabrielle felt herself being lifted up and his voice pierced the haze of unreality that still engulfed her. "I'm sorry, little one," she heard him say thickly into her hair as his arms closed around her, holding her close against his heaving ribs. "God, I'm . . . sorry."

She drew a hand up between them, and the awful crashing of his heart against her palm frightened her. It hurt to breathe, but her knees were quaking so badly she knew they would give out on her if he were suddenly to let her go. Somehow, she managed to draw in a ragged gasp of air, and her fingers closed around a fistful of his shirt. "Please . . . hold m-me."

His strong arms tightened around her, and a great calloused hand brushed against her jaw as it found its way into her hair and held her face against his chest, the brass buttons on his uniform blouse pressing into her chest. "I'm so sorry," he murmured over and over against the top of her head, and as the pain receded, Gabrielle's world gradually came back into focus and she realized that she was not shaking as much as he was. Compassion surged through her at the thought of this tall, broad-shouldered man trembling uncontrollably. She reached up to wrap her arm about his neck, inadvertently touching his face, and was surprised when her fingertips came up against something warm and wet. Lifting her head to look up at him, she barely had time to see the glimmer of moisture in his eyes before his mouth came down over hers in a fierce, demanding kiss that set liquid fire through her limbs.

The same warm, tingling sensations she had felt last night when he'd kissed her returned with even greater force, rendering her weak-kneed and trembling and filling her with dizzy, drugging delirium she wished would never end. Her heart beat rapidly, then slowly, then missed a beat entirely as his hands moved down her back, pressing her even closer against the hard length of him. Knowing nothing of this type of intimate touching, except what he had shown her, she copied his movements and returned them as best she could; molding her tender young body to his, entwining her fingers in his crisp

167

black hair as she teased the corners of his mouth with her tongue, totally unaware of the feverish passions her innocent caresses were unleashing in him.

All too soon, the spell was abruptly broken as Dan dragged his mouth away from hers. "Gabrielle, stop," he ordered, a ragged huskiness in his voice that she had never heard before, and he reached up to pry her hands from behind his head and force them down to her sides.

Wondering frantically what she had done to displease him, Gabrielle drew her head back, hoping to find the answer in his face, but he immediately took her back into his arms. "Don't move," he said thickly, his strong arms tightening around her. "Just let me hold you."

"But, I—"

"Don't. Don't say anything."

Hurt and bewildered by his odd behavior, she obeyed, acutely cognizant of his labored breathing and the erratic pounding of his heart, and of the unmistakable evidence of his male desire pressing urgently against her abdomen. Uncertainly, she wedged a hand up between them to rest it against his chest. His muscles leapt reflexively at her simple touch, and she blushed at the thought that she could affect him in that way. Encouraged, she let her hand slide upward to touch his face, but he caught it in an intense grip and stilled it against his cheek. "Gabrielle, don't!"

"Why? What are you afraid of?" she pleaded softly, only half-aware that she had spoken aloud, and she began to tremble uncontrollably, in part from fear and in part from something else—something she did not understand.

A choked curse tore from his lips. "I swore I'd never let that happen again," he whispered with such restrained violence that she would have bolted had he not been holding her so tightly.

Instead, her head jerked back and she stabbed him with a wounded look. "What?" she demanded, more hurt than she was willing to admit. "Kiss me?"

He did not answer, nor did he look at her, but she saw the answer to her question in the knotting of muscles along his jaw and she went crimson with humiliation. "I didn't realize you found kissing me so distasteful," she snapped, trying to hide her confusion beneath a veneer of cynicism. When Marcus had kissed her and she had not liked it, she had thought that there might be something wrong with her. Now, she knew there was. She had recoiled from Marcus's touch and now Dan Catlin had recoiled from hers. Her throat tightened and bitter tears stung her eyes. "Let go of me," she said miserably.

Dan took her by the shoulders and set her away from him, but slowly, deliberately, as though it cost him a great effort to do so. "I don't find kissing you at all distasteful, little one," he said gently as he turned and took several steps to distance himself from her, but not before she'd glimpsed something in his eyes. Tempted to believe it was compassion, Gabrielle desperately hoped that maybe there was nothing wrong with her after all.

"Then kiss me again," she demanded with a small, expectant laugh, as she bent down to retrieve his hat from the ground where it had fallen. If he really had meant what he'd said, then he should be more than happy to kiss her again. After all, people didn't willingly do things they found distasteful.

"No."

"Why?"

His shoulders went rigid. "Because, young lady," he said tersely over his shoulder, gripping the side of the wagon so hard his knuckles looked as though they might burst through his skin, "if I do, I won't want to stop with a mere kiss, and I am *not* in the habit of *seducing children*."

Her own words came back to her like a slap in the face. "I only said that this morning," she hastened to explain, humiliation staining her cheeks, "because I was angry with you. I-I didn't . . . mean it."

"But I do mean it, Gabrielle."

"I'm not a child," she insisted, determined not to let him off the hook so easily. "I'll be eighteen next month."

"And I'll be thirty-six the month thereafter. Good God, woman! Do you have any idea what that means?"

A dawning smile spread across Gabrielle's face. While he was trying to convince himself that she was a mere child, he had called her *woman*. "I think it means," she said slowly, and with as much solemnity as she could muster when her heart was singing with joy because she realized he was trying—desperately trying—to resist her, "I think it means . . . that you are very well preserved for a man in his dotage."

He spun around to stare at her, wordless surprise at her improbable statement frozen on his face. And then, though he tried to maintain a serious front, she saw the expression in his eyes soften and the corners of his mouth twitch just before his broad shoulders began to shake with silent laughter. Gabrielle was filled with wonder at the notion that this towering, powerful man whom she had always thought invincible was actually having to put up a fight to resist her!

Her previous anger at him forgotten, she went to stand before him, her expression solemn as she rose on tiptoe and reached up to place his hat on his head. "I won't make you kiss me," she said, struggling to maintain a straight face at the thought of anyone trying to *make* him do anything. "But I never swore I wouldn't kiss *you!*" With that, she flung herself against him and planted her soft full mouth squarely against his.

"Christ!" Dan staggered backward beneath her unexpected assault before he caught her arms and tried to pry them from around his neck, but she merely giggled into his mouth and tightened her hold on him. Finally, he tore his mouth away from hers. "Gabrielle!"

With a jaunty little laugh, she abruptly released him and sprang away. "You could definitely use more practice," she said authoritatively, giving him a haughty toss of her head as she whirled around to climb back up onto the wagon seat.

A low, throaty chuckle sounded from deep down in Dan's throat as he gave her an indelicate boost from behind. "You try that again, young lady," he taunted, the merry twinkle in his eyes belying the severity of his tone, "and I'll turn you over my knee and paddle your rear end!"

Gabrielle folded her hands demurely on her lap and impaled him with an imperious look, but she was pressed to keep the smile from her lips. "No, you won't."

"And what makes you so certain?" he asked, cocking a meaningful eyebrow at her.

"Because you don't trust me," she said frankly, a devilish gleam in her laughing green eyes. "You'd never know when I might poison your food or put a horned toad in your bed or—"

"Or run away?"

Her smile died and she felt something tighten around her heart. "I'll never run away again," she said in a low, pain-edged voice. "I promise."

Dan picked up the bag of marbles at her feet and placed them on her lap. Seeing the look of hurt that flashed through her eyes at the sight of them, he placed two fingers beneath her chin and tipped her face toward his. "In spite of what you may think, little one," he said gently, inclining his head toward the marbles. "I didn't deliberately keep them. But I do believe the gift would mean more coming from you."

As Gabrielle stared at his strong-boned, weather-hardened face, she realized with a pang that, for the past fourteen years, he had provided an unbreakable thread of continuity to her life by simply being there when she needed someone, regardless of whether she liked, acknowledged, or even *wanted* his presence. He had been there for her when her mother had died. He had come for her when she'd run away, and had stayed with her when she'd been ill. He had rescued her from the excessive attentions of both Marcus Epperling and Chase Dalton just as he had, twelve years ago, when she'd been in first grade, rescued her from Terence Overton's cruel tormenting. She never knew what he had said to Terence that day he'd taken him aside and had a quiet "man-to-man" talk with him before walking her home from school. All she knew was that the obnoxious fourth-grader had never again pushed her down in the mud or called her "buzzard bait." She had never realized it before now, but Dan had always been her friend. And, at times, he had been her *only* friend.

Her pensive scrutiny of his face was cut short by his amused chuckle. "What? No comeback?" he teased, a troubled look in his amber-flecked eyes.

Embarrassed by the unfamiliar turn her thoughts had taken and by the fact that she was openly gawking at him, Gabrielle forced her gaze away from his face, then said in her most withering tone, "I think Major Catlin, it's time you acted your age and contemplated getting gray hair!"

She was rewarded with a deep, warming laugh.

*　　　*　　　*

By the time they reached the Indian camp, Gabrielle's nerves were stretched to the snapping point. Her eyes darted anxiously back and forth, taking in the dozens of pole-and-brush wickiups that had been erected since her last visit. The rancheria was swarming with Apaches. Fear gnawed at the pit of her stomach as she watched four adult males, clad only in breechclouts and moccasins, start toward the wagon, and when Dan touched her hand, she came up off the seat with a start.

Realizing what she had done, Gabrielle laughed hollowly and cast him a sheepish glance before sitting back down. But she held herself unnaturally erect and, in spite of her efforts to appear nonplused, began to tremble violently.

Dan slid a reassuring arm about her slender shoulders. "This is why I didn't want to bring you here today," he said quietly, tightening his hold on her when she tried to pull away. "I didn't think you were ready for it."

"I-I'm fine . . . really," she stammered, but her eyes remained fixed on the four men who were approaching them. Dan lifted a hand in greeting and said something Gabrielle found unintelligible, and the Apaches walked on past the wagon.

Gabrielle did not realize she had been holding her breath until it burst from her lungs in a ragged gasp of relief. As an uncontrollable shudder rocked her, she squeezed her eyes shut.

Dan pulled her against him and held her tightly. "It's all right, little one. I'm here."

She turned her face into his shoulder. "I didn't . . . I mean, I thought. . . ." She was shaking so badly she could hardly talk.

Dan inwardly cursed himself. She wasn't ready for this. Not after what had happened to her when she'd run away. He should have known better than to bring her along. *He should have known better.*

"I know . . . they're not the . . . same ones." I'm . . . sorry."

"There's no need to apologize. Nor is there anything to fear. I'll be here with you. All right?"

Withdrawing from his embrace, Gabrielle busied herself with smoothing out the folds of her skirt. "If you don't stop putting your arms around me, Major Catlin," she said stiffly, not meeting his gaze, "people are going to think you have designs on me."

He chuckled. "Would that be so awful?"

"It would be . . . horrendous!"

He caught hold of her chin and tipped her face up toward his. In spite of her waspish tone, her eyes were brimming with unshed tears and he knew she was putting up a valiant struggle not to cry. "You'll be fine. I promise." He planted a kiss on the tip of her nose. "Now, young lady," he announced, getting down and going around to her side of the wagon, "unless I am mistaken Datigé is very anxious to see you again."

"Da-ti-gay?" Gabrielle asked, her tongue twisting awkwardly around the syllables.

Dan lifted her down from the seat. "The little girl you befriended the last time you were here."

Gabrielle felt as though every pair of eyes was fixed on her as Dan, keeping a firm grip on her arm to prevent her from bolting, propelled her across the camp. "Where are you taking me?" she asked, half-running, half-walking.

"You'll see."

"Major Catlin . . . please!"

He brought her to an abrupt halt in the shade of a ramada where several women were kneeling before stone metates, grinding corn. They stopped talking and turned curious gazes on Gabrielle, who was wishing she were somewhere else. Just then, two young boys ran through the group, upsetting a basket of dried mesquite beans. An older woman whose straight black hair was streaked with gray spoke sharply to them, then turned piercing black eyes on Gabrielle, surveying her as though she were a heifer at a cattle auction. Gabrielle's pulse raced, and even the wink Dan gave her did little to calm her rattled nerves.

Dan spoke to the women in her own language and pointed toward the bag of marbles in Gabrielle's hand. The woman then turned and said something, and a young girl with coal black hair that fell past her knees moved to stand before Gabrielle. Suspicion was reflected in her big doelike brown eyes as she studied Gabrielle intensely them suddenly turned and walked proudly toward one of the wickiups, her long hair swinging freely down her back.

"That's Zayigo," Dan explained in a low voice. "She's the little girl's mother."

Gabrielle jerked her head up to stare at him. "But she's not even as old as I am!"

"Probably not," Dan agreed. He inclined his head toward the older woman. "This is Datigé's grandmother. Everyone just calls her Anna. She'll look after you while I—"

"You're not leaving me here!" Gabrielle blurted out, gripping his arm in a fit of panic as the color drained from her face.

Dan pried her fingers from his arm, and clasped her hand in his. "I am merely going over to the other side of the camp to meet with the families who arrived last night."

Gabrielle vehemently shook her head, and her eyes were wide and dark with terror. "No . . . you can't."

"Gabrielle, I'm not going to argue with you," Dan said firmly. "You are going to stay here. Anna will see that no one bothers you. I shouldn't be over there for more than an hour."

"But—" Her words were cut short as something small and warm barreled against her leg from behind, nearly knocking her down, and she looked around to find the little girl, Datigé, clinging to her skirts.

The child was dressed a little better than she had been the last time, and her hair looked cleaner, but she was still so pitifully thin that her deep black eyes seemed too large and too dark for her little round face.

Dan released Gabrielle's hand and smiled. "Don't worry. You'll be fine here."

She threw him an imploring look and nearly cried out to him, but Datigé had already discovered the bag of marbles and was tugging impatiently on her other hand. *Damn him!* Gabrielle thought as she watched his departing back. Now she knew why he had not punished her for running away; he had been biding his time so he could think of something sufficiently torturous—like abandoning her here in the middle of an Apache camp with a horde of savages who were liable to lift her scalp!

Datigé was trying to pry her fingers away from the bag of

marbles. "Here, take it!" Gabrielle snapped, shoving the bag into the child's hand. Then she bit her lip and cast a remorseful glance around her as she realized what she had done. The women were all watching her coldly, their dark eyes brittle with disapproval. Zayigo was hovering a few feet away, like a small wild animal ready to spring. Gabrielle felt her face grow warm. Then she stood there awkwardly, shifting back and forth from one foot to the other and twisting her fingers into a fold of her skirt. She was beginning to feel not only foolish but downright detestable. These people had never done anything to hurt her, yet she was behaving in a manner that would have made her own mother furious.

Datigé turned the leather pouch upside down and shook it. Her squeal of delight drew the women's watchful gazes to the brightly colored glass spheres that rolled across the ground.

Not certain whether she even dared move, Gabrielle dropped to her knees despite the women's pointed stare, and began gathering up some of the marbles. Picking up a rock, she drew a circle in the dirt, then arranged the marbles inside it in the pattern of a cross. Her lively black eyes ever curious, Datigé squatted down, dropping her handful of marbles into the circle and giving Gabrielle a smile that would have melted even a granite heart.

Gabrielle picked up a marble that was deep cornflower blue. "This," she said softly in a quiet tone that made the little girl's eyes light up as though they were sharing some intimate secret, "is a shooter. And you hold it . . . like so. Remember? I showed you before." She handed the blue marble to Datigé and picked up a different one. Catching her bottom lip between her teeth as she concentrated on the game before her, Gabrielle bent down until the marble she wanted to hit was in her line of sight. She took aim and shot.

Her shooter hit its target with a sharp click, sending the marble a good three inches into the air before spinning out of the circle. Moving around to where her shooter had finally rolled to a stop, Gabrielle picked it up and shot again. Only this time her aim was off. Her shooter bypassed the player marbles completely and spun out of the circle to hit one of the ramada posts with a dull thud. Sitting back on her heels, she grinned at Datigé and motioned toward the circle. "Your turn," she said, glancing up in time to see Anna smile before turning away. The women went back to their work, and Gabrielle began to breathe a little easier. It looked as though she might be allowed to keep her scalp after all.

It wasn't long before little Datigé's infectious laughter drew attention to the ramada where the women worked. The two youths Gabrielle had seen earlier returned, along with a third, and soon the three boys were down on their hands and knees taking turns at the game of "ringer" that Gabrielle had taught Datigé. Gabrielle glanced up at Zayigo and saw her watching them, a look of longing in her dark eyes. Then Zayigo, realizing that Gabrielle was looking at her, quickly lowered her eyes and resumed pounding the dried corn on the metate before her. Gabrielle wasn't certain whether she felt sorry for Zayigo or annoyed. Even though the girl could not be more than fifteen or sixteen at the most, Zayigo was considered adult, while everyone at Camp Carleton—Major Catlin especially—treated Gabrielle as though she were still a child.

When another boy and two girls joined the game, and the jostling and the squeals of laughter threatened to overrun the ramada where the women were trying to work, Anna finally took matters into her own hands and shooed the children outside. After gathering up a handful of marbles, Gabrielle stood and, once again catching Zayigo's eye, smiled hesitantly and motioned for her to join them.

The Apache girl's hands stilled on the mano she was using to grind the corn, and a look that was a combination of hope and uncertainty flitted across her young face. She glanced hesitantly at Anna and the older woman said something in harsh, guttural tones that made Gabrielle flinch. She'd thought Zayigo had been ordered to get back to work, but the Apache girl dropped her mano onto the metate and jumped to her feet, her broad smile telling Gabrielle she had been mistaken. Zayigo's smiling regard for Gabrielle changed into something that bordered upon reverence as she joined her, and Gabrielle could not help but wonder how often she was permitted to put aside her adult task and simply be the child

176

that she was.

Away from the ramada, a bigger circle was drawn and the game of ringer was resumed with even more players than before. Gabrielle glanced around for some sight of Dan, but could not see him. He had promised her he would not be gone for more than an hour, yet she knew he had been away much longer than that. The sun was almost directly overhead now, and thunderheads were quickly gathering along the horizon for an afternoon storm. As Gabrielle reached up to wipe away a trickle of perspiration that streaked through the dust on her face, she could not help feeling vaguely uneasy.

The morning dragged on, and Gabrielle became increasingly uncomfortable. Her rib cage throbbed with a dull ache that she was beginning to think would never go away, and the bindings around it had become damp with perspiration and were making her itch. She began to lose interest in the game of marbles as they became more and more competitive, and finally she dropped out of the game entirely and sat down to rest.

As minutes ticked slowly by, Gabrielle became more and more uneasy. Though the harnessed wagon was still where he had left it, there was still no sign of Dan. Gabrielle silently cursed him, though she was more scared than angry. It wasn't like him to lie. He'd said he would return for her within an hour, so he would have returned—unless something had happened to him.

A thundercloud passed in front of the sun, casting the entire valley into shadow, and a sudden gust of hot, dry wind blew dust up into Gabrielle's face, causing her to grimace. She wrapped her arms about herself and shuddered. In spite of the intense heat, she felt chilled.

Then she saw him emerge from one of the wickiups. Jumping to her feet, she waved and called out for him to stop, but he did not hear or see her. That made her angry. At least he could have told her his business was going to take longer than he had anticipated, instead of leaving her to worry, she thought. But why should he tell her anything? she fumed. After all, to him she was just a *child*, not even worthy of his consideration. "Well, I won't stand for it," she muttered aloud, her chin jutting out. "He had better have a darned good reason for leaving me here and forgetting about me." Squaring her shoulders, Gabrielle started across the camp to where she had seen Dan disappear between two wickiups.

But defiance began to flag before she had taken more than a dozen steps.

There was something different about this side of the camp. She could not quite put a finger on it, but the wickiups were set apart from the others and appeared to have been hastily built, as though they were meant to be nothing more than temporary shelters, and the stares she received seemed to be less curious and more hostile. Her heart pounding loudly in her ears, Gabrielle started toward the spot where she had last seen Dan.

Suddenly she stopped.

From within the wickiup directly before her came a long low moan. It rose and fell and rose again until it became a shriek, then a series of shrieks, and finally a shrill, blood-chilling scream.

Chapter Eight

Terror such as Gabrielle had never known swelled in her chest, cutting off her air. Blood pounded furiously through her veins, yet icy shivers rippled over her, raising prickles on her skin. The screams from inside the wickiup faded into sobs. Someone—a woman—was in trouble or was hurting or needed help or God only knew what. Gabrielle looked anxiously about her, but there was still no sight of Dan, or of anyone else for that matter. She was totally alone with the strange woman inside that wickiup. Not knowing what to do, yet knowing she had to do something to help, Gabrielle took a hesitant step toward the wickiup, and then another, until she was standing before the low opening. "Are you all right in there?" she asked, bending down to peer through the portal. Her pulse raced, and it was all she could do not to turn and run.

A lone woman was squatting in the center of the wickiup, rocking to and fro and wailing at the top of her lungs. "Excuse me," Gabrielle ventured, squinting at the sudden dimness as she ducked into the wickiup. "I heard you crying. Are . . . are you all right?" Beyond the woman, a young man was lying on a pallet, his face the color of wood ash and his black hair matted with dried blood. He did not move. He did not even seem to be breathing. Gabrielle sucked in her breath as she realized with a start that he was dead. Inexplicably, she gagged. She had never seen a dead person before. Clamping her mouth shut to keep from being sick, she forced her gaze away from the lifeless figure and stared in fascinated horror as the woman, still wailing loudly, clawed at her face and arms until blood flowed from the deep scratches in her flesh.

Then the woman picked up a knife and, seizing a handful of her coarse black hair, whacked it off close to her scalp with the finely honed blade.

Not understanding, Gabrielle rushed toward her. "No, don't!" she cried out, horrified, as the woman severed yet another hank of hair. "Stop it! For God's sake, please stop!"

The woman abruptly ceased wailing and turned toward her as though noticing her for the first time, and there was a crazed look in her coal black eyes.

Gabrielle froze. She wanted to reach out to the woman, to comfort her, but when she opened her mouth to speak, nothing would come out.

Hate suddenly filled the Apache woman's eyes. Her expression turned ugly and her upper lip curled back in a snarl, making her look like a wild beast, ready to attack.

Her compassion turning into fear, Gabrielle began to back away from the grief-stricken woman.

But she lunged.

Gabrielle screamed and twisted away as the knife ripped through her skirt, barely missing her thigh. Blinded by terror, she groped wildly for the opening in the brush wall.

Someone screamed, again and again, and Gabrielle only half realized that the sounds were coming from her own throat. Through a dreamlike haze, she saw the Apache woman rise to her feet and come toward her, the deadly knife raised high above her head.

Gabrielle found the opening just as the knife descended, slashing through the bodice of her dress and grazing her shoulder. She bolted through the portal and out into the harsh sunlight, a shriek of panic ripping from her as she slammed face first into a rock-hard wall of blue twill.

Strong hands caught hold of her arms as she staggered backward, and Dan's angry voice pierced her daze. "What in the hell are you doing here?"

Uttering a strangled cry of relief, Gabrielle flung herself at him and jabbered hysterically, "Thank God . . . I-I didn't . . . couldn't . . . fi-ind you—"

"I told you to stay put! You have no business even being here." Dan took her by the shoulders and forced her away from him. Then he shook her hard. "If you ever disobey me again, I will punish you severely! Do you understand me?"

Before Gabrielle could answer, he turned on his heel and roughly dragged her after him toward the waiting wagon.

Gabrielle twisted around to see if the Apache woman had followed them, and was rewarded with a vicious yank that nearly sent her sprawling before Dan roughly hoisted her onto the wagon seat. By the time he climbed up beside her, she had wrapped her arms around her middle and was shaking so badly she could scarcely breathe. Dan snapped the reins, the explosive crack sounding like a gunshot, and Gabrielle huddled miserably on the seat as they left the rancheria behind them. Her lips clamped together, and her head was reeling with horrible visions of the crazed woman who had come after her with the knife.

Beside her, Dan sat without speaking, his eyes fixed straight ahead. Raw fury emanated from him like heat waves.

Gabrielle didn't understand why he was so angry with her. She hadn't done anything wrong. Yet every time she glanced in his direction, a taut muscle leaped in his jaw as though he were recoiling from the feel of her gaze on him. Screams of frustration rose in the back of her throat. She wanted to yell at him, but when she finally did manage to speak, all she could get out was an accusation. "You didn't come back for me."

Dan tensed, but said nothing.

"You didn't come back," Gabrielle repeated, more boldly this time. "You said you would only be an hour. I got scared. I was afraid something might have happened. . . ." Her voice faltered. He wasn't making this any easier for her. Taking a deep breath, she tried again. "I heard that woman scream. I didn't know what was wrong. I only wanted to help." Unable to stand his indifference any longer, she blurted out, "Damn you! Why don't you say something?"

"Don't swear," he said tersely, not looking at her. "It's unbecoming."

"I don't care! I'm trying to explain to you what happened and you won't listen! You're just sitting there like a tick on a

181

horse's ass, pretending I don't even exist."

He jerked on the reins, bringing the wagon to a stop, and glared so icily at her; she wished she hadn't made that crack about the tick. "All right," he snapped. "I'm listening."

Gabrielle could feel her resistance crumbling. She nervously moistened her lips. "I was worried about you. When you didn't come back . . . I was afraid something had happened. Then I heard that woman scream, like she was in some kind of trouble. I was only trying to help."

"That woman, Gabrielle," Dan said tersely, "was mourning for her son. She did not need your help."

"I-I didn't know."

"Is that all?"

Something inside her snapped. "No, it's not! You had no right to just go off and leave me like that. The least you could have done was come back and let me know your business was going to take a little longer. You're just like Father! To both of you, I am nothing more than a stupid child who is supposed to obey orders and not ask questions and not worry if something has happened to you. You don't care about me. Neither of you care about me." Her voice wavered and to her chagrin, her eyes began to sting.

"Are you finished?" Dan asked coldly.

Gabrielle looked away, unable to answer lest she do the unthinkable and burst into tears.

When he picked up the reins, and she had a sinking feeling in the pit of her stomach. She knew that whatever chance she'd had of getting through to him had been lost for good.

By the time they reached to post, storm clouds hung low over the valley, blocking the surrounding mountain peaks from view. Lightning flickered across the sky, and a hot dry wind had gusted up raising a flurry of dirt and debris from the desert floor and causing the horses to toss their heads and break their gait.

Captain Moreland was waiting for them on the veranda in front of the house. "Was wonderin' if you two was gonna make it back before the storm broke," he said, grinning. "Though, if you ask me, it mighta done the both of you good to have gotten rained on. You're both wearin' enough dirt to plant a crop of taters in!"

Dan met Bandy's gaze over the top of Gabrielle's head and he knew, in spite of the man's jovial manner, that something was wrong. Without waiting for him to assist her, Gabrielle jumped down from the seat.

"Howdy-do to you, too, Miss DuBois," Bandy teased as she flounced past him and up the stairs. His sharp eyes did not miss the rips in her dress or the tears in her eyes.

In response, Gabrielle gave him an insolent toss of her head before slamming the door shut behind her.

Captain Moreland's throaty laugh pierced the sound of the gusting wind. "What did ya do to get her all riled up this time, Danny boy?"

A tumbleweed rolled in front of the wagon and Dan had to tighten his grip on the reins to keep the horses from bolting. "Something happen here while I was gone?" he asked, deliberately avoiding any discussion of Gabrielle.

"Might say that," Bandy replied, his eyes narrowing as he studied his friend. "That rancher, Edwards, was here. He says someone's been cuttin' his herd and he's inclined to believe it's them Apaches from the camp. He's threatenin' to raise seventeen kinds of hell if they ain't moved outa here pronto. He might just be able to pull it off too, seein' as how he's got connections with the governor."

Dan swore under his breath. The last thing he needed right now was to have Bryce Edwards stirring up trouble. "Guess I'd better head on over to the ranch and have a talk with him. Anything else?"

Moreland hesitated a moment before answering. "We got a dispatch from Department this mornin'. General Stoneman has been relieved from duty."

When slamming the front door didn't do anything to relieve the anger building up inside her, Gabrielle slammed the bedroom door too. Not once, but twice. "Don't swear, Gabrielle. It's unbecoming," she mimicked, screwing up her face and sticking out her tongue at her reflection in the cheval mirror. "That woman was mourning for her son, Gabrielle.

183

She did not need your help. If you ever disobey me again, Gabrielle, I will punish you severely." Grabbing her pillow up off the bed, she hurled it at the closed door. "I am sick of being treated like a child!" she shouted. "Do you hear me? I am not a child!"

A hesitant knock sounded. "Is it safe to come in?" Grace asked, opening the door a crack and venturing a peek.

"Suit yourself," Gabrielle retorted as she yanked impatiently at the buttons on her bodice. "That man," she continued, oblivious of the puzzled looks Grace was giving her, "is the most obnoxious, insufferable, egotistical, autocratic, pigheaded, addlebrained—"

"Gabrielle, what are you talking about?"

"I am talking about Major Catlin, you dimwit! Do you know what he did to me today? He took me out to that infernal Indian camp and left me there! For hours! While he was off taking care of business, or so he says." Gabrielle jerked her dress down over her hips and stepped out of it.

"Oh, is that all?" Grace looked relieved. "For a moment, I thought he might actually have *done* something to you."

Halfway out of her petticoats, Gabrielle paused and gave Grace a look of total disbelief. "What do you mean, is that all? He didn't even show me the courtesy of letting me know his business would take longer than he had anticipated. He just left me sitting there to worry about him. And then, when I went looking for him, he yelled at me!"

Grace frowned. "Oh Gabrielle, sometimes you do fret over the most inconsequential things. Wait until I tell you what happened! General Stoneman was relieved from duty, and all because of that mess down at Camp Grant. And there's a good chance that Lieutenant Whitman and everyone else who was involved might be relieved too."

"Grace Simmons, haven't you heard a single word I've said? I was talking about Major Catlin."

"So am I! Do you know he might actually be court-martialed and sent to jail?"

Gabrielle froze. "What do you mean?"

"I don't know all the particulars, but it has something to do with him having Lieutenant Epperling bring all those Apaches up here to Camp Carleton."

"In what way?"

Grace shook her head. "It's too complicated to explain, but as I understand it, the Apaches we're keeping here are technically prisoners of war and Major Catlin is under orders to return them to Camp Grant. But Wilbur—I mean, Captain Moreland—says that he won't do it on the grounds that the Tucson Ring, or whatever it is they're calling themselves, is liable to go after them and murder them too, just like they did the—" She broke off abruptly. "Goodness, Gabrielle! What happened to your shoulder?"

Gabrielle followed her gaze. While it was not deep, the long scrape the Apache woman had inflicted on her shoulder was red and angry looking. "It's nothing," she said hastily. If Grace knew the truth, she might go running to Major Catlin. "I fell . . . and hit my shoulder on the wagon. Finish what you were saying."

"If Major Catlin doesn't send the Apaches back to Camp Grant, he'll be charged with disobeying a direct order and will be relieved from duty and court-martialed, maybe even be sent to a Federal prison!"

Federal prison! Still clutching her petticoat, Gabrielle sank down on the edge of the bed, her head reeling under a tumult of confused thoughts and conflicting emotions. Major Catlin couldn't go to prison. He just couldn't! She thought of the woman who had come after her with the knife and was filled with anger. Major Catlin should send every last one of those red savages back to Camp Grant! Then she remembered Datigé and Zayigo and the gruff but kindly Anna, and what was liable to happen to them if they were sent back. She couldn't bear the thought of Zayigo, who was not even as old as she, being brutally violated, or of sweet little Datigé being bludgeoned to death. Yet Major Catlin's career was on the line simply because he was helping them!

It's no wonder he's been so out of sorts lately, she thought, feeling utterly ashamed of the way she had behaved toward him. While she had been upset over the few harsh words he'd directed at her, *he* was in danger of going to prison.

Gabrielle thought of how Dan had spent yesterday evening

playing cards with her and trying to cheer her up, when all the while he had had more important matters on his mind. Her throat constricted and a stabbing pain burned in her chest. In spite of all her protests that she was not a child, she had behaved like one—a spoiled, selfish child, with no thought for anyone but herself.

"Gabrielle, you're not listening to me!"

There was a dazed expression in Gabrielle's eyes as she met Grace's admonishing look. "I-I'm sorry . . . did you say something?"

Grace's shoulders sagged in exasperation. "I said . . . don't let Lieutenant Epperling's behavior upset you so much. I'm sure he didn't mean those things he said last night. I overheard First Sergeant O'Donnell tell Pa that the lieutenant was in a bad mood all the way back from Camp Grant. Whatever he was in a tizzy about, I'm sure it had nothing to do with you. In fact, I know it didn't. Three times today he asked me if I'd seen you, and he seemed a little embarrassed. I'm sure he wants to apologize, and if you'll just give him a chance, he'll explain everything."

And Grace thinks I prattle on about inane matters! Gabrielle said to herself. "I don't want to talk about Marcus," she said aloud tossing her petticoat aside and bending down to unlace her shoes. "Right now, all I want to do is get out of these sweaty clothes and wash off." And think, she added silently. There had to be some way to get Major Catlin out of this mess he was in. Gabrielle knew her father wouldn't back him up. The colonel would never have allowed the Apaches to have been brought here in the first place.

Grace shook her head and eyed her friend woefully. "Everything will work out. Just you wait and see."

Any reply Gabrielle might have made was drowned out by thunder.

Picking Gabrielle's discarded dress up off the floor Grace placed it on the bed. 'I'd better go home before it starts to rain. I just wanted to be sure you were all right. You were crying so hard last night, I was afraid you might have made yourself sick."

And I ruined the evening for you, Gabrielle thought, impending tears making her eyes smart. "You're a good friend, Grace." And I'll make it up to you. I promise you I will.

But first she had to find some way to help Major Catlin.

"I'm afraid I don't know where Dan is," Captain Wilcox said when he finished examining Gabrielle's ribs. "The last time I saw him, he was talking with Captain Moreland. Hold this." He handed her one end of the muslin binding, and drew the other around behind her. "When you bring the two ends together in front, cross them. It will give the ribs added support without having to pull the bandage in as tightly. Here, you try it."

She did as he instructed, wrapping the long ends of the bandage three times about her rib cage before bringing them together for a knot. "How's that?"

"Not bad. With practice, you should be able to put them on without any assistance."

He showed her how to tie a knot that wouldn't slip, yet would still be easy to undo. "I thought you weren't going to be my doctor anymore," she said when he'd finished.

"I'm the only surgeon within ninety miles. Neither of us has the luxury of choice in the matter."

"But the other evening you said you weren't going to be responsible for—"

"I know what I said, and I regret allowing you to provoke me into losing my temper. You have a way of bringing out the worst in everyone, Gabrielle. Even I am not exempt."

She had heard that complaint so often from both Dan and from her father that it no longer fazed her. "How much longer will I have to wear these bandages?"

"Do you still have pain?"

"Only a little. Usually toward the end of the day. Or if I move too quickly," she amended, remembering how she had nearly fainted from pain just that morning when the major had jerked her to her feet.

"Then I would recommend that you continue to wear them for at least a few more days. Get some rest now. I'll examine you again next week. I might also suggest that you do not spend so much time in the sun. You're becoming as brown as an

187

Indian, and this desert climate can be unduly harsh on a female's tender skin."

"Yes sir," Gabrielle replied dutifully as she leaned back against the pillows and pulled the covers up over her nightgown, she was irritated at Captain Wilcox for being so forward as to point out that she was ruining her complexion. At least he had not said a *child's* tender skin.

She waited until she heard the front door close, then threw back the covers and bounded out of bed. Cursing silently, she yanked the nightgown up over her head and flung it across the room. Of all the times for Captain Wilcox to show up and order her into bed, just when she was in a hurry.

When Gabrielle had finished dressing, she slipped out the back door. It had begun to rain. Not wanting to take a chance on encountering Captain Wilcox, she avoided the parade ground and circled the post behind the buildings, keeping close to the walls to avoid being pelted by the huge raindrops that came at her from all directions.

When a peek through the window told her Dan wasn't in the Headquarters Building, she made a hurried dash for the stables, nearly colliding with Corporal Holmes as she ducked through the doorway to get out of the rain.

"Why, Miss Gabrielle, what are you doin' out here?" the corporal asked, taken aback.

"I was looking for Major Catlin. He wasn't at Headquarters, so I thought he might be in here." She wiped the water from her face and pulled her wet bodice away from her skin, laughing at the bedraggled appearance she knew she must be presenting. A vicious streak of blue-white lightning arched across the sky, so close Gabrielle felt her skin prickle. And somewhere an unbattened shutter banged repeatedly against a wall.

"The major ain't here," the soldier said after the thunder died down. "He rode out to Mr. Edwards' place about an hour ago."

Gabrielle's eyes widened in surprise. "The Rocking P? Why would he go there?"

"Beats me. Except that Edwards was here this morning raising holy hell with Captain Moreland about something or other." Corporal Holmes shifted nervously from one foot to the other, and she could tell from the look on his face that he was having a hard time finding words for what he wanted to say. "Miss Gabrielle . . . I know it's all over post about why the major kicked me outa the old man's house, and why I ain't your stricker anymore and . . . well"—his face reddened considerably—"I just hope you ain't mad at me. I didn't mean to sneak a peek at you when the major was tending you. It's just that . . . well . . . you're just about the prettiest girl I've ever known, and if you weren't the old man's daughter, I might even consider marrying you myself except that you're already betrothed to Lieutenant Epperling."

Marcus and I are not betrothed! Gabrielle wanted to scream. Instead, she forced a smile and said, "If that's an apology, I accept. And when Father comes home, I'll see if I can get him to make you our striker again. It's not the same with you gone. No one makes pecan pancakes quite like you do!"

A footfall behind them caused them both to turn, and something inside Gabrielle knotted at the sight of Marcus standing only a few paces away, feet apart and arms folded across his chest, a hard glint in his blue eyes. "When I give an order, Corporal, I expect it to be carried out immediately," he said tersely, his steely gaze fixed on the enlisted man.

"I was just on my way, sir."

"You were visiting with Miss DuBois."

The soldier's breath caught. "Er . . . yes, sir. But, only for a minute—"

"Private Wendle has been admitted to the infirmary. You will report in his stead for guard duty tonight."

"But, sir, I just pulled guard duty—"

"You will report for guard duty, Corporal Holmes. Is that clear?"

Something bristled inside Gabrielle. This was a side of Marcus she had never before seen. She realized she had never really seen him interact with any of the men. All of her dealings with him had been strictly personal, and even those had become sorely strained of late. Still, it annoyed her that he should chastise Corporal Holmes in front of her. Major Catlin would not have handled the situation like that, she thought. He would have waited until he was alone with the soldier before criticizing him. She took a deep breath. "It wasn't his fault. He was on his way out the door and I stopped him—"

"Don't interfere, Gabrielle," Lieutenant Epperling said in a clipped tone, arching an eyebrow by way of warning. "This does not concern you."

"But, Marcus, it does concern me. I'm the one who—"

"Corporal Holmes, you have your orders. I suggest you get to them, now!"

"Yes, sir," the soldier mumbled, his tone resentful.

Arrogant bastard! Gabrielle fumed. She fairly itched to slap Marcus Epperling's handsome face. Catching the surreptitious glance the corporal cast in her direction, she lifted her chin, whirled about, and started out the door after Holmes.

"Not you, Gabrielle," Marcus snapped, irritated by her childish display of temper. "Stay here. I want a word with you."

"Well, I have no wish whatsoever to speak with you," she flung over her shoulder, and kept going.

"Gabrielle!"

This time she did stop, and so did Corporal Holmes. Her heart pounding furiously, Gabrielle turned to face Marcus. She hoped she appeared more assured than she felt as she gave him a look of self-righteous indignation and said, "I would thank you not to use that tone of voice with me, Lieutenant Epperling."

"And I would thank you, Miss DuBois, not to turn your back on me while I am speaking to you." The implied threat in Marcus Epperling's tone caused Gabrielle's stomach to turn over. Marcus glanced at Corporal Holmes and his expression hardened even more. "I gave you an order, Corporal!"

Still, the soldier hesitated. "You gonna be all right, Miss Gabrielle?"

Torn by indecision, Gabrielle nervously moistened her lips. She wasn't at all certain she wanted to stay here with Marcus. Once the corporal left, they would be completely alone, and she was having the same feeling of unease she had experienced the night he had kissed her. "Yes, Charlie," she said softly, though her eyes were fixed on Lieutenant Epperling's face and she did not miss the tightening of his jaw at her use of

Holmes's given name. "I'll be fine."

Charlie Holmes glanced from her to the lieutenant and back again, bewilderment clouding his expression. It was the first time Miss Gabrielle had ever called him by his first name. Without another word, he turned and left, pausing only once to glance back over his shoulder.

The instant Corporal Holmes had gone, Marcus stalked to the door and pushed it shut. He then turned and seized Gabrielle's arm in a painful grip. "Just what was that little display about?" he demanded, yanking her around to face him. "I wasn't aware that you and Corporal Holmes were on a first-name basis."

Gabrielle jerked her arm free and took a step away from him, blinking as her eyes adjusted to the semidarkness. There was something suffocatingly possessive about Marcus Epperling. She had never noticed it before, though she was beginning to suspect that it had been there all along. She had simply been too blind to see it. "Charlie Holmes is my friend," she said flatly, hiding her hands in the folds of her skirt so that Marcus would not be able to see that they were shaking. She was having a hard time remembering what it was she had ever liked about him.

"In the future, Gabrielle, I would appreciate it if you were to limit your friendships to the wives of the other officers. It is unseemly for you to be fraternizing with enlisted men." After a second's hesitation, he added, "Or their families."

Raw fury erupted inside her. "Are you telling me who I may associate with, Marcus Epperling?" she demanded hotly, her green eyes blazing with unbridled anger.

Lieutenant Epperling's face softened, but the expression of contrition did not extend to his eyes. "Of course not, sweetheart," he said, in the indulgent tone one would use with a child, and closing the gap between them, he drew her into his arms. "I'm merely trying to point out the proper behavior for an officer's wife. And you *are* going to be my wife. Just as soon as I've had a chance to speak with your father."

Her face pressed uncomfortably against his uniform, Gabrielle stiffened and, laying her palms flat against his chest, pushed him away from her. "First of all," she said irritably, planting her hands on her hips and facing him squarely. "I will be friends with whomever I want, regardless of whether it suits your definition of proper behavior."

"Even Grace Simmons?"

"Especially Grace Simmons."

He chuckled. "Even if she is *only* the sergeant major's daughter?"

Hot color flooded Gabrielle's face at this not-so-subtle reminder of her own shabby treatment of the girl who had been her long-time friend and companion. She did not deign to reply.

One blond eyebrow arched upward at her stubborn silence. "Gabrielle, I am only concerned with—"

"I don't give a tinker's damn what your concerns are, Marcus Epperling!" she declared. "I used to like you. No, I take that back. I thought I was in love with you. But I'm beginning to see that all I was in love with was a pretty face. Inside, you're the most conceited, puffed-up—"

"As my wife," Marcus ground out from between clenched teeth, his face darkening, "you had better learn to curb your tongue. Since your father has been away, you have started talking like a common foot soldier. I won't tolerate gutter language from the woman who is supposed to help further my career, not hamper it with her unseemly behavior."

"Further your—!" Gabrielle sputtered, then broke off and clamped her mouth shut as realization dawned on her. Marcus must have found out that her father was being considered for brigadier general, and he was hoping a betrothal would pave the way for his own military advancement. "My, my, how quickly we forget," she said testily. "Yesterday I was *used merchandise* and today I'm supposed to help further your career. Are you certain, Lieutenant Epperling, that you are even speaking to the right woman? I don't see how I, with my gutter language and my dubious reputation, am supposed to contribute to your advancement." She cocked a critical eyebrow at him.

"Don't get sarcastic with me, Gabrielle. You know damned good and well that I didn't mean those things I said yesterday. I was angry over finding out that you and Major Catlin were

192

living under such intimate conditions."

"Conditions that my father arranged, you pigheaded oaf! And you're not the only one who's angry. *I'm* angry. I'm angry that you would even question my virtue or my—"

"Gabrielle, I'm not questioning your virtue. I simply want to be certain that the woman I marry is unsullied."

"Unsullied!" Gabrielle was so angry she could hardly think. "Well, I have news for you, Lieutenant. I wouldn't marry you if you were the last man on the face of this earth! Furthermore, the only thing that's sullied around here is your filthy mind!" She turned on her heel to leave, but he caught hold of her arm and yanked her back against him.

"One way or another, Gabrielle"—he gripped her arm so tightly that his fingers dug into her flesh and brought tears of pain to her eyes—"you will be my wife. If I have to, I will take you right here and now, on the floor of this stable. Then you won't have any choice but to marry me."

"Just you try it! I'll scream so loud—"

His mouth abruptly descended over hers, choking out her words and bruising her lips. He kissed her with a savageness that was meant to punish rather than to pleasure, and terror streaked through Gabrielle as she twisted in his arms, trying to break his grip on her. When his tongue plunged boldly into her mouth she gagged and jerked her head away. "Marcus!" she gasped on a single ragged breath. Wedging one arm up between them, she pushed as hard as she could splaying her fingers across his face.

Marcus slapped her arm away and, knotting his fingers in her damp hair, forced her face back up toward his. Gabrielle kept her teeth clamped shut, resisting his efforts to invade her mouth, and she brought the heel of her right foot down hard on his instep. He swore and jerked his head up, and in that instant Gabrielle threw her own head forward, striking him in the mouth with her forehead and wrenching free of his grasp just as the stable door flew open.

"What the hell's goin' on in here?" Captain Moreland demanded, his sharp eyes assessing the situation in a glance. Water dripped from the brim of his hat and streamed down over his buckskins.

Marcus reached up to gingerly touch his bloodied lip. "This is none of your business, Moreland," he snapped, eying the other officer coldly.

"It's *Captain* Moreland to you, Lieutenant, and I just made it my business. You be in Headquarters in five minutes. I want a little chat with you after I've taken Miss DuBois home." Turning, Bandy seized Gabrielle's elbow and steered her through the door, out into the rain, and when he spoke, something in his voice told her that he was just as angry with her as he was with Marcus. Perhaps even more so. "I believe, Miss DuBois, that the doc told you to stay in bed. Just what in blazes did you think you was doin' sneakin' out to meet Epperling? After the way he treated you last night, I woulda thought you had enough pride to keep away from the son-of-a-bitch!" he scolded as he propelled her across the parade ground toward Officers' Row.

Barely able to keep up with his angry stride, Gabrielle tried to catch her breath and speak. "I didn't . . . sneak . . . out to meet—"

"Lieutenant Johnson saw you skulkin' behind the Headquarters Building, and Corporal Holmes came and told me you was in the stables with Epperling, so don't go givin' me a line of crap missy, 'cause I ain't buyin' it."

"But, I didn't—" Gabrielle dug her heels into the muddy ground and succeeded in breaking the officer's stride. But when she tried jerking her arm free, he held fast. "I mean, I did go . . . around the back way . . . but not to meet Marcus. I was looking for Major Catlin."

Bandy pushed her up the steps of her father's house and through the door, slamming it shut with such force the pictures in the hallway almost leapt from the walls. When he spun her around to face him, the look in his eyes made her stomach knot in fear. "When I last saw Dan and you together, you wasn't even speakin' to each other, and now you're tryin' to tell me you was out in the stables lookin' for him? I might be runty, Miss DuBois, but I ain't stupid!"

When Gabrielle did not answer, Bandy folded his arms across his buckskin-clad chest and fixed a hard blue gaze on her. He was waiting for an explanation, she knew. As she dragged her wet sleeve across her face, she decided he probably would not believe her, but took a deep breath and met his gaze without flinching. He might not trust her, but she'd be damned if she was going to let him cow her. "I was told that there were going to be charges levied against him if he didn't return the Apaches to Camp Grant, and I wanted to find out if it was true. I didn't know Marcus was in the stables or I wouldn't have gone there. And the only reason I sneaked around behind the buildings was because Captain Wilcox told me to stay in bed and I didn't want him to see me. I know you don't believe me, but it's the truth. I know Major Catlin and I don't always get along, but that doesn't mean I want him to go to prison. So, if you will excuse me, Captain Moreland, I want to get out of these wet clothes." Gabrielle turned and started down the hall toward her room, acutely aware of the sharp blue gaze boring into her back.

Bandy spoke quietly to her retreating back. "Why do you want to help Dan?"

She stopped in the middle of the hallway and put out a hand to steady herself as she turned back to face him. Her knees were quaking and she didn't know why. "For the same reason I would have thought you might want to help. Or is your friendship with the major just something you remember whenever it's convenient for you?" She had not meant to be sarcastic, but her words came out that way and to her annoyance, Bandy Moreland chuckled. She stiffened. "Why haven't *you* done anything to help him, Captain?"

He fixed her with his infuriating grin. "Because, Miss DuBois, as you should know by now, Dan Catlin doesn't do nothin' he don't want to, and that includes acceptin' help from his friends."

"But can't you talk to him? Convince him to return the Apaches to Camp Grant? Surely if there are enough troops to guard the Indians until this mess blows over—"

"Dan won't do that."

"If he doesn't, he could go to prison!"

"He knows."

Frustration welled inside her. "And you're just going to sit back and let him destroy his life, aren't you? How can you call yourself his friend when you won't even lift a finger to help him?"

The humor left Bandy's eyes. "Miss DuBois, I'm gonna explain somethin' to you and you'd better listen up, 'cause I don't want to have to repeat myself. Dan Catlin wasn't more'n a year old when his ma died and his old man hightailed it outa Canada after killin' a British regular durin' the uprising at Red River. Knowin' he couldn't raise Danny and keep ahead of the law at the same time, his pa took him to Illinois where his ma had people, hopin' one of them would take the boy in. But that self-righteous bunch of Scots wouldn't have nothin' to do with Danny, 'cause he was *métis* and they didn't want no kid whose father was a breed, even if his ma was one of their own. So his old man took him to the Madison County Boys Home, then just plain flat disappeared.

"Fifteen years Dan spent in that hellhole, Miss DuBois, 'cause every time someone would consider adoptin' him, the story would get out about how his pa was a breed who was wanted by the law and how his own kin wouldn't have nothin' to do with him. Them kids at the orphanage was about as cruel a lot as a body'd ever chance to meet. They didn't miss an opportunity to remind Dan that he was a breed or where he'd come from, or to tell him that he'd never amount to nothin' 'cause of who he was. But, he held his own against every friggin' one of 'em. And when I wound up there after my folks was killed, the other boys would pick on me 'cause I was kinda the runt of the litter, but Dan would stick up for me every time, even if he wound up gettin' his face ground into the dirt, or takin' a beatin' that was meant for me.

"About the time Dan turned sixteen, old Silas McKenzie, his ma's uncle, showed up at the orphanage and announced that Dan was goin' home with him 'cause he needed an extra field hand. Well, Dan wouldn't have none of it. If he weren't good enough for the McKenzies when he was a little tyke, then he weren't about to go slavin' for them now that he was big enough to work a plow. So he ran off, but before he did, he promised he was gonna provide for me until he could come back to get me outa there. And he did, by God. He got himself into the Army and worked his way up through the ranks, and then he pulled every last string he knew of and collected on every favor that was owed him and got me into West Point. Danny was the smart one. He was the one who shoulda gone to the Academy. Not me. But he done for me like I was his own brother and he never asked for nothin' in return. So before you go accusin' me of not liftin' a finger to help him when he's in need, you just remember one thing. If I thought it would help, I'd give my life for that man, and there's nothin' or no one what could stand in my way. And, as for him roundin' up them Apaches and sendin' 'em back to Camp Grant, you can just forget it. He once swore he'd never turn another human bein' away simply 'cause they was Indian, and he's been true to his word ever since. Until them folks got someplace else to go where they'll be safe, he's gonna keep 'em right here. No matter what it costs him.''

By the time Captain Moreland finished speaking, Gabrielle was numb with shock and she felt as though the bottom had fallen out of her world. "I-I didn't know," she stammered.

"Of course you didn't," Bandy retorted, his temper dangerously close to exploding. "Not even the colonel knows the whole story, 'cause that's the way Dan wants it. He don't want folks feelin' sorry for him."

"I don't feel sorry for him. I feel ashamed—of myself. When I think of the way I acted—"

"You had darn well better be ashamed, missy, 'cause I'm tellin' you right now, if I'd been here that day of the festival and heard you callin' him a no-account breed the way you done, I'd of lit into you myself. By the time Dan got through blisterin' your rear end, it woulda been my turn. He's a fine man, about the finest you're ever gonna meet, and I won't stand for no one puttin' him down 'cause of somethin' what can't be helped. Now, if you'll excuse *me*, I got me one riled up lieutenant to tend to." He started for the door, then stopped and turned back to her. "And one more thing. The only ones who know the truth are Dan and me—and now you. And if you breathe one word of it to anyone, or let on to Dan that I told you, I'll come back here and cut your cursed tongue right outa your head!''

The front door slammed loudly after him.

Wrapping her arms around her stomach, Gabrielle slumped

against the wall and sank to her knees. She felt sick. For fourteen years Dan Catlin had been there for her, protecting her, trying to drill a sense of right and wrong into her. In his own way he'd looked out for her just as he'd looked out for Bandy Moreland years ago. And what had she ever done for him but antagonize him and treat him as though he were an outsider, jealously resenting any time her father—or anyone else—spent with him? She had been more than ungrateful. She had been despicable. Should she live to be a hundred, she would never be able to completely atone for her behavior.

Yet, she had to do something. She couldn't just sit back and let Dan go to prison simply because he had the guts to stand up to Department and refuse to send the Apaches back where they would face an uncertain, and possibly deadly, reception. She knew her father wouldn't support him. The colonel didn't want the Apaches anywhere near Camp Carleton, and he was going to be spitting mad when he learned Dan had brought them here. Without her father's backing, Dan would be court-martialed. The trick was to find some way to *make* her father stand up for Dan and support his actions. There had to be a way. . . .

It was not until late that night, when Dan finally returned from the ranch, that Gabrielle knew what she had to do.

Chapter Nine

Dan left the Rocking P feeling as though he had wasted his breath. Bryce Edwards had taken him over miles of range, heedless of the rain, and had shown him where his fences had been cut and his stock taken. He was convinced the Apaches from the camp were responsible, and nothing Dan said or did had made him change his mind. If the Apaches were not removed from Camp Carleton by the end of the month, Edwards intended to take his case to the governor. And Dan had no doubts that the rancher would win.

What disturbed him most, however, was that Edwards could very well be right. He did not believe the Apaches from Camp Grant were the thieves, but he had no such conviction about the new group that had arrived at the post just that morning. Unlike the others, they were Cibecue, and he had recognized one of the men as being from the war party which had taken Gabrielle captive. Bandy had warned him that it would be a mistake to release the two surviving warriors, and Dan was beginning to fear that he may have been right.The new arrivals at the camp did not seem to get along with the other Apaches. They kept to themselves, and Dan had an unsettling suspicion that they would prove to be troublemakers.

It was late by the time he arrived back in camp, and all he wanted to do was have a hot bath, sip a brandy, and hit the sack. He hoped Gabrielle was already in bed. The last thing he wanted was another confrontation with the girl. She had gotten under his skin and into his blood, and she was stirring up all kinds of crazy thoughts in his head. There were times when he wanted to throttle her, and times when he wanted to make love to her. Either way, she aroused something both dangerous and primitive in him—something that was best left alone.

A lamp was still burning in Gabrielle's bedroom. He could hear the wardrobe door being open and closed, and then a muffled curse as something hit the floor with a *clunk*. After a second's hesitation, he knocked lightly and waited for permission to enter before stepping within and being greeted by utter chaos. Dresses and shoes and lingerie were piled on the bed, draped over the cheval mirror, and strewn across the floor. In the midst of this clutter stood Gabrielle in nightgown and wrapper, her feet bare and her honey-colored tresses hanging forward over her left shoulder in a tumult of undisciplined curls. "I saved you some supper," she ventured, fixing on him an uncertain smile that gave no hint of her earlier anger.

Instantly, Dan was suspicious. "What is going on here?"

Her smile broadened. "What do you think of this?" she countered, retrieving a yellow, sprigged dress from the bed and holding it out in front of her. "Wouldn't this fabric look lovely on little Datigé? It would accent her black hair and her big brown eyes? And I'm sure this one"—she snatched a rose-colored silk from over the mirror and whirled to face him— "will only need to be shortened in order to fit Zayigo." She tossed both dresses onto the bed. "And then there are all these shoes. I never wear them because they pinch, so they've been sitting in my wardrobe all these months gathering dust. I thought some of the women at the Indian camp might be able to make use of them."

Bracing an elbow against the doorjamb, Dan pensively rubbed his forefinger back and forth across his upper lip, his eyes narrowing as he studied her. Though her wrapper had fallen open, she made no attempt to draw it shut, and it was all he could do to keep his gaze from dipping to the white cotton nightgown that might have seemed chaste had it not been for the beckoning shadow between her breasts. Her soft full lips were slightly parted and the misty look in her green eyes was

200

one part youthful innocence and two parts pure seduction. His pulse quickened. "You'll have to forgive me for being skeptical, Gabrielle, but I am finding this a little hard to swallow. When I left you this morning, you were slamming doors and swearing at me. Now you expect me to believe that you want to donate what appears to be a good portion of your wardrobe to the Apaches at the refugee camp?"

Gathering up her courage, Gabrielle went to him and placed her palms flat against his chest, her breath catching as she felt muscles leap reflexively beneath the fabric of his shirt. Her heart hammered loudly at the thought of what she was about to do, and an unfamiliar heat began at a point just below the pit of her stomach and rippled through her. She flushed less from embarrassment than from an awakening awareness of the intense masculinity that radiated from the man standing before her. What she was experiencing was not the revulsion she'd sometimes felt when she was alone with Marcus, but something entirely different. Something warm and wonderful . . . and just a little frightening. "This morning I behaved childishly. I should have obeyed you and waited for you to return," she said in a voice that was penitent and molasses smooth as she stared solemnly up at his chiseled face.

When he did not respond, but continued to study her with a marked degree of wariness, she demurely lowered her gaze, not out of any sense of shame but to keep him from seeing the mischief that danced in her eyes or the smile that tugged impatiently at the corners of her mouth. If he didn't stop giving her that grim look as though he half expected her take a knife to him, she was liable to burst out laughing. She dropped her hands to her sides and, her head still bowed, said in as sober a tone as she could muster, "I am truly sorry, and I hope you can find it in your heart to forgive me."

He sucked in his breath. "Gabrielle—"

She deftly dodged the hand that reached out to touch her hair, and slipped past him into the hallway. "I know you didn't have any supper," she said casually as she made her way down the dimly lit hall toward the kitchen. "Bryce Edwards isn't exactly known for his hospitality. So I saved you some fried chicken and biscuits. I also made a pot of coffee for you, but since it was my first time it's not very good. I won't be offended if you don't drink it."

Her first time! Dan swore to himself, for Gabrielle had managed to give the otherwise innocent statement a sexual connotation. And even in the semidarkness, there was no missing the beguiling sway of her hips as she padded down the hall in her bare feet. It took an inordinate amount of restraint of his part to remain at a safe distance behind her. Christ, but she is an inviting morsel, he thought irritably, and he suddenly wished he didn't have to be so damned honorable. Just what in the hell was she trying to pull anyway? If she twitched her derrière a little more, she was going to strain her back, not to mention his already stressed scruples. And did she have to parade around the house in that blessed nightgown? Good God, whatever had happened to the rules of etiquette that dictated what a woman was to wear in mixed company? He didn't believe Gabrielle did not know what she was doing to him.

She motioned toward the dining room and smiled bewitchingly over her shoulder. "We recieved a copy of the Prescott *Miner* today," she said sweetly. "I put it at your place. It's a week old, but I thought you might like to take a look at it while you're eating. Go ahead and sit down and put your feet up. I'll bring your supper from the kitchen."

Before he could say anything, she hastened down the hall, and he could have sworn he heard what sounded like a muffled giggle as she disappeared through the doorway. So she *was* up to something! He should have known. This morning she had been furious with him, and it wasn't like her to get over her animosity so quickly. Nor was it like her to wait on him hand and foot like a devoted wife. In fact, he couldn't quite picture Gabrielle catering to anyone except herself. So, whatever her scheme was she was certain to be the primary beneficiary. He chuckled to himself. In spite of her conniving, it was hard to be irritated by Gabrielle for long. Despite her faults, she could do the one thing few others had ever achieved: she could make him laugh.

Sitting down at the table, he unfolded the newspaper and began to scan the front page as he waited for Gabrielle to return. Two can play this little game, he thought; and he had every intention of turning the tables on her. One way or another, she was going to learn that she could not toy with him.

Gabrielle returned from the kitchen, carrying a tray laden with enough food to feed three hungry men. My dear Gabrielle, what devilment is going on in that devious little head of yours? Dan mused, a wicked gleam in his eyes as he watched her place the dishes on the table. With sun-kissed cheeks and long hair tumbling freely over her shoulders, she looked childishly vulnerable yet seductively alluring. A smile played at the corner of his mouth, but he wiped it away the instant she raised her beautiful green eyes to his face. "The coffee isn't very good at all. Perhaps you would prefer a brandy?" She made the offer apologetically, and her gaze was so guilelessly innocent that he decided against telling her brandy was meant to be savored on its own—after dinner—and was not to be drunk to wash down fried chicken. Instead, he inclined his head, careful not to give vent to his mounting good humor until after she left the dining room when his shoulders began to shake with silent laughter. Dan wasn't sure how much longer he could maintain this serious stance; the muscles in his face were already beginning to ache from the sheer effort of suppressing smiles.

His control was even further strained when Gabrielle returned from the parlor with a generously sized brandy snifter filled to within a quarter-inch of the brim. "Are you trying to get me drunk?" he asked when she set the glass before him, hiding his hilarity behind an ominous scowl.

Uncertainty flickered across Gabrielle's face as she wondered what she had done wrong. "Did I give you too much?"

One dark eyebrow arched upward. Did she honestly not know? "It's fine," he said flatly, his expression carefully guarded. For all her transparency, there were times when even he did not know when she was teasing from when she was being serious.

Gabrielle moved around to the side of the table and sat down in her usual place. "How was your meeting with Bryce Edwards?" she asked offhandedly, then broke a biscuit in half and nibbled on a piece of it as she studied Dan from beneath her dark lashes. "I heard he was here this morning, trying to stir up trouble."

Dan shot her a piercing glance. "He isn't trying to stir up trouble, Gabrielle. He has a legitimate gripe."

"About the Apaches?"

"Yes." Dan reached for the butter.

"He doesn't want them camped outside of the post, does he?"

"Why do you ask that?"

She shrugged, careful to keep her gaze fixed on the biscuit in her hand. "The residents of Tucson didn't want them quartered at Camp Grant. I don't think the people here are all that different."

Dan eyed her closely. Was she being perceptive or had she been talking to someone? "There are those"—he was trying to get a feel of just how much she knew—"who think I should send the Apaches back to Camp Grant."

Her heart turned over in her chest and her mouth went dry. *Lord, he was quick!* She broke off another piece of biscuit and put it in her mouth. Hoping she did not appear as nervous as she felt, she slowly licked the crumbs off her fingers with an exaggerated air of nonchalance. "What are you going to do?" she asked at last, lifting her lashes and looking straight at him.

His gaze did not waver. "Keep them here."

Gabrielle almost choked when she tried to swallow and she could feel blood pounding in her ears. It was not going to work! Her plan was going to fail before she could even put it into motion. Still, she had to try. "That's probably best," she said guardedly, putting what remained of the biscuit back on the edge of the platter. "After all, they wouldn't be very safe at Camp Grant, would they?"

He stared at her in disbelief. Was it possible that Gabrielle was the only person on the face of the earth who wasn't going to try to talk him into returning the Apaches to Camp Grant? Even Bandy Moreland, who was his friend, had not afforded him that courtesy. "No," he said slowly. "They wouldn't."

"Then I think you're doing the right thing."

Before he could say anything else, Gabrielle stood up and went to stand beside his chair. "I know I have no right to ask you this after the way I behaved this morning," she said, absently running a forefinger along the top of his shoulder, "but may I go with you to the camp tomorrow?"

Damn! His heart slammed against his ribs. Her very closeness and the provocative trailing of her finger across his shoulder were almost more than he could bear. "I'll think about it," he said noncommittally, an odd husky note in his voice.

Giving him an enigmatic half-smile, Gabrielle bent down and kissed him on the cheek, delight surging through her as a muscle in his jaw tightened beneath her lips. "Good night," she said in a softly seductive voice; then she bolted out of the room before she crumpled into a fit of uncontrollable laughter. Whoever would have guessed seducing a man could be so much fun?

She had already decided that the only way to save Dan from destroying his career was to get him to marry her. Her father would be furious, she knew, but he would also do everything in his power to get the charges against her husband dropped. In fact, he would probably do just about anything to avoid having his own name dragged into a scandal that might hurt his chances of promotion.

She knew Dan Catlin didn't love her; he didn't even like her. But once he had said that he did not hate her, and she knew that he was aware of her physically—in the way men are aware of women they find attractive, regardless of whether or not they like them. It wouldn't do any good to propose to him, for he would most likely refuse . . . after he finished laughing at her. And he would definitely refuse if he found out she was doing it for him. No, the only way to get him to marry her was to lure him into compromising her virtue, to leave him with no other choice but to make her his wife.

Closing her door, Gabrielle scurried about the cluttered bedroom, sweeping gowns up off the bed and dumping shoes into the trunk she had retrieved from her father's bedroom. She had to get all these clothes bundled up and ready to take to the Indian camp. Come morning, she was going to look like the most generous person in the world. If that didn't make Dan Catlin sit up and take notice, nothing would.

On top of the wardrobe were four large bandboxes she needed for packing the chemises and stockings and underdrawers she had outgrown. She thought of asking Major Catlin to get the boxes down for her, then decided against it. She wasn't certain just where the fine line between subtlety and overtness lay, but if the major had even the slightest inkling that she was trying to seduce him, summoning him to her bedroom would only serve to confirm his suspicions. Placing her dressing-table stool before the wardrobe, Gabrielle gathered up her nightgown and wrapper, and climbed onto the stool. She would just have to get the boxes herself.

In the dining room, Dan stretched out his long legs and slowly sipped his brandy, a frown narrowing the space between his brows as he puzzled over Gabrielle's behavior. He knew her well enough to be certain that she was not inclined to immediate forgiveness. Upon more than one occasion, he had seen her engage in week-long sulks that had tested the patience of everyone around her. Yet even though she had been furious with him this afternoon, she was now behaving as though nothing had happened, and being downright solicitous. He tried to attribute this unlikely change to a sincere desire to mend her ways, but that theory just wasn't credible. Gabrielle was plotting something; he wished he knew what.

A loud crash and a muffled scream brought him to his feet in an instant. He barged into Gabrielle's bedroom just as she was struggling to rise, using the overturned stool for support.

Dazed, she glanced up. "I'm all right," she hastily assured him as he approached, but despite the sheepish smile she gave him, her face was ashen.

Disregarding the hand she extended to him, he slid one arm around her shoulders, placed the other behind her knees, and picked her up.

"I'm fine, really," Gabrielle insisted in a shaky voice as he carried her across the room.

Dan lowered her to the bed, intensely aware of his body's inappropriate reaction to the feel of her in his arms. "What in the hell were you doing up there?" he demanded, disguising his kindling desire behind a harsh tone. *Damn, but she felt good!* "You could have hurt yourself."

Her breath caught. "I think . . . I did." There was an agonizing burning just beneath her ribs.

He laid her back on the pillows and, placing a hand on either side of her head, leaned over her, his expression solemn as he scrutinized her with an intensity that made her squirm. "Did you deliberately fall off that stool?"

Gabrielle's eyes widened. "It was an accident," she protested, hurt that he would even think such a thing. Then she caught her bottom lip between her teeth, unaware of how guilty the expression made her look.

In spite of her denial, Dan would have sworn she had staged that fall just to get him into her bedroom, just as he would have sworn she'd been making unseemly advances toward him earlier. What he couldn't figure out was, why?

Noticing that she was pressing her left arm to her side, he placed a palm against her rib cage. "Does this hurt?" he asked probing gently along the bruised area with his fingers. He could feel the tightly wound bandages beneath her nightgown, and had a sudden urge to strip her of both the gown and the bindings.

"Y-yes . . ." The words came out as a halting croak.

Dan's gaze slid up to her face, his eyes dark with longing. "And here?" he asked thickly, his fingers moving upward until they almost touched her breast.

Gabrielle's heart thumped erratically. His touch and the warmth of his brandy-scented breath alternately thrilled and frightened her. Instinct told her it would be a simple matter to lure him into her bed, and even though it was what she had planned to accomplish eventually, panic surged through her, raising goose bumps on her skin and choking the breath out of her. She wasn't repelled by him as she had been by Marcus. But she was scared. She wasn't ready to be bedded by any man, not even to one she was trying to trick into marrying her. She swallowed hard. "It doesn't hurt . . . as much now," she lied.

A veil passed over Dan's eyes and his expression became stern, as though he were deliberately distancing himself. Gabrielle felt an unexpected twinge of disappointment as he pulled away from her.

"You're staying in bed tomorrow, young lady," he stated

flatly, drawing the covers up over her.

Staying in bed! She gave him a wounded look. "But—"

"No arguments, Gabrielle. You're staying right here, in this bed, and that's final. I don't think you did any damage to those ribs when you fell, but if you're still experiencing pain in the morning, I'm going to get Wilcox over here to take a look at you."

"No!" The word was out before she could stop it, and Gabrielle felt her face grow warm with shame. She couldn't bring herself to tell him that she and the surgeon were liable to come to blows if their paths crossed. "I-I mean I'm feeling much better now. I really am."

"I don't want to take any chances. In fact, I intend to ask Miss Simmons to come over here and sit with you."

"I don't need a nanny! It doesn't even hurt much anymore. I'm fine." She flung back the covers and started to rise. "Look, I'll show you."

A firm hand descended on her shoulder and pushed her back against the pillows. "You're right," Dan said, drawing the sheet back up over her. "You don't need a nanny. You need a jailer. To make certain you follow orders."

"But you promised I could go with you tomorrow!"

"I promised no such thing."

"Yes, you did. You said—"

"I said I would think about it. Now"—he jerked his head toward the wardrobe—"What's up there that you want so badly you were willing to risk breaking your neck to get it?"

Her bottom lip curled out in a pout and she eyed him with contempt. She hated it when he treated her like a child.

One dark brow angled upward. "Well?"

"It's not important now," she said petulantly, glaring at him over the top of the covers she was clutching beneath her chin. Damn him! Why did he have to be so contrary? Just once, couldn't he see her as the woman she was and not some wayward child?

It took an incredible amount of self-control for Dan not to smile in genuine relief. The color had returned to Gabrielle's cheeks and she was back to being ornery, a sure sign that she had not seriously hurt herself, even if her fall was an accident as she claimed. His expression stoically noncommittal, he went to the dresser and blew out the lamp. "Good night, little one," he said with a nonchalance that made Gabrielle fume. "Pleasant dreams."

By morning, Gabrielle was feeling decidedly better. Her ribs hardly ached at all, and the only discomfort that remained from the previous night's fall was a slight soreness in her shoulder, the result of trying to catch herself when she had lost her balance. Furthermore, she had found a way to turn her confinement to her advantage.

"What is it now?" Dan asked, his tone deceptively tolerant, as he appeared at her bedroom door in answer to her third summons in less than ten minutes. He knew what she was trying to do, and he refused to back down on his decision not to take her with him.

She smiled sweetly over the top of the covers, knowing full well that she was starting to get to him. He didn't fool her for one minute. She knew exactly when his patience started wearing thin. "Could you take those things over there to the camp with you?" she asked, indicating a pile of neatly folded underthings on top of the dresser. "I'm sure the Indians will be able to find a use for them. But, before you do that, will you do something with these pillows? I can't seem to get comfortable."

You're treading on thin ice, little one. Determined not to let her wear him down, Dan allowed his mouth to curl into an indulgent smile. "Is there anything else you would like before I go?" he offered as he helped her sit up and adjusted the pillows behind her back.

He was so close she could smell the soap on his skin, and a tremor of excitement rippled down her spine. He certainly is handsome, she thought. Not pretty like Marcus, but rugged and manly looking. She fluttered her lashes at him. "A cup of coffee?"

Dan placed his palms flat on the mattress and bent down until his face was so near to Gabrielle's that she feared her eyes would cross, and he said in tone that was at once silky smooth and dangerously menacing, "Do you know what I do to little girls who push their luck?"

Gabrielle slid down against the pillows and peered up at him from beneath her lashes, her green eyes sparkling with mischief. "With milk and sugar," she replied, ignoring his threat. Then she added sheepishly, "Please?"

His eyes narrowed as he contemplated a suitable revenge, so Gabrielle demurely let her own gaze drop . . . to his lips. She wished he would kiss her. She liked the way he kissed. It made her feel all warm and liquid inside.

There was no mistaking either her unspoken invitation or his body's lusty reaction to it. Annoyed at being thrown off guard, Dan swore inwardly and jerked himself upright.

Recklessly close to bursting into giggles, Gabrielle allowed her gaze to slide back up to his eyes. "And toast. With butter and marmalade." She wondered what he would do if she called him by his given name.

He folded his arms across his chest and cocked an eyebrow at her, and though his expression was one of bored indifference, the lights in his hazel eyes shone like hard gold pinpoints. "How about an egg? Or two? After all, I have nothing better to do than make you breakfast."

She choked back a laugh and wrinkled her nose. "I don't like eggs."

A sardonic smile twisted his mouth. "Would you like a spanking?"

She shook her head, her green eyes aglow. "Not especially."

"It's on the menu."

"I'll pass, thank you."

Dan had never thought the day would come when he would be glad to see the sergeant major's daughter, but when Grace Simmons walked through the bedroom door he knew that her presence was the only thing keeping him from losing his patience with Gabrielle.

"What happened?" Grace blurted out, rushing to Gabrielle's side. "Major Catlin said you fell and hurt yourself and must stay in bed."

Aggravated because Dan had summoned Grace after she had asked him not to, Gabrielle cast him a censuring glance just in time to see a wicked grin disappear from his face. He was laughing at her! I'm trying to save your career, you ingrate! she wanted to scream at him. Instead, giving him a disdainful toss of her head, she forced her attention back to Grace and expelled her breath in an exaggerated sigh. "I wish the major hadn't bothered you, Grace darling. I'll be fine. You need not sit with me."

"Nonsense!" Grace retorted, tucking the covers up around her and fussing over her like a mother hen. "You just rest and I'll take care of you. Really, Gabrielle, you need to be more careful. Captain Wilcox has said several times that you have been overdoing it. You should listen to him."

"I can see that I am leaving you in capable hands," Dan said, the note of amusement in his voice infuriating Gabrielle. "So, if you ladies will excuse me . . ."

It was all Gabrielle could do not to jump out of bed and scratch his laughing eyes out. "You forgot the clothes," she said with an acid sweetness that did little to disguise her irritation. Her tone drew a bewildered glance from Grace that she stubbornly refused to acknowledge.

"Gabrielle, what on earth is the matter with you?" Grace demanded the instant Dan left the room. She had never known anyone to dare to repeatedly antagonize Major Catlin the way Gabrielle did, and there were times when she questioned her friend's judgment, if not her sanity.

"Hush!" Gabrielle hissed, her forehead furrowing in concentration as she listened for the closing of the front door. Then, the second she knew Dan was out of the house, she threw back the covers and barreled out of bed. "Come on. I'm starving."

Grace whirled around, her mouth agape, as the "invalid" flew past her in a flurry of uncombed tresses and billowing white nightgown. It took a moment for her to regain her wits and follow Gabrielle to the kitchen. "I thought you were hurt," she accused, none too pleased at having been tricked.

"Want a cup of coffee?"

"No, I want you to tell me what you are up to. Major Catlin isn't going to be too happy with you when he finds out you aren't really hurt."

"I've been running him ragged this morning," Gabrielle said

lightly as she stirred her coffee. "He will be vastly relieved to know that I have been cured."

"But why are you deliberately provoking him? He whipped you once. Aren't you afraid he might do it again?"

Gabrielle speared Grace with a withering look. "I'm not very proud of that, and I would appreciate it if everyone would stop reminding me of it."

"I'm sorry. It's just that it's becoming terribly hard to keep defending you. You're my friend, Gabrielle. My best friend. I hate it when people talk about you behind your back and say horrible things."

Gabrielle peered at Grace over the top of her coffee cup. "What things?"

Grace looked vaguely uncomfortable. "I'd rather not—"

"Grace!"

"Well . . . Pa said he overheard Captain Wilcox tell Lieutenant Johnson that your father might send you back East after all the trouble you caused while he was away this time, and Lieutenant Epperling said you weren't going anywhere because he was going to marry you and straighten you out. But then, after he left, Lieutenant Johnson said that if Lieutenant Epperling didn't marry you, no one would, because you would cause trouble no matter where your father sent you, and that no man wants that type of . . . disgrace . . . attached to his name. . . ." Grace's voice trailed off. The stricken look on Gabrielle's face made her sorry she had said anything.

Gabrielle put down her coffee cup. An odd queasiness in the pit of her stomach had destroyed her appetite. She knew she shouldn't care what other people said, especially when they were being spiteful, but she did. Well, she'd show them. She'd make the most desirable bachelor in the entire United States Cavalry marry her, and then see what the gossips had to say about it. Her only regret was that it would have to be at Grace's expense, because Grace was in love with Dan. A look of unshakable determination settled on her face. "I'm going to get dressed. I have a hundred things to do today. You don't have to stay with me, but if you do, I'm going to put you to work."

"Doing what?" Grace asked as she followed Gabrielle back

to the bedroom, ashamed of herself for feeling wary.

"Well, for starters, we're going to go door to door collecting clothes and whatever else people want to get rid of. Major Catlin can take the things to the Indian Camp."

"But you're supposed to be in bed!"

"I just recovered, remember?"

Grace shook her head. "I don't know. . . . Pa was saying that Major Catlin is in hot water for bringing the Apaches here. I don't think we should get involved."

Bitter resentment welled up inside Gabrielle, and her face flushed with anger, but when she spoke, her voice was quiet and carefully controlled. "You're right. *We* aren't going to do anything."

Grace flinched at the contempt in her friend's voice. "Gabrielle, I didn't mean—"

"Please, just go."

Grace shifted nervously and twisted her fingers together. "Are you sure? I mean . . . if you really want me to help—"

Gabrielle laughed, but it was a hollow sound, devoid of humor. "And have people talking about you the way they do about me? Heaven forbid!" She turned her back and yanked open the dresser drawer, not wanting Grace to see how hurt she was by her friend's reluctance to help.

"We might have some things at home that I can give you," Grace ventured uncertainly.

"Fine." Gabrielle tossed clean underclothes onto the bed and dumped fresh water into the washbasin.

"If you want me to stay—"

"No."

"Gabrielle, it's not that I don't want to help you. Really it isn't," Grace pleaded. "It's just that—"

"Grace please." Gabrielle turned around and gave her an imploring look. "You don't have to explain. I understand."

The older girl's shoulders slumped in relief. "Do you really?"

"Yes." Gabrielle didn't understand. She simply wanted Grace to leave.

"Well . . . I'd better go home, seeing as how it's wash day and all."

213

Gabrielle forced a smile. "Give your mother my regards."

Thirty minutes later, after she had bathed and dressed and started on her rounds about the post, Gabrielle was confronted with something she had never before experienced—she had a door closed in her face.

"Well, all you had to do was say no," she muttered under her breath, wondering what had gotten into Mrs. Crocker. The woman had always been polite to her in the past.

Shaking her head in bewilderment, she went to the next house, knocked on the door, then backed up two steps. If that one came flying shut in her face, she wanted to be safely out of the way.

"Why, if it isn't the colonel's little girl!" Mrs. Lewes exclaimed, wiping her hands on her apron as she opened the door. "My, my, how you've grown! I could swear it was only yesterday you were in pigtails and smocks. And look at you now! Won't you come in, dear, and have a glass of lemonade with me? You really shouldn't be standing out in this hot sun."

"No, thank you, Mrs. Lewes. I'm afraid I can't stay. But, if you don't mind, I'd like to ask a favor of you. I'm collecting old clothing and cooking utensils—whatever you can spare— to help out the Indians at the refugee camp. Most of them came here with nothing except what they had on their backs, and some of the children are almost naked. I thought it would be nice if—"

"We don't have anything," Mrs. Lewes said, her smile fading. "And even if we did, I don't think Mr. Lewes would want it to go to the Apaches. For heaven's sake, we are at war with those savages!"

"They're people, not savages. They were run out of their homes at Camp Grant and their families were—"

"I can't help you. I'm sorry." The expression on the woman's face had become downright antagonistic.

Gabrielle felt as though her heart had worked its way up into her throat and gotten stuck there. Mumbling a hasty apology, she went on to the next house, but her reception there was little better.

"Here, take these," Sergeant Bassinger's wife said. She shoved a pair of threadbare britches into Gabrielle's hands, then mopped her thick sweaty neck with a dishtowel. "I was going to cut them up and use them for cleaning rags, but you might as well have them. Only don't tell anyone I gave them to you. I don't want Harry getting into trouble just because I helped you out. There's going to be trouble enough when the colonel finds out Major Catlin is harboring them savages here."

"Mrs. Bassinger, they're not savages. They're people. And they have no place else to go."

"Nonetheless, if you tell anyone I donated those trousers, I'll deny it. I swear I will."

White-hot anger exploded inside Gabrielle and it was all she could do not to fling the trousers back into the fat woman's face. Her anger mounted as the morning wore on. At nearly every house she visited, she was treated with cool indifference or outright hostility. Only Mary Wilcox and Corporal LaSalle and his wife showed any enthusiasm for what she was trying to do and the LaSalle's had six children under the age of eight and could scarcely spare what they did give. By the time Gabrielle trudged home at midday, she was hot and tired and on the verge of tears, and had little to show for her efforts, only the clothing Mary Wilcox and Bonnie LaSalle had given her, a coffee pot with a hole in the bottom, and Harry Bassinger's tattered britches.

Never in her life had she been so disgusted with people. Even those who believed Major Catlin had done the right thing in offering the Apaches asylum refused to cooperate out of fear of her father's disapproval. If she heard one more person say "But the promotion board meets next month and I have to stay on the colonel's good side," she was going to scream. What was wrong with people anyway? Didn't anyone besides Dan Catlin have the guts to stand up for what he or she believed?

"Aw, c'mon, Miss Gabrielle," Corporal Bates said as he set her luncheon on the table. "You just caught folks at a bad time, that's all. Now, if you can wait until about July when all the transfers come through, everyone will be more'n willing to get rid of the stuff that goes over their weight limit."

Gabrielle had no appetite for the ham sandwich the soldier had made for her. "It's not that," she said in a choked voice, trying hard not to break down and cry. "Most of them are angry with Major Catlin for bringing the Apaches here, and the rest of them are worried about what Father is going to say. Just because Father is the post commander doesn't mean he's always right."

Corporal Bates rubbed his jaw pensively as he pondered the situation. He'd never seen Miss Gabrielle like this, torn up over folks less fortunate. Most of the time she was all wrapped up in herself. But then, maybe she was finally growing up. He felt sorry for her. Growing up wasn't easy for some people, and he knew she was one of them. He inclined his head toward her plate. "Are you gonna eat that sandwich?"

She pushed the plate toward him and gave him an apologetic glance. "I'm not very hungry."

"Split it with you."

She shrugged wearily. "Okay."

Corporal Bates pulled out a chair and sat down at the table. "If you want," he suggested, handing her a half of the sandwich and taking the other for himself, "I can talk to the fellas in the barracks and see if they got anything to donate."

She gave him a wan smile. "They won't be any different from the others. The excuses I got tended to be repeated all the way down the ranks."

The soldier was thoughtful. "Well, I can't speak for anyone else," he said at last, "but if I had to choose sides, I'd rather keep in the major's good grace rather than the colonel's—pardon me for saying so—because when we're out in the field, your father's gonna be sitting back here behind a desk while Major Catlin's the one who's gonna be out there covering our tails. Do you understand what I'm saying?"

"It just isn't fair!" Gabrielle protested, tears stinging her eyes. "Major Catlin can't send those people back to Camp Grant where they saw their loved ones murdered, but if he doesn't he'll be court-martialed."

Al Bates almost wanted to laugh. Hearing Miss Gabrielle defend Major Catlin was the closest he'd ever come to witnessing a miracle. Still, it did his heart good to know the two people he liked most in the world were finally seeing eye to eye on something. Suddenly, he did laugh. "I just thought of something."

Gabrielle had removed the meat from her sandwich. "What?" she asked, taking a small bite out of a piece of ham.

"Ruby Collins! Her and her girls got more clothes than anyone I ever seen! I'll bet she'd be willing to donate some stuff."

For a moment, Gabrielle just stared at him, horror and incredulity alternately reflecting in her eyes. Then a smile broke across her face and she jumped up from her chair. "Corporal Bates, you're wonderful!" she exclaimed, throwing her arms around the startled soldier before bolting from the dining room.

"Miss Gabrielle, wait!"

But the front door had already slammed shut behind her.

Gabrielle did not know what she had expected before she'd entered the brothel, but she was totally unprepared for what she found there. The main salon was dark and dingy, the mud plaster eroded from its wall and only packed earth for a floor. The room stank of cigar smoke and stale whiskey and looked as though no attempt had been made to clean up after the place had closed the night before. Chairs and several tables were overturned, and shattered bottles lay strewn across the floor, leaving dark stains where their contents had soaked into the ground.

Her bravado rapidly waning, Gabrielle cast a last nervous glance about the room and turned to leave. I should never have come here, she thought, picking her way through the broken glass as she headed toward the door.

"Can I help you, señora?"

She whirled around, her eyes widening and her mouth dropping open as she found herself face to face with a young Mexican girl who was standing barefoot near a side doorway. Clad only in a grimy shift, the girl was rubbing the sleep from her eyes with her fist.

My God, she's only a child! Gabrielle thought, but she averted her gaze when she realized she had been staring. How old could the girl be? Thirteen . . . fourteen at the most. A sickening lump formed in the pit of Gabrielle's stomach as she thought of the soldiers paying this child for her favors. She swallowed hard and forced the revolting picture from her mind. She had come here for a reason, and all she wanted to do right now was get her mission accomplished and then get as far away from this disgusting place as she could. She made herself meet the girl's curious stare. "I-I've come to see Miss Collins," she said, her voice wavering in spite of her effort to control it.

Though the girl's eyes widened slightly, she said nothing but merely turned and motioned for Gabrielle to follow her.

Gabrielle was aware of the blood pounding in her ears as she followed the girl down a wide corridor that was almost a room in itself, it's walls being lined with an occasional chair or table. Other rooms led off the corridor. Some of the doors were closed and others were carelessly left ajar, but Gabrielle kept her eyes fixed straight ahead. Too frightened to be even remotely curious, she wondered what had possessed her to come here!

Not once looking back to see if she was following, the girl forged ahead, twitching her backside saucily as she walked. For all her youth, Gabrielle reflected, the girl is no innocent. Suddenly she felt ashamed of her own efforts to seduce Dan Catlin. No wonder he thought she was that awful thing—a cock-teaser!

The girl tapped lightly on the closed door at the end of the corridor, then opened it and slipped inside, leaving Gabrielle alone in the hall.

Gabrielle pressed her fist into her middle, as much to keep her hand from shaking as to ease the gnawing pain of an empty stomach. Her knees trembled and threatened to buckle. The good intentions that had brought her this far had, by now, abandoned her completely.

The door suddenly opened and the girl stepped out into the hall, a sly look in her dark eyes as she motioned for Gabrielle to enter.

This area, unlike the public rooms, was bright and airy, and cheerfully furnished with a large wardrobe and a dressing table and several comfortable-looking overstuffed chairs. Sunlight streamed in through an open door that led out to a courtyard. Opposite it; a floor-length curtain was pulled shut, blocking the rest of the room from view. Gabrielle ran her tongue across her lips and glanced about, acutely aware of the door closing behind her and uncertain whether she was more bewildered or afraid. Unless Ruby Collins was waiting for her behind that curtain, she was alone. She stared at the curtain, her pulse racing, not knowing whether she should announce her presence or remain silent. Bringing one hand up to her mouth, she nervously cleared her throat. "Is anyone there?"

No answer.

She tried again. "Hello?"

"You wanted to see me?"

She caught her breath and whirled around.

In the courtyard doorway stood a woman whose mass of long auburn hair billowed about her face in soft curls. She was wearing a lacy white peignoir that exposed her neck and the tops of her breast, but not the heavy layers of makeup that Gabrielle had always associated with Ruby Collins. Her lashes were lush and naturally dark and there was a voluptuous beauty about her that made Gabrielle suddenly feel very young and very foolish. "Are y-you Miss Collins?" she asked, hating herself for stammering when it was so important that she appear grown-up and sophisticated.

The woman moved with a fluid grace as she stepped into the room, the sunlight shimmering off her hair and giving her an ethereal quality. "Of course," she said cheerfully, a note of amusement in her voice. "Only you can dispense with the *Miss*. Ruby will do fine. And you're the colonel's daughter. Gabrielle, isn't it?"

"How did you know?" Gabrielle blurted out inelegantly; then she wished she could retract the words.

The woman chuckled. "Every young buck who comes in here has mentioned you at one time or another. They weren't kidding either. You *are* pretty. I keep wondering which one of my customers I'm going to lose when you decide to get married."

Gabrielle blushed, because of the compliment and because of Ruby's casual talk of customers. Then a horrifying thought occurred to her. Was Dan Catlin one of Ruby Collin's customers? Not knowing how to respond, she clumsily returned the compliment. "You're very pretty, too, Miss—I mean—Ruby. You look different than I expected . . . up close, that is."

"That's about the nicest thing a *lady* has ever said to me," Ruby said, not at all offended by what could easily have been construed as an insult. She sat down at her dressing table and picked up a silver-backed hairbrush, favoring Gabrielle with an amused smile as she began drawing the brush through her beautiful tresses. "It's not often I get visitors of the female variety from Camp Carleton. Tell me, Gabrielle—may I call you Gabrielle?—what brings you here today?"

Gabrielle's mouth had gone dry, so she found it difficult to speak. This was crazy! She should never have come here. She moistened her lips and shifted uneasily. "I-I'm sure you know about . . . the Indians . . . camped down the creek," she stammered, while she stared fascinated, as Ruby deftly twisted her hair up into a perfectly executed chignon. "Major Catlin had them brought up here after the massacre at Camp Grant. And, well . . . most of them are pretty bad off and I was wondering if—I mean, you don't have to, of course—but if you had anything you might want to donate . . . Anything at all would be a help. Old clothes . . . whatever."

What started out as a chuckle soon deepened into a hearty, full-throated laugh. "Well, why didn't you say so right off instead of beating around the bush? Some of my girls are Mexican and won't take too kindly to having their things go to a bunch of Apaches, but I've got crates full of stuff that we collected the last time Camp Carleton had a charity drive. None of those prissy women would accept anything from us. I guess they were afraid our questionable morals might rub off onto their lily-white hands if they touched a dress one of my girls had worn. But I can tell you one thing, child, when you're hungry and going about in rags, you couldn't care less where your food or your clothes come from. Now, you just wait here, and I'll be right back. We'll get you fixed up. There won't be a soul in the Territory of Arizona who'll be able to say Ruby Collins didn't help out when there were folks in need."

After Ruby left the room, Gabrielle let out her breath in a long indelicate *whoosh*. Of all the people in the world, Ruby Collins was the last person she would have expected to donate anything. She remembered, to her shame, that she was one of those women who had once thought herself too good to sully her hands with Ruby Collins' castoffs.

The reporter followed Dan into the Headquarters Building. "Major Catlin, if the United States Government is planning to establish a permanent reservation here, the people of Yavapai County have a right to know. After all, aren't these savages the same ones who have been terrorizing Tucson and Eastern Pima County for the past—"

"Mr. Hyatt, as I have already told you"—Dan ground the words out, his hazel eyes narrowing until they were mere slits above the high sharp ridge of his cheekbones—"I refuse to comment. Now, unless you wish to be bodily removed from this post, I suggest you leave. Immediately!"

"But, Major Catlin—"

"And you can inform your employer, Mr. Hyatt, that the next journalist from the *Miner* who sets foot on this post will be arrested for trespassing on Government property. Good day, sir!"

There was no mistaking the note of finality in Dan's voice or the steely glint of anger in his eyes. With a sigh of exasperation, the reporter backed out of the building, and Dan ungraciously slammed the door shut after him before rounding on the four officers staring at him in mute astonishment. "All right," he said, his face dark with barely leashed fury. "Which one of you is responsible for that son-of-a-bitch being here?"

Thunder shook the valley and dust swirled up around the hem of Gabrielle's shirt as she emerged from Ruby Collins' establishment and started home with a dozen brightly-colored dresses and a promise from Ruby that she would send a boy over later with the rest of the clothing as well as some dishes and pots and pans that had been stored away and never used. Gabrielle was so wrapped up in her good fortune, she did not see anyone approach, and was crudely jolted back to reality when a hand closed about her arm in a bruising grip, and

221

she was jerked around so hard she dropped the dresses into the dirt.

"Marcus!" she gasped, terror surging through her as she noted the dark rage that contorted his handsome features. Her gaze flew to the dresses lying in a heap on the ground and she unthinkingly stooped to retrieve them, but Marcus Epperling yanked her back to her feet.

"What were you doing in that place?" he demanded, gripping her by the shoulders and shaking her so hard her teeth clacked together.

"M—Mar . . . c-cus. . . ." she managed to get out as her head snapped back hard enough to cause a blinding white pain to explode behind her eyes.

"Damn it, answer me!"

"Then stop . . . shaking . . . m-me!" Managing to wrench free of his grasp, Gabrielle took a step away from him. Her upper arms burned terribly and she knew that ugly purple bruises would soon appear where his fingers had dug into her flesh. Several seconds passed before she was able to catch her breath. "I was . . . collecting clothing. For the Apaches out at the camp," she said at last, fixing on him a hurt look. "Miss Collins was kind enough to donate—"

"*Miss* Collins? Gabrielle! Ruby Collins is a whore!"

"Don't say that!"

"Well, it's the truth, damn it! She's a prostitute and that place you just came from is a whorehouse! And don't you dare pretend you didn't know; even you aren't that naive!"

Gabrielle's face burned with shame. Ruby Collins might be a whore, but today she'd been more of a lady than most of the wives of the men at Camp Carleton. Still, Gabrielle had no desire to argue with Marcus. Not even bothering to respond to his crude remarks, she knelt and began picking up the dresses he had caused her to drop.

But he would not even allow her to do that.

Gabrielle uttered a startled cry as he kicked the dresses from her hands.

"I'll not have my wife touching that trash!" he bellowed.

Flinching at his cutting tone, Gabrielle rose, and though his fury frightened her, she refused to be intimidated. Her green eyes glittering with belligerence, she met his angry glare, raised her chin, and tossed her hair over her shoulder in a defiant gesture. "I am not your wife, Marcus Epperling, nor do I ever intend to be. So, you can just find someone else to—"

"You were willing to be my wife before you started living with that damned breed," he said accusingly, his face cold with anger.

"I was willing to be your wife before *you* started behaving like a jackass! Now, move out of my way and let me take these things home, or I'll scream so loudly everyone on this post will come running and I'll tell them you made an indecent gesture toward me."

He snickered. "It won't do you any good to create a scene, Gabrielle. No one will believe a word you say once I tell them where you've been." He cast a meaningful glance toward the brothel. "Believe me, my dear. The colonel will be none too pleased to learn that you have been panhandling for those mangy savages, much less cavorting with the likes of Ruby Collins and her brood of whores! In fact, he will most likely thank me for taking you to task for your unseemly behavior."

Her stomach churnng, Gabrielle reluctantly agreed, for she knew that he was probably right. "That's true," she said, trying to keep her voice steady in spite of her rapidly waning courage. "Except that Father isn't here. But Major Catlin is, and *he* is the one you'll have to answer to."

Icy contempt flashed in the officer's eyes, but anything he might have said was cut off by Ruby Collins' throaty chuckle. "Is there a problem, Gabrielle?" she asked with a familiarity that implied they were old friends, and both Gabrielle and Marcus turned to see Ruby standing near them, her arms weighted down by more dresses than Gabrielle had ever known any one person to own and a knowing half-smile on her face as her now kohl-rimmed eyes swept over the officer. With her were two of her "girls" and a Mexican boy of about ten, all of them with arms laden.

Gabrielle glanced at Ruby and then at Marcus, and she had an insane urge to giggle as she realized the sight she must be presenting to him, with what was generally considered Camp Carleton's basest element coming to her defense. Somehow she managed to tame the giggle into a subdued smile. "No, Ruby, there's no problem," she said with an exaggerated sweetness that hinted to the other woman that she was lying through her teeth. Her gray-green eyes glistened vengefully. "I merely dropped the dresses and Lieutenant Epperling was helping me pick them up. Isn't that considerate of him?"

The officer's face turned bright crimson as he struggled to avoid the amused stare of the curvaceous Justine with whom he had spent many an entertaining night.

"That is very considerate of you, sir," Ruby drawled conspiratorially, leaving Marcus no choice but to help Gabrielle pick up the dresses or make himself look like an ass by refusing.

Impaling Gabrielle with a brittle look that told her the discussion was far from over, Marcus bent down and retrieved the dresses from the ground, one by one, shaking the dirt off them and smoothing out the wrinkles before draping them across Gabrielle's arms.

Both Gabrielle and Ruby showered the officer with expressions of gratitude, and Marcus, his full mouth curving into a smile that did not extend to his eyes, touched his hand to the brim of his hat and stalked away, the stiff set of his shoulders failing to hide the anger roiling inside him.

The instant he was out of earshot, Ruby turned to her girls and, careful to avoid singling out the now-fidgeting Justine, told them in no uncertain terms that Lieutenant Epperling was no longer welcome at the "house."

"You mean, he's one of your customers?" Gabrielle blurted out, her eyes widening in shock as she stared at her flashily dressed rescuers.

Ruby chuckled at her charming innocence. "Not anymore, he's not! Come on, child, let's get these things inside before it starts to rain."

When Dan walked through the front door an hour later, Gabrielle thought she had never in her life been so glad to see anyone. All day long, she had been taking a battering. It had begun with Grace's repetition of the unkind remarks some of the officers had made about her, had continued through the rejections she had received from the soldiers and their wives, and had culminated in her unfortunate encounter with Marcus. Now, looking up at the darkly handsome man she was beginning to appreciate more and more with each passing day, Gabrielle felt tears of exhaustion and relief spring into her eyes, and it was all she could do not the fling herself into his arms.

"What is all this?" Dan asked sternly, indicating with a nod the piles of clothing and dishes that littered the hallway.

Suddenly, she wanted nothing more than to please him. "Isn't it wonderful?" she asked, giving him her warmest smile despite the aching uncertainty she was experiencing. "Everyone was so kind. When people saw you taking my old clothes out to the camp this morning, they brought by things they no longer had any use for and asked me to give them to you to take to the Apaches."

Ignoring the ill-humored look Dan was giving her, Gabrielle pushed past him and picked up a dress of tangerine satin trimmed with jet black tulle. "And look at this!" she exclaimed incredulously, giggling as she held the dress up before her. "Can't you see this on Anna? You do remember Anna . . . Datigé's grandmother?" Her voice wavered and the giggle died in her throat.

Then, without warning, Gabrielle buried her face in the gaudy satin and burst into tears.

Chapter Ten

Dan's arm slid gently about her shoulders, and Gabrielle turned against his chest, crushing the satin dress between them. She wept disconsolately in his arms, dampening the front of his uniform with her tears. She wept for herself, because of the shabby treatment she had received at the hands of those she had thought her friends and because of her disappointment in Marcus. But most of all, she wept from guilt over having tried to deceive the one man for whom she had any great measure of respect, the man who was now offering her comfort when everyone else had abandoned her.

Dan held her close as she cried out her misery, his chin resting against the top of her head. His eyes were fixed on the portrait that stared down at them from high on the wall, reminding him of all the times he had longed to hold Lisette and could not because she was the wife of his best friend. He felt almost as though he were being unfaithful to her memory by standing here and holding her daughter in his arms. Would he never be free of her?

After a while, Gabrielle's tears began to subside, but Dan kept his arms around her, not wanting to let her go just yet. "Tell me the truth, little one," he said, gently stroking her hair as he held her securely against his chest. "What really happened today?"

The tenderness in his voice completely undid her resolution to keep the unpleasant truth from him, and, between hiccups and choked sobs, the entire story spilled out, from Grace's defection to the ugly scene with Marcus. Through it all, Dan said nothing, but when Gabrielle pulled away and ventured to glance up at him, the smoldering anger on his face made her feel utterly ashamed. "I'm sorry," she finally managed to get out. "I know I should have obeyed you."

He pressed a handkerchief into her hand. "I'm not angry with you," he said, the gruffness of his tone bewildering her. "There is one thing, though, that puzzles me." His look quelled any notice Gabrielle might have had of lying to him. "First you give me your clothes to take to the Apaches, and then you spend the day trying to get others to donate. I don't want to imply that you aren't capable of such generosity; I merely did not expect it from you. I'm surprised. And pleased."

Guilt sliced through Gabrielle. "Please don't say that," she admonished, her chin quivering as tears threatened anew. "I didn't do it to be generous. I mean, my clothing I wanted you to take. But the other—what I did today—I thought it was the only thing I could do to annoy you that you wouldn't be able to find fault with," she explained contritely as she wiped her eyes. "Because you had ordered me to stay in bed. But everything went wrong. Almost everyone behaved as though the Apaches weren't even people. I tried to tell them about little Datigé, but they wouldn't listen. And even the ones who didn't feel that way were worried about what Father would say if he returned and found out they had helped you. They didn't stop to think that Father might be wrong."

Dan's brows came together he studied her with an intensity that made her uneasy.

"I don't know why I keep doing things that make you ashamed of me," Gabrielle continued in a choked voice as she smoothed the wrinkles out of the tangerine dress and placed it with the others. "I just want you to see me as something other than a selfish child."

When Gabrielle finally drummed up the courage to look at him, she was surprised to see a tender smile of sympathy on his face. "I think, little one, you would be amazed at how many supposedly generous acts are, in reality, prompted by selfish motives. But you" he chuckled—"are the only person I know with the gall to admit it."

Relief surged through her. "Then you're not angry with me?"

"I told you I wasn't."

Her head reeling with a crazy mixture of happiness and confusion, Gabrielle threw her arms around him and surprised them both by blurting out against his chest, "Now I know why I love you so much!"

She felt his muscles tense and, feeling sheepish over what she had just done, lifted her head and smiled up at him through her tears, humor sparkling in her misty eyes. "I didn't say I *liked* you."

Dan smiled and his entire body shook with silent laughter. "I didn't think you had."

On impulse, Gabrielle rose up on tiptoe and locked her hands behind his neck; then tenderly, lovingly she brushed her lips against his. No response was forthcoming. Dan stood without moving, the expression in his amber-flecked eyes mysteriously guarded, but he did not to stop her. Encouraged by the lack of resistance, Gabrielle kissed him again, more boldly this time; teasing his lips with the tip of her tongue as she slid her fingers up through the dark soft hair at his nape. There was a warm tingling in the pit of her stomach and her heart thumped so wildly she was positive he could feel it, but if he did, he gave no sign. Not certain whether she was more humiliated or dismayed by her inability to provoke a reaction, Gabrielle slowly lowered her heels to the floor and then dropped her hands to her sides. "That's odd," she mused aloud, giving him a wounded look as she turned away. "I could have sworn it was better the last time."

Before she had taken two steps, he seized her arm and yanked her to him, crushing her against his chest as his arms went around her with such savage strength a cry came from her lips. Then his mouth came down on hers and moved back and forth with a hungry intensity that caused Gabrielle's blood to pound. Her knees turned to jelly as his tongue plunged boldly into her mouth, probing, searching, while his hands roamed possessively down her back to cup her buttocks and press her so close against the hard length of him until her feet nearly cleared the floor.

Gabrielle's head reeled, and wave after wave of pleasurable shock rippled through her as Dan's strong hands caressed her body with a knowing familiarity, awakening in her both a heated passion and a chilling fear of her uncontrollable reactions. Feeling sinfully greedy for wanting this moment to go on and on, Gabrielle wantonly pressed her body against his. She was caught up in the wonderful, awful thing he was doing to her, yet terrified. If he chose to take her now, there would be no stopping him. He was a hundred times stronger than she and a thousand times more practiced; without half trying, he had her completely under his control, helpless to do anything but tremble impotently as he aroused a fiery ache in her.

She gasped for air as his mouth left hers to caress her neck, his breath hot and moist against her skin.

"God, I want you," Dan murmured into her ear, teasing the lobe with his tongue.

Gabrielle's knees quivered and she could not suppress the molten tremors that tore through her.

He cupped her face in his hands as his lips traced a line down the bridge of her nose and then flickered across her eyelids before recapturing her mouth in another deep, lingering kiss. He did want her, more than he had ever wanted a woman, and that annoyed, rather than pleased, him. She was a child, an innocent, not some common trollop whom he could enjoy and then discard without a second thought. Yet she had gotten into his blood. Day and night, she haunted him. Hardly a moment went by when she did not cross his mind. He could not even try to sleep without her image forming the instant he closed his eyes. It was becoming increasingly difficult to remember that she was his ward and he was responsible for her.

Dan pulled back and gazed at Gabrielle's upturned face. Dark lashes rested against soft, sun-flushed cheeks still damp from tears not yet dried. She's so young, he thought as he studied her perfectly-shaped mouth, unable to disregard the years that separated them. So young, yet so beautiful. And dangerous. Unless he misread the signals Gabrielle was sending him, she was actively encouraging his advances. But why?

He planted a gentle kiss on one corner of her mouth, reveling in the sweet scent of her.

Only a short time ago, she had hated him.

He kissed the other corner of her mouth, then drew away, his brow creasing as a disturbing thought crossed his mind. Why now? After all these years . . .

Countering his withdrawal, Gabrielle pressed closer to him and lifted her mouth invitingly.

He stiffened, reacting instinctively to the suspicions that invaded his thoughts. Was Epperling putting her up to this? Were the two of them in it together? He knew the lieutenant hated him. And, until recently, so had Gabrielle. Perhaps she still hated him. If so, what was their plan? Was Gabrielle to seduce him, then scream *rape*, spelling certain death to his Army career? A sick feeling knotted in the pit of Dan's stomach. There was only one way to find out.

Slipping one arm beneath her knees, he swept her up into his arms.

Gabrielle's eyes flew open as he did so, and she threw her arms around his neck as her feet left the floor. She opened her mouth to ask him where he was taking her, but, before she could utter a single word, the answer struck her like a blow, rendering her speechless. He was taking her to his bedroom! Panic coursed through her, and only through sheer determination was she able to subdue it. This was what she wanted. This was what she had planned for. Once it was done, he would have no choice but to marry her.

And his career would be secure.

She closed her eyes and buried her face against his neck, unable to stop trembling as she fought the misgivings that churned in her mind while he carried her down the hall. She had to do it. For him.

Not for him, you goose! For yourself. Because you can't bear the thought of him marrying anyone else. In spite of the excuses of trying to save his career, Gabrielle knew she truly cared for Dan. She *loved* him. A tortured sob rose in her throat as she fought to deny the admission. But she couldn't. She loved him so much her heart ached, yet she didn't dare tell him. He would never believe her. She loved him! Why, oh why, had it taken so long for her to realize it? Things could have been different between them. She could have shown him kindness and respect instead of spite. She could have obeyed his orders instead of going out of her way to antagonize him. And she could have used the time while her father was away to bring them closer together. Now the month was nearly over. Her father would be home soon, Dan would return to his own quarters, and she would never see him again except in passing. He would never hold her again, or kiss her or play cards with her or listen to her silly stories. Time was running out. She *had* to go through with this. If she didn't, she would lose him for good.

Gabrielle was startled when Dan kicked the bedroom door shut, and for a split second stark terror was reflected in her eyes. As he lowered her to the bed, the urge to flee was so great she nearly screamed. When he settled beside her on the mattress and gathered her into his arms, she gritted her teeth and forced herself to be still. She was doing this because she loved him. *She loved him.*

Like a warm, sheltering cocoon, his arm folded around her and pulled her close against him, and when his mouth once again found hers, Gabrielle's fears slowly began to ebb. He kissed her gently at first, teasing her lips with firm, but tender, caresses that lulled her into a pleasant languor while they sparked an odd warmth between her thighs. Bedding with him might not be so bad, she decided, finally gathering up the courage to return his kisses timidly at first, then more boldly. She liked it when he touched her. She liked the feel of his mouth on hers and his hands—

His hands! Her heart leaped as she realized he was unbuttoning her dress. He had seen her naked before, she nervously reminded herself as his long tanned fingers moved deftly down the length of her rib cage, slipping each tiny pearl button through its respective hole, then peeling back the halves of her bodice to expose her throat and the swells of her breast the top of her thin chemise revealed.

A chill went through Gabrielle as his kiss deepened, smothering any protest she might have made, and when his hand moved up over her breast, cupping its softness and molding it to his palm, her head reeled and an unfamiliar tingling swept over her. As her emotions crashed back and forth between fear to desire, her body reacted of its own accord, her back arching until she was pressing hungrily against his hand. In response, he pulled down the top of her chemise, baring her breasts, his strong fingers teasing her sensitive nipples until they were emboldened by his touch. Powerless to escape the dizzying effect his caresses had on her, Gabrielle finally gave up trying, and the instant she relaxed, the sensations became even more pronounced, then built rapidly until she was rocked by a violent tremor that exploded into a million white lights behind her closed eyes, and a startled cry tore from her lips.

No sooner had the first explosion begun to subside than she felt him guiding her toward yet another, and she moaned helplessly, terrified of the uncontrollable reactions he was so expertly coaxing from her, yet even more frightened that his caresses would stop. She had never, even in her wildest dreams, imagined that lovemaking could be so pleasurable. Or so overwhelming.

"So, you like that, do you?" Dan murmured into her ear just before his mouth began to forge a molten trail down her neck, a harsh raspiness to his voice because of the sheer effort it took to keep his own burgeoning desires under strict control.

Half-delirious, Gabrielle nodded.

He frowned. "Do you like this?" He brushed his lips across the naked ivory flesh of her soft full breast, planting scores of feather-light kisses just where he knew they would create the most pleasurable torment.

Gabrielle sucked in her breath and ground the back of her head into the pillow. "Yes . . ."

"And this?"

Her body leaped reflexively as he teased the rosy tip of one soft full breast with his tongue, and she was unaware that he was studying her reaction with a cold, clinical intensity.

When drew her dress down over her shoulders, she unwittingly aided him by pulling her arms free of the sleeves. She did not protest when he found the pink ribbon lacing her chemise and gave it a hearty tug that loosed the bow, letting it slide unobstructed through the embroidered eyelets, so he suddenly asked, "Shall I stop?"

Gabrielle flung her head back and forth on the pillow, the absurdity of his question escaping her. "Please . . ."

His hands were warm and rough against her bare skin. "Please what? What do you want me to do?"

"I-I don't know. . . ."

He eased the chemise off her shoulders.

"Do you want me to make love to you?" he asked quietly, still fondling her breast.

"N-no . . . yes . . ." She couldn't think.

Fury flashed in his amber-flecked eyes, but he kept his voice low and steady. "And then what, little one?" His moved sensuously over her bare flesh. "Do I go to the gallows for raping the colonel's daughter? Is that what you and Epperling plan for me?"

A paralyzing fear slowly invaded Gabrielle's passion-dazed senses as she realized what he was saying. What did Marcus have to do with this? Her eyes flew open, but before she could look at him, Dan shifted his weight so that she was pinned beneath him and his mouth descended over hers in a kiss that was punishing and angry. For the first time in her life, Gabrielle was truly afraid of him. Blood pounded furiously in her ears as she placed her palms against his chest and pushed hard, tearing her mouth from his at the same time. "Please . . . stop! You're hurting me!"

He seized her wrists and forced her hands over her head, pinning them to the mattress, and wedged his knee between her thighs. "What's wrong, Gabrielle?" he taunted, anger glinting in his eyes. "Isn't this what you wanted? For me to force myself on you so that you and your baby-faced lieutenant could complain to your father that I had robbed you of your innocence? Isn't this why you've been prancing around here in your nightgown half the time, playing the part of the devoted courtesan? Teasing me and trying to trick me into forgetting I am responsible for your welfare?"

"No!" She tried to wrench her arms free, but his fingers tightened around her wrists with bone-crushing force, bringing tears of pain to her eyes.

"Deny it, Gabrielle. Deny that you have been trying to seduce me."

A sob broke in her throat, "I c-can't."

His nostrils flared. "Damn you!"

"Please . . ."

His face descended on hers.

Gabrielle twisted her head away, dodging his mouth, "I can explain. . . ."

He released her wrists and knotted his hands in her hair, forcing her head back.

She opened her mouth to scream, but his mouth closed over hers, smothering her outcry. Consumed by fear, she fought back with all the desperation of a cornered animal, but the more she struggled, the more demanding he became, and more brutal. There was no gentleness to his touch now. His angry kisses bruised her lips, and her ribs ached from the force of the weight bearing down on her. Gabrielle's mind whirled and tears scalded her cheeks. She had to explain. She had to make him understand. She had to—

Suddenly, he released her. "I'll give you five minutes to get your things together," he said harshly as he rolled from the bed onto his feet. "You'll be staying with the Wilcoxes until your father returns." Pivoting on one foot, he stalked toward the door.

Gabrielle struggled to sit up, her breath coming in huge ragged gulps. "I did it because I love you!" she blurted out to his retreating back, sobbing and trying to cover herself.

He came to an abrupt halt in the doorway and turned back toward her, his eyes narrowing with surprise and suspicion. "What did you say?"

Her chin dropped to her chest and her slender shoulders moved with wrenching jerks. "I love you," she repeated, pulling her bodice over her breasts, too ashamed to look at him. Hot tears ran down her chin and spilled onto her hands. "I love . . . you."

"Then why did you set me up?"

"I didn't—"

"Don't lie to me! You set out to destroy my career!"

She shook her head vehemently. "No!"

"And just what do you think would have happened when your father returned to discover I had bedded his daughter? I sure as hell wouldn't have been promoted!'"

He came toward her, and, in panic, Gabrielle scrambled across the bed, coming to her feet on the opposite side. "I-I was trying to help," she implored, backing away until she bumped into the wall.

Dan stopped, annoyed by her retreat and by the fear in her eyes. "Oh? And just how did you plan to accomplish that?"

Fresh tears coursed down her cheeks. "By making you marry me," she said. Miserable now, she clutched the dress to her bosom, and when he did not respond, she continued in a halting, tear-choked voice. "I didn't want you to go to jail because you let . . . the Apaches come here. I thought . . . if you m-married me . . . Father would get the charges dropped and—"

"Gabrielle, there are no charges!"

"But, there will be!"

"You don't know that. And even if there were, what in blazes makes you think your father would come to my defense if I were married to you? He doesn't support my position with the Apaches. He never has."

"He would for the same reason he went on this trip to San Francisco." She was desperately trying to make him believe her. "He only went to Division so he could influence the promotion board. And if you m-married me—"

"If I married you, the scandal alone would destroy your father's career, not to mention his chances for promotion."

"No, it wouldn't. Don't you see? There wouldn't be any scandal if you married me. Father would do anything in his power to get this promotion, even if it means going against his beliefs and getting any charges against you dropped so that his name isn't sullied."

"Gabrielle, if I married you solely to get myself off the hook, I would be using both you and Stephen. I can't do that."

"But, I *want* you to!"

"And your father?"

"He uses you. He didn't think twice about dumping me on you when he decided to go to Division. I know you didn't want the responsibility of looking out for me. I heard you."

"You what?"

"I was listening at the door when you were in the study with Father. I heard you say you had better things to do with your time than play nursemaid to a spoiled brat. And you said I didn't have enough sense to fit on the sharp end of a cactus spine." Gabrielle hesitated. "That was why I went out of my way to aggravate you," she explained, hoping he wouldn't be too angry with her. "I was trying to pay you back for the things you said. But then . . . then everything changed. Sometimes you acted as though you were really concerned for me. When I got hurt you took care of me, and you didn't punish me for running away, even though I deserved it. And then, I . . . I started thinking about all the times you were there for me when no one else was and—I know you don't love me, but sometimes I think we're almost friends and if you liked me . . . even just a little—"

"First of all, young lady, there have been no charges filed against me, and—"

"But, what if there are? I don't want you to go to jail, and if you marry me, Father will have to help you. Please . . . believe me. I didn't do it to hurt you. Honest, I didn't."

The muscles in Dan's jaw knotted. Of all the crazy things Gabrielle had ever done, this one had to be the most insane. He took a deep breath and struggled to get a grip on his anger. Then he began slowly, deliberately "Did it ever occur to you, little one, that I would be far more likely to receive a jail sentence for bedding you than for bringing the Apaches here?"

She flinched. "I only wanted to help."

His face darkened. "If I had wanted your help, damn it, I would have asked for it!"

"But—"

"You're to stay in this house until I get back. I'll deal with you later."

Without another word, Dan turned and stormed from the room.

Feeling miserable, Gabrielle flinched when she heard the front door slam, then dropped her face into her hands and burst into tears.

*   *   *

"One thing is certain; we can't keep feeding them," Lieutenant Johnson insisted. "We don't have enough rations to get us through the next four weeks as it is. If more Apaches come here seeking asylum, we are going to have to turn them away."

Bandy shook his head. "I already told you, Dan won't—"

Marcus interrupted him, his eyes like bits of hard blue ice in his tanned face. "The colonel doesn't want them here. Department doesn't want them here. The people of this county don't want them here. Major Catlin is only one man. Sooner or later, he's going to have to give in."

Captain Wilcox nodded, his expression glum. "Normally, I would side with Dan, but, like Johnson, I have a wife to think of. And now, a child on the way. After what happened to-day—"

The surgeon broke off as the door swung open and Dan entered the Headquarters Building, his brow furrowed and his face dark with silent fury.

Dan stopped short and suspicion flickered in his eyes as he glanced at the gathering of officers. Then his gaze came to rest on Epperling. Even though he had been unable to prove it, he had suspected the lieutenant had been the one responsible for bringing the reporter from the *Miner* to the camp. But now, with his officers staring at him with guilt-ridden faces, he found them all suspect. Even Moreland, and that pained him greatly.

"Something wrong?" Dan asked, lifting a quizzical brow as he pushed the door shut.

Bandy handed him a folded paper. "A messenger brought this from Tucson while you was out at Edward's ranch. There's been trouble up at the Ciénega. A stagecoach ambushed. One of the drivers and a passenger killed. The governor's got his feathers ruffled over this one, Dan. Wants to know what you're gonna do about it."

Dan's face was expressionless as he scanned the dispatch. Ciénega Pass was nearly sixty miles away, and it was unlikely that any of the Apaches quartered near Camp Carleton were responsible for the attack. But Governor Safford apparently felt otherwise. "When does he want a reply?"

237

"Immediately," Bandy said. "His messenger's in the mess hall now, but he's gotta hit the road before the storm breaks or he'll never get across the wash."

Dan tossed the paper onto his desk. "Lieutenant Epperling, I want half your men posted at the stage stop east of the pass, the other half at Dripping Springs—for the sole purpose of escorting travelers through the mountains."

Marcus bristled. "My men just returned from Camp Grant—"

"Moreland will relieve you at the end of two weeks," Dan said tersely, cutting short Epperling's protest. He looked at the quartermaster officer. "How are we fixed on rations?"

Lieutenant Johnson shook his head. "The supply train is more than a month overdue. We've got enough beans and flour to last us till the end of June. Coffee's almost gone though, and I had to destroy what was left of the salt pork. It was so rancid, the dogs wouldn't eat it. Got plenty of sugar and molasses, both. Tried to work out a swap at the trading post for some canned vegetables and dried fruit, but Sully's got a good thing going with that store and he wasn't too keen on the idea. A couple more weeks, sir, and we're going to be up the proverbial creek without a paddle."

I did it because I love you. Gabrielle's voice encroached on Dan's thoughts and he had to force it from his mind. Damn her! Why couldn't she just leave him alone?

The other officers exchanged glances, and suddenly Dan realized that they were waiting for him. "We'll give them another week," he said flatly, breaking the awkward silence. "If the supplies aren't in by then, we'll change contractors."

Lieutenant Johnson looked relieved. "We could go with Parson's sir. Department will have a fit because their rates are higher than we've been paying, but I've heard they're reliable."

"There is another solution," Marcus interjected, his voice taut. "We can stop feeding that damned bunch of renegade Indians. Send them back to Camp Grant where they belong, and let Whitman take care of them. He's the one who offered them asylum in the first place."

"Dan, he's right," Ben Wilcox said apologetically. "I know you mean well, but the truth is . . . not only is it becoming outrageously costly to keep them here, their presence is endangering the lives of everyone on this post. Sooner or later, we're going to be facing the same kind of trouble Whitman had down at Camp Grant."

Going to the window, Dan stared glumly out at the roiling clouds and swirling dust. Once again, Gabrielle's voice intruded. *I didn't do it to hurt you. I only wanted to help. Please believe me. I love you.* "What about you, Moreland?" he asked over his shoulder. "Where do you stand?"

"You know I'd back you up one hundred percent, whatever you decided."

Something knotted inside Dan, but he did not turn to look at his friend. "That's not what I asked you."

Bandy's expression was unreadable. "I know how you feel about this, Danny . . . but the truth is, this time I gotta side with the others. Wilcox is right. The longer we keep 'em here, the greater the danger."

I love you. I love you. I love you. . . .

Dan sucked in his breath. "Epperling, have your men ready to move out in the morning. And before you go, I want you to prepare the paperwork necessary for recommending LaSalle for a promotion."

Marcus snickered inelegantly. "What in the hell has that no-account done to deserve—"

"Do it or I will," Dan said sharply, turning away from the window, his eyes blazing. "And if I have to do it, I will also prepare a recommendation for your dismissal. Is that clear?"

The other officers present exchanged glances, and Marcus shifted uneasily. "Yes, sir."

"You're all dismissed."

Bandy lingered behind after the others had gone. "Mind tellin' me what's eatin' at you?"

"Nothing," Dan said curtly. Going to his desk, he yanked open the drawer and removed a sheet of paper. "Find the governor's messenger and tell him I'll have a response ready in ten minutes."

Bandy thoughtfully rubbed one hand over his whiskery chin. "Listen, Dan—"

"I gave you an order, *Captain*."

"Don't you go pullin' rank on me, Danny. You're talkin' to Wilbur Moreland. Your old buddy. Remember?"

Dan slammed the drawer shut, but said nothing.

Bandy took a deep breath and tried again, "Just 'cause we don't see eye to eye on somethin' don't mean—"

"Forget it."

"No, I ain't gonna forget it! We go back a long way. I wouldn't even be here today if you hadn't looked out for me all them years I was too little to fight my own battles. You and me, we're like brothers. If something's troublin' you, I want to help."

Dan's lips thinned with anger. "Then why didn't you support me? I'd thought if anyone would understand how I felt about letting the Apaches stay here, you would."

"I told you I'd back you up."

"That's not the same thing, and you damn well know it." Dan shook his head, disgust hardening his already severe expression. "There is only one person on this entire post who believes in what I'm trying to do. Only one. And it's not even my best friend, but some seventeen-year-old brat who . . ." His voice trailed off. "Just forget it," he said instead.

There was a knowing look in Bandy's sharp blue eyes. "So that's what's got you so fired up. It's got nothin' to do with them Apaches. It's *her*, ain't it?"

"No."

"What happened? You get into another squabble or somethin'?"

"No."

"She do somethin' to piss you off? Talk back to you? Turn all your underdrawers wrong side out? Refuse to drink that godawful milk you been crammin' down her throat?"

"No!"

"Then what? For cryin' out loud! Whatever it is, you gotta talk about it instead of keepin' it all bottled up inside you!"

"All right, damn it! I'm in love with her! Are you satisfied?"

Bandy chuckled. "Shee-it! I coulda told you that!"

Sinking down in his chair, Dan propped one elbow on the desk and wearily rubbed a hand over his face. "I want to marry her. I want her to be my wife."

"So, what's stoppin' you?"

"For chrissake, Moreland! She's young enough to be my daughter!"

Bandy's expression became pensive. "Your daughter by whom? The colonel's old lady?"

Dan's eyes riveted on his friend's face, and his heart thundered against his ribs. "And just what in the hell do you mean by that?"

"You tell me."

"I swear to you, there was never anything between Lisette DuBois and me! Yes, I loved her. And if you had known her, you would have loved her too."

"Well, I never met the lady. But I seen her picture, and I can't help wonderin' if when you look at the girl, it's her ma you're seein' instead."

Dan crumpled the paper into a ball and hurled it across the room. "I'm beginning to wish I'd never told you about Lisette," he declared, his voice harsh with barely controlled anger.

"How does the little girl feel about all this?" Bandy asked, ignoring Dan's display of temper. "Does she love you?"

Though Dan said nothing, he could not help remembering the blatant overtures Gabrielle had made. Or how she'd felt in his arms. Even now, just thinking of the way she had pressed her body against his made his loins tighten. She'd said she loved him. But only last week she had been in love with Epperling. Hell, what did she know of love? She was just a child!

A child with whom he was thoroughly, insanely, obsessed . . .

I did it because I love you.

Damn! Dan silently upbraided himself. He would never forget the terrified look in her eyes when he had become rough with her. What had begun as something warm and beautiful had turned ugly because he had cruelly, deliberately driven a wedge between them. He had hurt her because that had been easier than acknowledging his love for her.

I love you.

"I'll be back later," he said abruptly, and started toward the door.

"What about the messenger?"

"You handle him. There's something I have to do."

Before Dan was halfway across the parade ground, a lone rider entered the quadrangle at breakneck speed and headed straight for him. It was Cy Harmon, Bryce Edwards' foreman. "You Major Catlin?" he called out, reining in his lathered mount.

"I am."

"Mr. Edwards wants you to come quick. There's been trouble over at the Rocking P."

In the darkened parlor, Gabrielle sat in a chair by the rain-lashed window, her bare feet tucked up beneath her, staring unseeing out into the stormy night. Lightning streaked across the sky, illuminating the room and making her nightgown glow with an eerie blue white light, and she flinched at the explosive crack of thunder that followed almost immediately. It was not the storm that frightened her, but being in the house alone. The clock in the hall had struck eleven only minutes before and still Dan had not returned. Gabrielle swallowed hard. It was all her fault. If she hadn't made a fool of herself by trying to seduce him, he would never have left. She had no idea where he could be; the lights in the Headquarters Building had been extinguished hours ago, but he hadn't come home for supper. She thought of Ruby Collins and the girls at the brothel, and stinging tears welled in her eyes. *It isn't possible!* she told herself, denying what she suddenly feared most.

But it *was* possible. And if that was where he was, she had driven him there. She had teased him and flaunted herself until he could stand it no more. And now he hated her.

A single tear slid down Gabrielle's cheek, and she took an angry swipe at it. She couldn't blame him for hating her. She hated herself.

242

"Please, come home," she begged, but her plea was lost in the rumble of thunder. She dragged her sleeve across her eyes. "I'll never do it again. I promise. Please . . . just come home."

It was nearly dawn before Dan returned to the house, his muscles aching and his uniform soaked through and reeking of woodsmoke. He washed at the pump and donned dry clothes, then went to Gabrielle's room to check on her before turning in. Ever since the night he had entered her bedroom only to find her gone, he had not been able to rest until he had assured himself that she was safely in her bed.

The muffled sounds of hiccups reached him as he pushed open her door to find her curled into a ball in the middle of her bed. He realized she had cried herself to sleep and something inside him twisted. Damn it! Why did he have to hurt her? As her body jerked with yet another convulsive hiccup, Dan swallowed hard and wished fervently that he could go back and undo the pain he had caused her. Crossing the room, he bent down and grasped her shoulder. "Gabrielle."

She came up with a start, her long hair spilling about her, and in the twilight, he could see that her face was swollen from crying. Her hiccups had stopped.

"It's all right," he said quietly, sliding into the bed beside her and drawing her into his arms. "It's just me."

Gabrielle's first conscious thought was that she would be ruined if someone found them in bed together. But the second was that he had finally come home. To her. "I'm sorry," she mumbled as she settled into the crook of his arm and rested her head against the warm, comforting wall of his chest, so thankful to have him back that she didn't care what anyone thought of their flagrant disregard of propriety. "I won't do it again. I promise."

His arms tightened around her, and she could feel his heart beating against her cheek. "Go back to sleep, little one," he said softly, stroking her hair. "It'll be morning soon, I just want to sit here awhile and hold you."

"You're not angry with me anymore?" she asked.

"I'm not angry."

Her eyelids drooped and she relaxed a little, comforted by the steady beating of his heart against her cheek. "I

243

love . . . you," she murmured sleepily against his shirtfront. Within minutes, her breathing changed and Dan knew she had fallen asleep.

He brushed his lips against the top of her head. His own troubled thoughts making sleep the furthest thing from his mind, he said to himself, I love you, too, little one. More than you'll ever know.

Chapter Eleven

It was midmorning when Gabrielle finally rubbed the sleep from her eyes. She stretched out indulgently on the long bed, a warm blush staining her cheeks as her thoughts turned to the previous night, and when she closed her eyes, she could almost feel Dan's strong arms around her. She wrapped her own arms around herself and squeezed tightly, a tiny squeal of delight bursting from her lips. He loved her; she just knew it! He had not said as much, of course, but he had come home, to her, and had held her in his arms until morning broke. He wouldn't have done that unless he loved her. Dan is going to marry me, Gabrielle decided, an impish smile touching her lips. He simply doesn't know it yet.

Kicking back the sheet, she dropped her feet over the side of the bed and stood up. "Oooh!" she muttered aloud. Clinging to the edge of the mattress with one hand, she pressed the other side to her aching temple. Lying awake and crying for half the night had left her feeling as heavy-headed and dizzy as she had when Lieutenant Dalton had given her champagne. At least this time she wouldn't have to suffer a dose of that nasty rattlesnake piss.

Gabrielle did not so easily accept the next unpleasant surprise to hit her. She recoiled in shock at see her reflection in the dressing-table mirror. Appalled by the swollen, red-rimmed eyes that stared back at her, she reached up to gingerly touch one puffy eyelid before letting out a horrified shriek.

Seconds later, Corporal Bates appeared in the doorway. "You

all right, Miss Gabrielle?"

"Don't look at me!" she blurted out, whirling away from him and covering her face with her hands. "Go get Grace. Now!" When he'd left she ventured another punishing peek in the mirror. She looked positively hideous! Even her nose was swollen and misshapen. Major Catlin would never marry her now. He wouldn't even want to be seen with her. She couldn't woo him looking like this. She had to do something, fast—before he came home.

Dumping water into the washbasin, Gabrielle splashed it onto her face, praying all the while that the swelling would hurry up and go away. If the major—Dan—walked in and saw her like this, she would surely die. "Oh, Grace," she moaned, sputtering as water went up her nose. "Please hurry!"

After what seemed an eternity, Grace finally appeared. "It's a sea of mud out there this morning," she commented as she removed her shoes by the front door. "Do you know it rained all night? The wash overflowed its banks and—"

"Forget that," Gabrielle admonished, grabbing her by the hand and pulling her into the bedroom. "You have to help me!"

"Gabrielle, what's—"

"Look!"

Grace's eyes widened as she stared in mute surprised at her friend's tear-ravaged face. Then she expelled her breath in a ragged gasp. "Oh, my word!"

"Don't just stand there!" Gabrielle wailed. She felt that her world had been turned upside down. "Do something! I splashed cold water on my face and I still look like a fat lady at the circus! You have to help me, Grace, before he sees me like this!"

"Well, there's no chance of that," the other girl said dryly. "Lieutenant Epperling moved out early this morning. Really, Gabrielle, I don't understand why you keep pining for him. I know he's handsome, but looks aren't everything. Personally, I think he is the most arrogant man I have ever known. And he treats you shamefully."

"I'm not talking about—" Gabrielle broke off abruptly upon realizing with a start that she could not very well tell Grace she had meant Dan Catlin. Grace was in love with him! She hastily changed what she had been about to say. "Marcus . . . left?"

"All of B Company did. A stagecoach was attacked at Ciénega Pass, so they have to patrol the area. And that's not all. Wilbur—I mean Captain Moreland—told me that Mr. Edwards' stables were torched last night and one of his hired hands was shot. Major Catlin spent most of the night over there, helping put out the fire and conducting an investigation. They think the fire might have been set by Indians, because they found moccasin prints behind the house before the rain washed everything away."

Gabrielle felt her face grow hot. And she had thought he had been at Ruby's place. "Where's Major Catlin now?" she asked, careful to keep her expression neutral.

"At Headquarters— Oh, Gabrielle! You didn't get into another squabble with him, did you? He's such a good man and Wil—Captain Moreland says he has a terrible burden on his shoulders right now, especially with—"

"Grace, please! There's no time for that. You must help me repair my face. Good heavens! I look . . . I look abominable!"

Grace shot her a disapproving glance. "Gabrielle DuBois, sometimes you can be so exasperating! Don't you ever think of anyone but yourself?"

Gabrielle gave her a sheepish grin. "Not if I can help it."

When Grace shook her head and went to the door to summon Corporal Bates, Gabrielle breathed a sigh of relief. She had managed to fool Grace into believing that she hadn't the slightest interest in anything concerning Dan Catlin—at least for now.

Bates swore aloud when Grace told him what she wanted, and even Gabrielle began to feel a little uneasy about what the other girl had in mind. "Mud?" she asked, incredulous.

Grace gave her an enigmatic half-smile. "And cucumbers."

Gabrielle grimaced. "Are you certain this will work?"

"Positive. First, we'll have to pin your hair up—don't you have a housecap? No matter. We'll just have to be careful not to get the mud in your hair, although I have heard that the Apaches use mud plasters to get rid of lice."

"Grace Simmons, you get even a speck of mud in my hair

and I swear I'll never speak to you again!"

"Sit down," Grace commanded, and pointed toward the dressing table, displaying an authority Gabrielle was not accustomed to encountering in her.

Gabrielle obeyed without question, too bewildered to protest. There was something odd about Grace that morning. She seemed more confident than usual. Gabrielle studied her friend closely in the mirror as Grace began pinning up her hair. There was a glow to Grace's normally pallid cheeks, a sparkle in her eyes. She was almost . . . pretty! Guilt stabbed Gabrielle. Grace Simmons was pretty because she was in love. Gabrielle shifted nervously on the seat. She wanted so much to be able to share with Grace the news that she, too, was in love, with Dan Catlin; but she couldn't. It would break Grace's heart. "Did you . . . did you see the major this morning?" she asked, and then cringed inwardly when Grace blushed and appeared to be fighting an involuntary smile.

"I did," Grace said, annoying Gabrielle by not disclosing anything more.

"You said he was at Edwards' place all night," she prompted, trying hard to keep her own blush under control. "I imagine he was exhausted."

"Actually, he was more furious than tired. Mr. Sully just got in the latest edition of the *Miner* down at the trading post, and there was this big article, right on the front page, about—"

"This what you wanted?" Corporal Bates called out from the doorway. He held a bowl of mud in one hand and a bowl of peeled and sliced cucumbers in the other. On his face was a dubious expression.

"That will do quite nicely," Grace replied, taking both bowls from him and setting them on the dressing table.

Corporal Bates hovered in the doorway. "What are you gonna do with that slop?" he asked and Gabrielle, realizing that she was still in her nightgown, glared scathingly at his reflection in the mirror.

"Don't you have something to do?"

"Naw . . . just finish heatin' up some water so the major can take a bath and shave later is all."

"You'd better leave," Grace advised with a smile. "She's

been known to throw things."

"I'm going. I'm going!" the soldier said, and to Gabrielle's chagrin, she could hear him chuckling as he retreated down the hall.

"Impertinent clod," she muttered peevishly, then reached for a slice of cucumber.

Grace smacked her hand, causing her to utter a yelp of surprise and drop the cucumber before it could reach her mouth. "That's not to eat, so put it back," the older girl ordered sternly.

"You're a regular tyrant this morning," Gabrielle complained but she obediently placed her hands on her lap, although her expression was anything but submissive.

Grace smiled again, but said nothing.

Gabrielle forced herself to assume a posture of demure acquiescence. "Now, tell me what you were going to say about Major Catlin before we were so rudely interrupted."

Something flickered in Grace's eyes. "You're awfully inquisitive about the major this morning. I didn't think you were that interested in what he did."

Gabrielle's chin inched upward. "I'm not. I'm simply trying to determine what kind of a temper he is going to be in when he comes home. Sometimes," she added with an exaggerated note of jadedness, "he can be as testy as a bear."

"Well, if I were you, I'd steer clear of him, at least until all the ruckus surrounding the article in the *Miner* dies down." Grace took her by the arm and propelled her toward the bed. "You'd better lie down while I'm doing this or else it's liable to drip all over your nightgown. And here, put this towel under your head so it doesn't get on your pillowcase."

"Are you absolutely certain this is going to make the swelling go away?"

"Most of it."

Giving her friend a skeptical glance, Gabrielle followed the instructions and lay down and closed her eyes. Her breath caught as Grace placed an icy-cool cucumber slice over each eye.

"Keep your eyes closed," Grace warned.

"Do I have any other choice?" Gabrielle retorted, wriggling

249

her nose when it suddenly began to itch.

Grace frowned. "If you have to scratch, do it now."

For the next five minutes, Gabrielle lay rigid and unmoving while Grace smeared mud over her face except for the area around her eyes, which was hidden by the cucumbers. "How long do I have to keep this muck on?" she asked, wriggling her nose again as the mud drew her skin taut.

"Don't do that!" Grace chided. "You have to keep real still so the mud can dry without cracking."

"It itches."

Pressing her lips together in a frown of annoyance, Grace removed the cucumber slices from Gabrielle's eyes and replaced them with two fresh, cool ones. "Behave yourself," she hissed.

Then, both girls jumped as the front door banged shut and Dan's voice boomed throughout the house. "Gabrielle!"

"Jeezus!" The oath burst from Gabrielle's lips before she could stop it. "Don't let him see me!" She leaped from the bed and grabbed a towel.

Gabrielle, don't! It's not dry yet!"

But Gabrielle already had a good portion of the mud wiped away. "Grace, you have to help me get this off! I can't let him see me like this!"

"I thought you wanted the swelling to go away!"

Gabrielle ran to the washbasin. "I need more water!"

Dan's footsteps reverberated down the hall, drawing closer.

Grace bent down to pick up the cucumber slices from the floor where they had fallen. "Gabrielle, I don't know what's gotten into—"

"Hurry, please!" Gabrielle gave the other girl a shove in the direction of the door, nearly sending her sprawling; then she slammed the bedroom door shut after her.

"Whoa!" Dan ordered, catching Grace by the shoulder as she barreled head first against his broad chest.

They both heard the key turn in the lock.

Dan held Grace away from him and impaled her with a piercing glare. "What is going on in there?"

Grace's heart thumped mercilessly. "N-Nothing."

"Hurry up with the water!" Gabrielle pleaded anxiously

from the other side of the door, her words muffled by the towel she was holding over her face.

His patience waning, Dan lifted an inquiring brow.

Grace nervously moistened her lips. "I have to get more water for her . . . washbasin."

Dan jerked his head over his shoulder, uncertain as to whether he was more annoyed by the Simmons girl's peculiar behavior or his own mounting dread of the new scheme Gabrielle was hatching. "You may leave now."

"But, the water—"

"Go!"

Grace did not need to be told again, and when she had gone Dan rapped impatiently on the bedroom door. "Open up," he ordered.

Dead silence.

"Gabrielle, I'm not in any mood for your games. Open this door. Now!"

"I can't," she responded in a small voice.

In spite of the lack of sleep and his already strained patience, Dan felt his anger slipping away from him. A smile tugged at the corners of his mouth as he leaned against the doorjamb and folded his arms across his chest. "I'll give you to the count of three, then I'm going to kick this door down if you haven't opened it. One . . ."

He heard a sharp intake of breath from the other side. "You can't come in here!"

"Two . . ."

"I—I'm getting dressed!"

"Three."

Dan made no attempt to move from his leisurely position against the doorframe, but he nearly burst out laughing when a muttered oath was followed by scurrying footsteps.

Her heart in her throat, Gabrielle unlocked the bedroom door and eased it open a bit.

Dan waited, his face aching from the strain of maintaining a serious expression.

Gabrielle inched the door open a shade more and peeked sheepishly through the crack. "I really am getting dressed," she said in a hoarse whisper.

One corner of Dan's mouth twitched as he gazed down into the single beautiful green eye peering up at him. "Open the door," he siad sternly.

Her shoulders sagging in concession, Gabrielle sighed and opened the door.

Dan jerked upright, surprise registering on his face.

Gabrielle stood before him, exasperated and defeated, her arms hanging at her sides, her hair pinned in a lopsided mass atop her head. Dan swore silently. Mud streaked her face and stained the front of her once-white gown.

His mouth twitched and a low chuckle rose in his throat.

Gabrielle knotted her hands, wishing they were around his neck and glared at him. "If you laugh, I'm going to punch you in the nose," she declared through clenched teeth.

Dan's eyes narrowed in solemn concentration, and he extended a forefinger to lightly touch the curve of her cheekbone. "You missed a spot."

"You!" She lunged at him, fists flying, and Dan burst into hearty laughter as he ducked to avoid the blow aimed at his head.

"Pipe down!" he commanded, still laughing as he caught hold of her wrists.

Stung by his laughter, Gabrielle retaliated by kicking him in the shins. "Don't tell me to pipe down!" she screamed, and jerking her hands free, she backed away from him. "I told you not to come in here," she said, trying to wipe some of the remaining mud off her face with her fingertips. "And I'll thank you not to laugh at me!"

Sensing that she was more embarrassed than angry, Dan immediately attempted to curb his mirth, but there was no hiding the merriment that danced in his eyes. Even with her hair askew and her face caked with clay, Gabrielle was still the most beautiful thing he had ever beheld. "You're never going to get all the mud off that way," he said decisively.

She gave him a ferocious scowl and dragged her sleeve across her brow. "Perhaps you have a better idea?"

"Of course."

"Then what would you—" She broke off and let out a squeal of panic as he closed the gap between them in a single stride and, ramming one arm behind her knees, swung her up into his arms. "Put me down!"

"In good time, little one. All in good time." He eyes gleaming with amusement, he turned on one heel and strode from the room. "Corporal Bates! You got that bathwater ready?" he shouted down the hall.

Gabrielle stiffened and her heart somersaulted. 'No!"

Corporal Bates came running as fast as his limp would allow. "Yes sir! The tub's all—" The striker broke off and his mouth dropped open when he saw Gabrielle, her face streaked with the very same mud he had collected from outside the kitchen door, kicking and protesting loudly as Major Catlin carried her down the hall. To top it all off, the major was laughing!

"Coming through," Dan announced, and Corporal Bates, still gaping, hurriedly backed out of the way.

"Put me down right this minute!" Gabrielle demanded hotly. She again tried to squirm out of Dan's arms, but he merely tightened his hold on her and kicked the kitchen door open.

Sitting on the floor in the middle of the kitchen was the copper tub, filled with steaming water.

Managing to wedge one elbow between herself and his chest, Gabrielle pushed hard, causing Dan to expel his breath in a loud grunt. "I told you to put me down!" she commanded.

He did.

Water surged up over the sides of the tub and onto the kitchen floor as Dan unceremoniously plunged Gabrielle, nightgown and all, into the bath that had been awaiting him.

"Arghhh!" she shrieked and started to rise, but he placed one hand firmly on top her head and shoved her beneath the water.

Hands, feet, and water flew everywhere.

Then Gabrielle came up sputtering, water streaming from her hair and down over her face. "I hate . . . ugh . . . you!" When she got out of the tub, she was going to kill him!

Chuckling, Dan pushed a washcloth into her hand. "You'll pay for this," Gabrielle threatened as she wiped water from her eyes.

Hunkering down beside the tub, Dan picked up the bar of

soap and held it out to her. "You'll need this."

Gabrielle's nostrils flared as she glowered at him, and it was all she could do not to rise up out of the tub and scratch his blasted eyes out! Her fingers tightened around the sopping washcloth, and she hurled it at him.

The cloth struck Dan across the face with a wet *plop!*

Realizing what she had done, Gabrielle clamped one hand over her mouth to stifle a giggle.

There was a menacing twist to the set of Dan's mouth as he took the washcloth and, with agonizing deliberation, held it over the tub and dropped it back into the water.

Laughter danced in Gabrielle's eyes as she shrank away from him, then shrieked as he lurched toward her, seizing her by the arms and hauling her halfway out of the water. But before she could utter a single word of protest, his mouth descended over hers in a hungry, passionate kiss that left her moaning and clinging to him.

His hands moved down her back to cup her buttocks, lifting her even further out of the water, and through her wetly clinging nightgown, she felt his strong fingers knead her flesh in a way that caused wave after wave of delicious heat to ripple through her.

And five minutes later, when Corporal Bates finally summoned the courage to peek into the kitchen, he found Miss Gabrielle, half-in and half-out of the tub he had filled for Major Catlin. Her wet nightgown molded provocatively to her body, she was locked in an embrace with the major—one that would have made even Ruby Collins blush. Chuckling to himself, Bates quickly eased the kitchen door shut and then limped down the hall.

Dan was the first to break the spell that had settled over them. "If I don't stop now, little one, I won't be able to stop at all," he murmured huskily against her soft throat as he eased her back down into the tub, unable to resist a smile as undisguised disappointment flickered across Gabrielle's face when he released her.

He loves me, she thought as her arms slid from around his neck, and the glowing warmth his kisses had sparked deep down inside her flared and grew. Whether Dan admitted it or not, she had his love. This wonderful, strong, handsome man had just made her the luckiest woman alive. She was happy. Happier than she had ever been in her entire life.

Then, without warning, Dan stood up to leave. "We need to have a talk," he said, his expression so solemn Gabrielle's eyes widened in alarm.

"Why?" she demanded, starting up out of the tub. "What did I do this time?"

He chuckled and reached for the door. "You haven't done a thing." His eyes swept over her, desire reflected in their gold-flecked depths as they lingered where her wet gown clung to her breast. "But I just might," he added thickly, "if you don't get back in that tub."

Blushing furiously as she realized what he was staring at, Gabrielle sank back down into the water and self-consciously folded her arms across her bosom. Lifting her chin, she countered his probing gaze with an accusatory one, and her bottom lip curled out peevishly.

That look of hers was almost his undoing. Dan's eyes darkened considerably and he was sorely tempted to go over and kiss the infuriating pout right off her beautiful pink mouth. He yanked open the door, determined to get out of the kitchen before he did somethin he might later regret. "Wash your face!" he ordered tersely as he headed out the door.

By the time Gabrielle had cleaned the mud from her face, changed into dry clothes, and tamed her wet hair into a single long braid, Dan had nearly finished loading all the clothing and utensils she had collected into one of the Army ambulance wagons. "I'm afraid your bathwater isn't hot anymore," Gabrielle said as she stepped aside to allow him to pass with an armload of clothing.

The half-smile he gave her told her nothing of what he was thinking. "I washed at the pump."

He didn't *seem* angry. Still, Gabrielle had a gnawing feeling in the pit of her stomach, and she suspected she wasn't going to like whatever it was he was going to say. Picking up a packing carton filled with shoes, she followed him out the door, careful to avoid the mud at the bottom of the steps. "Are you going to the Apache camp?" she asked with feigned lightness, wishing

255

he would just tell her what was wrong so she wouldn't have to wheedle it out of him.

He took the box from her and placed it in the bed of the wagon. "I wanted to get these things out there before it rained. From the look of those clouds gathering on the horizon, we could be in for another squall before the day is out."

"May I go with you?"

"As long as you don't mind taking a chance on getting wet."

Gabrielle's stomach knotted even tighter. He wasn't making this any easier for her. She moved out of his way as he returned to the house for the final load. "What did you want to talk to me about?" she finally asked, entering the front door on his heels.

"We'll discuss it on the way to the camp." Dan stooped to gather up the last of the clothing, nearly backing into Gabrielle when he stood up.

She jumped back. "Sorry."

"Your friend, Miss Simmons, was inquiring about you," Dan said, as he carried the last armload out to the ambulance wagon. "She was determined to impress upon me that it was her idea to put a mud plaster on your face.'

Gabrielle realized she had completely forgotten about Grace.

Dan eyed her closely, a puzzled expression on his face. "Just what have you two been discussing behind my back? I could swear the girl thought I was going to hit you."

Her earlier good spirits vanishing, Gabrielle swallowed hard and her face grew warm under his pointed scrutiny. "You did . . . once."

The muscle in his jaw tightened. "If I remember correctly, you deserved it."

"I never said I didn't," Gabrielle said sullenly. Then she averted her gaze, uneasy with the turn the conversation had taken. The last thing she wanted to think about was that awful day she had goaded him into losing his temper.

Dan caught hold of her chin and tilted her face up, forcing her to look at him. "I hope you know I would never deliberately do anything to hurt you, Gabrielle."

She so wanted to believe him. "Are you angry with me?" she asked warily.

"For what?"

"I don't know. You just seem angry . . . sort of."

She looked so young, so vulnerable, standing there and looking at him as though she half expected him to scold her, and Dan realized for the first time that the unanticipated changes in their relationship had probably confused and frightened her even more than they had him. He wanted her. Even in her innocence, she knew that, though it was not likely she understood it. There was still so much of the child left in her, but that, too, was rapidly changing. Quelling the urge to take her in his arms and tell her everything would be all right, he lifted a still-wet curl off her cheek, allowing it to wind around his fingers before smoothing it back from her face. "I'm not angry with you, little one," he said quietly, his eyes warming as they met hers. "I have other things on my mind right now."

Gabrielle's pulse quickened as his fingers, rough and warm, brushed against her cheek. "Like the . . . stagecoach attack?" she ventured hesitantly, wishing she didn't feel so awkwardly inmature. She liked it when he called her "little one;" it was a term of endearment no one else had ever used. And yet it also served to remind her that he still thought of her as a child. *That* she hated.

"Who told you about that?"

"Grace. She also told me someone set fire to Mr. Edwards' stables last night. Do you really think it was the Apaches?"

The crease between Dan's brows deepened. Grace Simmons was one unusually well-informed young lady. He turned his back to Gabrielle and began adjusting the harness. "I think it's a strong possibility," he said over his shoulder.

Gabrielle moved closer to him and placed a comforting hand on his arm. "There's going to be trouble, isn't there?" she asked quietly.

Dan straightened up. Though he was about to deny it, he knew from the look in her eyes that she would not believe him. "Yes. I'm afraid there might be."

She had half expected him to try to shelter her from the truth, and she was almost sorry he hadn't. She took a deep breath. "Do you think it will be as bad . . . as Camp Grant?"

"God, I hope not." No sooner were the words out than he regretted them. There was no disguising the fear that flashed in Gabrielle's eyes before she lowered her gaze. "Gabrielle, listen to me," he commanded, taking her by the shoulders and giving her a stern shake. "I won't let anything happen to you. You must believe that."

"I-I wasn't thinking about myself," she said in a choked voice, sudden tears welling in her eyes. "I was thinking about Datigé and . . ." Her voice broke, but before Dan could say anything, they were interrupted by Sergeant Reikowsky.

"All ready to go, Major," the enlisted man said. "These the goods you want driven out to the camp?"

Dan released Gabrielle and inclined his head. "You'll need a crowbar in case you get bogged down in the mud. Have my horse and a mount for Miss DuBois saddled. We'll meet you out there."

Being on horseback was a rare experience for Gabrielle. Her father seldom permitted it, preferring that she ride in a carriage or in one of the Army wagons instead.

Dan smiled inwardly at seeing the glow of happiness on her face when they slowed their horses to a walk, and he vowed that someday he would buy Gabrielle her own horse. Though she had little experience, she took to the sidesaddle naturally, and that pleased him. As far as he was concerned, too many women were skittish around horses. He wanted a wife who could ride, and ride well, even if he had to teach her how.

"This is fun," Gabrielle said, her eyes shining as she reined in her horse and fought to catch her breath. "Were we galloping?"

He chuckled. "Not quite. I want you to learn to control your horse a little better before you attempt a gallop."

Sergeant Reikowsky had reached the camp ahead of them, and when they finally crested the rise and rode into the rancheria, Dan laughed aloud at seeing the burly sergeant trying to fend off the half-dozen Apache women eagerly rummaging through the contents of the wagon. "Sir, I can't make 'em stop!" the enlisted man wailed, throwing up his hands in defeat.

Dismounting, Dan spoke to the woman Gabrielle recognized as Anna, and she immediately hurried off in the direction of the wickiups. Then he lifted the wagon seat and retrieved the blanket-wrapped bundle he had hidden beneath it. A mysterious gleam in his eyes, he shoved the bundle into Gabrielle's hands just as she slid from her horse. "Here. Hold this." He spoke in a low voice to the other women; then, taking Gabrielle's arm, propelled her in the direction Anna had taken.

Gabrielle's heart thumped a little unevenly, and she threw him a bewildered glance. "Where are we going?"

He only smiled.

More confused than ever, she allowed him to steer her along. Whatever he had intended to talk to her about, he had forgotten, or perhaps he had changed his mind. Skillfully diverting every question she had asked him, Dan had lured her into a lively ride on horseback that had caused her to forget momentarily all else but the thrill of doing something her father would have forbidden.

A squeal of excitement caught Gabrielle's attention, and she turned her head just in time to catch a glimpse of Datigé before the little girl barreled headfirst into her skirts and threw thin arms around her legs.

"I think someone is glad to see you," Dan whispered, and Gabrielle felt tears sting her eyes. No one had ever unquestioningly accepted her before. But Datigé had. Without reservation, without criticism, without demanding something in return. For the first time in her life, Gabrielle knew how it felt to be unconditionally loved.

If anything ever happened to Datigé, she would die, she realized.

Sweeping aside all thoughts of dirt and lice, Gabrielle dropped the bundle Dan had given her, and, kneeling, she wrapped her arms around the little girl and gave her a hug. "How are you, squirt?" she asked in a choked voice.

Watching her, Dan felt his own throat constrict. Gabrielle had more love pent up inside her than anyone he had ever known; she simply had never learned what to do with it. The colonel certainly had never encouraged any displays of affection, and he would probably be appalled if he could see his daughter sitting here hugging this scrawny child who was probably crawling with vermin. Struggling with his own emotions, Dan lightly brushed the backs of his knuckles against Gabrielle's honey-colored hair. "Don't forget the presents you brought," he prompted gently.

Bewildered, she looked up at him. "Presents?"

He inclined his head toward the bundle she had dropped on the ground, and she hesitantly reached for it.

"Is that what this is?" she asked. From the corner of her eye, she saw Zayigo and Anna coming toward them.

"Open it," Dan said.

Confused Gabrielle untied the string and folded back the blanket.

An aching tenderness surged through Dan as she uttered a surprised gasp before turning tear-glazed eyes on him. "You remembered," she whispered hoarsely. Turning back to Datigé, she lifted the dress of yellow sprigged muslin and wrapped it around the girl's bony shoulders. "Maybe your mama can cut a new dress out of this for you," she said, wishing she could make the child understand. Then Dan said something in Apache, and she realized with a start that he was explaining to Zayigo what she had just said.

Zayigo reached out to touch the sprigged muslin, wonder filling her dark eyes as she fingered the soft material.

Suddenly glad she had something to give her new friends, Gabrielle pulled the rose-colored silk from the bundle and held it out to Zayigo. "This is for you."

No translation was required. Zayigo's eyes widened like a child's at Christmas, and momentarily forgetting her shyness, she eagerly accepted the proffered gift.

"And this, Anna"—Gabrielle rose to her feet and unfurled with a dramatic flourish the jet-trimmed tangerine satin gown that had once belonged to one of Ruby Collins' girls—"is for you!"

Lacking her daughter's inherent reserve, Anna held the dress up before her and danced around in a circle, lifting the full skirt as she turned. Laughter now softened the lines of her weathered face.

Looking at Dan, Gabrielle caught him watching her with eyes that were surprisingly misty, and something inside her swelled to the point of bursting. "You're the most wonderful man in the world," she whispered, her face aglow with love.

He shook his head. "The dresses were your idea, little one. I merely salvaged them from the rest of the hoard. Speaking of which, you stay here while I go rescue Reikowsky. I think the man may be in over his head."

Gabrielle watched him as he headed back toward the wagon, which was now surrounded by scores of Apaches, all sorting through the things they had brought. She felt so happy she wanted to jump up and down and shout. That he had remembered which dresses she had wanted to give to Datigé and Zayigo and Anna touched her. He *was* a wonderful man and she loved him. She loved him with all her heart.

An impatient tug on her skirt drew her attention back to little Datigé, who, in trying to put on the vastly oversized dress she had been given, was unintentionally dragging its skirt in the dirt. Gabrielle pulled the dress back up over the child's head and turned to speak to Zayigo, but Datigé mother had already started across the rancheria toward the wickiup, her own new dress draped carefully over one arm. Frustrated at not being able to speak the Indians' language, Gabrielle cast a pleading glance at Anna, in the hope that the older woman would know what to do.

Without hesitation, Anna snatched up the sprigged muslin and motioned for Gabrielle to follow her.

Gabrielle's eyes widened in horror as Anna pulled out a hunting knife, and the memory of the grief-stricken woman who had attacked her with a similar weapon flashed through her head, reminding her that, in spite of the friendships she had made here, she was still among enemies. Enemies who would take her life without a second thought.

With several deft strokes, Anna slashed through the dress with the knife, cutting the unwieldy amount of fabric into more manageable lengths. Then, in what seemed to Gabrielle an impossibly short period of time, Anna fashioned a skirt for her little granddaughter, a miniature version of the full, gathered skirts the other Apache women wore. Datigé, her sweet young face alight with pleasure, modeled it gleefully, wearing it with her soft deerskin top, and twirling around and around so that the skirt would swirl out around her.

Then Zayigo, a pink blush on her smooth bronzed face, emerged from the wickiup wearing her new dress. Aside from needing to be shortened a little, it fit her perfectly. Her straight black hair had been brushed until it shone and it cascaded down her back like a shimmering dark waterfall. Gabrielle could not help feeling pleased with her choice. With the rose silk perfectly complementing her dusky complexion and her black eyes shining as she came toward them, Zayigo was the most beautiful girl Gabrielle had ever seen.

It did not take long before the others in the camp noticed Zayigo, and in no time, the Apache girl was surrounded by admirers, male and female alike.

For the first time, Gabrielle realized that she had never seen Datigé's father, and she wondered whether Zayigo was widowed or had never married. Then she looked at Datigé and decided it didn't matter. A child so beautiful could only have been conceived out of love, whether her parents were married or not.

It must be a wondrous thing, she thought, to have a child with a man one loves—a child like Datigé. A child to hold and nurture and love. Suddenly, she laughed aloud. No one would believe that she wanted to be a mother. Everyone would say that she was too selfish to know the first thing about mothering.

Drawn by her laugh, Datigé seized her hand and tugged hard.

"I'll show them, squirt," Gabrielle said, her eyes glowing as she allowed the little girl to drag her across the rancheria to where the other children were playing. "I'll be the best mother in the world. You just wait and see."

An hour later, after he had sent Sergeant Reikowsky back to post with the wagon, Dan found Gabrielle in the middle of a circle of noisy children. Her skirt hiked up to her knees, she was deftly dodging the medicine ball that was being thrown at her with deadly accuracy. He feared that she might be overdoing it. Scarcely two weeks had passed since the accident that had nearly taken her life, and even though each day had brought a marked improvement in her well-being, he knew she was not yet strong enough to be exerting herself so. Still, it was a rare thing to see her genuinely enjoying herself, and he decided to let the game continue for a few more minutes before he stepped in and brought it to a halt. Folding his arms across his chest, he stood, feet apart, a grin spreading across his tanned features as he watched her.

Her face and the front of her dress were streaked with dirt, for the ball had found its way into the mud more than once. And her hair had worked partially free of the braid and now hung in tangled curls about her face, giving her a look of untamed abandon which made Dan's loins burn with desire. God, how he wanted her! And she wanted him; she was simply too young and too inexperienced to know it. But he knew. He knew it by the way her body responded every time he held her or kissed her or caressed her tender flesh. Just below the surface of her childish innocence was a warm and passionate woman ready to learn how to love and be loved. And he wanted to be the one to teach her.

He wanted it to be perfect for her, from the very first time. He wanted to show her that the marriage bed was to be enjoyed, not merely endured. He wanted to coax her beautiful body to the very limits of sensual pleasure, and beyond, until she was delirious and moaning with desire.

Gabrielle squealed and tried to jump over the ball as it sailed past, only to be struck out. Laughing, she took her place on the perimeter of the circle, artlessly tossing her red-gold curls before bending and placing her hands on her knees in readiness to continue the game. Unknowingly she was affording Dan a provocative view of her posterior and her shapely calves. He groaned inwardly. Much more of that and he was liable to lose whatever restraint he still possessed. He wanted her more than he had ever wanted a woman, and she was sorely taxing his self-control.

Suddenly, Dan's pulse quickened and a chill traversed his

spine. His finely-honed instincts were alerting him to the presence of trouble. Careful not to move lest his attention be noted, he shifted his gaze to the brush that bordered the rancheria. There, partially hidden behind a stand of saltbush, stood one of the Apaches who had been responsible for Gabrielle's capture, his obsidian eyes fixed on her in a look of glittering hatred.

Chapter Twelve

Come on, come on, Gabrielle urged silently, and she bit her bottom lip as she took careful aim. Her target was a boy she had heard the other children call Nadé-ze, a bully of about fourteen who stood head and shoulders above the rest. He had a habit of throwing the ball with enough force to hurt, and she was determined to take him down a notch or two. Drawing back the ball, she hurled it as hard as she could.

Busy showing off for his friends, Nadé-ze did not see the ball coming until it was too late, and he let out a startled yelp as it grazed his hip. There was a thread of hysteria in the cheers that burst out around the circle, and Gabrielle, unable to suppress a surge of smug self-satisfaction, jumped clear off the ground and let out a rousing whoop before once more taking her place in the center of the circle.

The she spotted Dan.

Grinning from ear to ear, she waved to him, swinging her arm in a wide arc.

He chuckled. "Time to go," he called out, lifting his gaze skyward to indicate the dark clouds pressing down around them.

"Five more minutes."

"No."

"Please?"

"No!" While it pleased him to see her having fun for a change, his immediate concern was the Apache warrior still hovering in the brush only a few yards away.

Gabrielle grimaced. "Three more minutes."

A smile touched the corners of Dan's mouth as he started toward her.

Laughter bubbled up inside Gabrielle, and there was a devious gleam in her eyes as she backed away from him. "Two min—"

A fiery pain exploded between her shoulder blades as the ball struck her from behind, knocking her flat. She groaned and struggled to rise, then collapsed in the dirt.

"Gabrielle, answer me! Are you all right?" Dan grasped her by the shoulders and rolled her onto her back, but she lay without moving, her eyes closed, her breathing unusually shallow.

"I'll kill the little bastard," he muttered under his breath, and Gabrielle, trying hard not to laugh, opened one eye to venture a peek at him just as he sprang to his feet and turned on Nadé-ze.

The boy, seeing the murderous look in Dan's eyes, began to edge away from him.

Suddenly aware of what was happening, Gabrielle scrambled to her knees, *"Dan, no!"*

The shock of hearing her use his given name for the first time brought Dan up short, and he turned to stare at her in mute surprise. Suddenly it registered with him that she was not hurt.

Thunder rumbled throughout the valley, and a strong wind gusted out of nowhere.

Gabrielle pushed herself to her feet. "I'm all right," she said, grinning sheepishly and suddenly feeling guilty for scaring him. She held her arms out and pivoted. "See? All in one piece."

Nadé-ze turned and ran.

His anger rapidly changing to relief, then back to anger at the thought that she had played him for a fool, Dan started toward Gabrielle, his face dark with unbridled fury.

"Uh-oh," she muttered, starting to inch away him and nearly stumbling over the ball lying on the ground at her feet.

Dan's footsteps quickened. "You just stay right where you are, young lady," he commanded, leveling a warning finger at her. He intended to teach her not to pull another prank like that on him.

Far from immune to the tense silence that hung over the children, Gabrielle nervously moistened her lips. He was angry this time. Very angry. Still, there had to be some way to lighten his temper. . . .

Her heart thumping wildly, she picked up the ball and threw it at him.

Dan swore loudly as the ball clipped him in the knee, breaking his stride, and Gabrielle laughed. "You're it, now!"

Dan swore again, but stepping over the ball, he continued toward her.

Her eyes alight with mischief, Gabrielle put her thumbs in her ears and, to the noisy delight of the other children, wiggled her fingers at him and stuck out her tongue. Then, without waiting to see his reaction, she whirled around and broke into a run.

Cold fear surged through Dan. She was running straight toward the Apache hiding in the brush!

Sprinting after her, he caught her around the waist.

Gabrielle let out a shriek as he swung her up into his arms. "Put me down!" she cried out, pushing against his chest and trying to squirm free as he carried her across the rancheria to where their horses waited, the force of his strides jolting her and causing her teeth to knock together.

"Behave yourself," Dan growled.

"Put me down, or you'll be sorry!" Gabrielle threatened, though she was vacillating between hilarity and terror, having glimpsed the angry look on his face. She wondered what he would do if she kissed him. Stifling a giggle, she moved her face in closer to his and pursed her lips.

"Gabrielle, I'm warning you. . . ."

She brushed her lips against the smooth tanned line of his cheekbone.

"Gabrielle!"

He abruptly set her on her feet, but she lost her balance and toppled backward before he could catch her, to sprawl inelegantly in the dirt.

Dan folded his arms across his chest and glared down at her.

267

Still dangerously close to laughing in spite of his glowering, she sat up and began brushing the dirt from the front of her dress. "Did I get any on my face?" she asked with feigned innocence, coyly batting her lashes as she lifted her gaze to his.

Dan's fury rapidly disintegrated, and within moments it was all he could do to keep a straight face as he stared down into the beautiful green eyes twinkling mischievously up at him. No matter what she did, it was impossible to stay angry with her. *Impossible!* Like no one else had ever done, the little minx had wormed her way beneath his skin and had found the soft spot in his heart. The corners of his mouth twitched. He'd been of a mind to throttle her, yet here she was, making him want to laugh. Clenching his teeth lest she see the mirth bubbling up in him, Dan extended a hand toward her. "Get up," he ordered.

She eyed the proffered hand with overt suspicion. "What are you going to do to me?"

"What do you think I'm going to do to you?" he retorted, grasping her wrist and hauling her to her feet.

She choked back a giggle. "I know what I'd like to do to *you*."

One dark brow shot upward.

She threw her arms about his neck. "Kiss you!"

"Gabrielle!"

When Dan pried her hands from his neck, Gabrielle rose up on tiptoe and kissed him on the chin.

Swearing inwardly as heat swept through him at the feel of her body, Dan took her by the shoulders and set her away from him. "Enough!"

She solemnly folded her hands behind her back and peered up at him from beneath her lashes, but the smile that hovered on her lips was far from demure. Or obedient.

Still, there was so much love glowing in her gray-green eyes, Dan wished there were some way around the unpleasant task that lay ahead. He untied their horses. "I must leave for Tucson in the morning, little one," he said as he gave her a boost up.

Lightning crackled overhead, causing Gabrielle's mount to give a startled neigh and pull against the bridle, its large brown eyes rolling back in fear. Her hands tightened on the reins. "Why? Are you in some kind of trouble?"

Dan easily swung up into the saddle. "General Crook just took command of the Department. Every area commander must report to him immediately. I'll be filling in for your father."

"Will you be gone long?"

"Only a few days. Come on. Let's get out of here."

A hot dry wind kicked up as they started down the trail toward the post.

Gabrielle's horse tossed back its head and sidestepped nervously, and it was all she could do to keep her grip on the reins. "Who's going to take over here while you're away?"

"Moreland. Don't hold the reins so tightly. Give the animal some slack." Dan cast her a sideways glance, aware that she wasn't going to like what he was about to say. "You'll be staying with the Wilcoxes while I'm gone. I've already cleared it with Ben, and Mary said she'd welcome the company."

The Wilcoxes!

Gabrielle abruptly reined in her horse. "I don't want to stay with the Wilcoxes."

"Gabrielle, listen to—"

"No!" She could not explain what came over her at that precise moment; she only knew that her happiness had been shattered. Last night he had held her. This morning he had kissed her. And now he was treating her like a child again. Nothing would ever change. He would always think of her as a child, never as the woman she wanted to be for him, and for that, she suddenly hated him. "I am perfectly capable of looking after myself while you are away," she said hotly, the love that had sparkled in her eyes only moments before hardening into resentment. "I do not need a nursemaid and I refuse to stay with Captain Wilcox, so you can just *un*clear it with him."

Without warning, her horse shied.

Closing the distance between them, Dan seized her reins, temporarily bringing both her and the horse back under control.

"Let go—"

"Just calm down a moment and listen to me! It's for your own protection that Captain Wilcox has agreed to look after you. You are not staying in that house alone."

"It's my house!"

"And you are my responsibility! I don't want to spend the entire time I'm away worrying about you."

"Worrying about me or about the trouble I will inevitably cause?" Gabrielle's chin quivered. "I don't know why I ever imagined I was in love with you. I must have been out of my mind! I thought you cared about me. But you don't. You don't care about me at all!"

"I do care for you, Gabrielle. I care for you a great deal, and if you weren't so damned pigheaded, you'd have seen that by now."

"Save it!" she retorted, knowing full well that she was being unreasonable, yet too hurt to care. "Save it for some other flighty female who's stupid enough to fall in love with you, because I hate you! I hate you more than I've ever hated anyone in my entire life!" Gabrielle dug a heel into the gelding's side, and as the animal lunged forward, she jerked the reins from Dan's grasp.

Lightning crackled again, so close Gabrielle felt her skin prickle. Her horse screamed and rose on its hind legs as a cannon blast of thunder followed and the entire valley lit up as if it were on fire.

The gelding reared again, and Gabrielle's foot slipped from the stirrup. A searing pain slashed through her palms as the reins ripped flesh, and she was flung to the ground.

Her horse bolted.

Dan reached Gabrielle's side just as she was struggling to sit up. "What in the hell were you trying to do?" he shouted. "Get yourself trampled to death?"

Unable to catch her breath, Gabrielle took an angry swipe at the hand he extended toward her. "Go away!" she finally got out.

"Are you hurt?"

"Leave me alone!"

Ignoring her protests, Dan grabbed her hands and turned them over, frowning as he saw the torn skin on her palms. "Did you injure anything else? What about your ribs?"

Fire blazed in her eyes. "I told you to leave me alone! I don't need you fussing over me as if I were an old woman!"

"Or a child?" Dan asked sarcastically, his patience wearing perilously thin.

Not deigning to answer that, Gabrielle jerked her hands free and pushed herself to her feet, but when she tried to ward off his assistance, his hand merely tightened on her arm, and he was none too gentle in hauling her upright. "Stand still!" he ordered.

Realizing the futility of fighting him, she reluctantly obeyed, but she made no attempt to hide the hurt and anger she felt at his betrayal. She was utterly sickened by her own gullibility. Of all the men in the world, she had fallen prey to the one she should have had enough sense to avoid. Yet, he had made her fall in love with him.

Gripping her chin, he forced her to look at him. "That, young lady, was one of your more senseless acts. You damn near got yourself killed, and you caused a perfectly good horse to panic. If anything happens to that animal because of your foolishness—"

"If anything happens to the horse, Father will reimburse the Army for him. So you need not worry about—"

"No, my dear," Dan interrupted, his eyes flashing like molten stone. "That's where you are mistaken. If anything happens to the horse, the payment is coming out of your hide." Spinning her around, he shoved her in the direction of his own mount just as the first huge drops of rain began to fall.

Neither of them spoke the entire way back to post. Perched before him, with one knee hooked around the pommel in an awkward substitute for a sidesaddle, Gabrielle rode with her back rigid, trying in vain to avoid any bodily contact whatsoever with the man seated behind her, but ill-concealed anger pulsated in the strong arms that imprisoned her. The rain saturated her hair and ran down her face, streaking the dirt on her cheeks. She knew she was to blame for this latest rift; had she acquiesced to staying with Mary and the captain during his absence, the animosity now brewing between them would never have come about. Still, her pride had been sorely wounded by his persistence in treating her like a child. Wasn't it ever going to get through his thick skull that she was a woman?

Gabrielle choked back a sob, determined not to let him see her cry, although she knew that if he relented—just the tiniest bit—she would throw herself into his arms and cry. In spite of her anger, she wanted him to hold her and tell her that everything would be all right. She didn't understand what was happening to her, why she so desperately needed his love and his tenderness, or why, in spite of that, she was forever doing things to drive him away. She wanted him to love her. Completely and unconditionally. And yet she knew she was making it impossible for him to do so. He thought of her as a child because she *was* a child. To him, her not-quite-eighteen years seemed woefully insignificant.

Corporal Holmes ran to greet them. "What happened?" he called out over the thunder that shook the valley. "Miss Gabrielle's horse came back without a rider and we thought—"

Dan interrupted him as he dismounted and reached up for Gabrielle. "Is Wilcox in the dispensary?"

The soldier cast a hesitant glance at Gabrielle before answering. "Yes, sir, but he—"

"Tend to my horse," Dan ordered curtly. His fingers closed around Gabrielle's upper arms in a bruising grip, and he hauled her along after him in the direction of the infirmary.

Quickly growing winded from having to match his strides, Gabrielle struggled to keep up with him. "You're hurting my arm," she managed to gasp.

"I'd like to *break* it," Dan ground out ungraciously, although his hold on her did slacken somewhat.

Thankful for even the slightest reprieve, Gabrielle choked back an angry retort.

They nearly collided with Captain Wilcox on the steps of the dispensary. There was such absolute disapproval in his eyes as they swept over Gabrielle that she instinctively shrank away from him. "What happened?" Wilcox demanded tersely, and when Dan told him, he shook his head. "You'll have to see to her, Dan. I can't stay. Mary's having the baby. You know where the carbolic is. Here are the keys to the medicine chest."

Gabrielle's gratitude at having been spared any more of the

surgeon's censure vanished when Dan propelled her into the infirmary and pushed her down onto a chair. "Sit!"

"You need not shove me," she said between clenched teeth, and shot a venomous glance at him. "I know perfectly well how to sit."

"Do you know how to shut up?"

Stung, she clamped her mouth shut and retreated as far as the back of the chair would allow.

In spite of his anger, Dan's touch was surprisingly gentle as he cleansed the dirt from the torn flesh on her palm, but Gabrielle was too submersed in her own misery to take notice. Over the past weeks, she had defied him. She had tried to please him. She had even tried to seduce him. Why? Because she loved him or because she didn't want Grace to have him? Her heart told her it was the former. But a persistent, nagging voice in the back of her mind told her that her motives were suspect. She had not loved Dan when her father had entrusted her to his custody. She had not loved him when he'd rescued her from the amorous advances of Marcus Epperling, and later of Chase Dalton, only to confine her to the house for disobeying him. And she certainly hadn't loved him the day of the Cinco do Mayo festival.

So, when had she started to love him? When he'd risked his life to save her from the Apache war party? When he'd first kissed her? She could pinpoint neither the time when or the reason why she had stopped hating him and had started to be drawn to him. In fact, she had never actually *realized* that she loved him; she had *decided* it. Her mind was awhirl with troubled thoughts. Perhaps he had been right all along. Perhaps she was nothing more than a spoiled brat who manipulated people into giving her what she wanted. Perhaps she didn't *deserve* to be loved.

Dan had just finished cleaning and bandaging her hands, when Gabrielle opened her mouth to tell him she was sorry, that she would stay with Captain and Mary Wilcox after all, and that she wouldn't cause any more trouble. But before she could utter a word, he seized her arm and hauled her out of the chair, showing her about as much tenderness as he had when he'd shoved her into it, and she hastily swallowed the

273

unspoken apology. Why should she apologize when *he* was the one who was being ill-tempered and impossible?

Mud oozed up over the toes of her shoes as Dan half-steered, half-dragged her across the parade ground toward the house. The rain had stopped, but not for long. Already the clouds were regrouping and another downpour was coming.

Corporal Bates greeted them at the door, his eyes widening when he saw Gabrielle's bedraggled appearance and the bandages on her hands, but one look at the set of the major's jaws effectively stopped him from asking what had happened. "Set up the bath in Miss DuBois' bedroom," Dan barked and the soldier wasted no time in complying. Major Catlin was a fair man, but he could be a hard one, and Corporal Bates knew better than to cross him.

Gritting her teeth to keep back the angry words on the tip of her tongue, Gabrielle braced herself against the wall while Dan knelt to unlace her muddy shoes and remove them from her feet. She had a tremendous urge to kick him. He was being an ass. Well, she could be just as stubborn and disagreeable as he could. More so. She'd show him.

Having gotten her shoes off, Dan grasped her shoulder and marched her down the hallway toward her bedroom.

"You forgot to take your boots off," she snipped, casting a disdainful glance at his feet.

"I had the common sense to wipe the mud off my boots before entering the house," he retorted.

She bristled. "I would have had time to wipe my shoes off if you hadn't shoved me through the door."

"I didn't shove you through—"

"You did."

"Turn around."

Before she even had time to consider his command, he spun her about. Lifting what remained of the wet braid that hung down her back, he flung it forward over her shoulder.

She twisted her head around. "What are you doing?"

"I'm unbuttoning your dress. I seriously doubt you can manage it yourself with those bandages on your hands—stand still, damn it!"

Gabrielle seethed. "I don't suppose you intend to give me a

274

bath, too?"

"Unless you can come up with a better idea—yes."

"Oh, no, you won't!" She jerked away and whirled around to face him, her eyes blazing. "I am perfectly capable of washing myself, thank you!"

His face dark with barely restrained fury, Dan folded his arms across his chest while his toe beat an impatient tattoo on the floor. "And just how do you propose to do that without getting your bandages wet?"

"I . . . I'll use the backbrush!" A smug smile touched the corners of Gabrielle's mouth.

One black eyebrow arched provokingly. "On your face?"

Her smile faded. "Well . . . no."

"In that case, I'll wash your face, and then you can take over from there." Dan stuck his head out the bedroom door and yelled, "Bates, get a move on!" To Gabrielle, he said, "Get out of that dress."

Her chin shot up. "I most certainly will not! Not until you leave and afford me some privacy."

"*Now!*"

"And if I don't?"

Sparks flashed in Dan's eyes. "Defy me again, young lady, and you'll find out."

"The very least you could do is turn around."

Just then, Corporal Bates appeared in the doorway with the copper bath. "I'll just put it over here," he said, careful to avoid eye contact with either Gabrielle or the major as he set the tub on the floor. He didn't need to look at them to know they had been quarreling. He could *feel* the tension, it stretched between them like the tightrope walker's wire at a carnival. "I talked the mess sergeant out of some lemons," the soldier said offhandedly. "Made some lemonade earlier. With this heat, I thought maybe you'd like some—"

"Later," Dan said curtly. "Get the water."

"You didn't have to be so short with him," Gabrielle hissed, after the soldier had gone.

Dan shot her a withering glance. "I told you to get out of that dress!"

"And I told you to *turn around!*"

275

He took a step toward her. Then annoyed when she didn't even flinch he stopped short. He cursed silently, aware that he was becoming just as unreasonable and fractious as she was.

Corporal Bates appeared again. "I had the water sittin' in the hall," he said somewhat sheepishly, his face reddening because of snatches of conversation he had overheard.

Dan took the bucket from him. "I'll finish here. You're dismissed."

Al Bates shifted uneasily. "I was about to start supper, sir, and I didn't know what you wanted with—"

"Dismissed!"

Gabrielle sat down on the edge of the bed, stubbornly tilting her chin and resting her bandaged hands in her lap while she watched Dan pour the hot water into the bath. She would undress if and when *she* wanted, not because she had been browbeaten into doing it by the likes of Major Catlin!

Determined not to be drawn any further into a childish game of wills, Dan deliberately ignored her as he made the required number of trips to the pump and the kitchen stove and then back to her bedroom, though he found himself clenching his teeth when her stockinged feet made an annoying *swish, swish* on the wood floor as she idly swung them back and forth over the side of the bed. The little bitch! He was tempted to turn her over his knee and teach her a lesson she'd not soon forget!

By the time Dan returned to the bedroom with the final bucket of hot water, Gabrielle had relented and slipped out of her dress, not so much to appease him, but because she was afraid of what he might do to her if she did not. And it galled her to admit it. "You shouldn't have dismissed Bates before dinner," she said saucily, squelching an urge to stick her tongue out at him when he turned his back to empty the bucket into the tub. "Now you'll have to fix it yourself."

"*You* are going to cook dinner tonight," Dan retorted, unable to resist indulging in a sweeping glance down the length of her chemise-clad form as he came toward her with a soaped-up washcloth. "I have work to do."

She eyed him warily. "Me! Cook?"

"Yes, you. Now, stand still unless you want this soap in your eyes."

"But I can't cook! Grace was the one who made dinner that night you—"

"Then it's high time you learned."

"But I—"

Her reply was cut short, for the washcloth abruptly met her face and she clamped her lips together just in time to keep from getting soap in her mouth. Dan placed a hand behind her head to keep her from escaping, and though she fumed inwardly, she had no choice but to stand before him, her face screwed up and her eyes squeezed shut, while he none-too-gently scrubbed away the mud that had dried on her skin. He had no right to treat her this way! Well, she'd fix him. She'd show him just how far he could push her without getting his due!

"You got it in my eyes!" she gasped, grabbing the towel and pressing it to them the instant he released her.

He reached for the towel. "Here, let me see."

"Leave me alone!" Gabrielle twisted away from him, afraid he might find out that it was not the soap but tears caused by frustrated anger that stung her eyes. "Go away!"

Dan flung the washcloth into the tub. "Call me if you need help."

"I wouldn't ask you for help if you—"

"What did you say?"

"Nothing!"

Gabrielle waited until she heard the click of the latch, then gave in to a childish display of temper, sticking her tongue out at the closed door. Damn him! She jerked her chemise over her head and crushed it into a ball. She would have loved to cram it down Dan's throat. Cook dinner, indeed! She wanted to poison him, and he deserved it!

Fuming, she turned her attention to the sweaty muslin wrapped around her middle. Untying the knot with her hand swaddled in bandages was no easy task, and by the time she managed to get it undone, she had used up every colorful word she had ever heard. She decided she was never going to put the bindings on again, regardless of what Captain Wilcox said. She didn't care if he had apoplexy.

Bathing was no joy either—she had to hold the bar of soap between her feet while she worked the backbrush over it—nor was getting dressed. Her nightgown became twisted and she nearly broke her left arm trying to work it into the sleeve. To make matters worse, Gabrielle couldn't dry herself off very thoroughly, so when she tried to don clean underdrawers, the cotton stuck to her still-damp legs, and with her hands hampered, she could not get a good enough grip on the waist to be able to pull them all the way up. Finally giving in to frustration, which was quickly building to an explosive level, she yanked them off and hurled them across the room to land in a rumpled heap on the floor.

It was a peculiar sensation, wearing no underdrawers. Even with her wrapper on over her nightgown, Gabrielle felt naked as she made her way down the hallway in her bare feet.

Dan was in the dining room, poring over the ledgers he had spread across the table. He sensed Gabrielle's presence before he heard her, and did not start when her voice cut sharply through the silence. "You could do that in Father's study," she snapped, making no attempt to curb her ill humor.

He lifted his gaze to hers, the gold points in his eyes hard and cold. "I could. But, I won't."

She jutted her chin out stubbornly. "Then don't complain to me when you get food spilled all over your work." Scornfully tossing her damp, tangled curls, Gabrielle pivoted on one foot and then stomped off toward the kitchen.

Dan's gaze inadvertently dropped to the saucy sway of her backside as she left the room, and he uttered a muffled curse. Being alone with Gabrielle for hours on end was doing things to him, things he preferred not to think about. All the repeated warring between them was stirring up a heated passion he could no longer deny. He had been too long without a woman. The crease between his brows deepened as he strove to drive the provocative image of his best friend's daughter from his thoughts. He returned to his work, but his concentration had been broken, and after staring blindly at the figures on the pages before him for several moments, he slammed the ledger shut.

Ruby Collins, he decided. Tonight he would go to Ruby's. He

chuckled, some of his anger draining away as he pictured the look on Ruby's face when he would appear on her doorstep. The woman had been trying to get him into her establishment ever since he'd arrived at Camp Carleton, but he had resisted, preferring to think he was a cut above the soldiers who openly indulged in the vices Ruby's place offered.

But he wasn't. Damn it! He was a man. A man who needed a woman. And he'd have to swallow his pride and go to Ruby's or swing from the gallows for raping the colonel's daughter, because that was what it was going to come to if the little twit didn't watch her step!

With an uncanny sense of timing, Gabrielle appeared in the doorway. Ignoring the steely stare Dan fixed on her, she marched into the room and thumped the two plates she was carrying down on the table with just enough force to make a noise but not enough to break the china.

Her second trip to the dining room produced the cutlery, and she made even more noise as she placed it on the table.

Well aware that she was deliberately trying to antagonize him, Dan doubled his efforts to control his temper, but there was no mistaking the silent warning in his eyes as their gazes met and he matched her blazing glare with one of his own.

Gabrielle waited until she was in the relative safety of the kitchen before letting loose a string of epithets that would have succeeded in her getting her mouth washed out with soap only a few years ago had either Dan or her father heard her. Finally she shook her fist at the closed door "Damn you! Sitting there like *King Catlin* while I wait on you hand and foot! I can't cook. I told you I can't! I don't even know what I'm supposed to do with that . . . that . . . *thing*." She turned her nose up in disgust as she cast a wary glance at the chicken carcass Bates had plucked and hung above the sink to bleed.

Still swearing, she went into the pantry. Bread, she thought, picking up a loaf the striker had baked that morning. They would have bread. After all, what did she have to do but slice it? Standing on tiptoe, she reached for the preserved snap beans. If his royal highness thought she was going to soil her bandages preparing the fresh ones in the basket behind the pantry door, he'd better think again. He could eat these. And he could eat them *cold*. Lighting the stove wasn't in her repertoire either.

Setting the items she had selected on the work table, Gabrielle went back into the pantry to fetch a knife.

The puzzling array of cutlery on the shelf threw her into another quandary. There were knives of various lengths, all with pointed tips and smooth, finely-honed edges except the one with the blunt tip and serrated edge. And there was a somewhat smaller knife with a narrow curved blade that looked nothing short of treacherous. Next to it was the tiny black-handled one she had seen Bates use for paring potatoes. She sighed. *A knife is a knife. Right?* Choosing one of the long-bladed carving knives, she returned to the kitchen brandishing it like a rapier. "I shall cut out your black heart, Dan Catlin!" she threatened, pretending to stab her imaginary target. Her mouth curved into a taut smile as she gave the blade a vicious twist in midair.

Cutting the bread turned out to be harder than it looked, but Gabrielle, swearing furiously by now, never suspected that she had chosen the wrong knife. She simply attributed her disastrous results to ineptitude. Picking up a slice that tapered from thickness of one inch at the top to a crumbling, nearly transparent nothing at the bottom, she gave it a scornful glance before tossing it onto the plate with the rest of the bread. "You can eat it anyway," she hissed, hating Dan more than ever for making her do this.

Her green eyes shot daggers at him as she carried the plate of bread into the dining room and slammed it down on the table.

Since Dan had returned to working on the unit accounts, he merely cocked an eyebrow and eyed her steadily, but said nothing, fueling her fury with his silence.

"I'll fix you," Gabrielle muttered on her way back to the kitchen. "I'll teach you to order me around like I'm some—" She stopped, her gaze glued on the jar of lemonade Corporal Bates had prepared, inspiration surging through her like a lightning bolt. *No!* Her heart thumped erratically and her breath came in short sharp gasps. It was mean and it was wicked, but she was going to do it. By God, she was going to do it! Careful not to make a sound, she tiptoed back down the hall to the parlor, and in the sideboard, next to the brandy Dan favored, she found what she was looking for—the bottle of tequila.

It is time Dan Catlin got a taste of his own medicine, Gabrielle decided on her way back to the kitchen.

She even knew which peppers to use, although she wasn't certain how she was going to disguise their presence in the lemonade. Rattlesnake piss. And appropriate name, she thought. After all, she was making it for a *snake*.

It took several tries with the mortar and pestle before she obtained a steady rhythm, but the exercise had a positive effect, for, as the dark red-brown cascable chiles slowly turned to pulp, Gabrielle's frustration began to ebb, and to be replaced by single-minded determination. She was, once and for all, going to pay back Dan Catlin for all the grief he had caused her.

Scraping the last of the pulverized chiles into the jar of lemonade, she stood back to admire her handiwork. She would let that steep awhile and then strain it through cheesecloth into the pitcher before adding a hefty dose of tequila. She bit back a wicked smile. Dan Catlin would never know what hit him!

Again Dan looked up when Gabrielle entered the dining room, this time carrying a bowl of snap beans. Reacting instinctively, he jumped up and snatched the account ledgers from the table just as she forcefully deposited the dish onto it, sending the liquid in which the beans had been preserved splashing up over the rim of the bowl. Irritation snapped in his eyes as they followed her impudent exit from the room. She was dangerously close to getting a well-deserved punishment.

To his surprise, she was extraordinarily careful when she returned with a crystal serving pitcher filled with lemonade and two matching water goblets. "Aren't you going to abuse those, too?" he asked, puzzled by her abrupt change in behavior, but any suspicions he might have had were squelched when she gave him an empirical toss of her head and said flatly, "The crystal belonged to my mother. I have no wish to break it."

After she left the room, Dan closed the ledgers and placed his papers on a side chair. Later he would find a way to justify the cost of keeping the Apaches quartered near Camp Carleton.

Right now, he was too blasted tired.

By the time Gabrielle returned, carrying a covered platter, he had filled both their glasses. She stopped in the doorway. sudden panic flickering in her eyes as they riveted on the filled goblets, but swallowing hard, she marched boldly into the room and plunked the platter down on the table. "I've changed my mind," she said breathlessly, unable to meet his gaze. "I'm not hungry." Then, before he could stop her, she turned and fled.

Dan took a closer look at the *dinner* she had prepared.

The bread slices brought a curve of amusement to his lips. He could have done better with a bowie knife. And there was something odd about the beans; the pat of butter Gabrielle had placed on top had not even begun to melt. He touched the bowl. Just as he had suspected. The little minx had emptied the beans directly from the jar into the bowl without heating them. Expecting the worst, his pulse quickened as he reached for the cover on the silver platter and lifted it.

In the center of the platter, surrounded by parsley sprigs and sliced radishes, was one very dead, very naked, very raw stewing hen.

Dan slammed the cover down over it and sank back in his chair, choking back the laughter that attacked him in waves. He didn't want to laugh, but he couldn't help it. No matter how hard he tried to keep a firm grip on his anger, it eluded him. He had to give Gabrielle credit. When she set out to get even, she did a thorough job of it. Now he knew why she had not stayed to eat. She'd probably expected him to be furious. Well, he wouldn't disappoint her.

Still chuckling, he picked up his goblet of lemonade and raised it to his lips. . . .

Chapter Thirteen

The bellow of rage that shook the very walls of the house prompted Gabrielle's feet to fly. Paying no heed to where they carried her, she dashed through the first doorway she reached, realizing too late that she was in Dan's bedroom.

Not daring even to breathe, she pressed her body against the wall as his footsteps reverberated down the hall, each one exploding like a gunshot. He did not see her as he passed, but she knew it would be only seconds before he discovered that she was not in her own room. She looked frantically about her for some place to hide.

"Gabrielle!"

Without even thinking about what she was doing, she bolted across the room and dove beneath the bed.

"Damn it, girl! Answer me!"

She lay on the floor in mute terror as Dan retraced his footsteps, stopping just outside his bedroom door.

"Gabrielle, are you in here?"

It was dark in the room, night having fallen, and the only illumination was an occasional flicker of lightning.

Her breath caught as he entered the bedroom.

"Gabrielle?"

Without warning, her nose began to tickle. *Damn you, Bates! When was the last time you dusted under the beds?* She wrinkled up her nose, but the tingling sensation would not go away and her face felt as though it would burst from the effort she exerted to hold her breath.

Outside the window, lightning streaked across the sky and in the wavering flash of eerie blue-white light it created, Gabrielle could see Dan's feet beside the bed. Pressed to the floor, she felt her heart pounding so loudly she was certain the floorboards would pick up the sound and release it into the room, betraying her whereabouts.

And the tingling in her nose worsened.

Dan turned to leave and she relaxed.

Then she sneezed.

"Ow!" she cried out, as she banged the back of her head on a bed slat.

Like bands of iron, strong hands closed around her ankles and dragged her out from under the bed.

A cool draft brushed against her backside as her nightgown snagged on a floorboard and rode up around her waist. Uttering a shriek of horror, she grabbed the gown and yanked it back down over her buttocks, but the effort was for naught; before she could even catch her breath, Dan had lifted her off the floor, deposited her face downward across his lap, and yanked up the back of her gown.

Desperate to escape the punishment she knew she had earned, Gabrielle wriggled off his lap as his hand descended. The slap intended for her bottom grazed off her hip instead, and she landed on the floor on her hands and knees. Determined not to let her get away without some punishment, Dan caught hold of her wrapper, and as she desperately attempted to scramble away from him, Gabrielle heard the soft cotton tear. The robe ripped from bodice to hem.

For a moment, time seemed suspended and neither of them moved. Gabrielle stared in horror at the ruined garment, and Dan stared at Gabrielle as lightning illuminated her face, accenting the wild, wanton look in her eyes and the red-gold tresses that rioted about her shoulders.

It wasn't Ruby Collins he wanted.

A second bolt of lightning followed on the heels of the first and in the resulting flash, Gabrielle saw the burning look in Dan's eyes, a look that, had she been more experienced, she would have recognized as lust. Certain he intended to punish her, however, she turned to run, but his arms closed around

284

her and thunder drowned her shrieks as they sprawled backward across the bed. She threw her arms up over her face to protect herself from an anticipated blow, but he seized her wrists and pinioned them to the mattress, halting her flight as she attempted to twist away from him; and the panicked scream that rose in her throat was throttled as his mouth crushed down upon hers in a deep, penetrating kiss that shocked her senses and set her head to reeling. His knee thrust between her thighs and his broad chest pressed against her breasts, igniting an odd warmth inside her as his weight bore her deeper into the mattress.

She drew in a ragged breath of air as his mouth left hers, only to descend again into a kiss that was even more fiery, more demanding, than the first, and as she became aware that the charged heat that seemed to pulsate from his body was not anger, but ardor, her fear erupted anew. They were playing by his rules now, in a game which suddenly made her previous attempts at seduction seem hopelessly naïve. In this game, he wielded all the power and she was an unwilling participant. No, she told herself as a disturbing revelation shot through her. She was not unwilling. Only very, very scared.

Sensing her fear, Dan struggled to get his passion under control. Releasing her wrists, he cradled her head between his hands and lightly, tenderly, kissed her eyelids, her forehead, the tip of her nose, before raising his head to peer down into her wide, terrified eyes. "Don't be afraid of me, little one," he murmured huskily, gently brushing his thumbs across the delicate curve of her cheekbones. "I won't hurt you."

Lightning flashed again and Gabrielle flinched, but in the brief moment of illumination, she saw into his eyes and knew he spoke the truth. He would never hurt her. He *loved* her. His hand reached beneath the hem of her nightgown to travel up her thigh, and an aching heat uncoiled inside her as he stroked the soft naked flesh of her hip.

Dan studied her face closely in the darkness. He wanted her respect. He wanted her love. He did not want her to fear him. If she recoiled from his touch, he would stop.

Gradually, Gabrielle's heart slowed from its wild gallop to a steady, tranquilizing rhythm. The look in Dan's eyes puzzled her. He was waiting, but for what? Not understanding what he expected of her, she placed a trembling hand against his firm jaw, and her heart missed a beat as he turned his head to press a kiss into her bandaged palm.

Encouraged by the gentleness of his action, she lifted her head to touch her lips to his, and was surprised and more than a little pleased with herself when he responded to her gesture by gathering her close to him and continuing what she had started, smothering her with all manner of kisses—bold, tender, passionate—until the thoughts that coursed through her mind became disjointed and lacking in direction and she clung to him, aware only of a hot, pulsing need deep inside her that begged frantically for release.

Spinning slowly down from the dizzying heights to which his kisses had taken her, Gabrielle did not protest when he gently lifted her and drew both her nightgown and torn robe up over her head. Nor did she realize that he had also stripped off his own clothing until he settled back onto the bed and her fingertips encountered the crisp black mat of hair that swirled across his naked chest. Jolted out of her delirium, Gabrielle opened her eyes.

His face was only inches from hers, and he was staring down at her. Though it was dark, she imagined she could see every gold fleck and every tawny spoke that radiated out from the velvety black pupils that seemed to look into her very soul. Her body jerked reflexively as his hand sought her breast, his strong fingers teasing her nipple until it hardened into a tight little bud that proudly rose up against his palm. She reminded herself that he had promised not to hurt her and her panic ebbed. Then she nearly laughed aloud as she was seized by the sudden conviction that she was supposed to demurely close her eyes through all of this, but she kept her gaze cemented to his as his knowing hands worked their magic on her, and was filled with wonder at the new sensations that rippled through her.

It was Dan who first dragged his gaze away. He wanted to look at her. Not just at those mesmerizing sea green eyes. He wanted to look at all of her.

It was not the first time he had seen Gabrielle naked, yet, as before, he was struck by the sheer perfection of her beauty.

Though she was of average height for a woman, there was nothing average about her long, shapely legs or the satin-smoothness of her ivory skin; nothing average about the beguiling fullness of her soft breasts or the way they seemed to change shape so they might fit perfectly into the palm of his hand. And the burning passion that hovered in her just beneath the surface, waiting to be awakened, was decidedly not average. Deliberately refraining from thinking lest his conscience rudely intervene, Dan lowered his head to her breast.

Gabrielle gasped as his lips closed around her nipple and he drew it deep into his mouth. His tongue now performed the same erotic dance his fingers had earlier, relentlessly tormenting the sensitive peak as he gradually increased the drawing pressure of his mouth until she moaned and writhed beneath him, helpless to stem the sharp pangs of desire that shot through her. Whimpering softly, she knotted her fingers in his thick black hair and clutched his head to her breast, terrified that he would stop before she had gotten her fill of the exquisite sensations he was coaxing from her body.

Her back arched, and Dan opened one eye to find her other breast straining toward him, its luring peak staring him straight in the eye, and a chuckle sounded deep in his throat. "Afraid you are going to miss something, are you?" he said teasingly to the impudent nipple after he released its mate with a parting kiss.

Horrified by what she had just done, Gabrielle shied away from him and flattened herself to the mattress, but he pounced on the untried nipple like a cat seizing its prey, and once more Gabrielle felt herself being swept up into a swirling vortex from which there was neither escape nor release. His hand slid downward between her legs, and she instinctively opened to him, too caught up in the wildly wicked passions he was arousing in her to have a care for maidenly modesty.

She was ready for him; he could take her now if he so chose. Instead, stringently keeping his own burning ardor in check, Dan shifted his weight so that he could suckle one sweet breast and fondle the other while maintaining steady tempo with the fingers that now delved boldly into her moist warmth. He prolonged her torment until, his name bursting from her lips, she arched her hips against his hand and feverishly flung her head from side to side.

It was hearing her unthinkingly utter his name that nearly broke Dan's control, but he quickly restrained himself. She would have but one first time, and he wanted it to be perfect for her. Bracing his hands on either side of Gabrielle, he positioned himself above her and, to the sound of rain lashing against the window, entered her in a single swift, sure stroke.

A half-gasp, half-shriek escaped her as searing pain stabbed through her recently pleasured limbs, and she dug her nails into Dan's back, clinging to him out of fear and confusion. "It's all right, little one," he whispered, kissing her damp brow as he folded his arms around her and settled against her, alarmed by the frantic hammering of her heart against his chest. "It only hurts the first time. From now on, you'll only feel pleasure. I promise. I'll never hurt you again." While he had never been one to apologize for something that could not be helped, it suddenly became imperative that she understand he deeply regretted any pain he had caused her.

Gabrielle was still too stunned to know whether she had been more hurt or more surprised by what had happened. And then another sensation took over and the fiery ache between her thighs melted into a warm, comforting fullness. A moan of pleasure rose in her throat. She could feel him inside her! But it was more than that, for not only did he fill her body, he filled the aching void that had been a part of her for as long as she could remember. It was like finding the long-missing piece of a puzzle and fitting it into place. "You didn't really hurt me," she said softly, as she gazed into the eyes that studied her in the darkness. "I just never thought it would feel so . . . good. It feels better than good. It feels wonderful!"

His restraint dangerously close to shattering, Dan eased his weight off her and started to withdraw, but stopped short of doing so at her cry of disappointment.

"Please don't," she pleaded. "I don't want it to end just yet."

Dan stared down at her, a suffocating pressure swelling in his chest as he began to fully realize the extent of her innocence. "It's not over, little one," he said thickly, his voice hoarse with restrained passion. "It's only just beginning."

Before she could ask what he meant by that, he plunged partway into her, retreated, then plunged again and again, each time driving himself deeper and deeper into her incredible softness until she cried out in agitation and raised her hips beneath him, combating his forceful thrusts with movements of her own, breaking his rhythm in her eagerness.

He deliberately slowed down. "Easy now," he murmured, marveling at the myriad of emotions that rippled across her lovely face as he moved with agonizing slowness inside her. He could not believe the way she responded to him, giving herself completely and naturally, and his own body's ravenous hunger for her surprised him.

Gabrielle felt as though she were floating. Wave after wave of dizzying, drugging warmth washed over her, each one coming in the wake of the one before it, faster and faster, until she could no longer think over the trembling fury that raced through every nerve in her body. "Oh, please . . ." she begged, gasping when the tempo of his thrust suddenly changed, becoming hard and fast and deep. And the storm that had been rapidly building inside her broke, tearing a low scream from her throat as a shuddering ecstasy burst inside her, rocking her to the core. Smothering her cry with his mouth, Dan captured her lips in a long, desperate kiss before driving into her one last time.

When his labored breathing finally returned to normal, he gathered her into his arms and rolled onto his side, drawing her with him, feeling more contented, more at peace with himself and the world, than he had in a long time. God, how he loved this beautiful, precious, infuriating woman-child who lay snuggled against him like a warm puppy. He had loved her for a long time, without being able to admit it—he loved her so much it hurt.

Finally collecting her passion-dazed wits, Gabrielle grew restless in the silence that hovered between them, and she tilted back her head to look up into the strong, masculine face beside her, her wide eyes shining in the darkness.

Smoothing a tangled curl back from her brow, Dan smiled down at her. "How do you feel?"

289

There was a note of remorse in her voice. "Guilty."

His hand stilled on her cheek. "About what we just shared?"

She shook her head, her expression solemn. "No. About putting ten chiles in your rattlesnake piss. I think nine would have been sufficient."

"Why, you little—!" Her laughter burst around them as he flipped her onto her back and leaned over her, pinning her beneath him. "I should still punish you for that," he threatened, struggling to keep a straight face.

Secure in the certainty that he wouldn't, Gabrielle nodded agreeably, but her eyes sparkled impishly. "Yes, you probably should."

"But then," Dan continued, amused that she would dare call his bluff, "I think I've found a better way to tame the devil in you, little one." Even as he spoke, he was languorously running one hand down the length of her, raising tiny prickles of anticipation on her skin; and Gabrielle, with a sigh of happiness, surrendered willingly to his touch.

Later that night, after he had made love to her yet another time and they lay in each other's arms, listening to the storm crashing outside the house, Gabrielle finally found the courage to broach a subject that had been tormenting her. "If I have a choice," she said quietly, hoping her words did not destroy the fragile bond that had grown between them, "I would rather stay with Grace when you go to Tucson."

Dan's arms tightened around her, and several minutes passed while he hashed the suggestion over in his mind. He had not been oblivious to the look Wilcox had bestowed upon Gabrielle earlier. Indeed, he had been on the verge of telling Gabrielle he trusted her enough to let her stay home while he was away. And he did trust her. But he didn't trust Marcus Epperling. Dan did not doubt for an instant that the lieutenant would find an excuse to return to the post the minute word reached him that Gabrielle was alone, and he did not want to expose her to him. Still, he knew how strict Simmons was with his own daughter, and he had no illusions about how his rebellious little charge would react to the restrictions that would be imposed upon her in that man's household.

Disturbed by his silence, Gabrielle disengaged herself from

Dan's arms and sat up, her long hair spilling about her. "If you really want me to stay with the Wilcoxes, I will," she said, trying hard to keep the disappointment from her voice. "Mrs. Wilcox is always nice to me. I just don't think Captain Wilcox likes me very much."

"The sergeant major isn't exactly fond of you," Dan reminded her quietly.

She had no answer for that. It was true. Sergeant-Major Simmons didn't like her. Nor, she suspected, did Mrs. Simmons. Ashamed of all she had done to tarnish her image in everyone's eyes, Gabrielle lowered her gaze.

Dan caught her chin and forced it back up, not wishing to see her so unhappy. "Staying with the Simmons is an acceptable alternative. In fact, with Mary going into labor early, it's probably the only alternative."

She swallowed hard and took a deep breath. "Thank you."

"Come here."

Uncertainty flickered in her eyes. "Are you angry with me?"

"Should I be?"

Her mouth went dry as she realized yet another subject of contention demanded to be aired. "I—I'm sorry I pitched a fit earlier and that I scared the horse and—"

"No more apologies, little one. They're not necessary. I know you're sorry."

"But, I—"

"Shhh. It's over. It's forgiven. Now, come here."

She obediently settled back down in the comforting circle of his arms, but sleep was the farthest thing from her mind as she lay against the warm length of him, her fingers absently toying with the dark hair on his chest.

He could feel her restlessness, and he had a pretty good idea of what was troubling her. While he had not wanted to broach the issue just yet, he knew it would be cruel to prolong her anxiety.

As if reading his thoughts, Gabrielle suddenly burst out in a voice thick with emotion. "I won't tell anyone what we did tonight, so you don't have to worry about marrying me. I'll be all right. When I do marry, I can always pretend to be a virgin, so my husband need not know—"

In one swift, fluid motion he rolled her onto her back and pressed her into the pillows, half covering her with his body. "Look at me," he commanded, knotting his fingers in her thick hair and turning her face toward his. Even in the darkness, he could see the glimmer of tears in her eyes. "Do you honestly think I am the type of man who would take a woman's chastity without having any intention of marrying her?"

A tear streaked across her temple and into her hair. "You didn't take it," she protested stubbornly. "I gave it to you."

"You haven't answered my question."

The happiness she had felt earlier dissolved in a sea of misery and self-doubt. "I couldn't bear it if I thought you married me because you felt you had to," she confessed in a pained whisper. "Just knowing I had your love for a little while is enough for me."

"Well, it's not enough for me, damn it!" Dan barked, the unintentional sharpness of his tone causing her to flinch. His fingers tightened in her hair. "What happened between us tonight was as special for me as it was for you. I want you. I want you by my side every day and in my bed every night. Perhaps that sounds selfish, but you're just going to have to get used to it, because I'm a selfish man, Gabrielle. You're mine, and what's mine, I don't share. I sure as hell didn't make love to you just to send you on to another man's bed. I want you for my wife. Do you understand that?"

"You don't even like me most of the time."

"But, I love you, and if you haven't figured that out by now, then you're sorely lacking in common sense, young lady."

While she had seen it in his eyes, hearing him say he loved her was more than she had bargained for. Marcus had never told her he loved her, nor, for as far back as she could remember, had her father. Only her mother had ever spoken to her of love. And now Dan. "I only have enough common sense to fit on the sharp end of a cactus spine," she joked, trying unsuccessfully to inject some levity into the situation.

"Don't throw my words back into my face, Gabrielle," Dan cautioned, but he did release her hair to stroke her cheek. "It's not easy for me to say, because I never expected to feel this way about anyone, least of all about you, but I do love you. True, there are times when you try my patience, but I also know there are times when I try yours. It won't be a perfect union, little one, and I'm sure there will be some difficult times before we iron out our differences. But I'm willing to give it all I have . . . if you are."

It was one of the longest speeches she had ever heard him utter, and the fact that he was attempting to share his feelings with her, in spite of how difficult it was for him, warmed her heart far more than any socially acceptable courting ritual would have done. "Are you asking me to marry you?" she whispered, offering him her lips as she reached up to twine her arms around his neck and pull him down to her.

His kiss was slow and thoughtful, almost hesitant, and that surprised Gabrielle. She had never suspected that Dan Catlin would be one to have doubts about anything he did. Yet, when he finally did lift his head to fix her with a soul-probing gaze, there was no question in her mind that he loved her. He might be as uncertain about entering marriage as she was, but he loved her. And that was all that mattered.

Cupping her face between his hands, he gazed steadily into her eyes and said solemnly, "Miss DuBois, will you do me the honor of becoming my wife?"

Unable to resist teasing him just a little, Gabrielle frowned and feigned seriousness. "I don't know. I shall have to sleep on it."

Just then, a vicious bolt of lightning crackled and thunder exploded directly overhead, and Gabrielle, her heart leaping into her throat, gasped and clung to him in desperation. "I think God will strike me dead if I say no," she said breathlessly as the thunder faded into a low rumble and her pulse slowed.

"Not to mention what I'll do to you," Dan retorted, prying her arms from around his neck before she strangled him.

Settling back onto the pillows, she heaved an exaggerated sigh. "Then I suppose I have no choice but to submit."

"You have a choice, Gabrielle," Dan said quietly. "You'll always have a choice."

Feeling guilty for not behaving herself, Gabrielle immediately curbed the riotous joy inside her. "In that case, Major

Catlin," she said slowly, carefully enunciating each word in her monumental effort to be serious, "the honor is mine. I gladly accept your proposal of marriage."

"Do you promise to love, honor, and obey me?" he asked, so solemnly that it took her a moment to realize he had turned the tables and was now teasing her.

She immediately became mutinous. "I never said anything about *obeying*," she stated flatly, the feral gleam in her eyes betraying her addiction to their verbal sparring. "Only about marriage."

"It's part of the bargain."

She really became serious as a new doubt swept through her. "I promise I will try very hard to obey you, but if I fail and do something to displease you, will you love me anyway?"

There was so much painful uncertainty in her voice that Dan immediately regretted having teased her. He was only just beginning to acknowledge the depth of the fear and self-doubt that she endured, and he silently blamed Stephen DuBois for being the cause of his daughter's insecurities. To withhold love from one's own child was, to Dan's way of thinking, the cruelest form of abuse. While his own father had physically abandoned him, the colonel had emotionally abandoned Gabrielle.

In that instant, the respect he had been harboring for Stephen DuBois for nineteen years died.

Settling himself beside Gabrielle on the pillows, Dan drew her into his arms and held her soft warmth against him. "There is nothing you could do, little one, to make me stop loving you." He gently stroked her hair, a little awed by the way their hearts beat in unison. "When you love someone, you love the entire person, not just the good parts."

His hands moved down her back, pressing her closer to him, and Gabrielle could not remember ever having felt so lovingly comforted in her entire life. "Will you tell me every day that you love me?" she whispered into his chest.

"Every day," he promised.

"Even if you are very, very angry with me?"

"No matter how angry I am with you."

Feeling as though a terrible weight had been lifted off her

shoulders, Gabrielle snuggled against him, one arm wrapped about his waist. "I love you so much," she whispered sleepily, her eyelids drooping as she was finally overcome with exhaustion.

The trust she afforded him was a terrible burden, one Dan wasn't certain he wanted or needed, but as he lay there in the darkness, gently stroking the soft, warm, provocative little witch curled up next to him, he knew he would prefer the responsibility of shouldering her trust over the emptiness of living without her.

He only hoped nothing ever happened to kill that trust.

Dan awoke the following morning to find Gabrielle, the sheet clutched over her breasts, surreptitiously studying his nakedness through half-closed eyes, and his body responded instantly to the passion her inquisitive gaze aroused in him. He saw her eyes widen at what must have seemed to her no less than a miracle, then snap shut in feigned sleep the instant he moved to roll onto his side. Stifling a smile, he shifted so that he might more easily watch her expressive face while he indulged in his own game of possum.

He did not have long to wait.

Her long lashes fluttered against her cheeks, and first one eye, then the other, cautiously opened. After glancing at his face to make certain he was still asleep, her gaze once more found his now fully-aroused sex and inspected it with a thoroughness that would have made him uneasy had he not understood the reason for her curiosity; for a girl who had spent her entire life in the company of soldiers, Gabrielle DuBois had somehow made it almost to her eighteenth year without ever having seen a man unclothed. Suddenly he felt outrageously pleased that he had been the one to initiate her into the pleasures of womanhood.

He was also beginning to question his sanity. He had pledged the rest of his life to a woman who sparked his fury as easily as his ardor. That was not the behavior of a man in full possession of his senses.

Her eyes closed now in pretended slumber, Gabrielle sighed

softly and rolled toward him, her face nestling against his shoulder and one bandaged hand landing with dubious innocence on his chest. She lay without stirring for several weighted seconds; then, unaware that she was being watched through veiled eyes, she slyly began to inch her fingers downward, and it took every ounce of self-control Dan could muster not to flinch at her touch. *Damn!* When had he become ticklish?

Steadily downward the inquisitive hand traveled, across the taut planes of his abdomen, stopping short of the target Dan was fervently hoping she sought. Abandoning all pretense of sleep, he opened his eyes fully, saw the rapidly jumping pulse in the side of her neck, and knew that fear was preventing any further descent of her hand. "It's all right," he said quietly. "Go ahead and touch me."

She gasped and jerked her hand away as if she had been scalded.

A throaty laugh breaking inside him, Dan caught hold of her and rolled onto his back, pulling her atop him.

"You tricked me!" she said accusingly, then tried to untangle herself from the sheet and from her own tousled hair that had somehow become wrapped around her, but Dan's strong arms held her tightly, effectively preventing her escape. "You were pretending to be asleep!"

"Look who's talking!" he countered, a wicked gleam in his eyes as he moved one hand beneath the sheet to fondle a soft round buttock. "You, my dear woman, are an inveterate sneak!"

"And you, sir, are no gentleman or you wouldn't be manhandling me this way!"

One dark brow arched sardonically. "Is there a way that you prefer I manhandle you? Like this, perhaps?" Freeing a breast from the imprisoning sheet, he captured its dusky pink tip between his teeth while his hands gripped her waist and moved her struggling body in tantalizing circles against his hips.

"Don't do that!" she cried out, fighting back the flood of desire that threatened to drown her.

He immediately stopped, but the piercing look he afforded her made her want to run and hide. "Unless I dreamed last night, little one, I was under the distinct impression that you liked it when I touched you like that."

"I do! It's just that . . . it's . . . morning!"

"So?"

She swallowed hard, confused by the conflicting emotions that battered her already troubled conscience. "You mean people actually do this in the broad light of day?"

He almost chuckled, but stopped himself as he realized she was serious. "Probably more often than at night," he said gently, abandoning his erotic exploration of her body to reach up and smooth the tangled curls back from her face. "Desire doesn't operate by a clock, Gabrielle. It comes naturally, when two people are close enough and comfortable enough with each other to just let it happen. And, right now, my body desires yours. It's nothing to be ashamed of."

Feeling painfully like a schoolgirl being chided for her ignorance, Gabrielle sensed her cheeks grow warm. "I'm just . . . embarrassed to have you look at me," she said softly.

"I looked at you last night."

"But it was dark!"

"Not the entire time. Every time lightning lit up the room, I looked at you. I couldn't get enough of you. You're a beautiful woman, little one. An extremely beautiful woman."

His words only served to embarrass her further, and she couldn't think of anything to say.

"You looked at me this morning when you thought I was asleep," he reminded her.

Hot color stained her face all the way to the roots of her hair, and she nervously averted her gaze.

"Get up," Dan commanded, lifting her off him, and when she had returned to her own side of the bed, he swept the sheet aside.

Panic flickered in Gabrielle's eyes and she immediately sought to cover herself, but he seized her hands and brought them back to her sides.

Mortified, she lay rigid and unmoving while he stretched out on the bed beside her, their bodies as naked and exposed as on the day they were born.

"Turn toward me," he ordered, and she unthinkingly

obeyed, not certain what mental torture he had planned for her. Last night had been wonderful, but now all she wanted to do was to crawl into a corner somewhere and die. "Now, touch me."

She froze, unable to move a single muscle.

Summoning a pool of patience he had not known he possessed, Dan took her hand and placed it against the side of his face, and he did the same to her. "Now, tell me what you feel."

"You first," she said, relieved that it was only his face she was touching.

His gaze held hers as he stroked her cheek with his strong brown fingers, letting them linger on the curve of her jaw. "I feel what has to be the smoothest skin in the world," he said in a low, nonthreatening voice.

She followed his example. "It's prickly," she offered, giving him a feeble smile as she caressed his day-old growth of beard.

His fingers slid into her hair and toyed with the tangled mop of red-gold curls that framed her face. "It's springy. And thick."

"Your hair is springy too. And it's all there," she added a bit sheepishly, causing him to smile.

His hand traveled downward to rest against the pulse point at the side of her neck. "Thump, thump, thump, thump, thump," he mimicked in a rapid staccato that made her laugh. In response, she traced a corded muscle with her forefinger.

Her breath caught as he cupped his hand around her breast. "It's soft and vulnerable. Like you," he said, the expression in his eyes tender and understanding. "It changes to fit the shape of my palm, the way you sometimes change your moods to match mine. But"—he playfully tweaked the nipple that had hardened instantly in response to his caress—"it has a mind of its own."

His touch was doing odd things to her, making her feel warm and quivery inside, and she pressed her legs more tightly together to combat the restless longings stirring to life between her thighs. Catching her bottom lip between her teeth, she moved the flat of her hand down across his broad, powerfully-structured chest, her breath quickening as muscles leaped reflexively beneath her fingers. "It feels strong and . . . safe." She was acutely aware that his hand was descending over the faint yellowish bruises that remained from her accident, and further still. Suddenly, a totally irreverent thought streaked through Gabrielle's mind, and a glimmer of mischief broke through the soft desire in her eyes.

Dan lifted a querying brow and she blushed self-consciously. "I was just thinking," she explained with a naughty little laugh, "that the next time we play cards . . . we should gamble for higher stakes than salt-water taffy . . ."

Amusement danced among the amber lights in Dan's eyes. "It would appear that my bride-to-be has a decadent streak in her," he teased, and her response was lost in the delicious tremor that rippled through her as his knowing fingers slid through the soft curls at the juncture of her thighs to touch a spot so sensitive she feared she would forget herself and react with shocking immodesty. In fact, Gabrielle was so intent on maintaining her composure, she did not hear the soft words Dan murmured as his fingers methodically stroked the fire that was beginning to flare out of control within her. Her hand quaking terribly, she touched her fingertips to his rigid shaft.

And something melted inside her as a pleased smile softened Dan's stern features. "It's . . . warm," she ventured, closing her eyes lest he read the embarrassment in them. "Warmer than the rest of you. And it's hard and soft . . . all at the same time . . . like . . . stone covered in velvet."

"Open your eyes, little one. Don't be afraid. I want you to look at me while you touch me."

Swallowing, she did as she was bid. But her head reeled and it was becoming impossible to think clearly, for his skillful touch was unleashing a torrent of sensations in her. Her fingers closed around him and a cry shuddered from her throat. "I can't . . . stand it . . . anymore," she whimpered, squeezing her eyes shut and flinging back her head. "I c-can't . . ."

With incredible gentleness, he turned her onto her back and drew her beneath him, kissing her tenderly as he eased himself once again into her welcoming warmth.

*   *   *

"A full seven pounds!" Grace exclaimed, her face awash with a blush of excitement. "Can you believe it? Pa said you could hear her squalling all the way to the stables. They named her Constance May, but they'll probably wind up calling her Connie. Isn't it exciting? She is the first baby ever to be born at Camp Carleton."

"That's nice," Gabrielle said woodenly as she put the last of the dishes in the cupboard, recalling with a twinge of irritation that the hazy aftermath of passion had been rudely interrupted by Captain Wilcox's persistent pounding on the front door. "Here, help me empty this dishpan so I don't get my bandages all wet."

Grace eyed her quizzically as they carried the basin out into the yard and poured the water into the vegetable bed. "This is almost a wasted effort after all the rain we got last night," she joked, and when Gabrielle did not respond, her bewilderment turned to concern. "You didn't quarrel with the major before he left, did you?"

The guilt that had been festering deep down inside Gabrielle surged to the surface, but she could not bring herself to tell Grace the truth. "I don't want to talk about it," she declared. Propping the dishpan against the step, she went back into the house.

Her brows drawing together pensively, Grace followed Gabrielle inside and up the stairs. For a moment, she just stood in the doorway of her friend's room, her puzzled gaze fixed on Gabrielle's back, bent over the open valise on her bed. "Did I do something?"

"Don't be silly."

"Then, why won't you tell me what's wrong?"

Gabrielle straightened and whirled around. "Because I can't," she said, a silent plea for forgiveness in her eyes as she clutched a petticoat to her breast.

Grace stepped into the room. "Now look who's being silly. You can tell me anything. We're friends, aren't we?"

"Yes, but—"

"Then tell me!"

Gabrielle felt torn. Grace was going to find out the truth sooner or later; the entire post was going to know. And while

300

she feared her friend was going to hate her, she knew she should break the news to Grace herself. She took a deep breath. "Major Catlin asked me to marry him and I said yes," she choked out. "I know you love him, but I love him too. I can't help the way I feel. I'm sorry."

Surprise, then delight, reflected in Grace's eyes, and then understanding. "You don't have to apologize for being in love with Major Catlin. I think it's wonderful!"

Gabrielle frowned, not quite believing that her friend would relinquish her claim to Dan so easily. After all, were the situation reversed, she wouldn't. "You're not . . . upset?"

"Of course not!"

"But I thought you were in love with him."

"I was. And I still think he's a wonderful man. Wonderful for you, that is. Not for me. I quake in my shoes every time he barks at me. I don't think I would ever have the gumption to stand up to him the way you do. Quite frankly, he scares the daylights out of me!"

"Oh, Grace," Gabrielle blurted out, relieved to be able to unburden herself. "I love him so much! I know it sounds insane, what with the way we are constantly at each other's throats, but I've never in my life felt so safe or so loved as I do when he holds me."

"And he really wants to marry you?"

"He really does! He asked me last night—but you must not breathe a word of this to anyone. If Father hears about it before Dan has a chance to speak with him, he is liable to think Dan is marrying me simply to use Father's influence to keep himself out of trouble with the higher-ups. And Dan refuses to do that."

Grace could not help smiling. "It sounds so odd to hear you call him by his given name. And I still can't believe the two of you are actually in love! Pa says the reason you quarrel so much is because you're both as stubborn as Army mules—it's a miracle! Gabrielle, you must tell me everything!"

For the next hour, they sat amidst the piles of petticoats and underdrawers on Gabrielle's bed while she recounted every moment of the previous day, from the time Grace had left her stranded with the mud on her face right up to the incident with the rattlesnake piss.

"It's a wonder he didn't let you have it!" Grace gasped, laughing so hard tears streamed down her face.

"I thought he was going to, believe me. When he dragged me from under the bed, I could have sworn my life was over." At that point, Gabrielle no longer desired to tell Grace everything. What she and Dan had shared last night—and this morning— was something she wanted to keep to herself. Besides, Grace Simmons, who was always so good and perfect, who never did anything shameful, would be horrified to learn that her friend was no longer a virgin. Jealously guarding her real secret, Gabrielle continued in a low, thoughtful voice, "It was so wonderful when he kissed me, Grace. Not at all like it was when Marcus kissed me. And when he said he loved me, I wanted to get up on the roof and shout it to the entire post!"

"Well then, when is the wedding? Will it be a big affair or a small one? You will invite me, won't you?"

Gabrielle laughed. "In answer to your questions, I don't know, and of course you're invited! I want you to be my bridesmaid, and don't you dare refuse!"

Grace looked so genuinely happy for her that Gabrielle felt ready to burst with guilt. "Oh, Grace," she said, grasping the other girl's hand and clinging to it. "I'm so sorry for all the awful things I've done to you. Please forgive me."

"There's nothing to—"

"But, there is! I slapped you and called you names, not to mention teasing you about padding your bust. You're the best and dearest friend I've ever had. I only wish there was some way I could make up for the abominable way I treated you."

"You can make me godmother to your children," Grace said simply, quietly.

Gabrielle was momentarily taken aback. "You would want that responsibility?" she asked in stunned disbelief, then burst out laughing. "If my children are anything like me, they're liable to be little terrors!"

"If they're anything like you—and the major—they'll be the most beautiful children in the world. Now, before Mama starts wondering why we're taking so long, let's get the rest of your clothes packed and moved to our quarters. It's going to be fun, having you stay with me while Major Catlin is away. I'll finally have some help with the supper dishes!"

Gabrielle wrinkled her nose in disdain. "Maybe I should reconsider."

"Too late. Besides, we've been invited to go to the Wilcoxes' this afternoon to see the baby. I don't want to miss that for the world."

Suddenly, neither did Gabrielle. "Do you think Mrs. Wilcox will let us hold her?" she asked, jumping off the bed and stuffing several chemises into her valise. "I've never held a real live baby before."

"Never?"

Gabrielle shook her head, and then a wave of emotion threatened to overwhelm her. "Oh, Grace, I'm so glad you're my friend!"

This time it was the older girl's turn to grimace. "I'm beginning to think I liked you better when you were mean and odious! Here, hand me those stockings before you step on them and ruin them."

By the time they had finished packing and were trudging through the mud toward the noncommissioned officers' quarters, Gabrielle's spirits had risen considerably. Dan was gone, but he would return. And when he did, she would become his wife. They weren't foolish children, rushing into marriage after a brief acquaintance. She had known him almost her entire life, and found him to be a most honest, most dependable man. She was certain, as he had promised, he would tell her every day that he loved her, and nothing, nothing could ever drive them apart.

"Better wipe your feet before you go in, or Mama will have a fit," Grace warned as they lugged the valise up the steps, and Gabrielle, feeling as though she were on top of the world, brought her right hand up to her brow in a mocking salute, nearly sending them both toppling into the mud in a fit of giggles.

Mrs. Simmons' voice reached them the instant they opened the front door. "I spread some newspapers on the floor in the hall. You girls are to take off your shoes and leave them there. I don't want mud tracked through my house."

303

"What did I tell you?" Grace whispered and Gabrielle rolled her eyes.

With her hands hampered by the bandages, her movements were clumsy, and Grace managed to get out of both shoes before Gabrielle had unlaced even one. "I'll start unpacking your clothes," Grace said. "You can come back to my room when you're through."

Gabrielle finally managed to get one shoe off, and was about to place it on the newspaper when she saw Dan's name right on the front page. Her curiosity piqued, she set the shoe aside and picked up the paper.

As her eyes scanned the print, all color drained from her face.

Chapter Fourteen

"Gabrielle, what's wrong?"

Gabrielle did not know how long she had been standing there, staring at the newspaper, but Grace's voice snapped her out of her trancelike state. "Did you see this?" she demanded, shoving the newspaper beneath her friend's nose. "The *Miner* is encouraging the people of the Territory to petition the governor to have Dan removed from duty and tried as a criminal in a civilian court because he didn't place the Apaches under arrest and return them to Camp Grant!"

"Oh, Gabrielle, it's only words. You know reporters always blow these matters out of proportion just to stir up trouble. In fact, if you look closer, you'll see that the article was written by that Hyatt fellow, the one Major Catlin had thrown off the post only a few days ago. I'm sure that—"

"Grace, his career will be destroyed! Look at this. It says right here that Dan keeps the Indians at Camp Carleton because he 'has developed a taste for dusky Apache maidens.' I know it's not true. Dan would never do anything like that. Never!"

"Of course he wouldn't, silly. But you know how people are. They believe what they want to, and the more exciting the story, the better. Look how quickly word spread the time the major whipped you." Grace noticed the look of pain that flashed through Gabrielle's eyes, and she hastened to explain. "No one even mentions it anymore, but for days that was all anyone could talk about. That, and your running away.

Everyone had to be first with the latest tidbit of gossip about you, and most of what was said wasn't even true. It's the same thing with that news story. Everyone knows it's an exaggeration."

"Everyone *doesn't* know it's an exaggeration," Gabrielle protested, throwing down the paper and grabbing the shoe she had just taken off as the numbness of shock rapidly dissolved into heated waves of anger.

"Gabrielle, where are you going?"

"I'm going to get Dan out of this mess, once and for all."

"How?"

"I don't know! I just know I have to do *something*."

She found Bandy Moreland in the Headquarters Building. "Captain Moreland, I must go to Prescott right away, and I'll need a horse and an escort—"

"Whoa! Just slow down a minute, little lady! Now, would you mind tellin' me what's so all-fired important that you gotta go ridin' off for Prescott like your tail's on fire?"

"It's this," she said, handing him the article she had ripped out of the paper. "I need to talk to the reporter who wrote this and get him to rescind his story. It's just not true, and Dan will be ruined if something isn't done before word of this reaches the governor."

Bandy did not miss her inadvertent use of Dan's first name. "Sorry, Miss DuBois," he said, handing the paper back to her. "I gotta turn down your request."

It suddenly hurt Gabrielle to breath. "But why?"

Her chin quivered and her eyes widened slightly and misted over, and Bandy couldn't help thinking she was pretty adept at this. God help Dan; he was gonna need plenty of support if he married the little baggage. "Because, I wanted to tear outta here yesterday when I first seen that pack o' lies, but Dan said he'd have my hide if I did. He wants to work this out his own way, in his own time; and both you and me gotta respect that, whether it sticks in our craws or not."

"But—"

"No *buts*. If you want to help Danny, then you just stay put and behave yourself so he don't spend his time worryin' about what kind of mischief you're gettin' yourself into."

Nor was Sergeant-Major Simmons any help.

"Major Catlin got himself into this mess; he can get himself out," he told her tersely as they were sitting down to dinner.

"He would help you if the situation were reversed," Gabrielle insisted.

"Well, the situation *isn't* reversed, because *I* wouldn't be so damned thickheaded as to get myself into such a tangle in the first place. Now, if you don't mind, Gabrielle, I would like to eat my supper in peace."

Her heart sank. "Yes, sir," she muttered woodenly and lowered her eyes. Unfolding her napkin, she spread it across her lap before reaching for the bowl of mashed potatoes that had been placed near her, her hand stopping in midair at Grace's sharp intake of breath.

She looked up to find Grace, the sergeant major, and Mrs. Simmons all watching her in stunned silence, and her mouth suddenly went dry. "Did I do something wrong?" she finally managed to get out.

Mrs. Simmons speared her with a look of disapproval. "In this house, we give thanks to the Lord before we eat," she said sharply.

Feeling her face grow warm, Gabrielle lowered her hands to her lap. "Yes, ma'am."

"I wish you had come with me to see the baby this afternoon," Grace whispered in the darkness after they had gone to bed. "She's so *tiny*. I find it hard to imagine either of us ever being that small once." She smothered a giggle. "Can you imagine Major Catlin as a baby? Sometimes I think he was *born* six foot, three."

A choking lump ballooned in Gabrielle's throat at the mention of Dan's name. What kind of a future were they going to have together if he wasn't able to convince General Crook—and Governor Safford—that he was doing the right thing? What if he went to prison?

Grace raised up on one elbow. "Are you all right?"

Gabrielle turned her head to stare at the girl whose bed she

307

shared, her eyelids suddenly turning to sandpaper as she blinked back the tears that threatened. "Oh, Grace, I'm so scared. I have this awful feeling that something terrible is going to happen to Dan."

Grace found her hand beneath the covers and gave it a squeeze. "Nothing is going to happen. And, even if it does, with you by his side, he'll be able to get through anything."

Gabrielle shook her head. "But, there's nothing I can do—"

"Yes, there is. Just *be* there for him. Show him you believe in what he is trying to do. Give him someone to lean on."

"He'd be leaning on a coward," Gabrielle choked out.

Sergeant-Major Simmons' voice sliced through the darkness. "You girls stop that talking and go to sleep!"

With a sigh of resignation, Grace plumped her pillow and lay back down. "You're the bravest person I know," she whispered. "And you're the only person I know who would dare give Major Catlin *rattlesnake piss.*"

Later that night, Gabrielle turned restlessly, her slumber punctuated by troubled dreams.

"Not so loud," Grace whispered, casting an anxious glance over her shoulder at Gabrielle's sleeping form. "You'll wake her."

Bandy lowered his voice. "You gonna come walkin' with me again tonight?"

"Just for a little while. I don't want her to awaken and find me gone."

Grace climbed up on a chair and placed her hands on the Captain's shoulders as he helped her through the window.

Panic gripping her insides, Gabrielle cast a wild glance over her shoulder as a second set of footsteps pounded on the ground behind her, echoing her own.

The Apache pounced.

He slammed into her, knocking her to the ground with a force that drove the air from her lungs. She opened her mouth to scream but nothing would come out.

His weight shifted and she scrambled to her knees, but he grabbed hold of her skirt and pulled, yanking her legs out from under her, then, before she could cry out, he grasped her arm and flung her onto her back and she found herself staring up at Marcus Epperling.

"Marcus, help me!" she shrieked, but the boyishly handsome face suddenly became distorted as he threw back his head and laughed.

Suddenly, the evil-sounding laughter stopped, and as Marcus once more turned his gaze on her, the blue eyes Gabrielle had once loved changed to obsidian and golden curls became dark and lank hair.

She screamed and screamed.

Twisted by fury, his face loomed over her, teeth bared. He drew back his arm and, before she could dodge the blow she saw coming, crashed his fist into the side of her head.

Pain exploded in her, followed by waves of darkness. Eyes closed, she lay without moving, struggling to keep a grip on reality as total oblivion threatened to overcome her.

"That'll teach you to give that breed what should have been mine," she heard Marcus say. Then the clink of metal on metal came to her as he fumbled with his belt buckle.

Blackness hovered over her, alternately advancing, then retreating. She could feel the hardness of the ground beneath her, the rocks sharp-edged gouging into her back, and Marcus' hands groping crudely beneath her skirt.

"Whore!" she heard him shout, over and over, and she pressed her hands to her ears to shut out the awful sound. "I've been waiting a long time for this," Marcus grumbled as he worked her drawers down over her hips. "Cock-teaser!"

A wave of nausea swept over Gabrielle and she knew, with a calm certainty, that he was going to rape her.

"Gabrielle, answer me! Are you all right?" Dan's voice pierced her darkness.

She opened her eyes to the glint of sunlight on a steel blade. "Dan, look out!"

Dan leapt to his feet and whirled around as the Apache lunged, plunging the knife through his heart. . . .

With a strangled cry, Gabrielle bolted upright in the bed, her

309

breath coming in ragged gulps and her heart pounding so loudly each beat reverberated inside her chest.

It was a dream, she told herself as she glanced about the darkened bedroom, her pulse gradually slowing. Only a dream. Relief swept over her, and a shudder rocked her entire body.

Still, nothing could erase that awful picture from her mind.

Realizing with a start that she was alone in the room, Gabrielle lay back down, glad that Grace had gone to the outhouse and had not witnessed her fright. The other girl simply would not understand her fears. Grace would have thought she was turning into a silly goose.

The minutes ticked slowly by and still Grace did not return. Gabrielle shifted restlessly and rolled onto her side, pulling her knees up to her chest and tucking herself into a ball the way she always did when she was hurt or scared. She closed her eyes, but they snapped open the instant the disturbing dream images invaded her thoughts. "Please, God, keep Dan safe," she whispered into the darkness, unable to stop trembling.

She stiffened and her gaze riveted on the window as a movement from outside stirred the muslin curtain. Holding her breath, she watched, wide-eyed, as Grace climbed into the room. "She's still asleep," she heard Grace whisper. A man's muffled reply followed. *Grace had sneaked out to meet a man?*

"Good night, Wilbur," Grace whispered, and blew him a kiss.

Wilbur? Captain Moreland?

Gabrielle closed her eyes and forced herself to be still while Grace shucked off the dress she had pulled on over her nightgown and then slipped into bed.

Grace Simmons had sneaked out through her window in the middle of the night to meet Bandy Moreland!

Momentarily forgetting her own troubles, Gabrielle smothered a giggle as she rolled onto her side, still pretending sleep; and some of the tension left her. It was nice to know that perfect Grace Simmons had an errant streak in her after all.

Over the next few days, Gabrielle fell into a routine that once would have made her rebel. She dried dishes after every meal and even helped with the housecleaning, and she and Grace visited Mary Wilcox and ran errands for her. Mrs

Simmons still gave her an occasional wilting glance, but the sergeant major gradually eased up on his criticism. Meanwhile Grace continued to slip out at night to meet Bandy Moreland, completely unaware that her friend knew what she was doing. And Gabrielle was finally able to remove the bandages from her hands, but the ugly red scar tissue across her palms remained, a reminder of her childish behavior.

The rains stopped, and the ground became hard and cracked as the heat of June hit them with full force.

Supplies for the Apache camp arrived at the post, but the flour was wormy and the salted meat rancid.

No one spoke of Dan.

And Gabrielle kept her worries to herself.

"Happy Birthday," Grace said cheerfully the instant she opened her eyes after one particularly fitful night.

Pressing a hand to the side of her throbbing head, Gabrielle sat up and tried to focus her sleep-blurred gaze on the tissue-wrapped package Grace held out to her.

"Go ahead. Open it."

"I didn't think anyone would remember."

"Don't be silly! You remembered my birthday, didn't you?"

"Yes, but—"

"Open it!"

Giving Grace a wan smile, Gabrielle took the present. She did not open it immediately, but sat turning it over in her hands while fighting back a wave of melancholy. She missed Dan more than she would have thought possible; each moment that he was away passed with agonizing slowness. She wished he could be here to help her celebrate her birthday. Now that she was eighteen he wouldn't be so inclined to think of her as a child. At least, she hoped he wouldn't.

She untied the string and her breath caught as she peeled back the layers of tissue paper to reveal a handkerchief of fine lawn with a three-inch border of tatted lace. She touched a forefinger to the delicate lacework. "It's . . . beautiful! Did you do this?"

"Yes. Though I came close to giving up. I would get so frustrated every time the thread knotted on me."

Surprise reflected in Gabrielle's eyes. "Do you mean, this

311

doesn't come easily to you?"

Grace shook her head. "It never has."

"And I thought I was the only one!"

Grace bounded off the bed and went to the dresser. "There's something else." She removed an envelope and a tiny rosewood box from her dresser drawer and returned to the bed with them. "It's from Major Catlin."

Gabrielle's hands shook as she fingered the intricate pattern of grapes and leaves carved into the rounded top of the box, but she could not make herself open it. Setting it aside, she opened the envelope and removed the letter within. "My Dearest Little One," it read, "I instructed Miss Simmons to give this to you in the event that I am not able to return in time for your birthday. The box is of no particular value; I bought it after the war from another soldier in need of train fare home. But that which is inside belonged to my mother and is the only memento I have of her. I trust you to wear it next to your heart in the hope that someday it, along with our love, may be passed on to our children. While I am in Tucson, I shall buy you a real gift—one it will give me the greatest pleasure to present to you. Until then, remember that I do love you. Dan."

A warm glow spread over Gabrielle's face and engulfed her entire body. He loved her. He truly loved her!

"You don't know how hard it was pretending I didn't know anything when you told me he had proposed to you," Grace said. Drawing her knees up to her chin and hugging her legs, she went on. "I'm happy for you. And for the major. The two of you will be so good for each other."

Gabrielle uttered a rueful laugh. "If we don't kill each other first."

"Well, are you going to open your present or aren't you?"

"All right, I'll open it!"

Inside, against a bed of wine-colored velvet, lay a tiny spray of gold filigree roses suspended by a gold chain.

Grace's eyes glowed as she took in the stunned look on Gabrielle's face.

When Gabrielle lifted the necklace from the box, the morning sun streamed in through the open window and reflected off each perfectly-formed petal, each tiny-veined leaf, making the delicate roses appear to glow with a light of their own. "It's . . . beautiful," Gabrielle murmured, her head reeling with questions about the woman who had once worn this dainty piece of jewelry, and of the little boy who had, for years, held onto it until he'd finally entrusted it to the woman he planned to marry. There was so much she didn't know about Dan. And so much she wanted to learn. But what scared her the most was that she might not be able to live up to what he expected of her. She didn't want to let him down. She *couldn't* let him down.

"It's very old," Grace informed her. "Look at the clasp."

It was hard to make out the well-worn etching. "'Edinburgh, 1669,'" Gabrielle read aloud. "Oh, Grace! What if I lose it?"

"Major Catlin wouldn't have given it to you if he thought you might lose it. Why don't you put it on?"

Gabrielle turned her back and held up her hair while Grace fastened the clasp behind her neck, but her eyes remained fixed on the tiny roses that lay against the bodice of her nightgown. It was the first gift Dan had given her, and it meant more to her than she could put into words. For he had given her a part of himself, and that she treasured more than anything.

"Well, what do you think?" she asked, turning around so that Grace could see how she looked wearing the necklace.

"I think," Grace said slowly, sudden tears filling her eyes, "that Major Catlin is the luckiest man on earth."

Gabrielle laughed. "Or the most insane."

Grace joined in her laughter. "I'll second that!" she said, wiping her eyes with her fingertips.

Gabrielle suddenly remembered her new handkerchief. "Here, use this!"

"Saleratus, rose water, and preserved sweet cherries," the post trader said as he totaled up the purchase. "Will that be all, ladies?"

"Yes, Mr. Sully," Grace replied dutifully.

"Your mother didn't tell you to get cherries," Gabrielle whispered.

"I'm paying for the cherries."

"But, they're almost two dollars!"

Mr. Sully interrupted, "That'll be two dollars and twenty-seven cents, Miss Simmons."

Gabrielle seized Grace's hand as she tried to count out the coins. "It's too much money. Put the cherries back."

"No."

"You ladies making a cake?" the trader asked.

Grace jerked her hand free of Gabrielle's grasp. "Yes, sir. It's Gabrielle's birthday. Here you are, Mr. Sully. Two dollars and twenty-five . . . six . . . seven cents."

"Thank you. Come back again soon. And Happy Birthday to you, Miss Dubois."

"Are you out of your mind?" Gabrielle blurted out as they headed for the door. "You shouldn't have spent that much money!"

"Gabrielle, what's wrong with you? I declare, you're turning into an old fuddy-duddy! Where's your sense of adventure? Live dangerously! Have cherries on your birthday cake, for goodness sake!"

An old fuddy-duddy? Live dangerously? A frown of bewilderment creasing her brow, Gabrielle shook her head as though to clear it. Grace Simmons was telling her to live dangerously? Until now, it had always been the other way around.

"I wonder what they want?" Grace asked as they left the store, and Gabrielle followed her gaze to see Bryce Edwards, along with about a dozen men, ride into the quadrangle and head straight for the Headquarters Building.

"There's only one way to find out."

"Gabrielle, you can't go over there!"

"Now look who's being an old fuddy-duddy!"

Gabrielle recognized Bryce Edwards, his foreman, and a few of the hired hands from the Rocking P, but the other men were strangers. Some of them looked hard and mean, and their presence made her uneasy. She wished Dan were here.

Bandy Moreland emerged from the Headquarters Building. "Can I help you, gentlemen?" he asked, folding his arms across his buckskin-clad chest and facing the rancher squarely.

Bryce Edwards did not dismount. "I don't know who in the

hell you are, but I didn't ask for you. I want to see Major Catlin."

"Ain't here," Bandy said flatly, his sharp blue eyes narrowing as he assessed the situation.

"Well, then, you just give him a message for me," Edwards said, his tone derisive. "Tell him I caught this scum sneaking around my stock pens."

A gasp went up from the crowd that had gathered as one of the riders with the rancher, a dirty, unshaven man with a scar down the right side of his face, nudged his horse forward and dumped the bloody, bullet-ridden body of an Apache warrior onto the ground.

A woman began to scream, and Gabrielle pressed one hand over her mouth to keep from gagging.

The man had been stripped of his clothing, and his genitals had been cut off and stuffed into his mouth.

"Consider that a warning," Edwards shouted above the roar of the crowd. "You tell Catlin he's got two days. If the rest of them bastards aren't out of here by the end of the week, we're taking matters into our own hands. I'm sick of sitting by helplesslike while my men get shot up and my stock is raided."

"Get the women and children out of here!" someone shouted.

"Two days!" the rancher repeated.

Amidst a flurry of hooves and roiling dust, the men departed, leaving the mutilated body of their unfortunate victim lying in the dirt in front of the post headquarters.

"Go get somethin' to cover him up!"

Gabrielle squeezed her eyes shut and swallowed hard against the bile that rose in her throat.

"Oh, Gabrielle, let's go home," Grace wailed, clutching her arm.

"Get outa the way!" Bandy hollered at them, and they backed away just in time to keep from being knocked over as Captain Wilcox burst through the crowd.

Grace tugged her her friend's arm. "Gabrielle, please!"

Horror settled chillingly in Gabrielle's bones as she stared numbly at the gruesome sight before her. The men who did this wouldn't wait two days before carrying out their threats.

Nor would the soldiers be able to stop them. Before the week was out, Camp Carleton would hold as bloody a place in history as Camp Grant.

"Gabrielle!" Grace had seized her arms and was shaking her, all the while sobbing hysterically. "Please, answer me!"

I won't *let* it happen, Gabrielle thought.

Without considering what she was doing, she yanked her arms out of Grace's panicked grip and ran.

Her feet pounded the ground so hard each footfall reverberated through her with a vicious jerk, and she had to hold her skirts up high to keep them from becoming entangled with her legs as she ran, harder and faster than she had ever run in her life. Soon she'd left the safety of the post far behind. She had to reach the Apache camp before anyone else did.

Instead of following the trail, she cut across the wash. No water remained in the sandy bed, but the recent rains had eroded the banks and the crumbling earth gave way beneath her feet, causing her to pitch forward. A mesquite branch slapped her in the face as she fell and it snagged her hair, bringing a cry of pain to her lips. Picking herself up, she brushed the dirt off her dress and her hands. Perspiration now trickled down her forehead and into her eyes, and her heart pounded mercilessly. Struggling to catch her breath, Gabrielle pressed one hand to her chest, her fingers closing around the rose pendant which lay against her skin beneath the bodice of her dress. "Oh, Dan, please," she pleaded between gasps, her voice sounding unnaturally loud in the desert stillness. "Please, don't let me be too late."

By the time she reached the camp, her legs were shaking and her head was throbbing, but there was no time to stop and rest. Drawing curious stares as she tore through the rancheria, she dashed in and out among the wickiups until she found the ramada where the women of Anna's and Zayigo's clan did their cooking. "Anna!"

The old woman turned around, surprise registering on her weathered face at the sight of Gabrielle.

"Anna, you must go. All of you! It's too dangerous here. Do you understand? You have to leave. You can't stay here anymore. It's not safe!"

Anna eyed her closely and muttered something Gabrielle did not comprehend.

Desperate to make herself understood, Gabrielle grabbed the woman's arm. "Leave!" she shouted, pointing toward the foothills. "Go to the mountains! Go anywhere! Just go!"

Anna pulled her into the shade and indicated that she was to sit down.

"No!" Gabrielle cried out, her voice breaking on a sob. She had to make them understand her. "English! Does anyone here speak English?"

Anna said something in sharp gutteral tones to one of the other women who then hurried off to a nearby wickiup.

"Oh, Anna!" Gabrielle cried out, tears of despair welling in her eyes as she resisted the woman's efforts to make her sit. "What's going to happen to you? To all of you?"

A woman pushed a gourd into Gabrielle's hands, but she was shaking so badly she nearly spilled the water it contained. Her head reeled and the heat was beginning to make her sick to her stomach. "I—I can't drink . . . this," she stammered, and gave the gourd back.

Someone shouted, causing everyone to turn, and Gabrielle's stomach knotted at seeing dust rising in the distance, signaling approaching riders. They were not coming from the direction of Camp Carleton, but from the Rocking P.

An ominous silence hung in the air as six men, their hats pulled down low, rode into the rancheria. One of them spoke to a youth who pointed to one of the wickiups, then turned and ran. The men rode toward the wickiup, and Gabrielle's nausea gave way to a suffocating sense of doom. She heard a rush of whispers among the women and saw alarm ripple across their faces.

A tall lean man, who looked to be in his mid-forties, emerged from the wickiup.

"Are you the chief?" Gabrielle heard one of the men ask.

The Apache responded in what Gabrielle recognized as Spanish although she could not understand the words.

The rider leaned forward in the saddle and pushed back his hat, revealing a long jagged scar along the right side of his face; and Gabrielle sucked in her breath. He was one of the men she

317

had seen with Bryce Edwards at the post earlier. "I ain't here to cause no trouble," he said, and a Mexican companion hastily translated his words into Spanish. "Just to give you fair warning. We're sick o' you cuttin' our fences and runnin' off with our livestock. Edwards has lost darn near a hundred head to you redskinned savages in the past month and I lost more'n that. We ain't puttin' up with it no more. We caught one o' yer kin trespassin' on private property, and we're gonna do to you what we done to him if you don't get yer mangy asses outta here."

As the Apache responded in a low voice, Gabrielle, trying to stay as inconspicuous as possible, inched her way closer so she could hear him.

"The old man says his people do not steal your cattle, *señor*," the Mexican translated.

The scar-faced man spat on the ground. "That's a lie. There's no one else for miles around who coulda done it exceptin' you thievin' bastards. I ain't no fool. I know how it works. You folks sneak out at night and do your raidin'. Then you sneak back here afore the sun comes up so them old bluebellies at the fort think you been here all along. But you can't fool me. I know what's goin' on here. And I'm tellin' you, I ain't puttin' up with it any longer. I've had enough."

"*Señor*, he says you are mistaken. His people wish to live here in peace. They do not want trouble with the Americans."

Gabrielle noticed the warriors quietly gathering around their unwelcome visitors.

One of the riders drew his revolver. "You want me to give 'em a message, boss? Show 'em we mean business?"

Gabrielle gasped. It was Jack Doolen, the same man she had seen at the post the day of the Cinco de Mayo festival.

"Put the gun away, Doolen," the scar-faced man ordered. "We came here to put a stop to trouble, not start it."

"But, boss, there's a hundred-dollar bounty for every 'Pache scalp we take and—"

"We'll give 'em two days like Edwards promised, and if they ain't outta here, *then* we start collectin' scalps."

"But you promised we could barbeque us some 'Pache steaks for supper, and I ain't leavin' here 'til I got me some—"

He broke off as his eyes focused on a point in the crowd. "On second thought, mebbe what I want instead is a woman."

Gabrielle followed his gaze and her heart turned over. He was staring at Zayigo.

"Doolen, what the hell are you about? Get back on your horse!"

"Well, well, what have we here?" Jack Doolen said, pushing back his hat as he approached Zayigo. She took a step backward.

"Damn it, Doolen! I gave you an order!"

"In a minute, boss. Just give me a minute." His eyes raking over Zayigo, he grinned, revealing discolored teeth. "Come here and let me get a closer look, girl." He seized her wrist and pulled her toward him.

Her dark eyes widening in terror, Zayigo tried to pull away, but Doolen twisted her arm behind her back, causing her to cry out.

He snickered. "You know, you ain't a bad looker at that, even if you is nothin' but a 'Pache squaw. You got an old man hereabouts? Well, no matter, 'cause you're comin' with me." Turning, he roughly yanked the girl along after him.

Gabrielle pushed her way through the crowd. "Let her go!"

Doolen spun around. "What the—"

Her heart pounding so loudly she was certain everyone could hear it, Gabrielle stepped forward and faced the man squarely. "I told you to let her go," she repeated, her green eyes flashing with unbridled anger. "These people haven't done anything to you, and you have no right to come here and threaten them. And you," she added, turning a venomous glare on the man with the scar, "I saw what you did to that man you and Mr. Edwards brought to Camp Carleton. It was brutal and disgusting. You call these people savage, yet you are the savages. I don't know who you are, but if you're smart you'll take your own advice and get out of here before you have the entire United States Army down on your heads for murder."

"And who the hell are you?" Scarface demanded.

Though her courage was rapidly waning, she squared her shoulders and lifted her chin. "My father is Colonel DuBois, the commander of Camp—" Before Gabrielle could finish, little Datigé streaked across the clearing in front of her and ran toward her mother, grabbing her skirts.

"Get outta here, kid!" Doolen snapped, and gave the child a kick that sent her sprawling in the dirt.

Zayigo screamed.

Gabrielle ran to Datigé, who was now wailing loudly, and gathered her into her arms.

"Shut that kid up!" Doolen barked, waving his gun toward the crying child.

Fearing that he would shoot Datigé, Gabrielle sheltered the little girl with her body, and fixed on Doolen a look of glittering hatred. "Haven't you caused enough trouble? Just go away! All of you!"

"Damn it, Doolen, let the girl go and get back on your horse or you're fired!" the man with the scar ordered, but there was now a note of panic in his voice.

Gabrielle caught a movement out of the corner of her eye.

"*Señor,* we should leave," the Mexican said quietly.

Scarface shifted uneasily and nervously darted his eyes back and forth. "Let the girl go!"

Doolen pinned the squirming Zayigo against his chest. "She's mine!"

"*Now,* Doolen!"

Gabrielle's breath caught.

The Apaches had closed in around them. Each warrior held a rifle and those rifles were fixed on the rancher and his men. At this distance, they would not miss.

Suddenly Doolen realized what was happening. He dropped Zayigo's wrist as if it had burned his fingers and, shoving her away from him, made a panicked dash for his horse.

The man with the scar impaled him with a menacing look.

Without lowering their rifles, the Apaches moved aside to let the men pass, and Gabrielle did not realize she had been holding her breath until it suddenly burst from her lungs in a sigh of relief as she watched the men leave.

An ominous silence prevailed as the Apaches broke up, several of them casting guarded glances in Gabrielle's direction as they returned to their wickiups. Giving her a wan smile,

320

Zayigo took Datigé from her, then she, too, hurried off, and Gabrielle slowly rose to her feet, unable to shake the eerie feeling that somehow they all blamed her for what had just happened. As a hollow ache started in the middle of her chest, she touched the rose pendant safely hidden beneath her bodice, and blinked back tears.

"So, this is where you been hidin'. Miss DuBois, half the post is out lookin' for you."

Sitting on the floor beside her bed, Gabrielle hugged her knees more tightly to her chest. "I needed to be alone," she said, not looking up. She couldn't very well tell him where she had really been. She couldn't tell anyone. She knew she should report what had happened at the Apache camp that afternoon, but she was also acutely aware of the consequences. She would be punished for leaving the post, and the Indians would have their weapons taken away. How would they protect themselves then?

Captain Moreland hunkered down beside her. "Wanna talk about it?"

"No."

Bandy was silent a moment. "It was kinda ugly, huh?"

Gabrielle swallowed hard as her stomach rebelled at the horrifying memory. "Why do people do things like that, Captain Moreland? It would have been one thing for them to just shoot that Apache for trespassing. Why did they have to do . . . what they did?"

"I guess them fellas wanted to get their point across. The ranchers and settlers in the Territory have been puttin' up with this kinda bloodshed from the Indians for ages. Far as they're concerned, that Apache only got what he had comin'."

Gabrielle's gaze riveted on the officer. "You don't even care, do you?"

"I care."

"Then why aren't you doing something about it?"

The blue in Bandy's eyes turned cold. "Such as what?"

"Such as finding a place for the rest of the Apaches to go. A "safe place."

"And I suppose you got a whole list of recommendations," Bandy retorted. "Like it or not, Miss DuBois, there ain't a helluva lot I can do about it. The Apaches ain't welcome anywhere in the Territory. Even the other tribes don't want 'em around. You're askin' for a miracle, little girl, and unless the good Lord decides to cough one up, you're outta luck."

Gabrielle bristled. "You're always bragging about your six thousand acres. Why don't you let the Apaches stay there?"

"For the same reason a farmer don't let a pack o' weasels into his chicken coop."

"So, now they're weasels!" Gabrielle scrambled to her feet. "I didn't say nothin' about—"

"It was what you meant! You're no better than Bryce Edwards and that band of cutthroats he had with him. You don't care what happens to those people out there as long as you're not dragged into the middle of it. You talk about Dan fighting your battles when you were a child. From where I stand, it looks like you're still letting other people fight your battles for you. You have a responsibility to Dan to keep those—"

"My responsibility is to keep *you* safe, which is gettin' pretty hard to do seein' as how you don't like to follow orders and you got a bad habit of stickin' your nose into matters what don't concern you."

"Such as?"

"Such as leavin' the post without permission."

The color drained from Gabrielle's face along with her anger. "I—I never left the post," she stammered.

Bandy folded his arms across his chest. "Then, it 'pears to me Dan's gonna have to decide which one of us is tellin' the truth."

Panic rioted in Gabrielle's stomach. "You'd do that to him? You'd honestly try to destroy our . . . friendship?"

"If you're askin' if I'll do my damnedest to keep him from marryin' a woman who lies to him, the answer is yes."

Struggling to keep her fear from showing on her face, Gabrielle squared her shoulders and jutted out her chin in defiance. "Dan won't need to decide anything," she said slowly, surprised by the steadiness of her voice. "You're not going to tell him."

"And what makes you so all-fired certain I won't?"

"Because if you do, I'll tell Sergeant Major Simmons you've been sneaking out at night with his daughter."

Chapter Fifteen

"Father!"

The joyous surprise that had lit up Gabrielle's face when she'd opened the front door faded before the colonel's anger.

"Get your things together," DuBois said brusquely. "You're coming home."

Confusion clouded Gabrielle's face, and her hand went instinctively to the necklace Dan had given her, as if she sought solace from it. "Father, I—"

"That's an order. I'll send Holmes over later to get your clothes." He turned to go.

No hug. No kiss. Not even a hello.

"Corporal Holmes doesn't work for us . . . anymore . . ."

When the colonel turned back to look at her, Gabrielle cringed inside for disgust distorted his features. "I'll give you ten minutes."

"But, Father!"

"Ten minutes!"

Grace helped her pack. "Do you think he's angry because you're staying with us?"

"I don't know why he's angry," Gabrielle said in a choked voice. She was too hurt to make any sense of her jumbled thoughts. While her father had never been openly affectionate, she had always felt that, in his own way, he loved her. Until now.

Grace put a consoling hand on her arm. "You know you're always welcome here."

Gabrielle forced a smile. "I'll be all right. Father's moods usually don't last long. By the time I get home, he'll probably already have forgotten why he was angry."

However, twenty minutes later, when she was back in her own house, the colonel's ill temper showed no sign of dissipating.

"Gabrielle, get in here!" he bellowed from his study.

Her stomach churning nervously, she obeyed. "Did you have a pleasant trip?" she ventured, her voice wavering in spite of her efforts to keep it steady.

"I did not. You and Catlin managed to make my time at Division thoroughly *unpleasant*. Don't either of you know how to follow orders?"

Her thoughts immediately returned to the day of the festival. "Father, if I've done something to—"

"I had thought that by placing you in Major Catlin's keeping, I would be free to conduct my business without having to worry about you. Obviously, I was wrong. Do you have any idea how humiliating it is to be interrupted in the middle of a meeting with the Division commander only to be informed that my daughter has been making a public spectacle of herself—drinking, visiting unmarried officers in their quarters with no chaperon, and running around Camp Carleton dressed in men's britches? Not to mention running away. And then I discover that you have been going from house to house, begging for donations to give to that bunch of lice-ridden renegades who do *not* have my permission to quarter here!"

"But, Father, the Indians had no place else to—"

"That is a different matter entirely, one I intend to take up with Major Catlin when he returns. Right now, it is *your* behavior that is at question."

There was a cold ache in Gabrielle's chest where her heart should have been, and an emptiness that hurt as badly as a physical blow. A tart *Welcome home, Father* was about to spring to her lips, but she bit back the retort and, lowering her gaze, knotted her fingers in the folds of her skirt.

"I hope you know," Colonel DuBois gritted out from between clenched teeth, "you nearly cost me my promotion.

Fortunately, the general is broad-minded enough not to hold me entirely accountable for the actions of my second-in-command or of my hot-headed and irresponsible seventeen-year-old daughter."

Something inside Gabrielle twisted at this unintentional revelation that her own father had forgotten her birthday.

"I have, however," DuBois continued, "been placed in the awkward position of having to prove all over again that I am capable of assuming the responsibilities of a general officer. I no longer have the luxury of allowing myself to be distracted by your unseemly behavior. I cabled Charlotte from San Francisco and she has agreed to take you in."

Gabrielle's head shot up.

"The woman suffers from the delusion that having you under her roof will be no trouble at all. I trust you will at least try to behave yourself long enough for my promotion to be finalized."

Bandy Moreland appeared in the doorway.

"We will continue this discussion later," Colonel DuBois said briskly. "Come in, Captain."

The shock of her father's decision to send her away rendered Gabrielle immobile. Feeling betrayed, she gripped the edge of the colonel's desk, her eyes squeezed shut, for several long moments before she realized she had been dismissed, and when she finally did open her eyes to meet her father's gaze, the affection that had once radiated from their gray-green depths was no longer there. She had once kept alive a childish hope of love; now she felt only bitterness. In the span of only one day, the once-solid foundation of her entire world had begun to crumble. Too numb even to protest, Gabrielle turned to leave, blindly making her way past Bandy who stood watching her, a trouble expression clouding his blue eyes.

"Close the door on your way out," the colonel commanded.

"We'll get right down to business," she heard her father tell Captain Moreland through the closed door after she left the room. "First I want you to send a messenger to Ciénega Pass, to order Lieutenant Epperling and B Company back to Camp Carleton at once. Then you are to take a detachment out to that infernal Indian camp, round up every last man, woman, and

326

child; and escort them back to Camp Grant where they belong. This is an Army post, not a sanctuary for renegade Apaches."

Barely able to see through the tears that slid unheeded down her face, Gabrielle fled to the quiet safety of her room, unable to deal with this onslaught of disasters.

"An excellent choice," the attorney commented when Dan finished signing the papers. "I considered purchasing that tract of land myself, but my wife objected to living so far from town. There are several lovely building sites, and the frame structure that is already there will do quite nicely until you can get your new place built. Just don't be foolhardy enough to build near that grove of cottonwoods down by Arivaipa Creek; it's a mighty tempting spot, but that entire section of the valley is in a hundred-year flood plain."

Dan stood up. "Thanks for the advice. And I'm sure I can count on you to make certain the deed is issued in both Gabrielle's name and mine."

"Rest assured, the sale will be recorded this afternoon in full compliance with your instructions. You'll do all right out there, Mr. Catlin, with your land abutting that of your friend. You'll both have access to the best rangeland in the Territory. Mr. Moreland will have better summer grazing, but you're sitting on a better aquifer and your winters will be milder. It's amazing what a vast difference a few miles can make." The lawyer smiled and extended his hand. "I wish the best to you and your bride."

"Tell him you're getting married!"

Gabrielle shook her head. "I can't. I promised Dan I wouldn't say anything about it to Father until he returned. Oh, Grace, I don't want to go live with Aunt Charlotte!"

"When are you supposed to leave?"

"I don't know," Gabrielle said miserably. "I just hope I can stall long enough for Dan to return."

Corporal Bates stuck his head into the bedroom. "The colonel just left the Headquarters Building."

Gabrielle threw Grace an unhappy glance. "You'd better go before he gets here. He was so angry over nearly losing that promotion he'll probably vent his spleen on you too."

After Grace had gone, Gabrielle washed her face and smoothed her wayward curls back into their braid, but her heart sank when she looked at her reflection in the mirror. There was no hiding the fact that she had been crying; her face was splotchy, her eyes red-rimmed. But the confrontation with her father could not be put off any longer, regardless of how she looked. If nothing else, perhaps he would take pity on her and relent, she mused, then hastily pushed that thought out of her mind. She didn't want him to feel sorry for her; she wanted his respect.

She found her father in his study, going over the same ledgers Dan had spread across the dining-room table the night before he'd left for Tucson, and as she studied the graying head bent over the open ledgers, she was struck by the sudden realization that her own father was a stranger to her. Again, she felt betrayed. Only now that feeling of betrayal was intertwined with the feelings of abandonment she'd often experienced when she was alone, and she was torn between hating her father and wanting to grasp at any chance to *make* him love her.

"I'm busy," the colonel curtly replied to her knock, and a burning ache spread through Gabrielle's chest and rose into her throat.

Bracing herself, she took a deep breath and entered the room anyway. "Father, I need to speak with you."

Annoyance furrowed his brow as he looked up at her. "We can talk later."

"I'm not going to Baltimore."

"Gabrielle—"

"No, Father, let me finish," Gabrielle said, her outward calmness surprising her because inside she was twisted into knots. She stopped before his desk and faced him squarely. "I know you mean well and you think sending me to live with Aunt Charlotte, of whom I know absolutely nothing, is best for all concerned. It's not. I'm sorry I've disappointed you, and if you truly want to be rid of me, then I shall gladly leave this house today. But, I won't go to Baltimore."

Pushing back his chair and standing up, Colonel DuBois placed his palms flat on his desk and leaned toward her until his face was only inches from hers, anger glinting like shards of ice in his eyes as he glared at her. "And just where do you intend to go?"

"I'll stay with Grace until other arrangements can be made."

"You'll do no such thing."

"You can't stop me."

His nostrils flared uncontrollably. "I can, and I will."

Gabrielle fought to get a grip on her rapidly waning courage. "Why?" she asked in a quivering, pain-edged voice. "You don't want me here. I'm an embarrassment to you. You as much as said so. Why should you care where I go as long as I'm out of your hair?" For some crazy reason, she wanted him to say it was because he loved her.

"Because you are my daughter, damn it, and until you reach the age of majority, you will do as I say!" The colonel's voice had risen to a shout, but instead of intimidating Gabrielle, his outburst only served to antagonize her further.

"I've never done your bidding in the past," she retorted, disguising her hurt with sarcasm. "Why should I start now?"

"Because, my dear, if you take up residence in the Simmons' quarters, the sergeant major will see corporal again so quickly he won't know what hit him. Do I make myself clear?"

Gabrielle's breath caught in her throat. As the color siphoned from her face, her head reeled, yet she scrambled to come up with another plan. If she accepted Grace's invitation, the sergeant major—the entire Simmons family—would be made to suffer. She had never, in her wildest imaginings, thought her father would stoop that low. "In that case," she said haughtily, seizing the only alternative she could think of, "I will go stay with Ruby Collins at the cantina. If you think your precious promotion is in jeopardy now, just wait until—"

"How dare you!" the colonel thundered, and he slapped her across the face with a force that almost caused her knees to buckle. Raw fury pounding through his veins, he circled the desk and lifted his hand to strike her again, then froze at seeing

329

Bandy Moreland in the doorway, hat in hand. Panic gripped the colonel as he wondered just how long the officer had been standing there, but he quickly hid it behind a mask of outraged authority. "What do you want?" he bellowed.

"The Apaches are gone, sir," Bandy replied, but he was looking at Gabrielle though he was speaking to her father.

The colonel stiffened. "What do you mean, they're gone? All of them?"

"Yes, sir. Every last one of 'em."

A glimmer of joy pierced Gabrielle's wretchedness. The Apaches were gone! They wouldn't have to go back to Camp Grant, and they wouldn't be here when Bryce Edwards and his men came calling. Datigé and Zayigo and Anna and the others would be safe. Pressing a hand to her smarting cheek, she turned a tearful gaze on Bandy, but his own expression was unreadable and Gabrielle's stomach churned as she wondered anxiously whether or not he intended to tell her father she had gone to the camp the day before to alert the Indians.

"What in the hell is wrong with you people?" the colonel demanded. "You allowed several hundred Apaches to camp on your doorstep, yet you cannot account for their whereabouts! I should have both you and Catlin court-martialed!"

If Bandy was the least bit shaken by the colonel's threat, he did not show it. "They must've lit out sometime durin' the night," he said with a shrug. "They was here yesterday."

Her shoulders sagging in relief, Gabrielle smiled and mouthed a silent *thank you* to Bandy, then clamped her mouth shut when her father swung around on her.

He leveled a warning finger at her. "You are to go to your room and stay there until I give you permission to leave it. Set one foot out of this house, young lady, and I will make this the sorriest day of your life."

For two days, father and daughter did not speak to each other. The colonel left the house early each morning and did not return until long after Gabrielle had retired for the night. She was permitted no visitors, and was allowed to leave her room only for meals. Corporal Bates was under orders to report her every movement, and though Gabrielle trusted him not to betray her, she stayed in her room anyway, being too ashamed to have anyone see the purple-black bruise that had spread across her left cheekbone after her father had struck her.

But on the third day, when B Company returned to post and Gabrielle heard Marcus' voice as he entered the study with her father and then heard the door close after them, she defiantly left the confinement of her room and tiptoed down the hall to eavesdrop on their conversation.

"But, sir," Marcus protested loudly, "if it weren't for me, you would never have learned of the indignities your daughter was suffering at the hands of that arrogant, ill-mannered excuse of an officer. If I had not sent you that message—"

"If it weren't for you, I would never have been forced to place my daughter under Major Catlin's guardianship in the first place! I couldn't trust her to stay away from you, and I sure as hell couldn't trust you to keep your hands off her. So don't come sniveling to me about how your only concern was for Gabrielle's welfare. I wasn't born yesterday, Lieutenant!"

"Sir, my intentions toward Gabrielle have been nothing but honorable. I want to marry her, and I was hoping to obtain your blessing."

Seething inwardly, Gabrielle gritted her teeth. It was all she could do not to burst into the study and inform Marcus Epperling that she had no intention of marrying him, with or without her father's blessing. Even going to Baltimore was a preferable alternative, but she had no intention of doing that either. Without waiting to hear her father's reply, Gabrielle returned to her bedroom and closed the door, locking it behind her, then took her valise from under the bed. She intended to be packed and ready to leave the moment Dan returned.

"Glad to have you back, sir," Sergeant Reikowsky told Dan as he unsaddled his horse. "This place has been turned upside-down ever since the day you left."

"Has there been trouble?"

"Might say that. Before I forget, Captain Moreland's over at

331

A Company. He wants a word with you before you meet with the old man."

One dark eyebrow arched upward. "When did Colonel DuBois return?"

"A couple of days ago, sir. And I gotta tell you, he's been breathing fire down our necks from the minute he rode into camp. I don't know what went on up there at Division, but the old man sure came back pissed as hell."

A gnawing uneasiness gripped Dan's insides. "Is Gabrielle all right?"

"Wouldn't know 'bout that, sir. Haven't seen hide nor hair of her since the colonel got back. One rumor going around is that he locked her in her room. Another has it that she locked herself in and flat refuses to come out." He chuckled. "Either way, that girl of his can sure stir up a fuss without even doing anything."

Bandy did not ease Dan's misgivings. "I'm waitin' for payday," he declared, "and then I'm gettin' the hell outta here. I don't care if I have to spend all this winter sleepin' on the ground. That six thousand acres of mine is lookin' better 'n' better all the time, but even it ain't big enough by half to put me at a tolerable distance away from that puffed-up asshole sittin' over there in Headquarters. Now, I know he's your friend, Danny boy, and I know you feel like you owe him somethin' 'cause he picked you up off some St. Louis back alley and filled your gullet, but if that daughter of his was my woman and the old man busted her upside the head the way I seen him do, I'd whup his butt, then clean up the floor with what was left of him. I don't give a shit if DuBois is buckin' for brigadier general—I can't abide the bastard!"

Bandy's bitterness disturbed Dan. Gone was the easygoing, imperturbable man he had known, the soldier who was quick with a grin and liked by damn near everyone he met; in his place was a man with hatred glinting in his eyes.

And the thought of Stephen DuBois striking Gabrielle filled Dan with rage.

By the time Dan reached the colonel's quarters, his anger

was simmering dangerously just below the surface, like lava about to blast forth. Not bothering to knock, he stormed into the house and headed straight for the colonel's study, explosive fury surging through him as he burst into the room.

Both Marcus and the colonel whirled around to stare at him, their surprise frozen on their faces.

Dan looked at Marcus and jerked his head toward the door. "Get out."

Marcus bristled. "Now, listen here—"

"This is my house!" Colonel DuBois snapped, suddenly finding his tongue. "*I* decide who stays and who leaves here, Catlin. Not you."

His blue eyes glittering with self-righteous indignation, Marcus bit back an angry retort, and struggled to get his temper under control. He had just secured the colonel's permission to court Gabrielle; he was not willing to jeopardize that coup for the simple pleasure of plowing his fist into Dan Catlin's arrogant face. Squaring his shoulders and drawing himself up to his full height, Marcus turned to Colonel DuBois and said with forced graciousness, "Thank you, sir."

"And now, Major Catlin," the colonel continued, making no move to dismiss Lieutenant Epperling. "Would you mind telling me who gave you the right to barge into my house and order my guest out of it as if you owned the place?"

"I really don't think you want Epperling to hear what I have to say to you, Stephen."

"I'll decide that," DuBois ground out, a vein on his temple distending ominously from his anger-flushed face. "Get on with it."

Dan lost no time in getting to the point. "Why did you order B Company back from the Ciénega?"

"I didn't want the men there."

"They were there under my orders and at the governor's request."

"The last time I checked, *Major,* I am the commander of this post. Not you. Not Governor Safford. Nor am I under any obligation to answer to you. Is that clear?"

"You can stop trying to pull rank, Stephen. I resigned my commission two days ago. And you're right. You don't have to answer to me. But you do have to answer to General Crook. I hope like hell you have a good explanation to give *him* when four hundred Apaches don't arrive at Camp Thomas next week as planned."

"What are you talking about?" Colonel DuBois sputtered. He had been too stunned by the announcement of Dan's resignation to make sense of anything else that had been said. "General Crook never gave me any such directive."

"It's right here," Dan pulled a sheaf of papers from his pocket and flung them onto the desk. "Orders, signed by General Crook, authorizing all Apaches quartered at Camp Carleton to be transferred, at Government expense, to Camp Thomas where they are to receive temporary asylum until such time as a permanent Indian reservation can be established. Except now there aren't any Apaches to transfer!"

"It wasn't my fault the mangy sons-of-bitches decided to steal out of here in the middle of the night!" The colonel's voice had risen to a shout. "They were gone before I ever got back from Division."

"Did you honestly think they were going to stick around and wait for you to send them back to Camp Grant?"

"I wasn't going to send them—"

"You issued orders to that effect, and don't deny it."

The vein at the colonel's temple throbbed. "Unless you have something else to say, I suggest you start packing. I want you off this post. Now!"

"I'll leave," Dan said icily. "But I'm taking Gabrielle with me."

Marcus had been staring absently at an imaginary spot on the carpet and gloating over Dan's falling-out with the colonel rather than paying much attention to what was being said. Suddenly he jerked his head up.

"And just what does my daughter have to do with all of this?" Colonel DuBois demanded, remembering yet another issue that had been nagging at him since he'd received Epperling's dispatch in San Francisco.

"I love her and I intend to marry her," Dan said curtly, fully aware of the scathing look Marcus was giving him.

The colonel's eyes narrowed. "So there is an element of

truth to the rumors I've been hearing about you and Gabrielle. I had hoped they were false, but it's obvious I was mistaken about you. I thought I could trust you to keep my daughter safe while I was gone. Instead, I find that you had your filthy hands all over her the minute I turned my back!"

"I love her," Dan repeated slowly, deliberately, not certain just how much Gabrielle had told her father.

"Like hell you do! You're not capable of loving anyone. I fathomed that much about you the day we met. The truth is, Catlin, you couldn't have my wife so you set your sights on my daughter!"

Dan's face darkened and the muscles in his jaw knotted. "There was never anything between Lisette and me, and you well know it."

"Just what kind of an imbecile to you take me for! Do you think I didn't notice the sly looks that passed between the two of you or the way you couldn't keep your eyes off her whenever she was in the room? Do you think it never crossed my mind that you were always forcing your presence upon my household for dinner, for family outings, for holidays? I couldn't even spend a goddamned Christmas with my family without having you underfoot, ogling my wife!"

In the taut silence that followed the colonel's outburst, the three men suddenly became aware that they were not alone and three pairs of eyes turned to the doorway. Gabrielle stood in it, her stricken gaze fixed on Dan. Her face was devoid of color, save for the bruise which stood out in garish contrast to her unnatural pallor. Even her lips had turned pale. "Is it true?" she whispered brokenly, barely able to get the words out because of the terrible pressure bearing down on her. "Were you in love with my . . . mother?"

Dan felt his entire body grow numb as he realized what she must be thinking. He took a step toward her. "Gabrielle, let me explain—"

"I don't want explanations," she stated coldly, her voice stronger now and knife-edged. "I want the truth. Were you in love with my mother?"

The sight of her visibly bracing herself for his answer cut through Dan like a knife, and at that moment he would have given up his life to erase the agony he saw in her young face. Yet, if he lied to her, she would know it, and that lie would hang over them like a curse for the rest of their days. He took a deep breath. "Yes," he said gently, and flinched inwardly as pain flashed across her face. "I was once in love with your mother."

Gabrielle started as though he had struck her.

Disparate thoughts barraged her. *He is lying. He used me. When he looked at me, I was not the one he saw, but my mother.* After all, how many times had people mistaken the girl in the portrait for her? But what really hurt was thinking of him holding her, touching her, and wishing she were Lisette. In a blinding flash, the tender intimacies they had shared changed into something vile and abhorrent as what was left of her childish innocence came crashing down around her. The warm and precious memories she'd cherished of the night spent in his arms now sickened Gabrielle, and she suddenly felt she was about to retch.

The changing emotions that rioted across her face did not go unnoticed. Fear of losing her ripped through Dan, and he closed the distance between them in three long strides, but when he reached for her, Gabrielle recoiled. "Get out!" she ordered, her voice quaking, anguish in her pain-darkened eyes. "Get out of this house. Out of my life! Get out! Get out! *Get out!*" Choking on a sob, she turned to leave, but he grasped her by the shoulders and sharply brought her around.

"Let go of me!" she screamed, but that was the one thing he would not—could not—do.

"Gabrielle, listen to me!" he thundered, shaking her hard. "It was a long, long time ago. I was a young man infatuated with a beautiful woman. That was all. There was never anything more than friendship between your mother and me. *Never.*"

But his words fell on ears deafened by humiliation and fury. Wrenching free of his grasp, Gabrielle drew back her hand and swung as hard as she could, slapping him full force across the face.

Dan caught her by the arms and yanked her against him, but it took all his strength to hold her for she struggled against him like a demented wildcat, kicking and lashing out with her fists, striking blindly, wanting to hurt him as he had hurt her. "You bastard!" she sobbed hysterically. "I loved you! But you used me! You made me fall in love with you, and you used me! *You used me!*"

Remorse stung Dan and he closed his eyes. Never before had he felt so utterly helpless or deserving of contempt. "I'm sorry, little one," he whispered thickly into her hair. "I'm so sorry."

Gradually, she stopped fighting him, and he held her close as she wept brokenly in his arms, tortured sobs wracking her. How could he have done this to her? How could he have hurt this beautiful woman who was so dear to him and who had become so much a part of his life? He opened his eyes and met the colonel's gaze over the top of Gabrielle's head. Stephen DuBois was looking at him with such hatred that Dan knew he had ascertained precisely what had transpired between him and Gabrielle.

Marcus was a little slower to arrive at the truth, but when he did, his reaction was no less vehement. "My God!" he shouted, shock and horror rippling across his face. "You ruined her! You ruined the woman who was to become my wife!"

Gabrielle's crying stopped abruptly when Epperling's words pierced her dazed misery. Tearing herself from Dan's embrace, she whirled on Marcus, her tear-ravaged eyes glittering with scorn. She railed at him. "You pompous ass! I wouldn't marry you if you were God Himself! And you—" She swung back to face Dan, but when she opened her mouth to speak, her pain erupted anew and all she could manage was a constricted whisper. "I don't ever—ever—want to see you again." She reached to unfasten the gold clasp at her neck, but her hands were shaking so badly the pendant he had given her for her birthday slipped through her fingers before she could hand it to him. She bent to retrieve it from the carpet, paused, half straightened, reached for it again, and stopped. Then, with a tortured cry, she turned and fled the room.

"I've brought you some supper," Grace said gently as she

placed the tray on the table beside the bed.

Once more at the Simmons' quarters, Gabrielle was lying on her side of Grace's bed, facing the wall, a pillow clutched to her stomach. "I'm not hungry," she said woodenly.

Grace sat down on the edge of the bed. "You need to eat something. Your father is worried about you."

Angrily hurling the pillow against the wall, Gabrielle sat up, her long hair falling about her shoulders and down her back to lie in silken swirls on the quilt. "He's so worried, he left for Tucson already," she retorted sarcastically, drawing her knees up to her chest and hugging them tightly.

"He didn't have a choice. He had to go explain to General Crook why the Apaches—"

"He had a choice. He left because he was ashamed of me."

"Gabrielle, that's not true!"

"It *is* true! He couldn't bear to have people talking behind his back, whispering about his daughter, the *harlot*." In spite of her haughty tone, tears glimmered in Gabrielle's eyes. "He ordered Captain Moreland to take me to Prescott on Wednesday and put me on a stagecoach to Baltimore."

Disbelief slowly spread across the older girl's features. "That's the day after tomorrow."

Gabrielle snorted derisively. "He doesn't want me here when he gets back."

Too embarrassed to think of anything to say, Grace blushed uncomfortably and averted her gaze. In the strained silence that followed, she sat picking nervously at a loose thread on the quilt. She did not look up until she heard Gabrielle swallow, then swallow again.

"He said I was a disgrace to the family name and that . . . Mama would turn over in her grave if she knew what I had done," Gabrielle said in a choked whisper, the tears she had tried so hard to contain rolling down her cheeks in scalding waves. "He said . . . I had shamed him and that it would be a long time before he forgave me. He said—"

"Stop it!" Grace blurted out, jumping to her feet. "I don't care what your father said, and neither should you—because he's wrong! And if Major Catlin were here now, he would take him to task for saying such awful, hurtful things to you!"

Sudden anger blazed through the tears in Gabrielle's eyes. "Don't you ever again mention that man's name in my presence, Grace Simmons! Not ever!"

"And, why not?" Grace demanded, plunking her hands on her hips and returning Gabrielle's heated glare with one of her own. "You love him and he loves you, and don't you dare try to deny it. Do you think he would have gone after you when you ran away and risked his life to save you if he didn't love you? Do you think he would have sat by your bed for days and nights on end, nursing you through that fever, if he didn't love you? Do you think he would have asked you to marry him if he didn't love you?"

A torrent of conflicting emotions battered Gabrielle as Grace continued. "Dan Catlin is the kindest, most generous man I have ever known, and if you let him get away from you simply because of foolish pride, then you are a fool! Do you have any idea what that man did for you? He bought the ranch bordering Wilbur's so that you and I could be neighbors after we are married, and so you would be close enough to Camp Carleton to come see your father. And he told Wilbur that he was going to build you a big, beautiful house with a view of the mountains and with lots of bedrooms so you could have as many friends as you wanted come to visit you and that you would never have to worry about being lonely. If that's not love, then I sure as blazes don't know what is!"

Two totally unrelated revelations emerged from Grace's tirade to tease Gabrielle's already overwrought mind. One was that, somehow, Dan had discovered her fear of being alone, and the other was that Bandy Moreland and Grace were getting married. Then a third realization worked it's way into her consciousness: Dan had bought a ranch. For her.

"Well, I don't know what it is either," she remarked angrily, forcing all feeling save hatred from her. "But it certainly isn't love. *Love* is what he felt for my mother. He *used* me."

"He loves you."

"He loved my mother!"

"So what? You used to love Lieutenant Epperling!"

"That's different."

"Hogwash! It's not different at all. You're just too stubborn

339

and too selfish to admit that you're wrong. If you had any guts at all, Gabrielle DuBois, you would swallow your blasted pride and go to him. You're not the only one who's been hurt by all this. He's been hurt too. Very hurt."

Gabrielle knew Grace was right, but she also knew she could never face Dan again after what had happened that day. When he had held her and tried to comfort her, she had turned on him and told him she never wanted to see him again. He wouldn't even *want* her back now. No man in his right mind would. "I wish you would stop playing Cupid," she retorted, the anger she was feeling at herself ricocheting off Grace. "It's over and he's gone."

"The only thing that's gone," Grace snapped, "is your common sense!" Whirling about, she stalked to the bedroom door and yanked it open, then turned back to face Gabrielle while still clutching the doorknob in a white-knuckled grip. "The house on his ranch is eighteen miles east of the Dripping Springs Stage Station. Wilbur said to tell you he will be glad to take you there if you ever decide to come to your senses." She slammed the door after her with an explosive bang.

Fresh tears formed behind Gabrielle's eyelids, and there was a throbbing ache in her chest where her heart should have been. She tried in vain to remember Dan as he used to be, before she had been foolish enough to lose her heart to him. She tried to remember when he had punished her by confining her to her room, but what she thought of instead was the way he always called her little one in that special way that made her feel cherished and loved. She tried to remember the countless times he had scolded her, sometimes humiliating her so badly she wanted the ground to open up and swallow her whole, but what streaked through her mind was the way he had held and comforted her when she'd been frightened and alone. She tried to remember the time he had dragged her out of the Cinco de Mayo festival and spanked her in full view of the entire post, yet her mind betrayed her by dwelling on the memory of the night she had spent in his arms, and the exquisite sensations he had aroused in her with his lovemaking.

She thought of his promise to tell her every day that he loved her.

Then she remembered that he had never really loved her at all. He loved her mother.

Gabrielle placed her valise on the floor in front of the ticket window. "Excuse me, sir, could you please tell me when the next Eastbound coach is due to arrive?"

The man behind the counter lowered his head and peered at her over the top of his spectacles. "The San Diego to Mesilla stage is scheduled to pass through here in about thirty minutes—providin' it's not running late. You expectin' someone?"

Thirty minutes! That soon? She swallowed hard. "I'd like to book a . . . a seat." Gabrielle suddenly wished she had waited for Bandy. Why was this so damned difficult?

"You travelin' alone?" came the curt reply.

She nodded. "Yes, sir."

He gave her a disapproving look. "It's not safe, womenfolk travelin' alone, 'specially one as young and pretty as you. Long stretch between here and the Mesilla Valley, and lined with Apaches all the way. Anything's bound to happen on that road, especially since them Apaches from Camp Carleton took to the hills, burnin' and lootin' everything in their path. In fact, we lost one of our drivers just last—"

"How much do I owe you?" Gabrielle interrupted. She suddenly felt sick, and her stomach knotted as she thought of Datigé and realized she would never know what was to become of the little girl.

The man eyed her closely. "That all depends. You stayin' in El Paso, or are you transferrin'?"

"I'm transferring."

"Final destination?"

Her mouth unexpectedly went dry. *She would never see Dan again or feel his arms around her. He would never call her little one* . . . The room reeled around Gabrielle and she closed her eyes and rubbed one hand across her brow, suddenly feeling faint.

"Final destination?" the man repeated, his voice cutting through to her fogged mind.

Gabrielle's eyes flew open and she blinked as the man's face shifted in and out of focus. "B-Baltimore."

The man consulted a chart. "That'll be two hundred and thirty-six dollars."

For a moment, she just stared at him, thinking she might not have heard him correctly. When she and her father had taken the train from New York and then the stage only three years before, the combined fare for *both* of them had been less than half that amount. "The cost has gone up," she said at last, her hands shaking as she retrieved the bills from her reticule.

The man shrugged. "So have the dangers."

"Thought I told you to wait for me," Gabrielle heard Bandy say.

She turned. "I was buying a ticket. The stage should be here in half an hour."

"Good. Gives me time to try and knock some sense into that thick skull of yours."

Gabrielle bristled, anticipating another lecture, but the man behind the ticket counter nodded approvingly. "I tried to tell her it weren't safe for womenfolk to travel alone."

Bandy shot him a piercing look. "No one *asked* you." Taking Gabrielle's arm in an almost painful grip, he led her away from the prying ears of the ticket agent.

"Don't start," Gabrielle hissed through clenched teeth, acutely aware of the curious glances of the other passengers in the station.

"You just shut your trap and listen up," Bandy ordered, jerking her around to face him. "This is your last chance, little lady. You can come out to the ranch with me right now and try patchin' things up with that man of yours, or you can just get on that stagecoach and run away like a scalded dog. What's it gonna be?"

She jerked her arm free. "I'm going to run like a scalded dog. Are you satisfied?"

He nodded. "Yup. Danny's lucky to be gettin' rid of you. After what you done to him—"

"After what *I* did to *him!* What about what he did to me?"

"So he made a woman outta you. Better him than some

spineless idiot who don't know his head from a hole in the wall."

Embarrassment blazed across her face. "For God's sake, Captain Moreland! Will you lower your voice?"

"Why should I? After all, it's what you want everyone to think, ain't it? That Danny forced himself on you? That he took you against your will just 'cause you happen to look a little bit like your ma? You don't got the guts to admit that you bedded with him 'cause you wanted to."

Raw fury glittered in Gabrielle's eyes. "Are you quite through?"

Dropping onto a chair, Bandy tilted it back until it rested only on its rear legs, leaving her to stand and awkwardly stare at him. "Yup."

Her shoulders sagged as breath left her lungs in a *whoosh*. "Why are you doing this to me?" she pleaded quietly. "Why are you trying to punish me for what happened? You and Grace both keep doing it to me."

One of Bandy's brows arched upward. "I ain't tryin' to punish you. I was just hopin' if I couldn't sweet-talk you into goin' back to Danny, maybe if I pissed you off, you'd go back to him just to spite me." Suddenly, the corners of his mouth turned up in a lazy grin. "Guess it ain't working, huh?"

Gabrielle swallowed and shifted her gaze until she was staring blindly at a spot on the wall behind his head. "I-I'd rather not talk about him."

Bandy patted the chair next to him. "Then sit down and keep me company 'till the stage gets here."

She did as she was told, her hands trembling as she nervously adjusted the folds of her skirt.

"You ever been to the East Coast?" Bandy asked offhandedly.

It hurt to breathe. "I went to New York . . . once."

"Close enough, I guess. You like it there?"

She shrugged. "It was all right.

When Gabrielle didn't elaborate, Bandy cast a glance at her, concern creasing his brow. "You gotta promise to write to Grace as soon as you get to Baltimore."

She nodded numbly. "I promise."

Setting the front legs of his chair down, he leaned forward, dangling his hands between his thighs. "Grace was hopin' you'd stand up for her at the wedding," he said absently, not looking at her.

A sharp pain shot through Gabrielle's lungs. "I know."

They fell silent after that, and Gabrielle huddled forlornly in her chair, drowing in her own misery. No matter how hard she tried to dismiss Dan from her thoughts, he was always there, tormenting her. If only she could forget about the feelings he had once harbored for her mother, their love might have a chance to grow and flourish. But every time she thought of him touching her, an aching chill coursed through her, making her shudder.

"Did Dan go out to his ranch?" she asked after a while, hating herself for needing to know.

"Yup."

She moistened her dry lips. "Are you . . . and he going into the cattle business together?"

"Doubt it. Danny'll probably fix up the house and make some 'provements to the land, then turn around and sell it. Ain't no reason for him to keep it now."

Guilt stabbed Gabrielle. "Where will he go?"

"Thought you didn't want to talk about him."

Hot color flooding her face, she shrank back in her chair. "I don't."

It seemed an eternity passed, yet all too soon the stagecoach pulled into town. "Don't fret none about the rest of your things," Bandy told her, after he had given the driver her valise. "We'll get your trunks to Ehrenberg and on the steamer sometime next week."

Ehrenberg. That was where Dan had sent Chase Dalton after the young officer had invited her to his quarters and gotten her drunk on champagne. Dan could have had Lieutenant Dalton court-martialed, but he hadn't. He'd given him another chance. Gabrielle's throat constricted.

She was the last one to board. Bandy again made her promise that she would write to Grace, and then, just as she was preparing to mount the steps, he put a hand on her arm, stopping her. "You're ill-mannered and you're sassy and you could stand to have your butt paddled," he said tersely, "but I love you just the same."

It was almost Gabrielle's undoing. "Oh, Captain Moreland!" she whispered hoarsely, then flung herself into his arms. "I love you, too. You and Grace both."

He pried her arms from around his neck. "Now don't you go bawlin' on me, 'cause I don't got a handkerchief to lend you. But, here—you can take this." He pressed a small, square, velvet box into her hand. "I wish I could say this is from me, but it ain't. Now, skedaddle!"

Clutching the velvet box in one hand and her reticule in the other, Gabrielle entered the coach and slid back on the seat, flinching as the door slammed after her with a frightening finality. She twisted around to look out the window, but tears misted her eyes and she could barely make out Bandy Moreland standing on the boardwalk in front of the stage station. Before she could lift her hand to wave, the coach lurched forward, and she was on her way.

For several minutes, she sat stiffly, her body fighting the jolting rhythm of the moving stagecoach, her anguished gaze fixed on the velvet box in her hand. It was from Dan. She knew it. And she hated him for it. If he thought he could bribe her into coming back to him, then he didn't know her very well. Perhaps her mother would have accepted a bribe—"

Gabrielle abruptly forced that thought from her mind. Lashing out at someone else, alive or dead, would do nothing to ease her misery. Opening her reticule, she shoved the box inside. She had no desire to know what Dan had given her.

There were five other passengers on the coach: a woman, probably in her early thirties, with two small children—the girl was about Datigé's age and the boy slightly older; a gaunt gray-haired man who nodded over the newspaper he was reading; and a man in dark, dust-covered clothing who smelled of horses and sweat and who wore his hat pulled down over his eyes. Gabrielle smiled a tentative smile at the woman, but she merely gathered her children closer to her and looked away. Shifting nervously, Gabrielle pressed herself into the corner and then turned to stare absently out the window.

The road stretched across mile after seemingly endless mile of barren desert before finally turning east toward the mountains. Gradually giving herself up to the rocking of the coach, Gabrielle let her eyelids droop and, abandoning the attempt to force herself to stay awake, rested her head on the window frame and dozed.

The dream returned, stronger and more vivid than ever, only this time, instead of a knife, the Apache was holding a revolver. Gabrielle saw Dan's face, pale and taut with pain, saw the Apache level the gun at him as he staggered to his feet . . . pull back the hammer.

The explosion pierced the steady, persistent rumbling of the wheels, and Gabrielle awakened with a startled cry, then gripped the edge of the seat to keep from being thrown about at the coach lurched sharply. Night had fallen, and the steep walls of the canyon kept out the moonlight, leaving them in an eerie darkness that made her shiver in spite of the June heat.

The little girl began to whimper. "Hush dear," the woman said in a loud whisper, her voice oddly sharp.

The last vestiges of the nightmare slowly slipping away, Gabrielle planted her feet firmly on the floor and braced herself as the coach swayed. Her heart was thumping so loudly she was certain everyone in the coach could hear it.

Suddenly, a shot rang out, sounding uncannily like the gunshot in her dream.

The little girl shrieked, "Mama!"

The coach pitched again.

Gabrielle caught her breath. As another shot ripped through one of the canvas window flaps and lodged in the doorframe just above her head, a scream rose in her throat.

A terrifying vibration jolted the coach, and the air was filled with an ear-shattering roar and a splintering sound. Over the din, Gabrielle could hear the panicked screams of the horses. She thrust out her hand, frantically grasping for something to hold onto as she was flung from the seat, but found only air, and she was thrown to the far side of the coach, to land with a thud that knocked the air from her lungs.

A man's body slammed against hers with crushing force, pinning her beneath his weight, then it was abruptly wrenched

346

away as the coach rolled again and she was hurtled through the air like a rag doll.

A blinding white pain exploded inside Gabrielle's head, and burst into a million fiery sparks behind her eyes. She opened her mouth to scream, but no sound would come out; and a suffocating numbness washed over her, sweeping her into oblivion.

Chapter Sixteen

The voices seemed so far away.

Gabrielle tried to open her eyes, but could not.

"She'll live," she heard a man say. "Just took a knock on the head, is all."

"She's comin' to."

The smell of horses and sweat pierced her consciousness as someone slid an arm beneath her shoulders and lifted her up, and she sucked in her breath and gritted her teeth against the throbbing in her head. Everything around her reeled, making her feel sick to her stomach.

"Here, ma'am. Drink this."

Gabrielle forced her eyes open and found herself staring into the dark, piercing gaze of the man who had been on the stage, the one who'd worn his hat low, partially hiding his face.

"Go easy on it," he said as he handed her the canteen. "It's all the water we got left until we get to Dripping Springs."

The house on his ranch is eighteen miles east of the Dripping Springs Stage Station.

Gabrielle pushed that thought from her mind and mumbled a hasty thanks to the man who had given her the canteen.

Feeling a little steadier after taking several small sips of water, she handed the canteen back to him and glanced about the night-shrouded canyon, her gaze drawn by the fire that had been built next to the overturned stagecoach. It glowed eerily through the blanket that had been hung up to conceal it from anyone passing along the road above them.

"Don't want the light to beckon trouble," the man explained, following her gaze. "They should have that wheel fixed soon."

Gabrielle turned back to him and then brushed a stray curl back from her face. "I heard gunshots."

"Don't let *her* hear you say that," the man retorted, jerking his head toward the woman sitting about fifteen yards away with her two children. "She just spent the past hour trying to convince them two kids of hers that they *didn't* hear gunshots. Frankly, I think it's a mistake to try to pull the wool over young'n's eyes like that, but I guess it's none of my business what she tells them."

Gabrielle's throat tightened. The man reminded her of Bandy, even if he did smell as though he hadn't bathed in a month.

I was just hopin' that if I couldn't sweet-talk you into goin' back to Danny, maybe if I pissed you off, you'd go back to him just to spite me.

The man stood up. "I'd better get over there and help them right that stage and push it back onto the road. If you need anything, just holler."

"Sir?" Gabrielle blurted out as he started to leave.

He turned back to her.

She took a deep breath, and her heart thumped wildly against the wall of her chest. "Sir . . . how far east does this road run?"

The man rubbed his chin. "Till it reaches Dripping Springs, if I remember correctly. Then it turns south and cuts through Ciénega Pass."

The house on his ranch is eighteen miles east of the Dripping Springs Stage Station.

After he had gone, Gabrielle reached up to touch the back of her head with her fingertips, and winced as they came into contact with a large, tender lump. Her head hurt and her entire body felt as though it had been trampled by wild animals. She wanted to go home. She wanted Dan to hold her and tell her everything would be all right.

Will you tell me every day that you love me?

Every day.

Tears stung her eyes and she squeezed them shut.

Even if you are very, very angry with me?
No matter how angry I am with you.

The man from the stage returned. "You about ready to head out of here?"

Her eyes flew open. Taking a hasty swipe at the tear sliding down her cheek, Gabrielle nodded. He gripped her arm, holding her steady as she rose uncertainly to her feet and pressed a hand to her throbbing temple. "If you get dizzy, tell me," the man said. While Gabrielle was grateful for his help, his presence in no way even began to fill the aching void inside her.

By the time the stagecoach pulled into Dripping Springs, she had reached a decision.

When she told the driver what she wanted to do, however, he looked at her as though she had just taken leave of her senses. "Ma'am, if you think I'm going to rearrange all that freight just to get to your valise—" He broke off and clamped his mouth shut, but there was no mistaking the disapproval in his eyes as he glared at her. Finally, he sighed and shook his head. "All right. Tell you what. I'll reload at Ciénega Pass and put your bag off there. You can send someone to fetch it."

She inclined her head. "That'll be fine, thank you."

"I hope you know that leaving you here this late at night with no one to watch over you goes against my better judgment."

She glanced over her shoulder toward the stage station. "I won't be alone. There are other people in there."

The driver snorted inelegantly. "Only people you're going to find in there are riffraff that're not welcome at a poker table anywhere else in the Territory. If you ask me, I think you'd be better off going on to Ciénega Pass and getting a ride back from there."

Gabrielle said nothing but shifted uneasily from one foot to the other, cold dread building in the pit of her stomach. Perhaps he was right, she thought, looking around her. The stage station here at Dripping Springs was isolated. Too isolated. Maybe she would be better off going on to Ciénega Pass.

The relief driver emerged from around the side of the

building, buttoning his pants, and climbed up onto the seat.

Cupping his hands around his mouth, the driver yelled out, "Board up! You got two minutes!" He turned back to Gabrielle. "Sure you don't want to change your mind?"

She shook her head.

The man who had let her drink from his canteen hung behind after the other passengers had boarded the stage. "That fellow who put you on the stage in Prescott . . . he your man?"

There was never anything more than friendship between your mother and me. Never.

Her throat ached with unshed tears. "No, sir. He . . . he's a friend . . ."

The man rubbed his jaw thoughtfully before casting one more glance at her. "You sure you're going to be all right here?"

Unable to speak, she nodded.

The driver joined his relief on the seat and picked up the reins. "You just be careful, you hear?"

All too soon, they were gone and Gabrielle was left standing alone in the darkness outside the stage station, nursing a raw ache for the warmth and safety of Dan's arms. *If only I had listened to him, if only I'd given him a chance to explain,* she thought miserably, *I wouldn't be stranded in the middle of nowhere.*

Inside the station, a man laughed, and the sound was harsh and frightening.

Gabrielle shuddered and gritted her teeth to keep them from chattering, but whether that reaction was due to fear or the night air, she did not know. Taking a deep breath to steady herself, she turned and went into the station.

She had been here before, three years ago, but with her father and in broad daylight. After dark, the stage station changed into a noisy, smoke-filled saloon open to drinkers and gamblers rather than to travelers. Fear knotted in Gabrielle's stomach, and she began to understand why the driver had been so reluctant to leave her here.

A man at one of the tables nudged his companion and the two stared at her. One by one, every man in the room fell silent. All eyes were on her.

Her pulse racing, Gabrielle wrapped her arms about her stomach, and glanced anxiously about. She swallowed hard. "Is the station manager here?" she asked, her eyes dark with apprehension.

One of the men leaned back in his chair and yelled over his shoulder, "Hey, Charlie, get your ass out here! You got a payin' customer!"

A fat, sweaty, unshaven man emerged from the kitchen, wiping his hands on a greasy apron. He stopped short, his chin dropping when he saw Gabrielle. "Where in the hell did you come from?"

It hurt to breathe. "I . . . I was on the coach from Prescott."

The man's eyebrows shot up. "Then, why aren't you on it now? You stay in the outhouse so long the driver left without you?"

Hot color stained Gabrielle's cheeks as a titter spread through the room, and her lips tightened as annoyance slowly began to crowd out her fear. "I'm going to a ranch eighteen miles east of here," she said firmly, meeting the station manager's probing stare without flinching. "I'll need a ride."

"Then you'll have to go back to Prescott to get one."

Gabrielle's palm was fairly itching to slap the smug look off the man's face. Instead, she knotted her fingers in the folds of her skirt and her chin inched up mutinously. "All right. When is the next stage to Prescott due to pass through here?"

"Saturday, if you're lucky. Otherwise . . ." He held his hands out, palms up, and shrugged.

Three days. Dismay flickered in Gabrielle's eyes. "Then I shall require a room until then."

The man snickered. "Listen, lady—"

"I can pay you in advance," Gabrielle said hastily, and reached for her reticule, panic knifing through her when she realized she no longer had it. She must have dropped it when the stagecoach overturned.

"What I was trying to tell you, lady, is that I don't got any rooms. This is it. This and the kitchen."

For a moment, she just stared at him, too stunned to speak. Then her eyes slid from his face and slowly made their way around the room. All the men stared back at her. And waited.

She caught her bottom lip between her teeth as her confidence rapidly deserted her. If there were no rooms, where was she going to stay until Saturday? And if the stage did not arrive as scheduled, what then? Only one thing was certain— she could not stay here. She gave the man a pleading look. "Sir, are you sure you have nothing at all?"

He shook his head. "Nope. You can stretch out on the floor if you get tired. Other than that, you're out of luck." He turned to go.

"Wait!"

He turned back to her, aggravation hardening his eyes. "Listen, lady, I told you I don't have no rooms. Now, if you don't mind, I got work to do."

"Could you rent me a horse . . . or a wagon and a team?" she blurted out, desperation making her voice sharper than usual. "I don't have any money, but when I reach the ranch, my . . . my *husband* will reimburse you—"

"You've got to be crazy!" The man's eyes bulged.

Gabrielle's shoulders sagged. "Not right now," she hastened to explain, misunderstanding his reaction. "In the morning. After it gets light."

"Sorry, lady. I don't have nothing I can rent to you. You're just going to have to wait until the stage comes through."

"But, I know you have horses here! The driver of the last stage just changed teams not twenty minutes ago!"

"Yeah, I got horses here," the man said sarcastically, his patience wearing thin. "One spare team, and that's it. And if the next driver pulls in here with a lame horse, the same as yours just did, I'm up a creek. Sorry, you're just going to have to wait for the stage or find some other way to get to your husband, I can't help you." He did an abrupt about-face and stomped back into the kitchen, leaving her standing awkwardly in the main room, embarrassment coloring her cheeks.

Careful to avoid the curious stares that followed her, Gabrielle crossed the room and sought out a chair against the far wall, placing as much distance as she could between her and the men. Sitting down, she smoothed out the folds of her skirt, then squared her shoulders and stared straight ahead, her hands folded in her lap.

Gradually, the men turned away from her and went back to their card games. But they kept their voices low, and though she did not look at them directly, Gabrielle could feel the occasional glance cast in her direction and she knew she was the topic of discussion at more than one table.

Oh, Dan! Why didn't I listen to you? she wailed silently, and berated herself for the predicament she was in. Dan had given Chase Dalton a second chance. Why hadn't she given *him* one? Why was she so blasted willful and hardheaded, so quick to take offense and so slow to forgive?

She squirmed uncomfortably in the chair. She had to get out of there. As soon as it was light, she would go, even if that meant she had to walk all the way to Dan's ranch—or back to town.

An eerie feeling settled over Gabrielle as she sat in the station, feeling that she was being watched—no, studied—with an intensity that went beyond mere curiosity. Her pulse quickening, she nervously moistened her lips and turned her head.

He sat, leaning back, his chair tilted on its back legs, his hat pulled down low over his forehead, and watched her through half-closed eyes.

Gabrielle involuntarily sucked in her breath and her heart missed a beat.

It was Jack Doolen.

She forced her eyes away from him, but her hands tightened in her lap, causing her knuckles to turn white, and a terrible pressure bore down on her, making each breath painful. Of all the people she could possibly have encountered, Doolen was the last one she'd ever expected—or wanted—to see.

He brought his chair down to the floor with a thud that made her flinch, and stood up.

Panic erupted within Gabrielle as he approached her, but she gritted her teeth and braced herself.

Doolen stopped in front of her chair, so close she could smell the unwashed scent of him. "Well, well. What have we here?" he drawled, pushing back his hat. "If it ain't our little busy-body colonel's daughter from Camp Carleton."

She forced herself to look him in the eye. "Good evening,

Mr. Doolen."

For several seconds he looked surprised; then he burst out laughing. "You hear that?" he called out over his shoulder. "She called me *Mister* Doolen!"

A few snickers echoed throughout the room, to be followed by a taut silence. Gabrielle nervously shifted her gaze away from Doolen's face. No one said a word.

"What you doin' so far from home, little girl?" Doolen asked. "You run out of 'Paches to defend?"

She did not answer.

"I hear you're wanting to rent a horse."

It was a statement, not a question, and something about his tone of voice sent a shiver down Gabrielle's spine. She pressed her lips together, silently praying he would go away and leave her alone.

"How much you willing to pay?" he persisted, his annoyance flaring when she continued to ignore him.

She ran her tongue across her lips. "I've decided to wait for the stage," she said in a low voice, not looking at him. Her heart was pounding.

He stiffened. "Just a little while ago, you was hot to get outta here. What changed your mind? Ain't I good enough for you?"

Gabrielle's mind raced. If she turned him down, she was liable to incur his wrath, and that could prove worse than simply accepting his offer and allowing him to take her to the ranch. Still, the memory of what he had tried to do to Zayigo was clear in her mind. She did not like Doolen, and the mere thought of being alone with him made her skin crawl. She wished one of the men in the room would speak up and come to her aid, but she knew that was a futile, childish hope. "I-I don't have any money," she stammered. "I lost my reticule when the stagecoach overturned."

"You said your husband had money," he reminded her. "That is . . . if you even got a husband."

Gabrielle's stomach turned over. Hoping she looked more confident than she felt, she lifted her eyes and fixed them on his face. "All right. I'll have my husband pay you fifty dollars to take me to his ranch."

His mouth went slack, and for one brief second, she knew

she had the upper hand. But she had no way of knowing whether Dan had fifty dollars or if he would be willing to part with that sum for the return of a woman who had scorned him.

Her victory was short-lived. A bowie knife miraculously materialized in Doolen's hand, and before she realized what he was about, he'd reached out and grasped a handful of her hair. A cry of horror escaped her as he severed a silken lock with a single swipe of his knife. "Insurance," he said, giving her a malicious grin as he twirled the red-gold curls about in his fingers. "Gotta make sure your old man'll pay up." He turned and started back toward his table.

Gabrielle jumped to her feet. "How dare you!" she cried out, suddenly finding her voice. "Dan will kill you when he finds out what you've done!"

Doolen turned around to glare at her. "And I'll kill *you* if you don't sit down and shut your trap!"

Clenching and unclenching her hands, Gabrielle glanced hesitantly toward the kitchen.

The move did not go unnoticed. Doolen aimed a warning finger at her. "And don't go getting no big ideas about running to Charlie for help. He's the last person who'd stick his neck out for you." He pointed at her chair. "Sit!"

A peculiar sense of calm settled over Gabrielle as she returned his stare. She knew she had made a mistake when she'd tried to bargain with Doolen, and if she wanted to get away without losing more than a hank of hair, she was going to have to keep her wits about her. Fear was a luxury she could no longer afford. Without a word, she sat back down and folded her hands in her lap, fighting desperately against the inane urge to reach up and feel her shorn hair.

Doolen rubbed the lock of hair against his cheek. "That's better," he grumbled, throwing her a warning glance before returning to his table.

The men returned to their whiskey and their cards, and except for the occasional glance Doolen cast in her direction, no one paid her any attention. But the silent message was clear: he had laid claim to her, and no one dared intervene.

The seconds, then the minutes, ticked by with interminable slowness. If only I had a plan, Gabrielle thought as she covertly watched the men from beneath her lashes. Surely there was something she could do to get away, but, in spite of her efforts, she could think of nothing. Besides, there were nine of them, counting Charlie, and only one of her. And, with the way the whiskey was flowing, she was willing to wager that whatever was left of their consciences—if they'd had any to begin with—would not be enough to fill a shot glass. Her best bet was just to sit tight and draw as little notice as possible.

After a while, two of the men got up and left. And then another. Those who remained pushed their chairs over to one large table, and a new card game began. It had been a long time, possibly hours, since Charlie had made his last appearance, and Gabrielle wondered if he had gone to bed. Her eyelids began to droop, then her head. She jerked it up and took a deep breath. Her back hurt, so did her head. She shifted in her chair, trying to get comfortable. She had to remain awake and alert. Her lashes fluttered against her cheeks. Stay awake, she silently admonished herself, over and over. You must . . . stay awake. . . .

Sweat rolled off the taut muscles of Dan's back and shoulders as he raised the ax over his head and brought it down on the mesquite bough with enough force to drive it a good three inches into the rock-hard wood. When he finished getting enough wood to last the winter, he planned to start making repairs on the frame cabin. He was no longer in a hurry to get started on the sprawling adobe ranchhouse he'd planned to build for Gabrielle. *She* wouldn't be living in it. He wrenched the ax free and raised it again, his face dark with the silent fury that had been building within him these past couple of days.

Get out. Get out of this house. Out of my life! Get out! Get out! Get out!

He brought the ax down again and the sound of the blow echoed throughout the canyon.

I don't ever—ever—want to see you again. . . .

His hands tightened on the ax handle, and, with a burst of violence that barely hinted at what he was feeling inside, he brought the ax down one final time. Leaving it embedded in the wood, he found his canteen and took a swig of water, then spat it out.

Damn! Everything had a bitter taste these days.

Retrieving his shirt, Dan put it on and sat down on the top step of the porch to watch the sun come up and try to get his rampaging emotions back under control.

She would have loved it here, he thought, his gaze scanning the mountains that hugged the valley like giant sheltering sentinels, imparting a feeling of permanence and security. He thought of the house he had planned to build for her, with thick solid adobe walls to protect her and rooms filled with the gay laughter of children who knew they were loved and wanted. "Come back to me, little one," he whispered aloud in the predawn stillness. "Let me hold you and make it all up to you. Let me show you that it's you and only you that I love. Let me—"

His pulse quickened and his eyes narrowed as he observed the rising dust in the distance, signaling an approaching rider. Instinctively reaching for his gun, he stood up. Someone was in a hell of a hurry.

The instant Dan recognized Bandy Moreland, the anger, the pain, the longing abruptly left him to be replaced by a cold cutting fear. If anything had happened to Gabrielle, he would never forgive himself.

"The stagecoach was ambushed by Apaches up at the Ciénega!" Bandy shouted, reining in his horse. "They can't find her! She wasn't with the other passengers!"

Gabrielle moaned and rubbed one hand across her eyes, wincing when sharp pain shot down her spine as she straightened her back.

Seizing her by the arm, Doolen hauled her roughly out of the chair. "Hurry up, damn you! I don't got all day!"

Struggling to get her bearings, Gabrielle cast a blurry-eyed glance about her as she stumbled across a room bathed in the dim light of dawn. Everyone had gone except two men who were asleep on the floor, their snores loud and grating in the stillness. The station manager, Charlie, was nowhere to be seen.

A blast of cold air slapped Gabrielle in the face as Doolen shoved her out the door, jarring her fully awake, and panic welled up inside her. Her footsteps slowing, she drew her arms about her and shivered, as much from fear as from the early morning chill. "P-please," she stammered, her teeth chattering. "I-I'd rather wait f-for the stage."

"Shut up!" he barked, his fingers closing around her upper arm in a viselike grip. "You're coming with me."

Making no secret of her reluctance to go with him, she dragged her feet as he pulled her across the yard toward the corral where his horse was tied to the fence. Her mind raced as her eyes darted fearfully back and forth, anxiously searching for some way to escape.

But Doolen was not about to allow her to try to make a run for it. Grasping the reins firmly in one hand, he made Gabrielle mount first, then swung up behind her, wrapping his arms around her and pulling her against him.

Her arms pinned to her side, Gabrielle sat stiffly, making no effort to hide her revulsion for the man seated behind her. She resisted as best she could Doolen's efforts to hold her close, but the awkward position made it difficult for her to keep her balance and, as they took to the hills, she found herself sliding backward into Doolen's arms. Repulsed by his closeness and by the sour, unwashed odor of him, she gritted her teeth and it took every ounce of willpower she could muster not to gag.

Ahead of them, the sun was just breaking over the horizon.

By the time they reached the stage station at Ciénega Pass, Dan's horse was lathered and Bandy's was dangerously close to collapsing from exhaustion. Halfway up the porch steps, a soldier lifted his carbine and stepped in front of Dan, preventing him from entering the building. "You can't go in there, mister," the soldier said, then shrank from the murderous look Dan gave him. "Not until you clear it with Captain Saunders."

Dan opened his mouth to order the corporal out of the way, then stopped, suddenly realizing that he no longer had the authority to do so. He was a civilian now, and this soldier didn't know him from Adam. "Where's this Captain Saunders?" he snapped impatiently.

The soldier inclined his head. "Over there. With the prisoners."

Dan afforded the Apaches huddled in a circle nearby only a cursory glance. "I'm looking for a woman," he told Captain Saunders. He'd learned from Bandy that Saunders had been on patrol out of Camp Bowie when news of the ambush had reached him. "She's eighteen, about five foot, four—with red-gold hair and green eyes."

Saunders shook his head. "We only found one woman and she doesn't fit that description."

Bandy eyed the officer closely. "I put her on that stage myself."

"Sorry, I can't help you." Captain Saunders turned to bark an order at two soldiers who were piling up the trunks and valises salvaged from the wreckage.

Bandy stalked over to the pile and pulled out a valise that looked uncomfortably familiar. "This is hers," he said flatly. "I know because I was the one who gave it to the driver yesterday mornin' in Prescott."

The officer shook his head. "That might be so, sir, but the truth is, half this cargo was loaded on in San Diego. Just because there's a bag here that may or may not belong—"

"Goddamnit!" Dan virtually exploded, his frustration having become too great to bear. "Isn't there anyone here who can tell us where she might be?"

"Listen, mister, I know how you feel, but the truth is, I've got six bodies in there that I've yet to identify and there's one man who's not liable to make it past lunchtime. I have a dozen prisoners that Headquarters won't give me clearance to release or bring in, and a bunch of undisciplined, untrained recruits who think they have a right to the contraband we took off the prisoners. Take this, for example," Captain Saunders said, reaching into his pocket. "Two of my men beat each other to a pulp over this."

The color drained from Dan's face as he stared in mute horror at the ring the officer held up. On it, an oval-cut opal

360

was set in a circle of diamonds.

Captain Saunders tipped the ring so that the sunlight danced in fiery flashes off the precious stones. "I'll admit, it's a beautiful piece, but it sure isn't worth getting—" He broke off at seeing the hard glint of recognition in Dan's eyes. "Don't tell me," he said wearily, "this ring would look great on your wife. That's what Pearson and Jones said before they tried to kill each other for it." He started to return the ring to his pocket, but Dan's hand shot out, closing around his wrist in a bone-bruising grip.

"Where did you get that?" he demanded.

Annoyance flickered across the officer's face. "I don't owe you an explan—"

"*Where did you get it?*"

Sweat broke out across the captain's upper lip and it was all he could do to keep from flinching as Dan's grip tightened on his wrist. "Listen, mister," he said unevenly, certain this tall, dark, wild-eyed man was insane, "if you can prove the ring is yours, I'll let you have it."

Dan abruptly released the man's wrist and struggled to get his temper back under control. "There's an inscription inside the band," he said harshly. "It says . . ."—his voice faltered—"'Happy Birthday, Little One.'"

Casting an uncertain glance at Bandy and then appraising Dan, Captain Saunders turned the ring over and brought it up to eye level so he could inspect it closer. Instantly, his expression became somber. With an unspoken apology in his eyes, he handed the ring to Dan and said in a quiet voice tinged with regret, "I believe this belongs to you, sir."

Dan took the ring. "Where did you get it?" he repeated.

The officer nodded toward the prisoners. "He was wearing it."

Dan followed the captain's gaze and his blood ran cold. He did not need to ask which Apache the officer meant. The warrior's hands and feet were bound, rendering him helpless, but obsidian eyes stared back at Dan with the same glittering hatred he'd seen in them when they'd stared at Gabrielle from behind a saltbush that day at the refugee camp. His face twisted by contempt, the Apache leaned forward and spat on the ground.

The last threads of Dan's self-control snapped. A low, primal growl rose in his throat as he lunged.

Terror streaked across the Apache's face as Dan seized him by the shirtfront and hauled him to his feet. "Where is she?" Dan demanded, his words a frenzied mixture of English and Apache. He knotted a hand in the Indian's hair and jerked his head back. "Damn it, answer me! What have you done with her?"

"Dan, don't!" he heard Bandy yell. Strong hands grasped his shirt, but he shrugged them off and fastened his own about the Apache's neck, his thumbs gouging the man's jugular. "If you've hurt her, I'll kill you!" he threatened, shaking the fettered prisoner until the man's face turned purple and his eyes bulged from his head.

"Let him go!" Captain Saunders ordered.

Oblivious of the soldiers who seized him from behind and fought to subdue him, Dan tightened his grip on the Apache's neck. "Tell me where she is, you murdering bastard! What have you done with her?"

Something hard and cold jabbed into Dan's ribs. "Let him go," Captain Saunders repeated sternly, and only then did Dan realize that the muzzle of a gun was cutting into his side and the officer would shoot him if he did not relent.

His eyes blazing with unspent fury, Dan flung the Apache away from him. His arms were wrenched behind his back and he was forcibly dragged away from the prisoners, but only because he allowed the half-dozen soldiers to restrain him. He knew the rage roiling within him was enough to drive him to murder, and he swore inwardly that, if the Apache had hurt even one hair on Gabrielle's head, he would hunt him to the ends of the earth and kill him.

Captain Saunders ordered the soldiers to release Dan. "I suggest you get control of yourself, mister," he ground out, evidently distressed by his own inability to maintain order.

A muscle in his jaw jerking, Dan snatched his hat up from the ground where it had landed during the struggle. "I want to see the woman who was killed," he demanded.

"Sir, I told you, she wasn't the one—"

362

"Damn it! I want to see her!"

"All right! You can see her! And then I want you and your friend to get the hell out of here before I am forced to have you both arrested and placed in chains!"

The soldier who had been standing guard in front of the stage station scurried aside to let them pass, a mixture of fear and awe on his face. He had witnessed the commotion over the prisoner, and though he could only guess at the strength the big man with the hard-chiseled features possessed, he had no wish to make an enemy of him.

Another soldier—from his insignia Dan recognized him as a Medical Corps officer—tried to block his entrance. "They can't come in here!" the surgeon protested loudly, throwing Captain Saunders a pleading look, but Dan merely shoved him aside and strode purposefully into the building.

Captain Saunders inclined his head toward the shrouded bodies lying in a row on the floor by the far wall. "She's over there. Third from the left."

Gritting his teeth and bracing himself for the worst, Dan stepped over two small, lifeless forms that could only have been children, and bent down to yank back the blanket that covered the body of the woman.

Her face was battered and bloodied, her scalp partially torn from her head. She was naked from the waist down, and there was no mistaking what had been done to her before she'd died. Swallowing hard against the bile that rose in his throat, Dan lowered the blanket back over the woman and slowly straightened up. "It's not her," he said numbly, his face so ashen that Bandy gripped his arm, thinking he might pass out.

"Come on, Dan," Bandy said in a low, hollow voice. "Let's get out of here."

But Dan was not ready to leave yet. He turned to Captain Saunders. "You said there was one survivor," he prompted, still fighting the nausea that swept over him in retching waves.

"You can't—"

"I demand to see him!"

Wanting nothing more than to have this overwhelming, crazed giant of a man out of his hair and on his way, Captain Saunders relented. "You can have two minutes. No more. And if you attack him the way you did the prisoner a moment ago, I'll shoot you without a second thought."

The survivor of the attack looked like he would have been more at home on horseback instead of riding in a stagecoach. He had a hard, weathered face that defied description, but he could have been any one of the drifters who passed through the Territory on a daily basis. Still, there was something about the man's dark, piercing eyes that Dan knew he would never forget, because he had a sick feeling that this man was the last person to have seen Gabrielle alive.

"You her . . . husband?" the man asked in a pain-wrought voice when Dan knelt beside his cot and explained what he wanted.

Sensing that there was more to the man's question than mere assumption, Dan nodded. "Yes."

For a moment, the man just looked at him with those dark eyes, as though sizing him up. "She . . . got off . . . Dripping . . . Springs," he said at last, then dissolved into a fit of choking.

Hope and fear shot through Dan at once. "Did she say where she was going?"

The surgeon hastily intervened. "That's enough! The patient is in no condition to be grilled like this!"

"Where did she go?" Dan repeated, frantic insistence in his voice.

The man feebly shook his head. "Don't . . . know . . ."

Captain Saunders gripped Dan's shoulder. "He told you what you wanted to know. Now, leave!"

Ignoring the officer's command, Dan stood up. "I want you to take a search party out to the ranch," he told Bandy. "If she's not there, start working your way back toward Dripping Springs. If we have to, we'll comb every inch of these mountains." Halfway out of the building, Dan turned and leveled a finger at Captain Saunders. "My man will need a fresh horse and a half-dozen of your best scouts."

Captain Saunders bristles. "Now, listen here—"

"That's an order, *Captain!*"

After the door had slammed after Dan, Captain Saunders whirled on Bandy. "Who in the hell does that arrogant, demanding, self-righteous bastard think he is?"

"Dan Catlin," Moreland replied sharply. He was already halfway out the door.

Captain Saunders' entire body went rigid with disbelief. "*Major* Catlin?"

"Yes!" Bandy barked over his shoulder, not bothering to inform Saunders that Dan had resigned his commission. The door slammed again.

"Oh, shit!" Captain Saunders groaned, and his shoulders slumped in dismay as he figured his once-bright career had taken a fatal plunge.

Dan lost no time in reaching Dripping Springs, but when he dismounted and entered the tumbledown shack that served as a stage station at the isolated watering hole, his hopes of finding Gabrielle there rapidly vanished. Stinking of sweat and cigar smoke and stale whiskey, the main room of the station was empty save for the bottles and trash strewn about the floor. He called out, "Is anyone here?" and was met by the hollow echo of his own voice.

Moving silently through the dirty, dusty room, Dan pushed open a door that led to an equally dirty kitchen. There, in one corner, on a soiled mattress, was a man deep in drunken slumber. Spittle ran from one corner of his open mouth as he snored, and an empty whiskey bottle lay on the floor next to his slack fingers.

"Hey!" Dan called out loudly, but the man did not budge.

A mouse scurried across the floor and disappeared behind the stove.

Because it was so hard to imagine Gabrielle in such a filthy vermin-ridden place, it was also hard to believe that she had ever even been here.

His mouth tightening in disgust, Dan turned his head to look once more around the main room. As particles of dust danced in the shaft of sunlight that streamed in through the dirty window, his gaze was inexplicably drawn to something bright and shiny on the littered floor.

Crossing the room, he bent down to take a closer look, and

for several seconds, it seemed his heart stopped beating. Then it began to pound furiously as he reached down to pick up what he had seen. It was a lock of hair. A sixteen-inch lock of soft, red-gold hair. Swearing savagely, he stalked into the kitchen, seized the sleeping man by the front of his grease-stained clothes, and hauled him up off the mattress.

Charlie cried out and clawed about him blindly as he was rudely dragged from the peaceful depths to which he had sunk in the wee hours of the morning. His head felt as though it would explode, and his mouth was so dry all he could do was sputter and gasp when Dan shook him so fiercely he feared his teeth would come loose.

"Where is she? Where is Gabrielle?" Dan bellowed. He wanted to fling aside this filthy, repulsive excuse for a man, but he needed to get information from him. "She was here last night. She got off the stage from Prescott. Tell me, damn it! Where is she?"

Charlie whimpered pitifully, "I-I don't know . . . what you're t-talking—"

Without a second's hesitation, Dan picked up the terrified, blubbering man as though he weighed nothing, and half carried, half dragged him from the kitchen, through the main room, and out the front door. Then, before Charlie knew what fate lay in store for him, Dan heaved him headfirst over the side of the water trough.

Charlie thrashed about wildly as water filled his mouth and nose, but before he could pull himself up out of the trough, Dan had pressed him under the water, and was holding him down. He began to feel a lethargy seep through him, and he knew without a doubt that his day of reckoning had come.

Suddenly Dan hauled him up out of the trough. "Tell me where she is! Tell me what happened to the woman who came here last night. Tell me, damn it, or I'll drown you, you ass!"

Charlie dragged huge gulping breaths of air into his lungs. "I don't know!" he gasped, not certain whether God had given him another chance or he'd died and gone to hell. "I don't know where he took her!"

"Who? Who took her?"

Charlie shook his head. Then panic rose in him as he felt

himself being shoved back down into the trough. "No, wait! I'll tell you! It was Doolen!"

Dan grabbed a handful of the station manager's sopping hair, and jerked his head back with a force that sent the frightened man to his knees. "Who is Doolen?" he demanded, giving Charlie's head a vicious shake.

"He used . . . he used to work for Bryce Edwards," Charlie said hastily. He suddenly remembered something he had forgotten years ago: how to pray. "Edwards fired him 'cause he raped and murdered a Mexican girl down in Tubac. He works for Sam Penley now . . . least he used to, but Penley fired him last week 'cause of some trouble he caused with them Apaches staked out near Camp Carleton."

Dan struggled to get a grip on his dangerously escalating temper. "Why is she with Doolen? Where did they go?"

"The girl said she needed a ride . . . to her husband's ranch. Doolen offered to take her."

Still clutching Charlie's hair, Dan hauled him to his feet. "Offered? *Offered?*"

Charlie began to sob openly. "She said her husband would pay him fifty dollars if he would take her there!" he wailed.

Enraged, Dan lifted the man clear of the ground and hurled him into the water trough.

Chapter Seventeen

They had not gone more than a few miles before Gabrielle came to the sickening conclusion that, although they were headed in the right direction, Doolen had no intention of taking her to Dan's ranch. Her fears were confirmed only moments later when the horse was guided off the road and down a steep rock-strewn trail.

Doolen said nothing, but continued to direct the horse away from the road. Gabrielle twisted around, alarm flickering in her eyes as the ridges loomed over them, blocking out the sunlight. Why? she silently cried out, fear closing in on her along with the canyon walls. *Why hadn't she followed the driver's advice and waited until they'd reached Ciénega Pass before getting off the stagecoach?*

The horse momentarily lost its footing on the rocks, and Gabrielle gasped. Her heart leaping into her throat, she jerked her head around and gripped the saddle horn with both hands as the animal stumbled again before recovering its balance.

At the bottom of the ravine, Doolen reined in the horse.

Gabrielle's mouth went dry, and she had to swallow twice before she could speak. "Why are we stopping here?"

"You tell me," he retorted, lowering her to the ground before dismounting himself.

"I don't know why," she shot back, fear lending an edge to her voice. "I don't even know where we—" She broke off suddenly, the color leaving her face as it suddenly occurred to her that they were out in the middle of nowhere.

Noting the change in her expression, Doolen snickered. "I guess you ain't as dumb as you look," he taunted cruelly.

Feeling sick, Gabrielle pressed a hand against her stomach to suppress the churning there. "Why?" she asked in a low, uneven voice. "What do you want from me?" Perspiration beaded her upper lip.

"What do you think I want?" Doolen retorted, icy contempt in his eyes as they raked over her in a manner calculated to make her squirm.

She backed away from him, blood pounding in her ears. "I-I thought you were going to take me to my husband's ranch. I thought you w-wanted the money."

He grinned maliciously, his eyes narrowing until they were mere slits in his grimy, unshaven face, but he said nothing.

Gabrielle continued, slowly, to make her way backward in an attempt to put as much distance between them as possible. "If anything happens to me . . . my husband won't pay you a single penny."

Doolen burst out laughing at the look of distress on her face. "Wanna drink?" he asked unexpectedly, pulling a flask from his hip pocket and unscrewing the cap.

She shook her head, trying hard to keep her distaste from showing on her face. There had to be some way to reason with him. Her heel bumped into something hard and solid that brought her retreat to an abrupt halt. Her mind reeled frantically as she reached behind her and her fingers came into contact with the large boulder that blocked her path.

His sharp eyes not missing a thing, Doolen raised the flask to his lips and took a long draught, letting whiskey dribble from the corners of his mouth and down his chin. He wiped it off with his sleeve.

More frightened than ever, Gabrielle took a deep unsteady breath. "Listen . . . I know we didn't get along the first time we met, but those Apaches were under Government protection. If you had hurt Zayigo, there would have been—"

"Zayigo?" Doolen repeated, arching a brow. "Is that the squaw's name?"

"She's a girl. A very young girl. Not much more than a child. If you—"

369

"But you ain't." Doolen's gaze moved downward to linger on her bosom. "A child, that is."

Sudden color flooding her face, Gabrielle defensively brought one arm across her breasts. For the first time in her life, she wished that someone *would* think of her as merely a child, a faceless, nameless, sexless child.

Doolen rammed the flask back into his pocket and took a step toward her.

Panic flashing across her face, Gabrielle whirled about and dashed behind the boulder, putting it between them; but she realized too late that she had backed herself into a corner. With the canyon wall rising up sharply behind her, there was no place left for her to go but up. She was trapped and she knew it.

Doolen knew it too. Enjoying her dilemma, he made no further move to come after her. "You know, you could be a little nicer to me," he said, tilting his head to one side and peering at her through half-closed eyes, "instead of sticking your nose up in the air like you think I ain't good enough for you or something."

Flustered, Gabrielle nervously chewed on her bottom lip. "Why?" she asked, her voice quivering uncontrollably. "You promised you would take me to my husband's ranch."

He shrugged. "I lied."

In the back of her mind, she had known all along that he had never intended to take her to the ranch, but that had not stopped her from hoping, however foolishly, that she was wrong. Now his admission jarred her into reality. Fear chilled her. "If it's more money you want," she said hastily, "I can get it for you. If fifty dollars isn't enough, we can make it a hundred—"

"Shut up!" Doolen snapped, his patience waning. "Just shut up!" He started toward her.

Gravel rolled beneath Gabrielle's feet as she inched away from him.

"I got fired 'cause of you," Doolen spat out. "All I was after was a little bit of fun with that squaw and you had to go and stick your nose into it and get me in trouble with the boss." He started around the boulders. "You must've thought you was real hot stuff standin' up there defendin' them 'Paches like one

370

of them travelin' preachers spoutin' off about the poor and the meek. That's it, the poor and the meek." The gravel crunched under his feet as he drew closer, and there was a mean look in his eyes.

With no place to run, Gabrielle shrank back as he appeared around the boulder. "I'm sorry," she blurted out. "I didn't mean to get you fired. I didn't— Stay away from me!"

The pained cry was wrenched from her throat as he grabbed her arm and yanked her toward him, causing her to stumble and fall. "You're gonna pay," he said, jerking her roughly to her feet. "You're gonna get just what that squaw had coming."

"Let go of me!" Gabrielle lashed out with her foot, catching him in the knee with a sharp kick that brought a startled yelp to his lips and made him loosen his grip on her. Twisting free, she darted away from him, clambering up over the boulders she could not get around.

He lunged for her and seized the back of her skirt, but was thrown off balance when the dress tore in his hand, the sound of rending silk echoing through the canyon. He snatched at her skirt again, knotted his fingers in a fold, and pulled her down off the boulder. Seized by blind, unreasoning panic, Gabrielle balled her hand into a fist and swung wildly. He ducked, barely escaping her flailing arm, and instead of his head, she clipped the brim of his hat, sending it flying.

Doolen swore loudly as he nearly lost his grip on her. Then, locking his arm around her waist, he lifted her up into the air and swung her around. Together, they both tumbled to the ground.

Gabrielle gasped as the air was forced from her lungs, and she lay pinned beneath his weight, her face pressed against the rocky ground, unable to move. Shifting his weight, Doolen grabbed her by the shoulder and rolled her over onto her back. She threw herself at him, catching him off guard as she clawed at his eyes, and drove her knee into his belly.

Uttering a grunt of surprise, he faltered, and she nearly succeeded in pushing him off, but he flung himself on top of her, knocking her flat and grasping her wrists to force her hands out at her sides. "I'll teach you to fight me," he spat out, wedging a knee between her legs.

Driven by terror, Gabrielle twisted and bucked, trying to throw him off her. Screams that found no outlet rose to be strangled in her throat. She had an odd feeling that she'd lived this nightmare before, and in a flash of recognition, she realized that she had—in her dreams. Only this time her attacker was neither Marcus nor an Apache warrior. It was Jack Doolen. The only noise that came out of her mouth when she tried to scream was a small animal-like mewling sound, and her heart felt as though it would explode.

Releasing one of her wrists, Doolen reached for the hem of her skirt and dragged it up to her knees.

Without stopping to think of what she was doing, Gabrielle rose up and sank her teeth into his shoulder.

"Aaarghh!" he yelled, his eyes bulging with pain, and he backed off her. But she held on with all her might, coming up off the ground with him as he tried to rise. Forcing his hands between them, Doolen shoved her away.

Twisted by fury, his face loomed over her, and he drew back his arm. Then, just as she remembered from her dream, his fist crashed into her cheek.

Pain exploded in her head, followed by waves of darkness, and, eyes closed, Gabrielle lay without moving. But she struggled to keep a grip on reality as oblivion threatened to overcome her.

"That'll teach you," Doolen muttered, a self-satisfied look on his face as he fumbled with his belt buckle.

Blackness hovered over Gabrielle, alternately advancing, then retreating. She could feel the hard ground beneath her, the rocks gouging into her back, and Doolen's hands ripping at her skirt. Her lashes fluttered against her cheeks, and she opened her eyes to see a buzzard circling high overhead. An insane urge to laugh seized her. I'm not dead yet, she told herself, and was suddenly possessed with the courage to fight Doolen until she had drawn her last breath. With a calmness she did not know she was capable of showing, she shut her eyes and feigned unconsciousness while the fingers of her right hand closed securely around something hard and solid.

"I been waitin' a long time to have me a white woman," Doolen grumbled as he pulled her drawers down over her hips, his face set in a mask of crazed determination. He paused to lick his lips as his gaze rested on her breasts, torn between wanting to rip off the top half of her dress so he could see what she looked like underneath the fancy underthings she wore and wanting to get inside her and satisfy his lust. But his body gave him no choice. If he did not relieve himself soon, it would be too late.

It took every bit of willpower Gabrielle could summon to lie still while he pawed at her, the fingers of his left hand digging deeply into the tender flesh of her naked thighs while his right worked to free himself from his britches. And when he had his pants down to his knees and shifted his weight, readying himself to take her, her grip tightened on the rock under her hand, and, drawing on every ounce of strength she had, Gabrielle struck.

The rock cracked into the side of Doolen's head with a sickening thud. For an interminable second, he did not move. He did not even draw a breath. Then his mouth went slack and his eyes rolled back into his head as he slumped forward and collapsed on top of her.

Striking him with the rock had so sapped her strength that it took several minutes for Gabrielle to worm her way out from under him, but even as she pushed him off her, she knew he was not dead, merely unconscious, and could come to at any time. She staggered to her feet, her hands trembling violently as she pulled up her drawers and retied the string, grateful that she had lost no more than her pride to the filthy beast who now lay sprawled on the ground, his buttocks bared to the blazing noon sun.

He groaned and raised one hand to his head.

Gripped by panic, Gabrielle leaped over him and scrambled around the boulders to where his horse calmly waited. Blissfully ignorant of what had just happened, the animal turned its head to give her a velvet-eyed look of curiosity. The ground was shifting beneath her, and she had to grit her teeth against the reeling pain in her head. The bruise her father had given her was nothing compared to the one she was certain she now sported, for she could feel the skin stretching taut across her left cheekbone. Clutching the reins in one hand and the pommel in the other, she placed a foot in the stirrup and dragged herself up onto the animal's back, what was left of her tattered skirt bunching up around her knees as she straddled the saddle. Everything in view suddenly became blurred, and she felt peculiarly light-headed.

Not daring to look back, Gabrielle urged the horse toward the road, trusting the animal to find the best way up the rocky slope. Behind her, she heard Doolen groan, then utter an enraged shout.

A shot rang out, the bullet whistling past her ear, and her heart leaped frantically as she crouched down low against the horse's neck, silently begging it to go faster up the gravel-strewn trail.

Doolen fired again, and again he missed his mark. "Damn!" he muttered under his breath as he stumbled to his feet. Clutching the revolver in both hands, he aimed at Gabrielle's departing back and pulled back the hammer.

Upon reaching the road, Gabrielle turned the horse toward the east and dug her knees into his sides. The animal lunged forward, and the third bullet sailed past Gabrielle's head, the sound of the shot echoing through the mountain pass.

The stirrups were adjusted for Doolen's legs, and as the horse broke into a gallop, Gabrielle's feet slipped free and she had to grip the saddle with her knees to keep her balance. Loose gravel flew from beneath the horse's hooves as she clung to the pommel in desperation, terrified that she would be thrown. Her head throbbed and, where Doolen had hit her, her face was numb. The memory of his foul touch still burned on her skin, but she would not allow herself to think of how narrowly she had escaped being raped.

A second set of hoofbeats joined her, and grew steadily louder as they tattooed a quick staccato behind her. She urged her horse to go faster, certain that Doolen was closing in on her and forgetting in her panic that she had his mount. Her pursuer drew abreast. With one fluid motion, he swooped down and grabbed her reins, hauling both their horses to an abrupt halt. Gabrielle screamed as she lost her balance, then screamed again as a man's arm closed around her, pulling her off her horse and onto his before lowering her to the ground.

She broke free and turned to run, but strong hands gripped her shoulders and dragged her back.

"Gabrielle!" Dan thundered, his voice piercing her terror.

For a second, she went rigid, not believing that he had found her; then she flung herself at him and clung desperately to him out of fear that he would disappear into thin air like a mirage. "Stagecoach . . . sorry . . . shouldn't have gotten off," she babbled.

Dan set her away from him, alarmed. "Gabrielle!"

"Sorry . . . stage—"

"I said, stop it! Do you hear me? Stop it!" He shook her until her hysteria receded and she began to regain control of her senses.

She blinked at him in bewilderment as his face slowly came into focus.

His gaze went to her bruised cheek, then quickly returned to her eyes. "Did he hurt you?" Dan asked harshly, his fingers biting into her shoulders. "Did Doolen hurt you?"

Gabrielle reached up to touch her cheek. "He hit—" She broke off and shook her head vehemently as she suddenly realized what he meant. "He didn't have time. I-I got away . . ." Her face crumpling, she slumped against his chest and let out a half-choked sob. "Oh, Dan . . . Dan," she murmured, relinquishing herself to the violent tremors that shook her.

He gathered her into his arms and held her close. "It's all right, little one. Everything will be all right now."

"It was . . . awful," she murmured into his shirtfront.

"I know it was," he answered, his voice thick with emotion. "I know."

His arms were strong and comforting, and she never wanted to leave their secure warmth. "Please forgive me," she pleaded achingly. "I didn't mean those awful things I said to you. I'm so sorry I didn't believe you."

Setting her away from him, he gripped her chin and forced her head up, and for a brief second, she shrank from the dark intensity of his gaze. "Sooner or later, woman, you are going to have to get it through that thick skull of yours that I love you. Do you understand? I love *you*."

"And I love you," she whispered, her voice breaking. "I love you so much—"

A harsh laugh shattered the quiet and they both whirled around to find themselves staring down the barrel of Doolen's revolver.

"My, my, ain't this cozy?" Doolen sneered as he edged his way around the horses and seized their reins. His eyes raked over Gabrielle, and panic flickered in hers as she wondered frantically where he had come from. She thought she had put miles between them, but it was obvious that, in her fright, she had misjudged the distance. "And you thought you'd seen the last of me," Doolen taunted, a cruel grin spreading across his face. "Throws a bit of a kink into my plans, though. All I was after was a woman. I wasn't countin' on havin' to shoot her old man too." His gaze dropped to Dan's right hand. "You reach for your gun, mister, and you're a dead man."

Dan inched his hand away from his revolver, and Doolen waved his gun. "You! Get over here," he commanded, and Gabrielle reluctantly obeyed, a startled cry bursting from her as he seized her arm and jerked her against him. Doolen then motioned toward Dan. "Take that pistol by two fingers—two fingers, you hear me?—and *carefully* lay it on the ground. Make one dumb move and the lady here dies." As if to drive home his point, Doolen pressed the muzzle of his revolver to Gabrielle's temple.

Her heart pounded furiously and her mind raced as she watched Dan, who could not refuse to obey Doolen's command lest she suffer, ease his gun from its holster and lower it to the ground. In a sudden desperate attempt to divert Doolen's attention, Gabrielle stiffened and strained her neck to look down the road.

Without thinking, Doolen followed suit, and his gun momentarily dipped away from Gabrielle's head.

Dan lunged forward, catching him off guard.

Gabrielle screamed as Doolen's gun exploded and Dan reeled backward, clutching his shoulder. Without thinking, she ran to him, but he thrust her aside and staggered to his feet, blood from the wound in his shoulder oozing between his fingers and down over his hand. Doolen raised his gun, but before he could fire again, Dan charged into him headfirst, knocking him off his feet.

Gabrielle watched, horrified, as the two men crashed to the ground and rolled over and over in the dirt. They were like madmen, both of them, and she wasn't certain whether she was more frightened by Doolen's calculating cruelty or Dan's murderous rage. "Stop it!" she screamed, but neither man heard her. Her face white with fear, she edged away from them, her hands clenched so tightly that her nails dug into her palms, breaking the skin. A terrible foreboding gripped her, and once more she seemed to be caught in the throes of that awful, recurring nightmare.

Breaking free, Doolen hurled his gun at Dan's head, but Dan ducked and the revolver sailed past him, then skidded across the rocky ground toward Gabrielle. Dan was on his feet instantly. Oblivious of the bood pouring from his shoulder, he smashed his fist into Doolen's stomach, making him grunt and double over. Dan then brought his fists up under Doolen's chin in a savage blow that sent him reeling backward, blood trickling from the corners of his mouth. Dan seized the front of Doolen's shirt and dragged him to his feet, but Doolen, upon regaining his footing, drew back and plowed his fist into Dan's face.

Both men were bloodied now, and the crimson splatters that stained the ground increased as blow after vicious blow was dealt.

Sick with fear and revulsion, Gabrielle crept toward the gun that had been sent spinning her way. With trembling hands, she picked it up and shakily got to her feet. Somehow, though she could not remember doing so, she managed to pull back the hammer, but her hands were shaking so badly she nearly dropped the weapon.

Doolen locked his hands around Dan's neck as they both rolled in the dirt, and he slammed Dan's head into the ground, over and over. There was a crazed look in his eyes, and his upper lip was drawn back.

Dan wedged a knee between them and shoved.

In one unbroken movement, Doolen hit the ground and rolled to his feet, his hand dropping to his boot.

Sunlight glinted off metal as the bowie knife he'd used to shear off a lock of Gabrielle's hair appeared in his hand and he drew back his arm.

Gabrielle pulled the trigger.

Doolen's face went slack with surprise; then blood gushed from his mouth, spilling down the front of him. Still clutching the knife he had not had a chance to throw, he slumped face downward onto the ground and was still.

For a moment, no one moved. Dan stared at Gabrielle in mute surprise, and she stared at the man she had just killed, horror and revulsion clearly etched on her face. Then she took a deep shuddering breath and closed her eyes.

Dan staggered to his feet and went to her. Prying her fingers from the revolver, he took it from her and then drew her into his arms.

She buried her face against his chest. "He was going to kill you," she whispered into his shirtfront, and began to tremble violently as the impact of what had happened hit her. "Oh, Dan—"

"Shhh, it's all right," he said, holding her close and resting one cheek against the top of her head. He was shaking as badly as she was and was beginning to feel weak from loss of blood.

She lifted her head to stare up at him through the tears that glistened in her eyes. Her face and clothes were smeared with his blood. "I'm sorry," she said, her voice a hoarse whisper. Her chin quivered. "I'm sorry I ever doubted you loved me . . ."

He drew her back into his arms, terrified by the thought of what might have happened had she not acted as quickly as she had. "It's all right, little one," he murmured into her hair. "The worst is over now."

Dan lifted his head as hoofbeats thundered through the canyon, a puzzled frown creasing his brow as Bandy Moreland and a half-dozen soldiers appeared. Then he was seized by an urge to laugh as he remembered that he had actually *ordered* Captain Saunders to furnish Bandy with his best scouts.

"Got here fast as we could," Bandy called out as the men reined in their horses, his quick eyes assessing the seriousness of Dan's wound and the look of exhausted relief on Gabrielle's face. "When we heard the shots, we thought you was a goner for sure." Bending down, he rolled Doolen onto his back. "Who in the hell's this ugly bastard?"

"Name's Doolen," Dan said. His face was pale and he needed to sit down, but he wasn't about to relinquish his hold on Gabrielle. "I've seen him before, but right now I can't recall where."

Bandy straightened up. "He was with Bryce Edwards the other day when that bunch showed up at Camp Carleton with that gelded Apache, tryin' to stir up trouble."

"He was out at the Indian camp too," Gabrielle said in a small voice, feeling, rather than seeing, the sharp glance Dan gave her. "He was going to rape Zayigo."

Dan looked at Moreland, one dark brow arching ominously, and Bandy shifted uneasily and rubbed one hand along his jaw, not quite meeting Dan's glowering scrutiny. "Well . . . er . . . that's water under the bridge and—"

"I've seen him before too," one of the scouts put in, drawing everyone's attention. "He was arrested down in Calabasas last year for torching a rancher's barn, but no one had any proof it was him so they led him go."

Dan and Bandy exchanged glances.

Venturing a hesitant glance at Doolen's blood-splattered body, Gabrielle shuddered and buried her face against Dan's chest.

His arms tightened around her. "Come on, little one," he said gently. "Let's go home."

Garbed in one of Dan's shirts until her own clothes could be washed and mended, Gabrielle sat at the kitchen table, nervously staring out at the mountains that hugged the valley. The scouts were already on their way back to their detachment at Ciénega Pass. The bullet had been removed from Dan's shoulder, and after the wound had been cleaned and bound, Bandy had assured her that Dan was going to be all right. Bandy was in the bedroom with him now, the door closed. Gabrielle squirmed uneasily on her chair. He had been in there an awfully long time.

She jumped to her feet as the bedroom door opened and Bandy emerged, a sheepish look on his face. "Your turn," he said, dryly, giving her a rueful grin and glancing appreciatively at her long legs which the tails of Dan's shirt only partially covered.

Gabrielle bit her lip. "Is he terribly angry?"

"Chewed me up one wall and down the other."

She felt her face grow warm. "I'm sorry I got you into trouble. I thought you had already told him I went out to the camp that day."

"I'll live. What about you? You gonna be all right here till I get back?"

She gave him an embarrassed smile. They both knew her father was going to have a fit when he found out she was staying at the ranch with Dan, but she didn't care. She nodded. "I think so."

"Well, I gotta get back to Camp Carleton before they list me as a deserter. I'll have Grace open your trunks and pick out the clothes and gewgaws you're gonna need until we can get the rest of your things down here."

"Thanks. You're a good friend . . . Wilbur."

He grinned at her. "You take good care of that man in there, you hear?"

"Believe me, I will."

After Bandy had gone, it took a full minute for Gabrielle to summon enough courage to stick her head through the doorway of Dan's bedroom. "How do you feel?"

He was sitting up in bed, atop the covers, clad only in his trousers, one arm draped casually across a drawn-up knee, his back propped against the pillows. Bandages torn from a sheet spanned his broad tanned chest diagonally and horizontally, tightly binding his wound, and much of the color had returned to his face. But, in spite of his calm appearance, amber lights snapped in Dan's hazel eyes as they grazed over Gabrielle, stripping her of his shirt as she stepped into his room, then stopped several paces short of the bed. He wondered if she knew what a fetching picture she made in his shirt, her legs and feet bare and her freshly toweled hair tumbling down over her shoulders in damp curls. It was even hard to tell exactly which lock Doolen had ravaged. She was beautiful, more beautiful than he had remembered, and he had to exercise a firm restraint on the desire unfurling inside him. "Come here," he said quietly.

Reluctantly, she obeyed. She did not like having to answer to him, especially when she knew he was right.

He reached for her arm, and began rolling up the shirtsleeves that were far too long for her. "I believe you have some explaining to do, young lady," he said sternly as he adjusted first one sleeve, then the other.

She fidgeted. "I know it was foolish of me to go to the Apache camp alone," she said, wanting nothing more than to put the entire episode behind her. "But . . . someone had to warn them that they were in danger." She paused to laugh hollowly before continuing. "Not that it did much good. No one spoke English."

Dan grasped her hand and held it firmly, as if her were afraid to let go of her lest he lose her again. "Oh, you warned them, all right. But did it ever occur to you that Moreland knew enough to send troops out to the camp to protect the Apaches from an attack?"

Hot color brightened Gabrielle's face. "I didn't think of that."

"I thought I was going to be sick when I heard what you had done. Do you have any idea of the danger you were in out there?"

She tried to make light of the situation by shrugging indifferently. "You said yourself I didn't have enough sense to fit on the sharp end of a cactus spine," she retorted. "I guess you were right."

His expression softened, and he reached up to brush the backs of his knuckles across her bruised cheek. "No, little one, I wasn't right. You are impulsive, hard-headed and willful, but you are certainly not lacking in common sense. If you were, I might not be alive. Now," he said, the change in his tone signaling the end of the conversation, "come here."

This time she went to him willingly, not realizing until she settled into his one-armed embrace just how much she had missed him. "I'm also sorry I caused so much trouble by getting off the stagecoach in Dripping Springs," she whispered into his chest, anxious to unburden her nagging conscience.

Dan did not have the heart to tell her what would have happened to her if she had *not* gotten off that stage. He knew he would have to break the news to her eventually, but not yet. Right now, he just wanted to hold her. His arm tightened around her. "It's all right, little one. I'm just thankful that you're safe with me now."

Gabrielle was not so easily satisfied, however, and she grew increasingly restless as she fretted about how she was going to face the future without him, for, though he had assured her that he loved her, he had not said one word about marriage. She could not blame her if he no longer wanted to marry her. After all, *she* had broken off their betrothal.

She lifted her head and caught him grinning broadly at her.

"If you think I'm going to release you from our betrothal, Gabrielle, think again. You will marry me if I have to corral you and physically drag you to the altar."

She sat up and stared at him in surprise. How did he know what she had been thinking?

He chuckled. "It's written all over your face," he said, answering her unvoiced question. "You're very transparent, my dear. How do you think I always know when you are up to something?"

How, indeed? she mused, smiling involuntarily as she remembered the effort she had put into keeping two steps ahead of him only to have him thwart her. Then her expression became serious. "Father is going to try to stand in our way."

"He can try. He won't succeed."

"But, what if—"

"Gabrielle, listen to me. It took me a long time to come to terms with the fact that any debt I owed your father has long since been repaid. Now Stephen is going to have to come to terms with the fact that I love his daughter. There is nothing he can do to change that. Besides, the next time we see your father, he is likely to be standing here with a loaded revolver, demanding that I marry you."

Before she could ask what he meant by that, he gripped her around the waist and flipped her onto her back, pinning her beneath him. Surprise, then desire, then concern flashed across her face in rapid succession as he pressed her down into the mattress. "Your shoulder—"

A throaty chuckle escaped him, silencing her protest. "I intend to compromise you, my dear," he explained, his eyes darkening with unabashed lust as his hand slid down to caress her naked thigh. As his lips descended over hers, he added in a husky voice that both teased and threatened, "Thoroughly . . ."

LOVE'S BRIGHTEST STARS SHINE
WITH ZEBRA BOOKS!

CATALINA'S CARESS (2202, $3.95)
by Sylvie F. Sommerfield

Catalina Carrington was determined to buy her riverboat back from the handsome gambler who'd beaten her brother at cards. But when dashing Marc Copeland named his price — three days as his mistress — Catalina swore she'd never meet his terms . . . even as she imagined the rapture a night in his arms would bring!

BELOVED EMBRACE (2135, $3.95)
by Cassie Edwards

Leana Rutherford was terrified when the ship carrying her family from New York to Texas was attacked by savage pirates. But when she gazed upon the bold sea-bandit Brandon Seton, Leana longed to share the ecstasy she was sure sure his passionate caress would ignite!

ELUSIVE SWAN (2061, $3.95)
by Sylvie F. Sommerfield

Just one glance from the handsome stranger in the dockside tavern in boisterous St. Augustine made Arianne tremble with excitement. But the innocent young woman was already running from one man . . . and no matter how fiercely the flames of desire burned within her, Arianne dared not submit to another!

SAVAGE PARADISE (1985, $3.95)
by Cassie Edwards

Marianna Fowler detested the desolate wilderness of the unsettled Montana Territory. But once the hot-blooded Chippewa brave Lone Hawk saved her life, the spirited young beauty wished never to leave, longing to experience the fire of the handsome warrior's passionate embrace!

MOONLIT MAGIC (1941, $3.95)
by Sylvie F. Sommerfield

When she found the slick railroad negotiator Trace Cord trespassing on her property and bathing in her river, innocent Jenny Graham could barely contain her rage. But when she saw how the setting sun gilded Trace's magnificent physique, Jenny's seething fury was transformed into burning desire!

Available wherever paperbacks are sold, or order direct from the Publisher. Send cover price plus 50¢ per copy for mailing and handling to Zebra Books, Dept. 2667, 475 Park Avenue South, New York, N.Y. 10016. Residents of New York, New Jersey and Pennsylvania must include sales tax. DO NOT SEND CASH.